MERE MORTALS

RILEY PARRA: SEASON THREE

Geonn Cannon

Supposed Crimes LLC • Matthews, North Carolina

This book is a work of fiction. Names, characters, places, and incidents are products of the author's imagination or are used fictitiously. Any resemblance to actual events or locales or persons, living or dead, is entirely coincidental.

www.supposedcrimes.com

This book is typeset in Goudy Old Style.

To Marem Hassler and Liz Vassey
And everyone at Tello Films
for bringing these characters to life

TABLE OF CONTENTS

MERE MORTALS

"WOULD YOU like a cup of tea?" He turned and motioned toward the house. A servant approached and placed a tea service on the table. The man across the table smiled in anticipation as the drink was poured. "I love tea."

Riley closed her eyes and tried to focus. Her host thanked the waiter and moved to the edge of his seat to prepare a glass. He glanced up at her when she remained where she was.

"I would feel self-conscious if I was the only person at the table drinking the tea. So I would refrain if you refused. However, if you would simply take a cup, I could enjoy a beverage."

"Fine."

"Good! Thank you. I appreciate it." She heard the sound of tea pouring into the porcelain cups like it was the only sound that existed. He took a sip, sighed happily and cradled the cup with both hands. "We don't have long. What would you like to discuss?"

"Why me?"

A bellowing laugh. "Oh, you get straight to the heart of the matter, don't you? Well, Detective Parra. Why not you?" He took a sip of tea, and then placed His cup back onto the table. "Now our time runs short. What do you really wish to ask Me?"

Questions began to form in Riley's mind.

"Early this morning, one of our detectives, working with

outside contractors, successfully identified the serial killer known as the Angel Maker. Upon raiding his residence, our people attempted to arrest the suspect, who responded violently. Our detective responded with appropriate force, and the Angel Maker was killed in the resulting confrontation. Unfortunately, he was also able to~"

Lieutenant Zoe Briggs closed her eyes and put the paper back on her desk. It was terrible. A sound byte for the local news, something to stand in front of the crowd and recite before throwing out a 'no questions' and running for the exit. She wanted to honor Riley's sacrifice but, at the same time, she didn't want to make it real. She'd only just discovered how much Riley had done for the city, and now it was over. Riley Parra was lying in the morgue waiting to be autopsied, photographed... buried.

There was a knock on the door and her temporary assistant leaned in. "Boss. The natives are getting restless. I think someone leaked that the Angel Maker was killed."

Gail Finney, no doubt. Priest and Gillian had both warned her that the reporter was bad news, but she didn't need their warning. Finney was a muck-raking journalist who didn't belong in a supermarket tabloid, let alone all over the radio and prominently printed in the newspaper. She would cross the street to spit on a cop, and seemed hell-bent on making the police department villains. It was hard enough doing their job without~

"Ma'am?"

"Yeah. I'm coming." She picked up the press release - even if it was cold and impersonal, it was better than she trusted herself to do off the cuff - and stepped around her desk. The press would be gathered in the lobby, so she'd give her statement from the stairs. It would be easier to make a hasty retreat that way.

She was almost to the stairs when the elevator doors opened and Gillian Hunt burst into the bullpen. She looked like she was on the run from the devil and, knowing this city, she might very well have been. Briggs slowed and moved to intercept her, eager for the distraction from her grim duty. "Dr. Hunt?"

Gillian spun, skidding to a stop next to an empty desk. Her eyes were red from crying, but her scrubs were still pristine. *She's coming to beg off the autopsy after all. Can't say as I blame her.* She held up her hand to tell her it would be reassigned, but Gillian spoke first. "I need to speak with you in private. Right now."

Briggs looked at her assistant. "Tell the press I'm dealing with some loose ends. I'll be down when I can." She crossed to Gillian and followed her back to the elevators. She put her hand on Gillian's shoulder and lowered her voice. "If you need someone else to do Riley's post-mortem, I understand."

Gillian laughed, a quick and desperate bark of a sound. "No. You don't have to do that."

The elevator doors closed behind them and Gillian pressed the button for the morgue and began to pace.

"You need to take some time. What happened last night was hard on all of us..."

"Riley's alive."

Briggs furrowed her brow and then closed her eyes. "I'm still dealing with the revelations you guys dumped on me a few weeks ago. Angels, demons, the whole... situation. I know that there are some amazing things I have no idea about, but I saw her. I held her hand while she..." Briggs looked away as her voice trailed off. "She couldn't have survived that, Gillian."

The elevator doors parted upon their arrival at the morgue. Riley Parra stepped into the car, saw Briggs, and then turned to face Gillian. Gillian put her hands on Riley's shoulders and sagged against her, eyes closed like someone who had just discovered a good dream turned out to be real. Riley kissed Gillian's eyebrow. "Did you tell her?"

Briggs stumbled back until she could lean against the door of the elevator. A bell rang, and the door bumped against her shoulder, but she ignored it. "That's impossible." Her voice was barely a gasp, forced out by sheer force of will. Riley turned to face her, dressed in her jeans and a green scrub top. Her face was scrubbed of even the minimal makeup she usually wore, and her hair was down and wet, but it was undeniably her. She spoke the only word that occurred to her.

"How?"

"A miracle," Gillian whispered.

Riley shook her head. "That's as good a word as any. But we're not out of the woods yet." She motioned for them to follow her, and Briggs found the strength to walk out of the elevator. Gillian walked alongside her and put a hand on her elbow, supporting Briggs while using her to keep herself upright. Gillian tightened her grip and leaned closer to Briggs to whisper, "Thank you."

"For what?"

Gillian blinked back a fresh round of tears. "For seeing her. For letting me know it's real."

Briggs squeezed Gillian's hand as Riley pushed through the morgue doors. Briggs thought that the surprise of resurrection would have prepared her for anything, but the sight of Caitlin Priest lying unconscious on an exam table was another unexpected shock. Her face was pale and drawn, her hair fanned out on either side of her head like a golden pillow.

"What happened?"

"When angels take human form, their true form surrounds that body like a... an aura." Riley looked down at Priest. "It's called their divinity. It's what makes them more than human. Priest tapped into that to save me. The well ran dry."

Priest's eyes were closed, and her breathing was so shallow that Briggs had to stare to make sure she was still alive.

"What does that mean?" Briggs asked quietly.

Gillian put her hand on Priest's head, stroking her hair. "It means she's dying."

Gail Finney checked the battery on her voice recorder for the tenth time since arriving at the police station. She felt elated, almost giddy, at the thought of hearing the news. Riley Parra, dead at the hands of the Angel Maker. She knew that hadn't been the planned endgame, but damned if it wasn't perfect. The city was terrified, the cops were shell-shocked, and the champion of good had fallen. When Marchosias controlled the city completely, Gail would get her reward for being such a good and faithful servant.

Well. Maybe not "good" or faithful.

She smiled as Lieutenant Briggs came down the stairs. The scrum of reporters moved forward, representatives from most of the major news outlets in the state. Gail was near the front of the crowd since she'd arrived immediately after the impromptu press conference on the lawn of Terrence Bishop's house. She extended her arm so that the recorder was as close to Briggs as possible. She didn't want to miss a word.

"Good morning, everyone. I'm sorry to have kept you waiting, but it's been a pretty hectic evening and morning for us here as I'm sure you can guess. I'd like to begin by reading a prepared statement. Last night, working on information acquired from an anonymous source, two of our detectives working with outside consultants were able to identify the serial killer known as the Angel Maker. They confronted the man, who responded violently, and our detectives were required to respond with deadly force. The suspect in the case was killed in the resulting action. Unfortunately, one of our own was gravely injured at the same time..."

Gail tried to hide her smile. Her heart was pounding. Briggs still looked shell-shocked all these hours later, her hands trembling slightly on the side of the podium.

"Detective Caitlin Priest is currently in critical condition—"

The rest of the words were drowned out, and Gail felt like the room was closing in on her. *Priest, the angel? No, impossible. According to Gremory, Priest wasn't even present at the crime scene.* She withdrew the recorder and turned on her heel, pushing through the crowd as she tried to make sense of this unexpected news. She was almost to the door when she heard Briggs say her name.

"Leaving already, Miss Finney? I guess you got enough facts for your column. I look forward to see what you make up to fill in the blanks."

The crowd snickered, and she felt her face burning red. They had been so close to triumph. To have it snatched out of their hands so effortlessly, to go from the champion to a laughingstock... She turned and stormed out of the building. Behind her, she heard Briggs begin to speak again.

"Okay, where were we? Detective Priest..."

"Riley, can you come here?"

Riley was standing next to the bed where Priest was unconscious, dying, whatever. Gillian had called to her from the door of her office, and Riley brushed Priest's shoulder before she obliged. She put her hand on Gillian's arm, and Gillian drew her into the office. "What's wrong?"

Gillian cupped Riley's face. "Nothing." She kissed Riley softly, just brushing her lips across Riley's. Riley smiled and put her hands on Gillian's hips, returning the kiss. They didn't need passion, and the kiss wasn't an invitation to more. It was just something that had to be done, to reaffirm their connection and Riley's humanity. Riley pecked Gillian's upper and lower lips, the corners of her mouth, and then rested her forehead against Gillian's.

Gillian took a deep breath of Riley's scent. "You scared me."

"Sorry about that."

Gillian brushed her cheek against Riley's, leaning into her embrace. She rested her head on Riley's shoulder and kissed her neck. Riley closed her eyes and stroked Gillian's back, supporting her weight easily as Gillian began to sob. "Shh. Hey, it's all right. I'm here. I'm okay."

"You've died twice. You got thrown off that building when you were on patrol all those years ago, and now this and... next time you won't be so lucky. Next time might be for good."

"Right. And that makes me just like everyone else on the planet."

Gillian leaned back and looked into Riley's eyes. "I couldn't bear it. I couldn't go on. If you really died, I would have to go... right after you."

Riley brushed Gillian's cheek with her thumb. "Then I'll have to do my best to stay alive from now on."

Gillian smiled. "You mean you haven't been trying?"

Riley chuckled and kissed Gillian again. This time they held the contact longer, breaking apart just long enough to breathe before they came together again.

Briggs cleared her throat to announce her arrival. "Are you two done reaffirming life in there, or should I take a walk?"

Riley broke the kiss and brushed her cheek against Gillian's before she pulled away from her. Briggs was standing next to Priest, looking down at her. She didn't look up as she spoke.

"I dealt with the press conference. I'll adjust my reports later to mention Priest was with us at the Angel Maker house, that she was the one who was injured by him." She shook her head. "Falsifying police reports to cover up a resurrection. There's a new one." She finally looked up at Riley. "Now we need to figure out what the hell we're going to do next. Is she...?"

"Caitlin is still alive." Gillian moved next to Priest and checked her pulse, just to be sure. "Her heartbeat is weak, but steady. She was only conscious for a few seconds after... what she did..." She glanced at Riley and then back at Priest. "She complained of a deep pain and then just passed out."

"Will she pull through?"

Gillian shrugged. "I don't know. This body was only created to be a host for the angel Zerachiel. Zerachiel is... gone. So I don't know if it's like a car without a driver or a skin after being shed by a snake. She might just fade away."

Riley was staring at Priest. "Is there anything you can do for her?"

"If she's dying, there's no cure for what's killing her. If she's not, she just needs time to deal with the shock of losing part of herself. I think all I can do is be here for her and make sure that she's comfortable when and if she wakes up."

Briggs nodded. "Okay. And what about you, Detective Parra?"

Riley was thrown by the question. "What about me? I'm fine."

"You were *dead* two hours ago." Gillian winced and Riley apologized by rubbing her shoulder. "I don't care if it was an angel's divinity that brought you back. The human body and the human mind doesn't just rebound from something like that. I want you to go home and rest."

"I won't leave Gillian."

Gillian put her hand on Riley's arm. "I appreciate that, but I think you should go. If just to get a clean outfit and lay down in our bed for a while. You went through a horrible trauma, and you had a huge night before everything else happened. You need to rest. I can stretch out on the couch here. I'll call you if anything happens with Cait." She kissed Riley quickly. "I'll be fine. I'll feel better knowing you're at home and safe."

"All right." Riley squeezed Gillian's hip and then looked at Briggs. "Fine. I'll go home."

"Thank you. Dr. Hunt, you had the same rough night. I know I don't really have authority over you, so consider this a strong suggestion. Take the rest of the week off. I'll call in your backup to take over for you. Priest will still be your responsibility, of course, but for everything else, I want you sitting out."

"Yes, ma'am."

Briggs exhaled. "Thank you for making it easy on me, ladies. I want updates on Priest's condition as warranted. I'll be upstairs if either of you need anything." She looked at Priest and shook her head. "Crazy day."

"Really crazy." Gillian put her hand on top of Riley's. Riley looked at it and realized that Gillian had been touching her almost constantly since her resurrection. She knew that it was just a personal reassurance that Riley wasn't a hallucination. She turned her hand upside down and linked their fingers together. She squeezed. Gillian could hold onto her as much as she needed; Riley wanted the contact as badly as she did.

"Stop, stop," Kenzie gasped. She put her hand on Chelsea's forehead and pushed her away, bringing her legs together as she twisted her lower body to the right. Chelsea rolled over Kenzie's hip and slid up her body, embracing her from behind. They were both dripping sweat, and Chelsea was still struggling to catch her breath.

She kissed Kenzie's neck and shoulders, and Kenzie closed her eyes as a fresh round of tears threatened.

Chelsea spooned against Kenzie from behind, and Kenzie gripped Chelsea's arm. She didn't know where their marathon lovemaking session had come from; as soon as they stepped into the office, they were on each other. They barely made it upstairs to the apartment they shared before Chelsea was undressed, and they hadn't come up for air since. Her heart was pounding, her skin was slick with sweat... she was alive. They had survived. As much as she hated herself for spending Riley's wake like this, another part of her knew Riley wouldn't want it any other way. She wouldn't want her friends weeping; she'd demand they appreciate the fact they were still alive. It didn't make her feel any better.

"How are you holding up?" Chelsea kissed Kenzie's ear.

"She can't be dead. I was the idiot, I was the risk-taker, and I was the one who went overseas. I had a bomb blow up in my face. If anyone should have died~"

"Shut your mouth." Chelsea turned Kenzie's head and kissed her lips. Kenzie twisted until she was on her back, pulling Chelsea onto her as her tongue slid into Kenzie's mouth. She slid her hands down Chelsea's back, cupping her ass and pulling her closer.

Someone started knocking on the office door downstairs.

"Leave it," Kenzie gasped between kisses.

"It could be a client."

"I don't care. Not today." She kissed Chelsea harder, rolling her hips up to meet Chelsea's. "Make love to me again."

Chelsea decided to ignore the knocking and, eventually, it did stop. She moved her hand between Kenzie's legs, touching her just as they heard the alarm begin to sound as the uninvited guest let themself in.

"Son of a bitch," Chelsea grumbled. She pushed herself up, and Kenzie scrambled to the edge of the bed.

Kenzie grabbed her robe and tugged it on, tying the belt as she moved toward the door. "I'll take care of it. Stay here." She picked up her gun as she left the bedroom, checking the magazine before she headed down to the office. The stairs led into a small vestibule behind their workspace, and she paused there to scan the interior of the office. The light filtering through their greenhouse cast jungle-like shadows of flowers, leaves and vines on the walls. She stepped out when she saw movement, focusing her gun on the shape moving behind one of their desks.

"Freeze, asshole."

The desk light turned on and Riley held her hands up. "Take it easy, Kenzie."

Kenzie's eyes widened. "Jesus..."

"Just~"

Kenzie fired.

"Riley..."

Gillian was up and off the couch by the time Priest finished speaking. Riley had helped her transfer Priest to a cot in her office before leaving, and Gillian had curled up on the couch to try getting some rest. She knelt next to Priest and took her hand. "Hey, there you are. I was starting to get worried."

Priest's lips were dry and cracked, and her eyelids looked too heavy to keep up. "Thought... you hated... me."

"Bringing my girlfriend back from the dead covers a multitude of sins." Gillian brought Priest's hand to her mouth and kissed the knuckles. "How are you?"

"Shooting pain... inside." She blinked and stared up at the ceiling as she touched her abdomen. Her eyes were watery. "Never meant to survive this long."

Gillian said, "Yeah, well. You and Riley both have a bad habit of coming back from the brink. Don't end the streak now."

Priest closed her eyes. "Is Riley here?"

"No, she... she went home. I thought she needed to get some rest." Priest nodded. "I can get her for you."

"Mm-mm." She shook her head slowly. "She hates me. Just... needed to do this. For her. For you. To apologize for what I did. For the hurt. The Angel Maker was my fault. I deserved to pay the price, not Riley." She grunted and folded slightly as if trying to protect her midsection from a blow. "Oh, Father. It hurts."

"I can give you something for the pain." Gillian moved to her desk and opened a drawer.

"No. Let me go."

Gillian closed her eyes. "You saved Riley. I can't just stand by and watch you die in agony."

"So... make it... happen quicker."

Gillian turned. Priest was staring up at her with pleading eyes, her bottom lip quivering. "I'm mortal now. Human, just like you. Easy to kill. Easier... so weak." She swallowed, and it seemed to take a Herculean effort. "Mercy killing."

"I won't do that."

"I spared Riley," Priest whispered. "Spare me the pain. It hurts, Gillian."

Gillian turned away from Priest and looked down at her desk. She opened the drawer again and thought about what would be required to put Priest to sleep. Maybe if she just knocked her out, she would be able to pass quietly. If the pain was stronger than the drugs, however... but she could worry about that later. She sniffled and ran her hand under her nose.

"I'll see what I can do."

"You *shot* me."

"I shot *at* you. In your general direction." Kenzie looked chagrined.

"Splitting hairs. Which, incidentally, is what you just did to me." Riley reached up and touched her head for the fifth time, making sure the bullet really had missed her. She was sitting in the client's chair in front of Kenzie's desk, and Kenzie was on the other side staring at her. Chelsea had come downstairs in a baggy T-shirt and a pair of shorts, drawn by the gunshot. She was wearing her black glasses, but Riley knew Chelsea was using what limited vision she had to stare at her.

Kenzie shrugged and held her hands out. "I said I was sorry. Look, angels and demons are real. Why not zombies? Why not vampires? I saw your dead body, and then you break into our office and skulk around in the darkness. What was I supposed to think?"

Chelsea put a hand on Kenzie's shoulder. "Riley, why don't you explain what happened?"

Riley leaned forward. "Look, I know the two of you have some... thing going on with my partner. Priest. I don't know the details, I don't want to know. But she's the reason I'm sitting here. She sacrificed herself to save me."

She saw Chelsea's fingers tighten on Kenzie's shoulder. "What... what do you mean sacrificed?"

Riley wet her lips and looked down at her hands. "She surrendered her divinity. Zerachiel died, and Caitlin isn't far behind. She gave up her life to bring mine back."

Chelsea put a hand over her mouth and turned away. "My God. Literally, I guess. Can we go to see her?"

"She's at the morgue right now. Gillian's keeping an eye on her. I'm sure Jill would let you in if you showed up."

Chelsea bent down and kissed the top of Kenzie's head. "I'll go get some clothes."

Kenzie stood as Chelsea left. She walked around the desk and impulsively embraced Riley. "Not well."

Riley frowned, confused by the sudden affection. Kenzie had never been big on hugging. She patted Kenzie's back. "What's not well?"

"That's how I was handling this. Losing you. Not well."

Riley awkwardly returned the embrace from her former partner, in both senses of the word. "Sorry I worried you, Mackenzie."

Kenzie stepped back and quickly swept a hand over her cheek to catch any stray moisture. "Yeah. Just don't do it again, huh? At least you took the bad guy down with you."

Riley smiled.

"So what's next?"

"I go home and get some rest. Doctor's orders, not to mention the lieutenant. Try and figure out what the real next step is."

Chelsea came downstairs in a blouse and a pair of trousers. Kenzie's clothes were folded over her arm.

"I'll leave you two alone for now. I just wanted to share the good news and the bad news."

"We'll call you if anything happens with Priest," Kenzie said.

"It's good to have you back." Chelsea reached out and touched Riley's cheek. "You mean a lot to Mackenzie, so you mean a lot to me, too."

Riley nodded. "Yeah. You know that saying about watching your own funeral? I think I know how that would feel now. I'm going to get out of here. I'll see you guys later."

"Thank you for telling us about Caitlin." Kenzie took her clothes from Chelsea. "And about you."

Riley nudged Kenzie's arm playfully. "Thank you for the warning shot."

Everyone had been dealt with. Gillian, Kenzie and Chelsea were with Priest, Gail Finney had fled the press conference like her hair was on fire, and her duties were done. Riley entered the apartment she shared with Gillian in utter exhaustion. She unzipped her jacket and tossed it over the back of the couch instead of hanging it up. *Is it really that much more effort to just hang it on this hook?* Riley stared at the way it draped. She had come so close to never again hearing Gillian gripe at her for that. She picked up the coat and hung it on the closet door.

She paused with her hand against the wall, eyes closed, listening to the sounds of the building. Traffic outside, people talking on the stairs, sirens somewhere distant. She didn't remember being dead, but the air seemed sweeter somehow. The sounds that would originally have been irritating were welcome now.

Riley went into the bedroom and took off her borrowed scrub top. The side of her jeans had a streak of dried blood running down the left leg, and she stared at it for a long moment before she took them off. At first she thought it odd that there was no dried blood on her skin, but then she realized that Gillian had probably washed her off in the morgue.

She couldn't control that shudder that ripped through her at that mental image. Her mind was a scrambled mess of *Oh, God, I died, I was dead, I died.* She pressed her fists to her face. She remembered the feel of the blade slicing into her, the feel of her heart trying to beat around the intruder. She had been dead.

But she was still alive.

She lifted her head, still trembling, and pulled herself up using the edge of the bed. She moved to the bathroom and stood in front of the mirror. The spot between her left arm and breast was unblemished, free of even a white-line scar. Priest's resurrection zap had really done a great job. She wondered how much of her had been healed and began searching for old scars. A few on her back seemed much lighter, and others were gone entirely. Her tattoo actually seemed fresher. She turned on the shower and took off her underwear as she waited for the water to warm up.

I wonder if I'm a virgin again. Gillian will have to check that out later.

She pulled the curtain and stood under the spray, angling her face up to wash off the cold water from the morgue sprayer. She shuddered again at the thought, but she kept it under control this time. She folded her hands to gather water and then swept it over the top of her head. She smoothed down her hair, worked her fingers into her ears, and made sure that she covered every inch as Gillian was sure to have done. The morgue water had evaporated on her body, and she wanted it as gone as it could get.

The hot water eventually ran out, and Riley reluctantly shut off the water and pushed back the curtain.

The brunette was standing in front of the sink. She had the

face of a Greek statue, with a pointed chin and a strong jaw. Her eyes were a vivid green, her Cupid's bow lips curled into a relaxed smile. Her hair was pulled back in a loose ponytail. She wore a thin white shift that joined at her hip to leave her haunches exposed.

Riley looked away to wipe the excess water from her face. She gestured at the sink. "Hand me that towel, would you?"

The woman turned, picked up the towel, and held it out. Riley took it and wiped off her face and torso, spreading the towel on the tile before she stepped out of the tub. "I guess you're an angel, right?" She took another towel off the rack and wrapped it around her body.

"Yes."

"Here to finish the job? Make sure things get set right?"

"No."

Riley walked into the bedroom and the angel followed. "By the way, I think I talked to your Boss. He's a crazy son of a bitch." The angel didn't respond. "So what's your name?"

"Sariel."

"Okay, Sara. Why are you here? If you guys are cool with me coming back, then is this just a service call? Are you here to make sure everything is in the right place?"

Sariel shook her head. "I'm here to tie up the loose ends Zerachiel left behind. Once that is complete, I will be taking over as your new guardian angel."

"Wonderful. Welcome to the team." She pulled back the blanket on the bed, dropped the towel, and stretched out. She hadn't expected it to be a big deal, but Gillian was right; she definitely needed to spend some time in her own bed. "Listen, don't take this the wrong way, but Priest and I went through a lot of ups and downs, but she was my friend. She's really the only angel I could ever stand, despite her faults. So don't expect you and me to get buddy-buddy right away. Once bitten, twice shy and all that. I'm happy to have you, you know, around. But we're not going to be friends. Got that, Sara?"

When there was no answer, Riley opened her eyes and scanned the bedroom. The apartment was empty.

"Good." She folded her pillow and put her head down. "Glad we got that out of the way."

The windows of Gail's apartment were covered by thick blackout curtains. She sat in the darkness with a bottle of beer sweating on her thigh, staring into the shadows. She felt the presence arrive, as usual, but this time didn't wait until the other woman broke the silence. She rose immediately and spun to face the demon. "What the hell went wrong?"

Gremory froze, a dark silhouette against the blackness of the room. It felt as if she was drawing the darkness to her, sucking it into her presence and leaving the rest of the apartment cold. She finally spoke in a low, measured voice. "You will do well to watch your tone."

Gail stepped closer, uncowed by the demon's tone. "No. You swore to me. You said Riley Parra had died last night, but she's alive and well."

"There was an unexpected occurance. Zerachiel stepped in and altered events."

"If you knew she could do that–"

"It has only been done once before, and it resulted in grave consequences. The angel is now gone, and the human shell will soon die. How long do you believe Riley Parra will survive without her angel watching over her? She knows who we are now, so there's no need to remain hidden from her. We no longer need to operate in the shadows. Parra is at her most vulnerable now, and we are at the peak of our abilities." One hand, as cold and smooth as a stone in a river, brushed Gail's cheek. "We will destroy her. She can only cheat death so many times before she pays the death she owes."

Gail closed her eyes. A part of her, a remnant from before she'd met Gremory, almost felt sorry for Riley. They were very alike, with their supernatural handlers. Gremory had been by Gail's side for just over fifteen months, but Gail didn't know what she would do without the demon's guiding hand. To think of the pain Riley must be going through with the loss of her angel... The compassion faded and a smile spread across her face as she thought of Riley in pain.

"Things will go according to plan. Riley Parra and her winged seraphim will not win this battle. You must be patient."

"Yes, my love."

Gremory stepped closer. "You doubted me. You know you must be punished for that."

Gail swallowed hard. "Y-yes, my love."

"Turn your back to me." Gail did as instructed and her slacks were pushed down. A few seconds later, when her punishment began, Gail began screaming with a mixture of pain and pleasure.

Tears rolled down her cheeks as she gave silent thanks to the special soundproofing Gremory had put on her walls. Without it, the neighbors would have put the police on their speed dials.

A section of the morgue was set aside for Priest, separated from the rest of the room by a pair of privacy curtains. Word quickly spread among the department that one of their own was clinging to life, and cops came by throughout the afternoon to offer moral support. Gillian, Kenzie and Chelsea held vigil beside Priest's bed. Gillian had just given Priest another sedative, but the injections were becoming less effective against the pain.

"The church." Kenzie straightened in her seat suddenly as the thought occurred to her. "She always said that churches healed her, they rejuvenated her spirit. Maybe..."

Chelsea shook her head. "It fed Zerachiel's spirit, babe. She's gone. Going to church would just make us feel better; it wouldn't do anything for Caitlin."

"That's doesn't mean we shouldn't try." Kenzie looked at Priest. "It's not fair. I feel like I'm choosing Riley over her. That if she dies, at least Riley is all right. It makes me feel like shit."

"You're not choosing anything." Gillian reached across the bed and squeezed Kenzie's forearm. "Priest made the decision herself. She decided to sacrifice herself so that Riley could live."

Chelsea touched Priest's cheek tenderly. "I won't say that it was the wrong choice to make. But I hate that it has to be one or the other."

Gillian said, "Yesterday I would have disagreed with you. This past year, she's been working with a serial killer. People died because of her. But now, I don't... I don't know. I feel like I'm forgiving her too easily. But she brought Riley back to me. That outweighs everything in my head. I think Caitlin deserves our forgiveness. And she deserves our respect." She brushed a hair away from Priest's face. Priest's eyelids fluttered, and she turned her head toward the touch. Gillian was shocked and checked to make sure she had really administered the new dose of sedatives. "Hey. You shouldn't be awake."

Priest groaned. "Hurts."

"I know, sweetie. Is there anything I can get you? Some water or food..."

Priest's stomach growled so loudly that Kenzie frowned at it.

Gillian furrowed her brow. "Caitlin, when was the last time

you ate?"

"Dunno. Don't need to eat."

Gillian closed her eyes in exasperation. "You do *now*, you stupid angel." She stood and hurried back to her office.

Kenzie stood and followed her. "You didn't check her out?"

Gillian shrugged. "She's an angel who lost her divinity and told me she was fading away. I didn't even think there could be a common medical explanation." She pulled her lunchbox from the bottom drawer and ripped it open. There was an apple, some granola bars, and a cookie wrapped in plastic. She handed it all to Kenzie. "Here, give her these. Break them apart into small pieces and feed her slowly. I'm going to see if I can find something more substantial in the break room."

The medical examiner called in to take over Gillian's workload for the day looked up from an examination at her sudden appearance, but she didn't even acknowledge him as she burst through the doors to the hallway. She took the stairs this time, too impatient to wait for the elevator. A few detectives were in the break room but she ignored them as she ran to the mini fridge and dropped to her knees. There were salads, all plainly marked with other people's names, and fruit in plastic bags. She found a container of soup with Lieutenant Briggs' name on it and grabbed it.

Briggs spotted her on the way back to the elevator. She held up the soup without slowing. "I'm taking this. Priest needs it."

Briggs frowned and followed Gillian to the stairs.

Kenzie was sitting on the edge of Priest's cot, her right shoulder propping Priest up. She had a piece of a granola bar pinched between two fingers, feeding it between Priest's lips as Gillian returned. "How is she doing?"

"A little better." Kenzie moved back to let Gillian take her position. "She's eating, but I don't want to rush it."

"No, rushing would be bad." Gillian opened the soup container. "Caitlin, do you think you could keep down some soup?"

Briggs had just arrived and quickly assessed the situation. "It's miso soup, if that matters."

Gillian nodded. "I'll just give her the broth." She folded the plastic lid to use as a spoon, scooping up some of the yellow-green broth and pouring it into Priest's mouth.

"Thank you, Gillian." Priest licked her lips after she'd had half the soup. "But all you're doing is managing my pain. Some of it was hunger, I guess, but... I'm still going to go away. It's just a matter of time."

"Well, I don't get to save my patients very often. And you've saved Riley so often that I..." Her throat closed and she choked back tears. She felt someone's hand on her back as she took another lid-full of soup. "Eat your soup. Doctor's orders. C'mon."

Priest took another sip.

The foreclosed church where Riley and Priest had set up the Cell looked utterly abandoned as Riley pulled into the back lot. She had dozed for almost half an hour before she threw back the blankets. She couldn't just lay there while there was still so much left unfinished. She crossed the weed-choked lot to the front door.

She checked the locks to make sure no squatters had taken refuge before she went around to the back. The storm shelter door was triple locked and Riley used her keys to get inside. Stone stairs ran down and to the right, leading into the church's basement. The walls were thick concrete, covered with sigils and signs that Priest had helped put in place before the Angel Maker's final moments.

Markus the Demon was still sitting in the middle of his trap, arms folded on bent knees, head pressed into the crook of his arm. He'd been imprisoned there since his attempt on the life of Leah Mason. She'd meant to free him, but things got a little out of hand before she could make the time. He didn't look up as Riley approached, but he snickered loud enough that she could hear.

"Hey, look who it is. The yoyo." He smiled. "That's the nickname for you that's been going around today. We heard some things about you." He looked up; his human face was contorted almost beyond recognition, his demonic side showing through. "I felt you die. Every demon and angel in this burg felt you die. For our side, was like an orgasm, only more fun. We were sure you were going to come and play in our playground. But then, shock of wonders... you went up to talk to the Big Boss. That impressed a lot of us. Well, all of us, really. Sat down and had a nice little chat with the Man Himself." He whistled. "And then... you come back to this place, and an angel dies. Do you know what it feels like to a demon when an angel dies?"

Riley stared at him.

"You better be glad you didn't see *my* boss. He would have been very glad to see you." He stood up. "He could have ripped you limb from limb. A decade for your right arm. A century for your left. He would spend five hundred years removing your eyes. One at a time. And he would have done it in the time you were gone. Time is funny down there. You know how 'time flies when you're having fun'? Well, imagine how slowly time goes when you are literally in hell."

"I want to test something." She opened her bag and removed a book. "I'm not going to be able to do this the easy way now that Priest is gone, but I planned for that. I knew I couldn't count on her help when I went after the Angel Maker, so I learned a few things. Let me know if I get anything wrong." She flipped to a page she had marked and began to read in Latin. "*Sacrit maritas nos lacrimit est triparceratis.*"

Markus flung himself forward and pressed his body against the confines of the trap. Smoke rose from inside of his clothes. "Bitch, stop, bitch." His words sounded like stones scraping together and accidentally forming the semblance of real words.

"*Promate illuc tyreratis est furimus cum servent cum tusculate tunicate est maritatrices.*"

Markus grabbed his head and backed away from her. He was looking less human with each word she spoke, steam so thick that it nearly obscured him entirely.

"*Recommentare stalare sum sagevi sic scitate sussurantis.*"

The smoke suddenly ceased as if a faucet had been plugged, and Markus collapsed to his knees. He was panting, his shoulders rising and falling with each breath. He looked like an outclassed boxer who'd just gone ten rounds with the champion, his eyes hooded and dark, his lips parted with the force of his exhalations. He lifted his head and glared at her.

"When I am released from this trap, I will flail you. I will let you live as I remove the skin from your body. I will remove your muscles from your skeleton. I will take you apart a piece at a time. And only when you are completely eradicated will I begin to kill the pieces of you."

"I don't need an angel to make a devil's trap." Riley closed her book. "And apparently I don't need an angel to exorcise you pricks. Thanks for the dry run, Markus."

"Where do you think Zerachiel went?"

Riley stopped with one foot on the bottom step.

"She went against her orders. Do you think her Boss looked very kindly upon her actions? There are rules in this little game of ours, Detective Parra. Zerachiel didn't play fair. Zerachiel broke the rules and brought you back. Zerachiel is ours now, Riley. My brothers are feeding on her as we speak. Remember how I said moments in Hell can seem like years? Zerachiel has been demon fodder for, oh, centuries now. She... is... delicious."

Riley turned to face him. "*Peragavi ipsos deminus exsangua.*"

Markus wailed and dropped to one knee. Riley turned and started up the stairs.

"Finish it! Don't leave me like this!" He howled in pain, smoldering in mid-expulsion as Riley left the Cell.

She was almost to the car when her phone rang. She recognized the ring tone she'd assigned to Gillian and answered as she unlocked the car. "Hey. I know you told me to stay home~"

"Hon, someone's here."

Riley straightened and looked over the top of her car as if she could see all the way to the station. "What do you mean someone?"

"She said she's an angel."

"Sariel?"

Gillian hesitated before she answered. "Yes. She's going to do something to Priest."

Riley closed her eyes and sagged against the car. She assumed whatever Sariel had to do, it would end Priest's life. She could tell Gillian and the others to just let her do what she came to do, but it felt wrong. She had to see Priest one more time, if just to thank her. She owed her that much. "I'll be right there. Don't let her do anything until I show up."

Sariel was wearing the same lightweight dress as before, but her hair was down on her shoulders. Priest was sitting on her cot with Kenzie at her side. Gillian and Chelsea were standing between the angel and her target when Riley came into the morgue. "Where's the backup ME?"

Gillian kept her eyes on Sariel when she answered. "I told him we needed some time. He's taking a long lunch."

Riley moved forward. "Caitlin, you okay?"

"No." Her voice was weak, rough with pain. "Tell them I need to do this."

"Gillian, the reason I told you to wait until I got here is because I needed to say this in person." She knelt in front of Priest and took her hand. "I wouldn't have made it through these past two years without you. You've saved my life time and again. But more than that, you were my friend. When it mattered, you always stood by my side even when it got you in trouble with... with your Boss. I wanted Sariel to wait so that I could say goodbye."

Priest closed her eyes and her tears finally slipped free. Riley leaned closer and kissed Priest's cheek.

"I love you, Caitlin."

"I love you, too, Riley."

"I just wanted to say that to you." Riley stood up and reached under her jacket. "And that's why I changed my mind." She twisted at the waist and aimed her gun between Sariel's eyes. "You're not going to do a damned thing to my partner. So turn around and walk away."

Sariel stared impassively at the weapon. "You must know that your weapon can't hurt me."

"Right." She bent her arm and pressed the barrel of the gun against the soft flesh under her chin. She heard Gillian shout her name but she was forced to ignore it. "You're my new guardian angel, right? Hell of a first day for you if I pull this trigger."

Priest struggled to her feet. "Riley, what are you doing?"

"Last year, you got torn apart by hellhounds so I had a chance to get away. You stood by me time and time again."

Gillian said, "She helped the Angel Maker, Riley."

"Zerachiel did that. And Zerachiel abandoned me for my trial. Come to think of it, every time I got pissed or annoyed at Priest, it was because of Zerachiel or some angelic shit. Priest was always my friend. Caitlin Priest may have been created as a shell for an angel, but she's a hell of a lot more than that now. You can't deny that. The fact that she's standing next to me right now should show you she's more than just a flesh suit. She may just be two years old, but she's alive. She has likes and dislikes. She has people who love her. She's a person.

"You wings have always said that it's my duty to protect all the people in this city. Right now, Caitlin Priest is one of those people. I don't care which side she's endangered by, I'm not going to stand back and watch you kill her."

Priest put her hand on Riley's shoulder. "I'm already dying, Riley. She just wants to make it easier."

Kenzie stood and moved in front of Priest. She stood with her shoulder against Riley's. "I won't let it happen, either."

Chelsea took a step forward and stood on Riley's other side. "Neither will I."

Gillian moved to stand between Riley and Priest, blocking

Priest with half her body. She put her hand on Riley's shoulder and squeezed.

Sariel stared at the women.

"Caitlin Priest has saved us. All of us, at one point or another. And now we need to return the favor." Riley moved her free hand and took Priest's. She squeezed. "If you can make her pain easier, then do it. If you can stop whatever is killing her right now, *do* it. Zerachiel did her duty as my guardian angel. I wouldn't let her protect me when I went after the Angel Maker, so she did it after the fact. She did nothing wrong. She doesn't deserve to be executed this way."

Sariel lifted her hand. Chelsea and Gillian were thrown back by a gust of wind, and Riley lowered her gun to instinctively grab for her lover. Sariel lunged forward and slapped Riley's hand. The impact stung far more than it should have, and Riley turned to face the angel. Before she had a chance to defend herself, the flat of Sariel's right hand pounded into her chest like a piston. Riley was lifted off her feet by the blow and landed halfway across the room. She skidded across the tile floor and slammed into an instrument tray that rattled like dry bones.

Kenzie grabbed Sariel's arm. Sariel spun and used her free hand to grab a handful of Kenzie's blouse. She lifted Kenzie straight up in the air, twisted at the waist, and swung her forcibly down like she was spiking a football. Kenzie hit the cot and bounced before falling face-first onto the floor. She tried once to get to her feet, but then fell and stayed down.

Riley crawled to Gillian's side. Gillian seemed dazed, but she managed, "I'm okay, I'm okay," and squeezed Riley's hand. Riley turned to face Sariel and Priest.

The two seraphim were facing each other, eyes locked. Sariel lifted her hand and pressed two fingers against Priest's forehead.

"No... no!" Riley couldn't even move; she knew it was pointless to try and reach Priest before what happened was finished.

There was a flash, and Priest collapsed like a marionette with cut strings. Riley closed her eyes and dropped her head. Gillian slid forward and pulled Riley to her, already sobbing as they clung to each other. Riley looked and saw that Sariel was already gone. The room felt suddenly silent, empty and hollow.

Chelsea had managed to crawl across the room and was desperately trying to rouse Kenzie. "Kenzie. Kenzie, wake up..."

"I wouldn't have done it." Riley's words were soft and warm

against Gillian's ear. "The gun was unloaded. I just had to make her listen."

Gillian lifted her head and kissed Riley's neck. "I'm so sorry, Riley."

"Gillian." Chelsea's voice was frantic, just one note below a scream. Riley helped Gillian to her feet and they moved to where she was kneeling. Kenzie was laying facedown, blood trickling out from under her head. Gillian pushed the cot out of her way and gently checked Kenzie before rolling her over. The blood was from a cut on her forehead, her eyes closed and lips parted.

Chelsea was trembling violently. "Tell me she's not~"

Kenzie groaned and Chelsea sobbed with relief. She turned her back on the group, hands pressed to her face as she trembled with relief.

"Just knocked out." Gillian stroked Kenzie's hair away from the cut. "She probably has a concussion. I-I need some bandages."

"I've got it." Riley got to her feet and went to the supply drawer. She ignored Priest's body for the moment; there would be time enough to deal with that later. She took handfuls of whatever supplies Gillian might need and carried it across the room. Chelsea had composed herself and was crouching next to Gillian to act as her nurse.

Priest's legs suddenly twitched, and her hands came up as if reaching for something.

Riley froze. Gillian and Chelsea both twisted to look as Priest rolled onto her stomach and slowly pushed herself up. She sat on bent knees, hands on her thighs, staring blankly until she turned her head and focused on the women.

"Caitlin?" Riley said.

Priest blinked and looked up at Riley. "Hello."

Riley dropped to her knees in front of her. "I thought Sariel..."

"I guess you made a convincing argument." Priest looked down at her hands. "My palms are tingling."

Gillian's surprise, relief, and panic gave way to anger. "If she was just going to give in, then why did she toss us around like rag dolls?"

Priest shrugged. "You pissed her off."

Riley couldn't stop herself from laughing. "Well, if she's going to stick around, she better get used to that."

Priest looked at her friends. "Is everybody okay?"

Riley saw that Kenzie was starting to come around, holding

Chelsea's hand with a loose grip. She nodded. "Yeah. Everyone's okay."

The doors to the morgue opened and the replacement ME returned with his lunch. He paused just inside the threshold and looked at the tableau. Gillian was still tending to Kenzie's forehead wound. Chelsea's tears were streaking down her face behind her black glasses. Priest had weakly laid her head on Riley's shoulder, and Riley was stroking her hair. Blood was smeared on the floor near Kenzie's body.

After a moment he held up his white to-go bag. "Does anyone want my fries?"

Priest blinked in surprise, raising one hand as she clutched her stomach with the other. "I think I do."

Gillian came out of her office with Priest a few steps behind her. "She's physically fine. The pain is fading a bit and she's feeling a little more... human."

Kenzie, lying on an exam bed, tenderly probed the bandage on her forehead. "Is that a good thing? I mean, considering."

Priest smiled. "It's acceptable. I'm still weak, but it's manageable. And I believe it is getting better."

"So what does that mean now?"

Priest shrugged and shook her head. "This has never happened before. When an angel returns Home, or dies in a manner such as Zerachiel, the host decays. We... they... have no further need for their earthly body, so they don't care much what happens to it."

"All the John Doe bodies that come into the morgue." Everyone looked at Chelsea. She shrugged. "It makes sense, doesn't it? All the unknown and unclaimed bodies that pass through this place. I'm sure some of them are people who just slipped through the cracks, but~"

"Yes." Priest had started nodding almost immediately. "We discard our... their..." She closed her eyes and focused. "Demons use human hosts, but angels don't like taking over a mortal's body. It's like stealing a car. So angels create bodies. When we are finished with them, there's no need to care for them. If we have to come back to this plane of existence, we just create another body. So yes, I'm certain some of the lost people the medical examiner's office has dealt with were former angels."

"But now you get to live." Gillian put her hand on Priest's shoulder.

"I guess so." She looked at Riley and held out her hand. "I'm so sorry. For the Angel Maker, for~"

"That wasn't you. That was Zerachiel." She shook Priest's hand. "You gave me back my life, I saved yours. We're even."

Kenzie slowly sat up, holding her head and wincing. "So what now?"

Riley looked at Gillian. "You still have the day off?"

"Uh, yeah. I think so."

She took Gillian's hand. "We're going to go. Kenzie, can you and~"

"We'll get Priest home."

"Thanks. I need to go talk to Briggs, let her know how the stuff with Priest worked out. But then there's someplace we need to go."

Gillian nodded. She looked at the women around her and exhaled sharply. "Turned out to be a pretty good day after all."

Riley smiled and pulled Gillian to her for a kiss.

Gillian knew that she couldn't hold Riley's hand while she was driving, so she settled for keeping one hand on Riley's thigh throughout the drive. At red lights, Riley would let go of the wheel and cover Gillian's hand with her own, stroking the fingers and tracing the lines of her palm until the light turned green again. The deeper they got into No Man's Land, the more nervous Gillian became. She watched out the windows, staring at people on the sidewalks who eyed the car like it was one stop shopping.

"Are you worried?" Riley asked.

"Yeah. Lucky I'm with a cop."

Riley smiled. Neither of them mentioned that having a cop wasn't an assurance they would be left alone. Not in this neighborhood.

Riley parked in front of an apparently random building and scanned the street before she got out of the car. Gillian waited until Riley came around to her side before she opened her door and joined her on the sidewalk. "What are we doing here?"

"Trust me." Riley put her hand on Gillian's elbow and guided her toward the building's front stoop. A slender black man stepped out of the shadows and moved toward them, and Gillian tensed. But Riley lifted her hand in greeting. "Just make sure it's left alone, Muse."

"Sure thing, Riley. That your girl?"

Riley smiled. "This is her."

"Dump her, baby," Muse said to Gillian. "Start datin' someone who takes you to *nice* places."

Gillian slipped her hand around Riley's waist. "She takes me to plenty of nice places. She just doesn't usually have to drive to them."

Muse laughed and moved toward the car while Riley led Gillian into the building. The lobby was vacant and poorly maintained; the paint was peeling, half the lights were burned out, and the floor was stained by what she hoped was just dirty water leaking down one wall. Riley led her up the stairs, making sure that she stayed close as they ascended.

"If you tell me you bought a new apartment..."

Riley laughed. "I can afford better than this even on a cop's salary. It's not far."

Not far turned out to be four flights of stairs to an emergency exit. Riley searched briefly until she found a length of wood, which she used to pry open the lock. She led Gillian out onto the roof. "C'mon."

Gillian cringed against the cold. She followed Riley across the roof and stopped at the stomach-high wall. From their position, she could see between two buildings and all the way down to the waterfront. From this high, even No Man's Land looked beautiful if she ignored the sirens and shouting from all around them. She pressed against Riley, who embraced her to help fight the cold.

"Okay, so what are we doing up here?"

Riley kissed Gillian's forehead. "I came here when I was fifteen. A guy I ran around with lived here, and he wasn't home. So I decided to come up and see what the roof looked like. And I stood here and I decided I was going to jump. There was no real reason. I wasn't depressed and it wasn't a particularly bad week. I just didn't want to go downstairs and pick someone's pocket, or rob a grocery store, or decide what I wanted to do with the rest of my day. I decided it would be so much easier to just jump and get it over with. It's the ultimate hobby. You only have to do it once and you never have to do anything again."

"Don't joke." Gillian's voice was rough, and Riley stroked her hair.

"Sorry. I stood here for a long time deciding it was the right thing to do. My father didn't care about me. My friends, well... I could be replaced easily enough. So I was ready to do it. And then I looked across the alley into that window right there." She pointed and Gillian saw a dirty window with pale green-yellow curtains obscuring most of the view. The apartment on the other side was dark. "There weren't any curtains back then. I could see right into the kitchen. A woman was standing at the counter and she was making dinner. It was exotic. I'd never seen someone prepare a meal before. Especially not that lovingly."

Gillian turned her head, her cheek against Riley's. She could smell Riley's soap and, faintly, her sweat. She breathed deeply and thought of how close she'd come to losing her forever.

"I watched her for a long time. She never looked out the window or saw me. Eventually, her husband came home and she changed. She went from biding her time to being really... alive. I realized that maybe I was so bored because I was just waiting, too. I didn't want to jump before I found out what I was supposed to be waiting for. A year later, I met Christine Lee. When she died, I became a cop. When I became a detective, I started spending a lot of time with a beautiful medical examiner."

Gillian leaned back and smiled at her. "Thanks for waiting."

"You're worth it." She kissed Gillian softly. When they parted, she brushed her thumb over Gillian's bottom lip. "If Priest hadn't... done what she did, I would have died in love with you. You would have been the woman I spent the rest of my life with. But it would have been by default. So I thought I'd..." She closed her eyes. "I thought I'd make it official."

Gillian pressed her lips together to make them stop trembling. Riley took a ring from her pocket and held it up between two fingers.

"I got this a while back, but I never mentioned it. I just wanted to have it on hand. I knew I'd need it eventually, but I never got around to it. If I'd died without giving it to you..." She exhaled and shook her head. "I don't want to do this in a corny way. But I got a second chance, and I'm not going to waste it. I should have done this the second you said you'd be with me. I should have told you that I never want to be with anyone else. And even if we can't make it official, even if it's too dangerous for you to wear the ring, I want you to have it. I got what I was supposed to wait for."

Gillian folded her hand around Riley's, closing the ring in her palm. "I love you, Riley. Yes." Riley smiled and pulled Gillian to her for a kiss.

Riley didn't get any sleep the first night of her resurrection. Gillian confirmed that she hadn't reclaimed her virginity, but that didn't affect their celebration. Riley was awake to watch the sunrise with her new fiancé dozing quietly in her arms. Life was good.

Briggs didn't want her coming in to work right away, ordering her to recover and make sure everything was working properly before she did anything strenuous, but that didn't mean she couldn't drive Gillian to work. And if she happened to stop by her desk for a while, where was the harm? They had a slow, leisurely breakfast together before they left, and Riley made a quick stop by Priest's apartment.

She got tired of knocking after five minutes, so she popped the lock and stepped into Priest's apartment. It looked much the same as the last time she'd visited, but she noticed a lot of small items were packed up in boxes. "Caitlin, you here?"

"I'm in the bedroom."

Riley crossed to the hall that branched off the living room. The bedroom door was open, and she saw Priest sitting on the floor with her back against the bed. She was holding a book open on her legs, but she was staring past it at the wall. Riley stopped in the doorway. "Hey. I'm taking Gillian in to work. Thought I'd see if you wanted to come with."

Priest lowered her head. "I'm not going in."

"Are you still feeling queasy? I can have Jill come up and—"

"No. I can't go in."

Riley stepped into the room and sat next to Priest on the floor. "Talk to me, Goose." Priest frowned. "It's a... movie reference. What's wrong?"

"Last night, I lay on top of my bed and tried to sleep. I could hear the music in the church downstairs, as always, but it was flat. It didn't feel... the way it always felt. And because it didn't feel good, it hurt. My entire body feels like it's wrapped in thick, thick cloth and I can only feel vague sensations through it. And it's not just the music; everything is vague. I appreciate what you did to save my life, but I know why I'm the first... vessel, I suppose, to continue existing. I don't think many other angels could stand this. It's unbearable."

Riley put her arm around Priest and drew her closer. "It's all right. It'll take some adjustment. You weren't as human as you thought."

"No." She rested her head on Riley's shoulder. "I saw a program about scuba divers on television. They wore suits and breathing masks. If one of those men decided they were a fish, and took off the mask... they would drown. That's how I feel right now. I feel like I'm drowning in mortality."

"We're going to help you. Me and Jill, Kenzie and Chelsea... even Briggs. We'll~"

"No. I have to do this alone, Riley."

Riley nodded slowly. She hadn't wanted to admit this, but it made sense. "How long do you think you'll be gone?"

"Not long. I just need to clear my head. I need to decide who Caitlin Priest is without Zerachiel."

"Do you need some money?"

Priest laughed. "In the past two years, I've bought six suits and a small meal once per day. Even on a police detective's salary, I have quite a bit of money saved up." She shook her head. "I am sorry, Riley. You stood up to defend me, and the first thing I do is leave you."

"I stood up to defend your right to live. If you need to clear your head first, then I understand. Just don't be gone too long, all right?"

"I'll do my best."

Riley held up her left hand to show off her ring. "Gillian and I are betrothed."

"Betrothed?"

"Gillian's word. I like it."

Priest smiled. "Congratulations."

"It took us long enough." Riley smiled, still amazed by the bit of gold around her right finger. "We'll wait until you get back before we do anything. I want you to be my maid of honor."

"Thank you," Priest whispered.

They sat together for a while longer before Riley pushed herself up. "Don't get lost. Don't let anyone take advantage of you. Come home soon."

"I will." Priest held out her hand, and Riley shook it. "See you later, Caitlin Priest."

"But not too much later."

Riley smiled and left the apartment. Gillian was sipping her coffee in the passenger seat of the car. "Is she getting ready?"

"She's not coming. Not yet."

"Ah. Is she okay?"

Riley nodded. "Yeah. She will be." She picked up Gillian's

hand, her left hand, and kissed her ring. "C'mon. We're going to be late for work."

Priest locked the apartment door behind Riley and turned to face her spartan apartment. "She's gone."

Sariel came out of the kitchen. "Then we should begin."

Priest took a deep breath, closed her eyes, and nodded before she followed Sariel into the living room.

THE FOLLOWING IS A REENACTMENT

Four years ago

RILEY TRIED not to toy with her necktie. She felt like a chess piece, an extra bit of decorating that added to the ambiance of the setting. She wasn't a real person, not an entity worth considering. She had her hands behind her back, as instructed, and she stood briefly by the side entrance before starting her third circuit of the room's perimeter. She was in full uniform, the brim of her cap pulled down over her eyes.

Sweet Kara crossed Riley's path and turned to walk beside her. "Someone's asking about you."

"Lieutenant Hathaway?"

Kara smirked. "No, I haven't seen her. Your *girlfriend*."

Riley rolled her eyes and turned her head so that Kara couldn't see her blush. They moved slowly, not eager to cover much space. They were still assigned to provide security for the fundraiser for two more hours. The floor to ceiling windows of the ballroom were lit from outside by small spotlights, so they could see out but no one could see in. It made her feel like she was enclosed inside of a bubble of decadence while ignoring the world outside.

"She's over by the drinks if you want to say hi."

"Just drop it, Kara."

Kara chuckled and rolled her shoulders, clasped her hands

tighter behind her back, and mimicked a Buckingham Palace guard.

"You have plans for when this godawful thing ends?" Riley asked. "Wanna grab a drink?"

"Sorry. I made plans with someone."

"Another conquest?"

"My niece."

Riley smiled. "Domestic Sweet Kara. I'd like to see that."

"You and my mom both." She caught the police commissioner's eye. "Uh oh. I think we're having a bit too much fun for the brass. Let's split up. See you on the other side of the room probably."

Riley nodded and again assumed her stoic expression. The police commissioner, the mayor, and more than a handful of muckety-mucks that Riley was sure would otherwise be in jail if not for their deep pockets. She and several other detectives had been assigned as security and forced to put on their old patrol uniforms for the aesthetic of it. She was just glad she was still able to fit into the trousers.

She told herself that it was a casual trajectory; that the drink table just happened to be in her way. She walked behind the table since the police weren't allowed to partake of the refreshments and eyed the crowd. She spotted Gillian standing a few feet away and averted her gaze. She glanced out the windows at the well-lit and the building's perfectly tended lawn before she looked back.

Gillian was already in motion, moving closer with a smile. "Well, hi there."

"Hi. I'm not supposed to... fraternize."

Gillian shrugged. "What will they do, relieve you of your duties? Let you go home early?"

Riley smiled. "In that case, hello, Dr. Hunt."

"Hi. You look nice."

"Yeah, my old patrol uniform. Really flattering. Unlike..." She finally allowed herself to notice Gillian's dress and the sight made her voice trail off. It was green, which helped bring out the color of her eyes, and her chestnut-colored hair was gathered behind her head. Somehow the style was reminiscent of how she usually wore it in the morgue, but fancier somehow. A few strands were free, and Riley resisted the urge to tuck them behind Gillian's ears.

"Unlike?" Gillian prompted.

"Sorry. I just meant you looked really nice."

She smiled. "Well, anything is an improvement over scrubs."

"No, you even make scrubs look good." Riley hadn't intended to say anything quite so come-on-esque and dipped her chin. "So are you enjoying the party?"

"I'm enjoying parts of the party." She picked up a plate with a small slice of red velvet cake on it. "I asked your partner if you were here. She got the strangest look on her face."

Riley shook her head. "That's just Kara. I wouldn't worry about her too much."

"Oh, I didn't say I was worried. Will you be here for the rest of the night?"

"I'm on the schedule for two more hours. If I have to stay longer than that, it's overtime. So the boss will most likely tell me to go home in one hour and fifty-nine minutes."

Gillian laughed. "Well, come say hi to me again before that happens. It's nice to talk to someone who doesn't just want to brag about how much money they have."

"That is one thing you never have to worry about with me, Dr. Hunt."

"Gillian."

Riley hesitated. "Gillian."

"Would you like a piece of cake?"

"Not allowed to partake while on the job."

Gillian narrowed her eyes. "I didn't ask if you were allowed, I asked if you wanted a piece. Besides, you don't strike me as a strict adherent to the rules." She picked up another plate and looked over her shoulder as she held it out to Riley. "No one's looking."

Riley picked up the cube, popped it into her mouth, and chewed as quickly as she could while Gillian kept a lookout.

"Now I need a drink."

"That would be harder to sneak." Gillian picked up a cup of punch. Riley suddenly had a mental image of Gillian taking a sip, holding it in her mouth, and then kissing her. She blushed as Gillian held the cup out to her. "Quickly."

Riley took the cup, sipped, and quickly passed her tongue over her lips. "Mm. Perfect, thank you." She looked past Gillian. "Ah, the people you were talking to earlier seem to miss your presence."

Gillian turned. "Oh, them. I should probably go over. State board, they appointed me to medical examiner, so I need to stay on their good side."

"Definitely do that. You're the best ME I've ever seen."

Gillian winked at her. "Thanks. If you need any more snack-related hookups, come and find me."

"I'll be sure to do that."

Gillian put down her empty plates and left the snack table to rejoin the party. Riley watched her go, paying close attention to how low the dress dipped in the back, and turned to resume her rounds. She found Kara standing a few feet away with a shit-eating grin on her face. Riley groaned and braced herself.

"She *fed* you."

"She just ran interference so I could get a piece of cake."

Kara chuckled. "Uh-huh."

"Shut up."

"I think it's sweet. And with you in the uniform and her in her gown, it's even romantic. The princess and the ranch hand."

"I think you're blending fantasies there."

Kara lowered her voice and affected a Southern accent. "Why, Missus Hunt. I didn't think this was a part of my duties. I can be gentle if you~"

"Kara... I'm warning you."

She chuckled. "I just want you to be happy, Riley. No, scratch that. I just want you to get laid. And if it happens with the lovely medical examiner..."

"I'm not going to have a one night stand with someone I work with."

"Right. That's why you and I have never hooked up."

Riley smiled. "That and your straightness."

"Eh, no one's *really* straight. Give me a couple of drinks and we'll talk."

Together they rounded the ballroom two more times, moving as slowly as possible. They paused to converse with other detectives forced to play dress-up, and Riley tried not to look at her watch every five minutes. She was standing by the back entrance of the ballroom when Kara approached quickly. "Hey, look outside."

Riley frowned. "What?"

"Just look outside, don't~"

But Riley had caught sight of the green dress moving through the crowd. Gillian was moving with a little more care than she had before, indicating she'd partaken of the champagne being passed out. There was little danger of her falling, however, considering how she was hanging off the bare-shouldered brunette in the black dress. As they stepped out the door, Gillian's arm went around the woman's waist and pulled her closer.

"I'm sorry, Riley."

"For what?" Riley said. She kept her eyes on the crowd, her jaw firm as she tried not to let her irrational feelings show. "I'll just find someone else to sneak me cake, that's all."

Kara didn't even fake a smile. "Yeah."

Riley looked at her watch. "Twenty more minutes and we can get out of here, too."

"If you want to go get a drink, I could~"

"What? Blow off your niece? I'm fine, Kara. I don't know what you're worried about."

Kara leaned against the wall beside Riley and didn't press the matter.

Present Day

"It was bad enough when I graduated from the academy and just thought I was surrounded by jerky bureaucrats. Now that I know half the people there are either demons or demon-adjacent, it's going to be torture."

"You'll be fine." Gillian was still in the bathroom applying her makeup. Riley was trying to make her tie work using a smaller mirror from Gillian's nightstand. "Lieutenant Briggs promised it's going to be as quick and painless as possible. A few pictures, a few handshakes, and you'll be free to go back to your regular job and your regular clothes."

Riley pulled her tie free. "This is why I took the detective exam. So I wouldn't have to deal with the damn uniform."

"Oh, you're such a child." Gillian came out of the bedroom.

Riley turned to let her deal with the infernal knot, and immediately forgot about her uniform. "*Qué pasada.*"

Gillian held her arms out and did a spin. She was wearing a gold toga-type dress that left her right shoulder bare. Riley closed the distance between them and lifted her chin so Gillian could knot the tie for her. She did it in record time, smoothing her hands over the shoulders of Riley's uniform and stepping back to admire how it looked on her.

"Mm. You always look so delicious in this thing."

Riley smiled. "Do you remember the last time you saw me in it?"

Gillian thought for a moment and then smiled. "The fundraiser. I had to get all dolled up so the state wouldn't replace me. And you... oh, I remember you, Detective Parra."

"Sweet Kara said that it was like an heiress and a stable boy, or something like that."

"Well, you *were* the hired help for the event."

Riley smiled and gently stroked Gillian's waist through her dress. "And you were the high society dame who I didn't have a shot with."

"Except you did. You should have asked me out. I would've said yes."

"Well, that's good to know *now*." She bowed her head and kissed Gillian. It was meant to be quick, but neither of them pulled back. Gillian parted Riley's lips with her tongue and gripped Riley's belt with both hands.

Gillian broke the kiss, but kept her forehead against Riley's. "This uniform. Riley, you have no idea what this uniform does to me."

"Yeah?"

"Mm. I wouldn't have just said yes if you'd asked me out that night. I would have done whatever you wanted, if you asked me while you were wearing this."

"Really?" Gillian purred and nodded. "Well, what if I'd asked you to step out of the party? Come with me into the hall?"

Gillian nodded. "I would have gone with you. Would you have kissed me?"

"For starters." Riley kissed her again.

Gillian pulled back and took Riley's hand. "Come with me." She led Riley out of the bedroom and into the small hallway that led to the bathroom and living room. Gillian pressed herself against the wall, hands behind her back. "Well, Detective Parra? What was so important you couldn't tell me in the ballroom?"

Riley closed the bedroom door, making the hallway darker. "I'm not sure, Dr. Hunt. I just know that I wanted to get you alone. I wanted to make sure I was the only thing you could see when I told you how beautiful you looked tonight." She brushed Gillian's hair out of her face. "Tonight and every day at work. I just wanted to tell you, without anyone overhearing, that however bad tonight is, it's worth it just to have seen you looking like this for one second."

Gillian bit her bottom lip. "Well, Riley. I had no idea you felt that way."

Riley stepped closer, pinning Gillian to the wall with her hips. "And I would really like to kiss you right now." She dipped her head, her lips brushing Gillian's lightly.

"Detective! Someone could come by at any minute."

Riley sucked her neck and Gillian's voice wavered.

"Although I've always been a sucker for a woman in uniform..." She put her hands on Riley's chest and toyed with her badge. "I won't lie... I've fantasized about this a couple of times."

"Really?" Riley said against Gillian's neck. Riley ran her hands down Gillian's arms, tickled her palms with her fingertips, and then lifted both of Gillian's arms over her head. Gillian gasped in surprise and sagged forward against Riley's body. "Keep your hands up, ma'am. I don't want to cuff you."

"Yes, Officer."

Riley tickled Gillian's arm as she dropped her hand, moving down Gillian's side to her hip. She lifted her head and kissed Gillian's lips as she began to draw up her dress.

"We're going to be late."

"How can we be late? We're already at the party."

Gillian chuckled against Riley's mouth. "Oh, right. Well, we'll have to be quiet. I wouldn't want the mayor to hear."

Riley pulled back and saw that she'd smeared Gillian's lipstick slightly. She brushed it with her thumb and Gillian kissed and sucked the tip before she pulled it back. Riley used her wet thumb to draw the letter R on Gillian's neck, and Gillian chuckled. "Nice."

"Thank you." She bent down and kissed the spot, her other hand drawing up Gillian's dress. She caressed the smooth curve of Gillian's hip, relieved she hadn't yet put on her pantyhose. Her thumb hooked on the waistband of her underwear and gently drew them down her legs.

Gillian chuckled and twisted her fingers together to resist the urge to lower them. "You wouldn't have done *this* that first night..."

"Are you sure?"

Gillian opened her eyes and smiled. "You would have gone this far?"

"Once I'd kissed you, I wouldn't have been able to draw the line unless you told me to stop." She licked her lips. "Dr. Hunt, I need you to tell me to stop."

Gillian blinked and struggled to slip back into character. "Okay. When you reach the line, I will definitely stop you."

Riley let Gillian's underwear fall, and Gillian stepped out of them without breaking eye contact. Riley twisted her wrist to rub the back of her hand against the spot where her leg met her hip. Gillian drew a sharp breath and rested her head against the wall.

"Can I touch you?"

"Yes."

Gillian's hands dropped to the front of Riley's uniform, toying with her badge before moving to the buttons. She undid a few, just enough to reveal the clean white undershirt. She drew in a breath and let it out slowly. "I really did fantasize about this, you know. About you."

"Yeah?" Riley cupped her, and Gillian groaned. "Tell me."

"I dreamt about you in the morgue. Lifting me onto the table and taking my scrubs off. Lying me down naked and..."

Riley was using two fingers, and words seemed to fail her for the moment. Riley nuzzled Gillian's cheek until she spoke again.

"...you'd make love to me."

"Nice fantasy."

Gillian sighed. "Yeah, it worked for me."

Riley kissed her way down Gillian's neck, dropping to one knee in front of her. She slid her hand down Gillian's leg, massaged the back of her knee until it bent, and she guided it up onto her shoulder. Gillian muttered something under her breath as Riley kissed her thigh and pushed up her dress just enough to see her. She licked her lips and then ran her tongue up Gillian's thigh.

"I'll tell you one thing," Riley said softly. Gillian murmured. "This would have been a lot better than a damn piece of cake."

Gillian laughed breathlessly. "God, you're baaa...d. Riley..."

Riley had pressed her thumb between Gillian's folds before slipping her tongue against them, spreading her open as her tongue ventured forth. Gillian put her hand on the back of Riley's head, looking down as her fingers curled in the braids. "If I mess it up, I'll rebraid your hair before we go," she sighed.

Riley murmured her agreement, and Gillian gasped as the vibrations washed over her. Riley curled her tongue, using her free hand to pull Gillian's dress out of the way so she could look up and watch her reactions. It didn't take long for her breathing to quicken, her lips parted and her chin lifted as she tightened her leg on Riley's shoulder. Riley didn't let up, flicking her tongue against Gillian's clit before pushing inside again.

Gillian moaned, her leg tensing and relaxing against Riley's shoulder until finally it relaxed and Gillian began to softly stroke Riley's hair. She sighed, moaned, and looked down to meet Riley's eyes as Riley pulled back from Gillian's dress. She lowered Gillian's leg and kissed her way back up Gillian's body.

"Very nice, Officer," Gillian whispered, wrapping her arms around Riley's neck and pulling her forward for a kiss.

"I don't usually do that on a first date, Dr. Hunt."

Gillian laughed and Riley kissed both her cheeks before trying to pull away. "We're going to be late..."

"Whoa, nelly." Gillian pulled Riley back to her. "My fantasy didn't end there. You think I fantasized about you and didn't have my fun?"

Riley looked toward the door. "We're... we're really going to be late, Jill..."

Gillian pushed off the wall and shuffled Riley back against the opposite wall. Riley's shoulders impacted gently, her eyes widening at being manhandled. Gillian's eyes sparkled as she slid her hands over the starched material of Riley's uniform blouse. She kissed Riley's lips as her hand moved down, following the line of buttons to Riley's belt. "You in this uniform? You were a regular player in my fantasies for a long, long time." She unfastened the belt one-handed, breathing hard as she pinned Riley to the wall.

"Yeah? Tell me more, Dr. Hunt?"

"No. You tell me your fantasies. Did you ever think about me?"

Riley moaned as Gillian undid her pants. "Half the women I slept with after meeting you could have been your twins. I dated an ER nurse just because she was wearing scrubs." She leaned in and whispered in Gillian's ear. "When I masturbated, I would call out your name."

Gillian tugged on Riley's pants and slid her hand down the front of them. Riley closed her eyes as Gillian bowed down and kissed her neck.

"Don't give me a hickey..."

"Sh." Gillian rocked her hips in time with her hand, easily avoiding Riley's underwear to touch bare flesh. Riley held onto Gillian's shoulders, arching her back as Gillian looked down at her. "God, I've wanted to do this forever."

"You should have asked. I wouldn't have minded putting it on. Not for you." She put her hand on Gillian's neck, curling her fingers under Gillian's hair.

Gillian sighed. "I'll remember that. Come for me..."

"This won't get you out of the ticket, ma'am."

"Oh-ho, Riley..."

"I'm gonna have to frisk you when you're done, you know that, right?"

"You're going to make me come again..."

"Me first."

Riley pulled Gillian forward and kissed her hard. Gillian slipped her tongue into Riley's mouth, muffling her moans as she came.

When they pulled apart, Gillian made a show of tugging Riley's trousers back into place, buttoning them and tugging the zipper up. Her first attempt to fasten the belt was too tight - "Honey, I'm flattered, but I can't breathe..." - but she got it right the second time. Riley retrieved Gillian's panties and helped her back into them.

"God, I'm not even ready... I need to redo my makeup." She looked at her watch. "Briggs is going to murder you."

Riley put her hand in the small of Gillian's back and pulled her forward for a kiss. "Worth it."

Gillian smiled and they both went back into the bedroom to finish getting ready.

Lieutenant Briggs met Riley by the backstage entrance. "It's about time, Detective. I was starting to get anxious." She sighed and brushed her hair back out of her face. She looked at the empty passenger seat of Riley's car. "Where is your girlfriend?"

"I don't know. Not here. Why?"

"Nothing. I think the photographers wanted a few pictures. Never mind, it doesn't matter. Come on, let's get this over with, huh?"

"Fine by me."

She adjusted her tie, made sure her cap was seated correctly on her head, and followed Briggs into the theater so she could receive her commendation.

After the ceremony, Gillian waited by the refreshment table. She was aware of someone standing beside her but ignored them until she decided on a cup of punch. She lifted it to her lips and turned to face her companion. "Oh, hello."

"Hi. I'm not supposed to fraternize." The uniformed officer clasped her hands behind her back and examined the food table. "And I'm not allowed to partake of food on the job."

"Well, that's a shame. The food is delicious."

"I'm sure it is." Riley turned to face her. "Dr. Hunt, may I speak with you for a moment outside?"

"About what?"

Riley slipped her hand into Gillian's and guided her away from the table. "I'm sure we'll think of something."

A VERY SORRY SAINT

"WELCOME TO Utopia."

"That was the message we were given, wasn't it? The headline being shoved down all our throats. All hail Detective Riley Parra who has delivered us from the Angel Maker! She saved us all from the fires of Hades by stopping one man with a knife, and now it will all be bliss and happiness from now on. Right? I mean, right? It's been eight weeks since the Angel Maker was killed, my gentle listeners, and I'm afraid I have to be the bearer of bad news. The city is still a mess. Crime is still rampant. A woman walking alone on the street at night stands a better chance of getting raped and killed than she does getting splashed by a passing car.

"Detective Parra got lucky, ladies and gentlemen. She is a police officer, like a hundred others in this town. The people in charge of the media, and the people pulling the strings at the police department *want* us to lay down our arms. They want us to feel content in our homes at night because it means they can pretend to be making a difference. They want~"

Riley looked up as Gail Finney's voice cut off mid-sentence. "I was listening to that."

"And I've told you not to." Gillian had come out of the bedroom dressed for work in green scrubs under a pale yellow sweater. Her hair was pinned back, and she wore her horn-rimmed glasses instead of her usual contacts. She bent down and kissed Riley's temple. "It just gets you riled up when you hear her vitriol. Why expose yourself to the grief?"

"Know thy enemy." Riley finished the last bit of her oatmeal and stood to carry her bowl to the sink. "Want a ride in to work?"

"Yes, please."

Riley rinsed out her bowl and checked her watch. She had enough time to wait for Gillian to eat her breakfast, so she returned to the kitchen table and sat down. Gillian cut a grapefruit in half, salted it, and sat down in her usual seat. She unfolded the newspaper Riley had opened to the funny pages and skimmed the headlines as she ate.

It was Breakfast Fifty-Three: the fifty-third breakfast that she and Gillian weren't supposed to have together. She couldn't bring herself to stop counting. The five fights they weren't supposed to have. Seventeen lovemaking sessions. Two movies. Eight weekends. If Priest hadn't sacrificed herself to save Riley, she would have missed so much time with Gillian. She couldn't stop thinking of each and every little thing they did together as a gift. She looked at the ring on the third finger of Gillian's hand. Not to mention the big important things she wouldn't have been able to do.

Gillian looked up, her hair caught in her glasses. She smiled. "What?"

Riley shook her head. "I love you."

Gillian pushed her glasses up with her pinky and looked down. "Flirt."

She finished her grapefruit, put on a sweater, and slid her arm around Riley's elbow as they walked out of the apartment. She kissed Riley's cheek and whispered, "For the record, I love you, too."

Riley nuzzled Gillian's cheek as they went downstairs to the car. She looked down the street as she walked around to the driver's side, Gail's editorial still ringing in her ears. The police department had certainly done their part to make Riley into the hero of the moment, and most reporters were willing to play up the hero angle. For the time being, Priest's plan of working with the Angel Maker had worked. Riley was someone for the public to set their sights on, a symbol of hope in an increasingly dark world. Riley just hoped that she could live up to the promise.

Gillian waited to speak until they were underway, turning to look at Riley when they reached the first intersection. "Are you still working solo?"

"For now. Briggs keeps trying to foist new partners on me."

"Any word from Priest?"

Riley shook her head. "I went by her place last week. It was cleaned out." Gillian nodded. "She'll be back. She just needed some time to get her head clear. I mean, she went from being one species to being another. That's gotta take some time to work through."

"Yeah. I just don't like the idea of you being out there alone with all this attention. You've been in the newspaper more often than the mayor lately."

Riley shrugged. "No more dangerous than before."

"Before you had an angel on your shoulder."

"I still have an angel watching out for me. Sariel."

Gillian raised an eyebrow. "The woman who gave Kenzie a concussion just to make a point?"

"Touché." She reached over and squeezed Gillian's thigh. "I'll be extra careful when I'm out."

Gillian shook her head. "Don't patronize me, Riley. I just want you to know I'm concerned. Keep that in mind before you go rushing headlong into something. Priest isn't around to pull your fat out of the fire."

Riley nodded. "I got it. I do."

"That's all I wanted. Now I'll turn off the nag."

"Don't." She let go of the steering wheel again and took Gillian's hand. She brought it to her lips and kissed the knuckles. "I like having someone bitching at me to be careful."

Gillian smiled. "Driving one-handed. Is that part of your 'being careful' initiative?"

Riley let Gillian's hand drop and made a point of taking the wheel in the perfect ten-and-two positions. "Better?"

"Much."

Riley wasn't sure what the opposite of pariah was, but she certainly felt the part whenever she arrived at work. Detectives glanced up as she passed their desks, uniformed officers nudged each other and tried to be subtle about pointing at her as she arrived at her desk and checked the memos that had accumulated during the night. Lieutenant Briggs' door opened and she stepped out, glanced at Riley, and clapped her hands to get everyone's attention. "Detectives, now that we're all here, let me have a moment of your time, please."

Riley leaned forward and rested her chin on her right fist. The other detectives in the room gathered, and Briggs checked the paper in her hands before she started speaking.

"Okay, everyone. Thanks to the efforts of Detectives Lewis and Delgado, we have a confession in the bodega shootings from last week." The room applauded the efforts while the detectives in question, exhausted and slumped at their desks, accepted it with lazy nods. "Franklin, they're expecting you in court this afternoon so dress nice. You know how Judge Nunn gets."

Franklin took a tasteful purple tie from his pocket and held it up like a flag. Briggs approved it with a thumbs-up.

"Very nice, very nice. Everyone else, you have your assignments. Get to them." The crowd began to disperse. "Riley, could I see you for a second?"

Riley resisted the urge to roll her eyes. Briggs stepped out of the way and Riley went into her office. Briggs closed the door and walked around the desk as Riley took a seat.

"How are you doing, Detective?"

"Fine. I closed a case last week, the shooting at the apartments. I have an interview with a witness at the gas station robbery before lunch, and I'm confident..."

Briggs held up a hand to stop her. "You know what I meant. How are things going since Priest left?"

"Priest is on paid leave."

"Technically. For now. But we can't leave it that way indefinitely, Riley. Eventually we'll have to remove her name from the roster and admit that she left."

Riley looked at the back of the framed photos on Briggs' desk. "Why do pictures always face the person at the desk? Shouldn't they face the visitor? You know what your family looks like." She reached out to take one of the pictures, but Briggs took it away before she could turn it around. "I'm not going to take on a new partner. We had this discussion two weeks ago."

"And two weeks before that. I remember. You need a partner, Riley."

"I have a partner. She's just not here right now."

Briggs closed her eyes and pressed her hands together as if in prayer. "I'm cutting you some slack because of your unique circumstances. Because of the fact that Priest is not an ordinary cop. But I can only stretch the limits so far, Riley. You need a partner by the end of the week or I'm going to be forced to put you on suspended duty."

Riley sighed and let her shoulders slump. "All right. I'll hold auditions on Wednesday. I'll give you my answer by Friday morning. You have my word."

She pushed herself up, and Briggs touched the intercom button on her phone. "Come on in, Detective."

The door opened just as Riley reached for the knob. She backed up a step as the man stepped inside.

"Riley Parra, meet your new partner. Ken Booker, Riley Parra."

Ken Booker was a bit shorter than Riley with pale hair and a square face. His eyes widened when he saw her and he backed up a step, straightening his blazer and reaching for the perfect knot in his bright red tie. He smiled and extended a hand.

"Detective Parra. I've been hearing a lot~"

"How old are you?"

"Ah..." Ken glanced past Riley to Briggs.

Briggs cleared her throat. "Ken is the newest detective on the force, Riley. He passed the exam a month ago."

"You've got to be kidding me."

"We've been waiting for a spot to open up and~"

Riley turned her back on him. "A spot has not opened up. Not with me."

Briggs pointed at Ken. "He's your only option, Riley. Either you team up with him now, or I put you on suspension."

The two women stared each other down over the desk until Riley finally surrendered. She turned and stormed out of the office past Ken. "C'mon, Bookie. We're burning daylight."

Riley ignored Ken's attempts at conversation as she drove. She mostly ignored his monologue about being at the academy, his years as a uniformed officer and his few forays into No Man's Land. The only contribution she made was to stop him so he could check the directions before she made a wrong turn. Their witness lived in an apartment building right next to the el train, crowded on one side by the wooden frame of the tracks. Riley parked in the alley and caught Ken up as they walked around to the front of the building.

"Here are the CliffsNotes. An all-night gas station slash convenience store got robbed last week. The clerk opened the register and handed over the money inside, but the robber decided to shoot him anyway. Security cameras were useless. Yesterday someone called the station and told us they could identify who the shooter was. We're going to take his statement and check it out. Hopefully we'll have someone to arrest by this afternoon."

Ken nodded along with her recap. "Sounds easy enough."

Riley winced and shook her head. "Never say... okay. Anything that goes wrong from this point in, I'm blaming you. Just keep your mouth shut when we get up there."

Their witness, Randall Griffin, lived on the second floor. Riley double-checked the apartment number before she knocked, stepping back so the badge on her belt was visible to the peephole. After a minute with no answer, she knocked again. "Mr. Griffin? This is Riley Parra. We spoke on the phone."

"Maybe he's not in."

"He set the time, not us. If he's not here~"

Something impacted the back of the door hard enough to back Riley and Ken up a few steps. Riley's hand instinctively went for her gun, and she waved Ken off to the side so he'd be out of the line of fire. "Mr. Griffin?" She tested the knob and discovered the apartment was unlocked. "Mr. Griffin, we're coming inside." After waiting for Griffin to make some sort of response, Riley pushed the door open. The animal that had pounded the door from the other side darted out between Riley's legs and dashed down the hall. She thought it might have been a cat.

Any fear she was jumping to conclusions faded when she saw the Jackson Pollack painting on the floor just inside the apartment. The cat had walked through something dark red and left a scattered pattern of prints all around the apartment as it sought an exit. Riley kept her gun drawn as she stepped into the apartment, sweeping her gaze from left to right as she moved. She was in the living room with the kitchen across the space by the doors that led to the tiny balcony. There was a wide empty space between the back of the couch and the kitchen counter, and that was where Randall Griffin's body was sprawled on the garish carpet.

Riley glanced back to make sure Ken was behind her. "Check the bedrooms." She walked forward and did a full sweep of the main rooms before she knelt next to Griffin's body. The pool of blood seeping into the carpet around him left little doubt, but still she checked his pulse.

Ken came from the back of the apartment. "No one back there." He looked at the dead body, gulped, and looked at her again. "Are you really going to blame this on me?"

"Go get that cat."

"What?"

"It has blood on its paws. It could have other evidence."

Ken blinked. "A-are you serious?"

Riley pointed at the door. "Go, Bookie!"

He turned and ran from the apartment. Riley looked at the body and took out her cell phone.

Ken was easily able to track down the errant cat. It left a trail of bloody paw prints down the hall to the stairs, down to the lobby, and then to a small supply closet where it was found hunkered behind a bucket. Animal control was called and gave the cat an examination while Gillian and her assistant headed upstairs to deal with the cat's former owner. She smiled when she saw Riley in the apartment.

"It shouldn't be so nice to walk into a room and see you standing over a dead body."

"We all get our kicks where we can. Hope you weren't too busy."

"The other dead bodies aren't going anywhere. Who do we have here?"

Riley looked at the body. "Randall Griffin, potential informant to a gas station shooting. We were coming to take his statement and found this."

Gillian knelt next to the body. "We?"

"Me and my new partner. Ken Booker."

"Is he..." She made a motion toward her back with one hand, indicating wings.

Riley shook her head. "I don't think so. He's mainly a pain in the ass. I'm going to look for shelters or a kennel on the way back to the station to see if I can drop him off."

Gillian chuckled quietly as she examined the body.

"What?"

"You hated Priest when you met her, too. And Sweet Kara hated you when you guys first met, if I remember correctly. You can be a real prickly bitch."

Riley shook her head. "I like who I like."

"I get that. But if Priest isn't around, you need someone to help you with the heavy lifting. Is there any reason Booker shouldn't be that person?"

Riley shook her head. "You and your logic."

Gillian laughed and Booker returned to the apartment. He

looked sheepish as he nodded a greeting to Gillian. "The cat is with animal control. I didn't see anything worth noting other than the blood on its paws."

"Dr. Hunt, Detective Ken Booker. Bookie, this is Dr. Gillian Hunt."

Ken smiled. "Hello, Doctor."

Gillian acknowledged his greeting with a slight nod of her head as she continued her exam. "He hasn't been here long; rigor mortis is just starting to set in. That gives us a two to six hour window, but..." She gestured at the bloody trail running around the apartment. "We should assume the later end of that spectrum considering how long the cat wandered back and forth through the red stuff. Looks like he was stabbed with a pair of scissors, which are absent from the scene."

"One attacker?"

Gillian nodded. She turned to her assistant and motioned for her to prepare the body to be moved to the morgue. "So much for a nice and easy case, huh?"

"Blame him." Riley hooked her thumb in Ken's direction. "I looked around the apartment when I got here, but I didn't see any signs of forced entry. Didn't see any bloody scissors, either. I need to find the landlord and see if there was anyone unusual in the building~"

Ken cleared his throat. "I actually did that while I was waiting for animal control." He took a pad from his pocket and flipped it open. "He said that between the hours of five and eleven, he only saw three non-residents enter the building. One was a mailman and he assumed the other two were just visitors. Nothing about them stood out."

Riley tried not to act too impressed. "Did he give you descriptions anyway?"

"Average height, Caucasian, brown hair, wearing a red baseball cap. The other guy could have been his twin, except for the baseball cap."

Riley watched as Gillian and her assistant escorted the body out of the apartment. Gillian offered a wave just before she stepped out of sight, and Riley returned it despite the fact Gillian couldn't possibly have seen. She dropped her hands to her hips and turned slowly to look around the entire room. "We don't know much about this guy, but we know a few things. He had information about the robbery, but he didn't come forward with it until a week after it happened. He sounded nervous on the 911 call. He didn't want to give his name at first but he finally gave in."

There was a small table next to the couch with a stack of mail, magazines, and a few beer cans. Riley picked up a handful of envelopes and turned them over. Randall Griffin's chicken scratch handwriting covered the back of several of them. She shuffled them until she found a familiar phone number: the police tip line. The rest of that envelope was filled with random information and doodles.

Ken cleared his throat. "The landlord also had information about Mr. Griffin."

"Yeah? Anything worth mentioning?"

"Late with the rent every month, always paid right before the notices went out. His neighbors never complained about him, or his cat. He worked at Moon's Automotive. It's a garage on W Street."

Riley groaned. "God, not Dubya Street."

"Yeah. What about it?"

Riley shook her head. "You must be new. Okay, are the uniforms downstairs?" Ken nodded. "Get them up here to keep an eye on the place until the crime scene guys are done with it. We're going to Dubya Street."

Riley informed Ken of W Street's sordid history on the drive to Moon's Automotive. During a nationwide bicentennial celebration, several streets in the city had been renamed after Presidents. As time marched on and new leaders were elected, streets were slowly added to the list. By the time the forty-third President's street was due to be dubbed, the man in office was unpopular enough that petitions began to circulate by business owners refusing to accept the name change.

Eventually a half-mile dead end road called Skyline Drive was chosen, and the city leaders christened it W Street to differentiate it from the other Bush Street. Vandalism quickly followed, along with several businesses choosing new locations away from the unloved designation. Realtors and property owners were forced to offer extremely low rent as incentive for new businesses to move in and take over the abandoned storefronts.

"Skyline Drive was already inside No Man's Land, so it's not like it was a plum address anyway. People were just frustrated at the time, and it never recovered."

Booker chuckled. "So it's just like every other street in No

Man's Land?"

Riley shrugged. "It's a matter of degrees. Every street is bad, but this is one of the worst."

Ken watched the city go by outside his window, and Riley wondered how often he had ventured into the bad part of town. It was like watching a time-lapse photograph of degradation passing by the window.

Moon's Automotive was a large building with four garages that faced the street. All of the garage doors were open, and three of the bays were occupied. Riley pulled into the roundabout driveway, past the "No U-Turns!" sign posted by the entrance, and parked by the empty garage bay. She got out of the car and hooked her badge on her belt where it was impossible to miss as she walked inside. Ken followed behind her, glancing to the left and right, obviously uncomfortable being in No Man's Land.

A man came out of the back office when Riley was halfway across the empty garage. He wore a polo shirt, but the grease on his hands implied he did more than just push papers. His eyes were on Riley's hip, the gold shield drawing the eye even in the dim light of the garage. Riley heard power tools quieting as the mechanics turned their attention on the new arrivals.

"Morning." Riley attempted a smile as she pushed her blazer back so everyone could get a good, clear look at the badge. "I'm looking for whoever is in charge."

"That would be me. Austin Dean." He showed his hands as an apology for not shaking Riley's. "What can I help you with?"

"Maybe we can talk somewhere a bit more private."

Dean shrugged and gestured at his office, turning around to escort Riley and Ken inside. Riley shut the door behind herself as the manager took his seat. "Do you know a Randall Griffin?"

"Employed him up until this morning."

Ken said, "What happened this morning?"

Dean shrugged. "Didn't come in to work, didn't answer when I called him. That's the third time in two weeks. I gave him a warning and apparently it didn't stick."

"Well, I don't know about the other two times, but he had a good reason today. He was killed in his apartment this morning."

Dean frowned, then rolled his head back on his shoulders and clapped a dirty hand over his eyes. "Damn it all. Well. I guess it doesn't change much for me, does it? I still gotta replace him." He dropped his hand, the grease leaving behind a raccoon mask over his eyes. "What do you guys need from me?"

"If Griffin had any friends or coworkers he might have confided in, we need to talk with them. We have reason to believe he had information in a case we're working on but he was killed before he could tell us anything."

Dean looked past them to the window in his office door. He jabbed a button on his desk phone and leaned toward it. "Brogan, Erwin, get your butts in here." They could hear his voice over a PA system echoing in the garage behind them.

He had barely leaned back before the door opened and a skinny, dark-haired man stepped inside. He looked at Riley and Ken before he wiped his hands on the chest of his jumpsuit.

"You wanted to see me?"

"You and Brogan. Where's he?"

The man, obviously Erwin, hooked a thumb over his shoulder. "He had to go get something out of his car. Said he'd be here in a minute."

Riley looked at Ken. "Stay with him." She brushed past Erwin and left the office, moving quickly toward the open garage door. She spotted a man in a pale blue jumpsuit walking quickly across the parking lot. His hands were in his pockets, his head down, but it was just a poor attempt to appear casual. Riley broke into a run. "Mr. Brogan! Stop right there."

Brogan didn't look back before he started running. Riley growled and ran faster, trying to meet his pace. He cut to the north, toward the weed-choked field where the street dead-ended.

"This is the police. Stop right where you are, Brogan!"

The last building on the street was abandoned, with a loading dock that dipped down below street level. As Brogan passed the wide entry to the driveway, someone Riley assumed to be a transient appeared running in an intercept pattern. The transient wore a hooded sweatshirt, the hood pulled up despite the heat of the day, and a pair of ratty and torn jeans.

"Back! Get back!"

The transient grabbed Brogan by the shoulders and pulled, the two of them stumbling to the ground. Brogan hit, his fall broken by the transient, and the two of them rolled across the pavement. Brogan started to get to his feet, but the intervention had given Riley enough time to catch up with him. She grabbed the back of Brogan's jumpsuit and forced him onto his stomach. "Down. Stay down. Don't move. Arms to your sides, palms on the asphalt."

She looked up to thank the transient for helping and to admonish whoever it was for risking themselves.

Caitlin Priest tugged the hood tighter around her face, but it was too late to conceal her identity. She looked around in a panic and began backing away. Riley furrowed her brow and almost forgot about the suspect she had pinned by her bent knee. "Caitlin."

"I shouldn't have been following you. Sorry, Riley. I-I'm sorry. Forget I was here." She turned and ran into the field, taking Brogan's attempted escape route and disappearing into the tall weeds. Riley considered following her since Brogan wasn't going anywhere, but she knew it would be a waste of time. Even if she wasn't an angel anymore, she was still wily.

She managed to cuff Brogan's wrists and hauled him up. "We just wanted to have a nice conversation about your friend. Now we have to take you downtown and make a whole thing out of it. Happy now? I'm sure your boss will be thrilled. C'mon. Get up."

She walked him back to the garage. Ken was standing by the car, and Riley could see Erwin sitting in the backseat. Ken opened the driver's side back door and Riley put Brogan inside.

Ken exhaled and pushed a hand through his hair. "I talked to the owner of the garage and told him we'd probably be taking two of his guys for the rest of the afternoon. He wasn't happy, but he did say it wasn't our fault. So. What do we do now?"

"We take them back to the barn and have a nice conversation about their dead friend."

Ken looked down the street and pointed at the field. "I thought I saw someone out there with you when you grabbed Brogan."

"Yeah. Someone heard me shouting for him to stop and knocked him down for me."

"Wow." Ken smiled. "Lucky for us, huh?"

Riley nodded and climbed into the car. "Yeah. It's almost like a guardian angel watching out for us."

Riley handed Brogan and Erwin off to a pair of uniformed officers with instructions to set them up in different interrogation rooms. Ken watched them go and followed Riley into the bullpen. "So what do we do now? Go in and sweat them?"

"This isn't *The Shield*. We're going to let them stew for a little while and then go see what they have to say. Ignoring them will do a lot better than pushing for information. Go get a snack, grab something for lunch. We'll check on them in twenty minutes or so."

Ken seemed reluctant to just do nothing, but eventually he went to a desk across the room and sat down. Riley planned to inform Briggs about the changes in their case, but first she had something else she had to do. She took the elevator down to the morgue and found Gillian in the midst of examining Randall Griffin's body.

"Jill. You got a minute?"

"No. I'll have a full report for you as soon as I can, though."

Riley looked at the body. "Right. Sorry. I... have to tell you anyway. I saw Priest."

Gillian looked up. "What? Where? Is she okay?"

"I don't know. She just showed up. We were on a garage on W Street~"

"What the hell were you doing on Dubya Street?"

Riley held up her hands to put off the concern. "Just following a lead. A person of interest was running from me. He was about to get away when Priest just came out of nowhere and tackled him for me. She apologized for following me and then just took off again." She leaned against the empty exam table behind Gillian. "I don't see her for two months after she saves my life, and this is how we run into each other again?"

"Are you okay?"

"She looked homeless, Gillian. I thought she was some transient who just happened to be around. I haven't been worrying about her because I assumed she was off getting used to her humanity. But if she's just circling the drain, and if she's sleeping in a cardboard box in some alley, how am I supposed to... just step over her?"

Gillian read between the lines with ease. "Like your mother."

"Priest saved my life. I can't leave her out there."

"If it's her choice, I'm not sure there's anything you can do."

Riley stared at the tile floor, her hands in her pockets. "I can at least give her the option. I can tell her that she's welcome to come back, and that she has a home and she has friends who care about her. That's all that I can do."

Gillian nodded. "Let me know when you find her. I'd like to be there."

"I will." Riley kissed her fingers and flicked the kiss at Gillian. "See you at the end of the day."

"See you then. Let's go out to eat tonight."

Riley nodded. "That sounds great. I'll think about where we should go."

"Okay. Wait, don't go. I don't have a full report, but I do have something interesting." She gestured at Griffin's body. "He was beaten up about a week ago. Most of the bruises are on his chest and back, but he had a black eye that was just starting to heal."

"Someone hit him where it wouldn't show."

"Seems that way."

Riley processed the information. "Okay. Thanks, Jill."

Gillian waved goodbye and turned back to her latest customer. Riley left the morgue and went to the elevators. With any luck, Brogan and Erwin would have extremely guilty consciences and she could still wipe the case from her calendar before clocking out for the day.

Nick Erwin had his head down on the table when Riley finally joined him in the interrogation room. He jumped when she slapped the table with the folder in her hand and she placed a plastic cup of water near his right hand. He blinked at her, looked at the water, and shifted uncomfortably in his seat. "You can't keep me here."

"You don't like our hospitality?" Riley sat down and casually opened his file.

Erwin sniffed and looked around the room. His gaze lingered on the mirror behind Riley. She skimmed his file. "We have a lot of stuff on you. That must be weird, huh? You've never seen me before, but I have all this good information. Like I know when you were thirteen you were picked up for joyriding."

"Those files were, uh, were sealed."

Riley shook her head. "No, they weren't. You were never charged. The officers gave you a warning. Three times, three different officers. You got lucky. If they'd bothered to check your file they would have seen you were a repeat offender. Might have been a different high school experience for you if they'd been a little meaner."

Erwin shrugged and looked down at his hands. "I don't wanna talk."

"Then how are we going to get to know each other?" She closed the file. "I only wanted to talk to you guys this morning. You and your friend Brogan. He made me run, Nick. Can you believe that? I hate running. You came right to the office when you were called, and that puts you on my good side. I'm giving you the opportunity to talk to me and maybe get some leniency. So let's have the conversation we were supposed to have at the garage this morning. Randall Griffin. You knew him."

Erwin nodded. "He worked with us at Moon."

"When was the last time you saw him?"

"Yes~" He cleared his throat. "Yesterday? At work. Sometimes we went out after work, a bunch of us, for drinks and stuff, but not yesterday." He crossed his arms over his chest and glanced at the door. Riley knew he was thinking of escape but he didn't have the guts to actually make an attempt.

"Was he acting odd?"

"No. Same ol' Randy."

"How about last week? Did your buddy Randy have any run-ins last week?"

Erwin blinked, shifted again, and glanced back at the door. "I don't know. I'm not his nanny."

"Well, I think you know something. And I know you want to be the one to tell me. We can have a good witness and a bad witness, and Mr. Brogan has a strong lead to be my least favorite witness of the week. Let me help you."

Erwin started shaking his head. "I tell you, I go to jail. Brogan goes to jail, too. How long you think I'll survive in there? He'll know that I told."

"We can protect you."

He laughed and shook his head. "I want to go home. Or back to work. I don't want to be here anymore."

"All right. I'll go get your discharge papers. Stay right here." She stood up and left the room. When the door was closed, she motioned to the guard who'd been stationed outside. "Make sure he doesn't leave."

"Yes, ma'am."

Riley walked past him and went into the observation room. There was one-way glass on either side of the room, one mirror looking in on Erwin and the other into Brogan's room. Ken was sitting across from Brogan trying to get him to talk without luck. Riley stared at Brogan, his expression carved into stone. It was obvious he wasn't going to talk anytime soon. If Erwin didn't get over his fear, they would have to let both men go.

Randall Griffin had been killed in his apartment a week after receiving a pretty severe beating. Riley looked at Brogan's crossed arms and saw slight bruising on his knuckles. The injuries could have been the result of working in tight quarters, bumping and banging around inside a car's engine led to all kinds of injuries. Or maybe he bruised his knuckles beating up Griffin. She could have Gillian check if his fists matched the bruises on Griffin's body.

Griffin had missed three days of work at the garage. He'd been nervous, anxious and twitchy on the phone when he called the tip line.

Erwin was afraid that he and Brogan would end up in jail if he told the truth. Griffin had been calling with information about the gas station shooting.

Riley left the observation room and went into Brogan's room without knocking. Brogan and Ken both looked at her as Riley rounded the desk and took a seat next to Ken.

"My apologies, Detective Booker. I need to talk with Brogan."

Brogan shrugged. "I have nothing to say to him, I got nothing to say to you."

Riley ignored him. "Erwin told me about the gas station last week."

Ken and Brogan both looked at Riley. Ken was confused, but Brogan looked ready to jump over the table. His fingers tightened against his biceps and his nostrils flared with anger.

"It wasn't the first time you'd done a holdup, but I think it was the first time someone got hurt. Griffin had a conscience, something you were severely lacking. It took Erwin a while, but he found his, too. Griffin wanted to confess. He couldn't live with the murder on his head, so he was ready to throw in the towel. So you gave him a beating to change his mind. It worked for a while, didn't it? But what happened yesterday?"

Brogan closed his eyes and shook his head. "I'm gonna kill that little prick."

"Tell us what happened at Griffin's apartment, Mr. Brogan. Were you just checking up on him, or did you know he was about to surrender himself? He called the tip line yesterday. Maybe he told you, or maybe you could just tell that he wasn't going to stay quiet for long. You argued, maybe you started beating on him again. This time he fought back, so you grabbed a pair of scissors and stabbed him with them."

"Erwin was lying. It was all him. He's just pinning it on me to keep his own fat out of the fire."

"So what really happened?"

"Yeah, we robbed the place. But Randy was just the driver. He didn't see anything. The clerk grabbed for my gun and it just went off. We all agreed we'd shut up about it. We took the car back to the garage and I tossed the gun into the field. But Griffin had to go and read up on the clerk. The clerk had a kid, and Griffin's kid lived with his ex, so... I don't know. He got all sentimental. He started skipping work, but me and Erwin convinced him to let the matter drop."

Riley nodded. "And yesterday?"

"Dunno."

Riley smiled. "Come on, Mr. Brogan. You're the one who ran when Detective Booker and I showed up this morning. You're the one who clammed up when you could have been pointing the finger at your friend. And I think you're the kind of person who *would* turn on your friend if given half a change. So your silence was to protect yourself."

Brogan leaned back in his chair.

Riley sighed and stood up. "It would have been a lot easier if you'd just confessed. I mean, killing a person is one thing. People in this town are desensitized to that. But you had to kill his cat, too. The press hates when a pet gets killed."

Brogan furrowed his brow. "The cat? The cat still alive when..."

Riley raised an eyebrow. "The cat was alive when... what, Mr. Brogan?"

Brogan closed his eyes, realizing he'd been snared. "The cat was still alive when I left."

"Yes, it was. William Brogan, you're under arrest for the murders of Randall Griffin and Brian Amos." She went to the door and knocked, bringing an officer into the room. "This fine officer will tell you what rights you have while you're being processed. Then we're going to have a nice long conversation while we take your statement. It'll be a great afternoon."

The officer handcuffed Brogan and lifted him from the seat.

"Oh, and by the way. Erwin knew both of you were going to jail. He wasn't going to risk his life by ratting on you. I had most of it figured out, but thanks for filling in the blanks."

The officer hauled Brogan out of the room and Ken stared after him in shock. He turned to Riley and shook his head. "You were guessing?"

"I prefer to call it conjecture."

Ken whistled. "Remind me to never play poker with you, Detective Parra. What now?"

"Now we get warrants to search Brogan's car, and Erwin's car. With any luck we'll find blood evidence and the missing scissors."

"I'll get on that."

Lieutenant Briggs crossed Ken's path as he went to his desk to start making calls. She glanced at him and then stopped at Riley's side. Briggs gestured at Ken. "Looks like he's doing pretty well."

"I closed the case in spite of him, not because of."

"But you have to admit, it was nice having someone watch your back again."

Riley shrugged. "He's competent. He'll make someone a good partner once puberty hits."

"How long are you going to wait, Riley? Six months, a year? How long before you accept that Priest might not be coming back?"

Riley had already decided not to tell Briggs about seeing Priest, at least until she had a little more information. The sighting gave her hope that Priest's sabbatical or exile was almost over. At the very least, she knew Priest was in No Man's Land. She could find her, talk to her, and either convince her to come back or accept she was gone for good.

"Give me a couple of days. After everything she's done for me, it's hard for me to just let her go and let someone take her place."

Briggs leaned against the wall between the interrogation rooms. "When I was a detective, a girl went missing from her apartment. It was my case, but everyone was involved in it. We had uniforms knocking on doors, we had the K-9 unit searching up and down every street in the neighborhood... I interviewed everyone the girl knew. Family, friends, neighbors, teachers. I never found her. I never found out if she was taken, or if she just wandered off and got hurt. It's very hard to admit that sometimes people just disappear."

"How long did it take you to give up on finding her?"

"I'll let you know." She smiled sadly. "I know she's gone, and I can't let her go. But I also didn't let it consume me. Don't sit around waiting for Priest to come back."

Riley nodded. "I won't take much more time."

Briggs patted her shoulder. "A couple of days."

"At the outside. Yeah."

Briggs pushed away from the wall and went back to her office.

Erwin was much more willing to talk when faced with Brogan's confession. He confessed that the three of them used vehicles left overnight at the garage for the heists, robbing a few convenience stores and gas stations a week to "supplement their income." The gun was usually empty, but Brogan had been growing more confident with each success, so he decided to up the ante and increase his power by loading it. Brian Amos, the clerk at the Corner Stop, fought back and Brogan fired without thinking. Everything else in Riley's version of events turned out to be mostly accurate; the second thoughts, Brogan roughing Griffin up to ensure his silence.

Forensics found pools of blood and a pair of bleached scissors in Brogan's car. Erwin went to work because he wasn't aware of what Brogan had done, and Brogan went to work because he didn't want Austin Dean to fire him for not showing up. He had planned to wash the car after work and get rid of the scissors at the waterfront after work. Erwin and Brogan were both booked and processed and taken down to holding, and Riley was able to close the case by the end of the work day.

She had just stood up, shrugging into her jacket, when Ken appeared beside her desk. He smiled and waited for her to acknowledge his presence before speaking.

"Pretty good day today."

"Yeah. Good guys won."

Ken smiled and looked down at the desk. "Uh, look. Detective Parra. I just wanted to say thank you for this. For today." He licked his lips. "I know you didn't want a partner. I was kind of forced on you. But it was really great working with you. I hope I get a chance to do it again sometime." He held out his hand.

Riley took it and squeezed. "You weren't so bad yourself, Detective Booker. Could have been a lot worse than it was."

"So will we be paired up again tomorrow?"

"I don't know. We'll see what happens tonight." She pushed her chair under her desk. "Have a good night, Bookie. You earned it."

Downstairs, she found the morgue quiet and as deserted as usual. Randall Griffin had been examined and deposited in a drawer, and the three tables in the center of the room were pristine and empty. Gillian was in her office, and Riley knocked on the door as she stuck her head inside. "I'm looking for my fiance. Is she around?"

Gillian smiled. "I think I saw her rattling around these parts. Are you all set?"

"If you are."

Gillian nodded and shut down her computer. "How was your day, dear? Catch any killers?"

"Just one." Riley put her hands around Gillian's waist and leaned forward to kiss her. "But he killed two people."

"My hero." Gillian smiled and nuzzled Riley's cheek. "Where do you want to eat?"

Riley nibbled Gillian's ear. "I want to eat you."

"Well, then we have dessert covered." She pulled back and kissed Riley's lips. "Italian?"

"Sounds good." She released Gillian so she could get her jacket from the locker behind the door. "Have you decided what you're going to do about Priest?"

Riley winced. "Yeah. I was thinking between dinner and dessert I would go out and try to find her."

"In No Man's Land, after dark, on Dubya Street." Gillian pulled her jacket on and buttoned it before she spoke again. "Okay."

Riley furrowed her brow. "What do you mean 'okay'?"

Gillian embraced Riley again. "I mean I trust you. You know what you're doing. And I know that you would be doing it anyway, but you decided to tell me and risk a fight rather than lie and hope you got away with it. So yeah. Okay."

Riley kissed her. "I love you, you know."

"Mm. Good. It'll make the whole marriage thing a lot smoother."

Riley put her arm around Gillian and walked her out of the morgue.

There were moments, rare and precious, when Riley was able to forget the big picture. When she could ignore the fact that she lived on the front lines of a literal holy war, when demons and angels were the furthest things from her mind. Sometimes it happened on the road, sometimes it happened in the morning when she was getting ready for work. The one constant was Gillian's presence. She made it easy to forget.

Sitting in a restaurant together, still in their work clothes and making no effort to pretend it was a special occasion, Riley had felt like a normal human being again. It was an odd feeling, and one that she could never repay Gillian for giving her. They sat on the same side of the booth, thighs touching under the table, and they held hands when they didn't have to let go for their food.

Their fingers were still laced together as they walked upstairs. Riley's plan was to escort Gillian to their apartment, kiss her goodnight, and then head over to W Street and look for Priest.

"And then?"

Riley smiled. "I don't know. It's not like I had a lot of real dates when I was a teenager. Why don't you tell me what you would have done?"

They had reached their apartment, and Gillian turned to face her. "Well, after my date took me out for a wonderful dinner and escorted me back to my door, we would have stood under the porch light that my father had oh, so subtly left on. And I would have turned to him~"

"Him?"

"I was a late-bloomer. I would have turned to him and said, 'I had a very lovely evening. Thank you.'"

Riley stepped closer. "And then?"

"Then I would have started to hope he would kiss me."

"Why couldn't you kiss him?"

Gillian's voice was soft as Riley's lips came closer. "I wouldn't want to look easy."

"Ah." Riley pulled back just before making contact. She could smell the after-dinner mint on Gillian's breath. "What if I promised I'd still respect you in the morning?"

"You don't have to respect me. Just treat me nice." She put her arms around Riley and pulled her close. "And I don't have to worry about looking easy. Kiss me, Riley."

Riley complied.

Gillian made a quiet noise of pleasure in her throat, moving her hands from the small of Riley's back to the nape of her neck. She tickled the hairs there, her fingers resting on the collar of Riley's shirt as she tilted her head slightly. Her lips parted and Riley's tongue took advantage of the invitation. Riley had her hands on the elastic waistband of Gillian's scrub pants, her blouse pushed up so that her fingertips were touching the warm flesh of Gillian's hips.

Gillian broke the kiss with a moan. "Okay. So I'll see you after gym class tomorrow?"

Riley smiled. "I thought you weren't worried about looking easy. Invite me in."

"You wanted to go find Priest. I don't want you to think I'm seducing you, forcing you to stay in when you'd rather be~"

"I want to be right here with you. Whatever I'm doing,

whoever I'm with, no matter how dire the circumstances, I will always want to be right here. With you. Doing this." They kissed, and Riley brushed Gillian's hair away from her face. Her fingers caught on Gillian's glasses, and she took them off. She folded them one-handed and stuck them into the pocket of her jacket without breaking the kiss.

The next time they broke for air, Gillian resumed her argument. "But Priest."

"Priest left. She ran away. If she's not ready to come back, then spending the night kicking around in an alley won't change her mind." She kissed the corners of Gillian's mouth. "I'm not going anywhere tonight. Invite me in."

Gillian took her keys from her pocket and twisted at the waist. She unlocked the apartment door, pushed it open, and looked at Riley again. "Do you want to come in for some coffee?"

Riley kissed her, and Gillian moaned with pleasure. She put her arms on Riley's shoulders and crossed her wrists. Riley moved her hands down Gillian's back to her thighs, crouched, and Gillian leapt. She hooked her legs on either side of Riley's waist and Riley carried her into the apartment. Riley broke the kiss. "Couch or bed?"

Gillian cupped the back of Riley's head. "Fuck me anywhere."

Riley growled and moved her hands under Gillian's rear end, grasping her wrists with each hand to more easily carry her. Gillian pushed the door closed and Riley walked her down the hall without turning on any lights. When they reached the bedroom, Gillian whispered, "Am I heavy?"

"Maybe should've skipped the appetizers..."

Gillian's laugh turned into a moan as Riley began sucking on her neck. At the bed, Riley bent her knees and gently lowered Gillian to the mattress and let her sprawl across the blankets. She straightened, Gillian's legs still spread on either side of her. She quickly took off her jacket and tossed it aside, pulling Gillian up for a kiss as she worked the buttons of her blouse. Gillian brushed Riley's hands away.

"Let me."

Riley looked down as Gillian undid the buttons expertly and then pushed the blouse off her shoulders. Her heart was pounding as she pulled on Gillian's scrub top. Gillian lifted her arms and Riley peeled it off, revealing her sleeveless V-neck undershirt. Riley exhaled, shook her head and closed her eyes as she kissed Gillian's temple. "I love undressing you."

"Then don't stop now."

Riley took off Gillian's shirt and blouse, kneeling to kiss between her breasts before she took off the bra. Gillian's nipples were hard and Riley took them into her mouth before she pushed her hands under the waistband of Gillian's pants. Riley leaned back and Gillian lifted her hips, and the scrubs were peeled away. Gillian's shoes hit the ground with hollow thuds, and Riley left her socks on for the time being; her feet tended to get cold at night. Riley's hands trembled as she took off Gillian's underwear and moved forward again. She lifted Gillian's legs onto her shoulders and kissed her stomach before sliding lower.

Gillian cried out when Riley's lips touched her. Riley quieted her, turning her head and brushing her lips against Gillian's thigh. "It's okay. It's okay, darling. It's okay."

"Sorry. I've been thinking about this all day." She stroked Riley's hair.

Riley kissed Gillian's thigh again before she returned to her sex. Gillian groaned, but managed to restrain herself as Riley's tongue touched her, spreading her open before darting inside. Gillian threaded her fingers through Riley's hair, down to where it was tied into a ponytail. She released it, Riley's hair falling free and brushing the sensitive skin of her thighs. Riley used her fingers to penetrate, her tongue and lips to caress. Gillian climaxed quickly, gasping an apology even as she moaned Riley's name. She lifted her hips to meet Riley, trembling as her thighs closed around Riley's head. She straightened her back, rolled her shoulders, and groaned as she sank down onto the mattress.

Riley kissed her way up Gillian's body, resting her head on Gillian's chest to hear the pounding of her heart.

Gillian finally recovered enough to kiss the top of Riley's head. Riley stretched up and they kissed, and Gillian undid Riley's bra. She shrugged out of it, slid up Gillian's body, and Gillian brushed her lips over the curve of Riley's breasts. Riley rolled to one side, and Gillian propped herself up on one arm as Riley turned away from her. They pulled the pillows out of the way, and Gillian spooned against Riley from behind.

She unbuttoned Riley's pants and pushed her hand inside, cupping her mound as she kissed Riley's neck. Riley found Gillian's free hand and gripped it tightly, lacing their fingers together as they'd been in the hall. She rocked her hips, moaning gently as

Gillian teased her with two fingers. She gently bit Riley's neck as she pushed two fingers inside of her. Gillian licked Riley's neck and Riley shuddered, and Gillian kissed the shell of Riley's ear.

She whispered things to Riley as she moved her fingers, whimpering as Riley moaned her responses just loud enough for Gillian to hear. Their fingers flexed and relaxed, Riley urging Gillian to move faster with a subtle tightening of her grip as their sweaty palms slid together. Gillian moved her hips against Riley, breathing heavily as she pushed Riley to the edge and stopped just short of letting her fall.

"Do you want to come?"

"Let me come," Riley moaned.

Gillian rested her head on Riley's shoulder and stopped teasing. She moved her hand faster, thrusting into Riley as her palm ran across Riley's erect clit. Riley pressed back against Gillian as she came, squeezing her hand and whispering her name when she finally relaxed. She rolled onto her back, her arms tangled with Gillian's, and they kissed.

"I think that date was a success."

Gillian laughed and kissed the tip of Riley's nose. "By anyone's definitions."

Riley pulled Gillian to her, closing her eyes and holding her as her breathing and heart rate returned to normal. By the time they were both breathing normally, Riley had dozed off with Gillian leaving a trail of kisses along her eyebrows. She smiled and thought back to the list she had made during breakfast and made an addition: they were now up to eighteen lovemaking sessions. She didn't plan to stop counting any time soon.

Riley was already partially awake when Gillian slipped out of her arms. She pulled Gillian's pillow to her chest, using it as a surrogate as the shower started running. She considered getting out of bed and joining her, but her body refused to cooperate. She didn't know if she fell asleep or if Gillian just took an extremely short shower, but she was suddenly aware of Gillian sitting on the edge of the bed and stroking her hair.

"Mm."

"Hey. Sorry. I was going to let you sleep, but..." Riley sat up and blinked at her. Gillian was wrapped in a towel, beads of water still visible on her shoulders and chest. "I wanted to give you the option of going to look for Priest."

"It's the middle of the night."

Gillian nodded. "I know. I think you're only here because of me. And I appreciate that, and I love you for it. But you want to find Priest. You need to do that for her because you're... who you are. I can accept that walking in dark alleys is who you are. I know you'll be safe and that you can take care of yourself."

Riley sat up and kissed Gillian's shoulder. She smelled like body wash and Riley closed her eyes to remember the scent.

"Of course if I'm completely off base and you want to just spoon naked..."

Riley smiled. "Priest sacrificed everything for me. I owe it to her."

"I know you do. If it wasn't for her, I wouldn't... h-have you at all anymore. I can spare a single night." Riley cupped Gillian's face and kissed her. "Go. Be careful."

"I'll go for an hour. If I don't find her by then, I'll come back and we can spoon naked until dawn."

Gillian smiled and turned her head to kiss Riley's palm. "Well, then you better get going. I'll be here when you get back."

Riley was very aware of the "could have been." Instead of standing on a corner, fingering the butt end of her gun while she watched two punks cross the street toward her, she could have been tangled in Gillian's arms and legs. The knowledge made her crankier than her lack of sleep. She was dressed as inconspicuously as possible; a hockey jersey she'd never thrown out after stealing it from a former girlfriend, ripped jeans, a hoodie, and sneakers. She had her gun, but her badge would only have caused problems rather than solving them. She thought about contacting Muse, but she didn't want to spread the word that her former partner was missing in No Man's Land. She could trust Muse, but information had a way of getting out.

She had started on W Street, moving north and east to start a clockwise exploration of the surrounding area. She asked a few people about Priest, giving a vague description of her, but most people waved her off without giving an actual answer. She had been walking for forty-five minutes and, in order to keep her promise to Gillian, had started making her way back to where she had parked.

As Riley walked, she couldn't help but flashback to her days as a teen. She had once called these streets home. She'd even robbed a few convenience stores in her time. She'd been a lot luckier than

Griffin and his coworkers and met Christine Lee. Any other cop, it would have been the end of Riley's freedom. Christine gave her a lifeline and saved her life. No Man's Land had changed since she was a teenage hellion. It was darker, less hopeful. There were very few cops like Christine Lee left to save the ones who slipped through the cracks.

She rounded the last corner before getting back to her car and saw someone was sitting on the trunk. Their feet were on the bumper, their arms draped casually over their knees. Riley cursed under her breath and approached quickly, taking her gun from the pocket of her jacket. She waited until she was close enough to be heard without raising her voice. "Did I forget to tip the valet?"

"Hi, Riley."

She lowered her weapon and closed her eyes. "Been here long?"

"About half an hour. I didn't want anything to happen to your car."

Riley climbed onto the trunk and sat down next to Priest. Her clothes were different but just as dirty, and she looked like she wasn't getting enough sleep. Her hair needed to be washed and her fingernails were longer than usual. "You could have achieved the same effect by showing yourself and letting me take you somewhere."

"But if I'd gone looking for you and missed you..." She shrugged. "I'm not as good at tracking as I used to be."

"You found me pretty easily this afternoon."

Priest shook her head. "That was luck. I saw your car, so I followed you. I was going to watch you from a distance until you left. But I couldn't just let that man get away. I spent too long watching out for you that it was basically an instinct."

Riley said, "I appreciate it. So what were you doing on W Street anyway?"

"Hiding. I haven't been anywhere for very long lately. I move from one place to the next."

"Sleeping where? On the street?"

"Sometimes. There are a few shelters that have room."

Riley resisted the urge to yell, rubbing her palms on the thighs of her jeans. "You didn't have to do that."

"I wanted to. I needed time away from the things I knew. What would you do if you woke up tomorrow morning and you were a man? What I've gone through is comparable to that. I've been changed on an essential, deep level. Sometimes it feels odd to breathe, and some days I forget that I have to eat. It frightens me to think of how little I know, and how unequipped I am to deal with normal things."

"Look, the way I see it, you've always been here. You were Caitlin Priest, and Zerachiel was just hitching a ride. So you spent your entire short life on this mortal coil with an angel running the show. Now she's gone, and you have to walk the tightrope without a safety net."

Priest nodded.

"You've spent your entire life looking out for me. You gave up more than I could ever comprehend for me. So let me return the favor. Let me look out for you for a change. Come home with me. Get a good night's rest on our couch and in the morning, let us take you to breakfast."

"And what then?"

"Then we take care of tomorrow. And then we do it all over again. It's what we humans have been doing for years."

Priest seemed reluctant. "Are you sure Gillian won't mind?"

"I'm offering you the couch. After what you did, Gillian would probably offer you our bed and get a hotel for me and her. I think you earned sainthood with that woman for giving me back to her." She shook her head. "God knows why she wanted that so badly."

Priest dipped her chin and smiled. "She loves you so much. Your pain is hers, and so is your joy."

Riley winced. "Oh, man. So all that corny platitude crap was you? I thought it was Zerachiel who was the lame poet."

Priest shrugged. "Some of her rubbed off on me, I suppose."

"All right, I promised Gillian I'd be home in an hour." She slipped off the trunk and turned to face Priest. "Whether you come home with me or not, I refuse to leave you alone in No Man's Land. Let me take you to a shelter or something."

Priest looked past Riley down the street. She blinked rapidly and then carefully lowered herself to the street as well.

"Being in a home sounds very nice to me, actually."

Riley smiled and pulled Priest into a hug. Priest stiffened at first but eventually returned the embrace.

"In case I didn't say it after you gave my life back, thank you. For that, and for everything you've done for me over the past two years."

Priest closed her eyes and rested her head on Riley's shoulder.

"You're welcome."

Riley stepped back and patted Priest on the arm. "Now it's my time to give some of that back to you. Get in the car. I'm going to take you home."

Priest walked around to the passenger side of the car and Riley got behind the wheel. She watched Priest fasten the seatbelt, her hands shaking as she looked out the windshield. "You ready to get back to the real world?"

Priest took a deep breath and then nodded. "Yes."

"Then let's get out of here."

She pulled away from the curb and headed out of No Man's Land.

OCCAM'S RAZOR

THE BLANKETS were tangled around their legs, ensnaring them both, but neither wanted to take the time to get free. Riley had her arms looped under Gillian's, her hands laced on the base of Gillian's neck. She was barely focused on the movement of her hips, her world narrowed to the beautiful face inches from hers. Gillian's eyes were closed, her lips slightly parted so she could make quiet noises of pleasure as they moved against each other. Riley bowed her head and kissed Gillian's cheek, and she felt each puff of Gillian's breath against her cheek.

"Don't stop."

Riley moved her lips to Gillian's neck and licked, tasting sweat as Gillian moaned and pressed down against her thigh.

"Riley..."

There was a knock on the bedroom door and Riley groaned in frustration. Gillian half-groaned and half-laughed, pressing her lips to Riley's temple.

"It's okay," Riley whispered to her. "Don't stop." She moved faster and Gillian dug her fingers into Riley's hips. Another knock, louder this time. "Shh." Riley kissed her way back up to Gillian's mouth. "Don't fake it, we have time. Come for me."

"Riley?" Priest sounded concerned.

"Hold on!" Riley shouted. Her voice was ragged, the words blurring together as she watched Gillian's eyes close, her bottom lip trembling as her hands softened and slid up Riley's flanks. Riley reluctantly peeled herself away from Gillian's suddenly limp body, pushing sweaty hair out of her eyes as she pulled on a T-shirt and stumbled, weak-kneed, to the door.

Priest was standing backlit by a flickering blue light, the living room television most likely. The past three nights, Riley and Gillian had heard the sound of syndicated sitcoms, infomercials and late night comics drifting down the hall from the front room until all hours of the night. Priest looked at Riley and then looked past her at Gillian. Gillian smiled sheepishly and wagged her fingers in greeting.

Priest ducked her chin. "Oh, my. I-I thought you were sleeping."

"Nope. What?"

Priest held up Riley's cell phone. "He said it was urgent."

Riley closed her eyes and sagged against the open door. "Why did you answer it?"

"I thought~"

"Never mind." Riley took the phone. "Who?"

"Detective Booker."

Riley held up a hand to let Gillian know she would be right back before she stepped out of the bedroom and pressed the phone to her ear. "Point of interest, Booker. Don't ever call me in the middle of the night again unless you're bleeding from the ears."

"I'm sorry, Detective Parra, but it's kind of an urgent matter. An officer brought in a suspect in a murder earlier tonight, but the guy is refusing to talk to anyone but you. He's tearing up the interrogation room screaming that he wants you to come talk to him immediately."

"Name?"

"Marcus Skaggs."

Riley shook her head. "I don't know anyone by~" She focused on the last name and pinched the bridge of her nose. "Wait. Yeah. I know him. Wait, you said he was a suspect in a murder?"

"Yeah. First responders found him on the scene covered with blood. He claims he's innocent, but he'll only tell you why."

"Great." Riley sighed and took the phone from her ear to look at the time display. A little past midnight. "Tell him I'll be down there as soon as I can." She hung up and sagged against the wall.

"I'm sorry."

Riley had forgotten Priest was hovering nearby. "Don't. It's not your fault. Muse is in trouble."

"Muse, your CI from No Man's Land?"

"Yeah. They have him down at the station. I should get down there."

Priest put a hand on Riley's arm. "When I apologized, it was for... i-interrupting. If I had known what you were doing I would have waited."

"So now I have to imagine you lurking outside the bedroom door waiting to hear us finish? It's okay, Priest, don't worry about it."

"Okay. Apologize to Gillian for me, though?"

Riley nodded and went back into the bedroom. Gillian was swaddled in the thick red blanket, leaving her head, one bare shoulder, and her right leg exposed. Riley moaned. "You're making what I have to say next so much harder."

"You have to go in." Gillian smiled. "It's okay. I'm just worried about taking without giving, if you catch my drift."

Riley crawled onto the bed and cupped Gillian's face to kiss her. "You'll owe me one. Rain check."

"Count on it. And Riley... never, ever, not once have I *ever* had to fake an orgasm with you."

"Good to know." Riley winked at her and slid off the bed to get dressed.

Detective Booker stood up as soon as he saw Riley, crossing the room to intercept her. "Hey. Thanks for coming so quickly."

"Couldn't exactly let him tear up the interrogation room all night. What are you doing here so late?"

"I couldn't sleep. I realized you'd never done the paperwork on Brogan and Erwin, so I thought I'd take care of it."

Riley raised an eyebrow. Having a partner who didn't mind doing her paperwork could actually be a godsend. "Thanks for taking care of that for me. I was going to get to it this weekend. Which room is Muse in?" Booker furrowed his brow. "Mr. Skaggs. What interrogation room is he in?"

"Oh, two."

Riley nodded her thanks. As she approached the closed door, she realized she didn't need Booker's help. A uniformed officer was standing guard, and Riley could hear Muse shouting within the room. The officer's shoulders visibly lost their tension as Riley approached him.

"Thank God. He's been shouting for you since we brought him in."

She looked at his nametag. "Don't worry, Officer Steiner. I'll calm him down. What do I need to know?"

Steiner cleared his throat and, when he spoke, sounded like he was reciting from his incident report. "My partner and I responded to an anonymous call of shots fired at the Camp/Green Factory. We arrived to find the chain link fence around the parking lot had been cut, and the victim was lying in plain sight in the middle of the pavement. We determined he was dead from multiple gunshot wounds and called for backup, and then we began to secure the scene. I discovered Mr. Skaggs on the opposite side of the parking lot with blood covering his clothes."

"Weapon?"

"Didn't find one. My partner is with the forensics team right now going over the crime scene."

"What was Mr. Skaggs doing?"

"Ma'am?"

"Was he just standing there in his bloody clothes or was he trying to escape?"

Steiner shrugged. "He was sitting down with his back to the loading dock. Just kind of staring off into limbo. He didn't resist when we handcuffed him, but once we started reading him his rights, he got all fired up. I thought he was going to kick out every window in the cruiser."

"Do you have an ID on the corpse?"

"Local punk named Burt Woods. Twenty-three, high school dropout, frequent guest of our fine establishment."

Riley yawned as she absorbed the information, covering her mouth with one fist. "Okay. Stay out here just in case."

He stepped aside and Riley went into the room. Muse was standing on the table with his back to the door, bent forward so he could shout directly at the one-way glass of the mirror. "In No Cent!" he shouted. His bloody clothes were gone, replaced by a wrinkled blue jumpsuit. He stomped his sneakers on the table, his shackled hands hanging down between his knees. "In No Cent! I wanna talk to Detective Ri~"

"Get your filthy sneakers off the table. Someone has to clean that."

Muse spun around, eyes wide. "Thank God!" He dropped to his knees and scurried off the table. He hooked his sneaker around the leg of his chair and pulled it close so he could sit down. "Thank God. I didn't think anyone was going to call you."

"I wish they hadn't. Thirty minutes ago I was on top of my girlfriend. So you better work really hard to get me on your side." She took the seat across from him. "The cops told me the last chapter of tonight's story. You tell me how it began."

The fight seemed to seep out of Muse's body, his shoulders sagging as his head dropped toward the table. "Man, I don't even know. I don't. We were down at this place called War Pigs, shooting pool. Guy comes in and starts trying to hustle me. I can spot a hustle from a mile away, but I wanted the cred for taking the douche down. So we played a game and I won. He told me he'd buy me a drink as a reward and I took him up on it. Free drink, whatever?"

"You ever see the guy before?"

Muse shrugged. "Guys like that don't get recognized. They move around so no one knows their game. He was light-skinned black, with a really thin beard. No mustache. Real big hair. Not an afro, like that kid from *Boondocks* only not as big. Huey, not Riley." Muse smiled, although it was a slightly terrified expression. "Hey, that's your name."

"Yep." Riley crossed her arms. "So this guy who bought you the drink. Did you get his name?"

"Milo."

"You think Milo might have been a little upset that you beat him at his own game?"

"He said it was nice to have a challenge for once. He said he'd been hustling crappy players so long that he forgot what it was like to really enjoy a game. I bought it. He seemed sincere, you know? But maybe he was just setting me up. If he was, though, he never came back to take me out."

Riley tapped her finger on the table, wishing the story would move along. "Okay, so you had your drink with Milo, and he left the bar?"

"Yeah, he walked out. I left about... I don't know. Half hour after him. I stopped for a smoke on the corner. And... after that..." He looked past her as if his speech was written on the wall over her shoulder. "Dunno. I guess I walked around for a while. Ended up at Camp/Green somehow."

"How far apart are the two places? War Pigs and Camp/Green?"

"'Bout three miles." He shrugged. "I've walked farther some nights. Don't usually head over to that part of town, though."

Riley pictured the area in her mind. "Okay, you're standing on the corner outside of War Pigs and smoking."

"And thinking of calling you."

Riley frowned. "What? Why?"

Muse seemed as confused as she was. "I dunno. I just remember standing there with my smoke and thinking that I should call ya." He scratched his chin, the handcuffs forcing him to lift both hands. "I don't know."

"Do you have any information you need to give me?" She had told Muse to be on the lookout for anything he might hear about Gail Finney and another person named Alyssa Gremory whom she'd first heard of from Chelsea Stanton.

"Everything I know, I told you already. Maybe I overheard someone say something at the bar and I just don't remember it."

"This Milo character only bought you one drink, right? Are you usually such a lightweight? Blackout drunk from one mug?"

Muse shook his head. "I had four glasses, and no. That ain't unusual. I don't blackout. I gotta keep up with everyone around me and keep my ears open so I can get info for you."

"All right. So you have no memory of being at Camp/Green or how you ended up covered with blood?"

"No. Not at all. Even a little bit." He shook his head emphatically.

"Do you know Burt Woods?"

Muse shook his head. "Who is he? A lawyer friend of yours?"

"He's the victim."

Muse rubbed his face. "Oh. Nah. Never heard of him. Was he a good guy?"

"No, not really."

"Well, there's something. Least it wasn't a minister or something, some good Samaritan."

"You think that'll matter?"

Muse shook his head sadly. "Nah. Makes me feel a little better though, that it wasn't a good person I'm accused of taking out."

Riley sighed and ran a hand over her face. "Okay. There's nothing I can do about this until the morning. I promise you, I will look into it first thing. Right now, what you need to do is let the nice man outside take you down to a cell. Get some sleep. I'll do my best to make sure you don't have to spend any more time there than necessary. Okay?"

Muse exhaled and nodded sadly. "Sorry I interrupted, you know. With your girl."

"Don't worry about it. After everything you've done for me, I owed you one. The other cops are probably going to run some tests. Gunshot residue, blood samples, urine samples. Please, cooperate with them. If you really didn't do this, everything they do will support you."

"Unless they fix the results. They already got me. It could be a case closed for them."

Riley closed her eyes. "Do you trust me, Muse? Do you honestly think I would let them get away with that?"

He lowered his eyes. "Nah."

"Trust me. Just remember that I'm the one in charge of what happens. Try to have a good night."

"You too."

Riley exhaled as she left the room, turning to Steiner. "I want blood and urine tests to see if he was drugged. Was he tested for GSR?"

"Yes, ma'am. He'd fired a gun recently."

That was bad. Riley rubbed the base of her skull, stress and lack of sleep starting to gang up on her. "Yeah, okay. Get the tests and give me the results in the morning. He shouldn't give you any trouble if you want to move him down to holding."

"You're a saint, Detective."

"No, I know saints. They would be a lot less grumpy right now." She bid him goodnight and looked at Booker's desk as she headed for the elevator. He looked up and the room was empty enough that she could speak to him by just slightly raising her voice. "Thanks for the call, Bookie. You saved the guards a noisy night."

"Hopefully I didn't wake you up."

"It would have been better if you did." She smiled at his confused look and waved it off. "Go home, Bookie. Get some sleep. Get laid. Life's too short for paperwork."

"I'll do my best."

She waved over her shoulder as the elevator doors opened and she stepped inside. Once she was alone, she sagged against the corner of the elevator car and closed her eyes. Muse had lost time, woke covered with blood and in a lethargic state... the gunshot residue test was positive, meaning he had fired a weapon. There was a very good chance that Muse had actually pulled the trigger, but that he hadn't been in control of himself when it happened.

The evidence was pointing to possession. If that turned out to be the truth, she had no idea how she was going to clear his name without exposing the war between Heaven and Hell that was raging in No Man's Land.

It was a hell of a time to be lacking an angel.

On the drive home, Riley couldn't help but see conspiracies. Her tattoo ensured that the demons couldn't get to her directly, so they went after Gillian. When that didn't work, they tried to blow up the station house with the most important people in Riley's life locked inside. And now Muse, her number one source of information in No Man's Land, was implicated in a murder. She had to figure out who was behind this attempt and, if she managed to get through it intact, what the demons would go after next.

She parked, her exhaustion finally overtaking her as she trudged upstairs. Priest was asleep with the television on and Riley watched her in the pale blue glow. Her expression was unguarded, slack, and undeniably human. She couldn't pinpoint the differences; she looked exactly the same as she had when she was the host to Zerachiel. But there was an undeniable... humanity... to her now. Riley switched off the set, pulled the comforter up to Priest's shoulder, and moved quietly to the bedroom.

Riley stepped out of her shoes before she went into the bedroom. The window cast a rectangle of light against the wall in front of the closet, and she was illuminated by it as she took off her jacket.

"Riley?"

"Sh. Sorry. Go back to sleep, babe."

She heard Gillian shifting on the bed, the blankets sliding over her legs as she sat up. "No. Take off your pants."

Riley paused and looked over her shoulder. She smiled. "What?"

"Take off your pants."

Riley turned to face the bed and unfastened her jeans. She pushed them down her legs before she straightened up again. She stepped out of the pants and kicked them aside. "Paying off the rain check already?"

"Mm-hmm. Take off your shirt." The T-shirt was pulled over

her head and tossed aside. "Now come here…"

Riley stepped into the darkness and climbed into the bed, Gillian's hands finding her in the shadows and they proceeded to finish what had been so rudely interrupted by the phone call.

The next morning, Riley arrived to work early. Booker's desk was empty, and she bypassed it as she crossed to Briggs' office. The door was open and Riley waited to be acknowledged before she stepped inside. Briggs waved her inside as she hung up the phone. "Good morning, Detective Parra. What favor can I do for you today?"

Riley was a bit taken aback by the brusqueness of her tone. "I need to talk to you, boss."

"Can it wait?"

"Not really. A man was brought in last night, Mu~ Markus Skaggs. He's accused of murder."

Briggs nodded. "I saw the update on the overnight bulletin. What's his significance?"

"He's one of my confidential informants. I spoke with him last night and I don't think it's going to be a cut and dry case."

"One of those, huh?" Briggs sighed and stood up. "All right. The assignment is yours. Anything else?"

"Yeah. I need an answer on Priest." Briggs closed her eyes, but Riley soldiered on. "I know you said you'd think about it, but it's been three days. She deserves to know if she has a job here. I need my partner back."

Briggs pointed at the door and Riley shut it. "Caitlin Priest collaborated with a serial killer. She used the resources of this department to provide a list of victims. I accept that we can't prosecute her for that, but I am… very reluctant… to give her a badge."

"Respectfully, ma'am, you're wrong. The person who did those things was Zerachiel. It's easier if you think of the woman you knew as someone suffering from multiple personalities. Zerachiel was willing to do whatever was necessary to further the angels' agenda. Priest was the one who watched my back. Zerachiel sacrificed herself to save me. Caitlin Priest was as much a victim to Zerachiel as we were. She's still alive, and I want her back."

Briggs sighed. "She'll be your responsibility. If anything happens… if she goes off the road in *any* way, I will hold you personally responsible. Are we clear?"

"Very."

Briggs took her seat again. "People died because of Caitlin Priest. And I know, dual personalities. But Priest knew exactly what Zerachiel was doing, and she let it happen. I'm willing to give her a little leeway for doing the right thing when the time came. She gave us the list and she pointed us toward the Angel Maker. But that doesn't mean I forgive her. It doesn't mean I'll trust her when our backs are to the wall."

"You won't have to trust her. Just trust me."

Briggs held Riley's gaze for a long moment before she nodded. "I'll start the paperwork. She can come back on Monday."

"Boss~"

"So you handle the Skaggs thing with Booker. Non-negotiable."

Riley knew that Briggs was making a huge concession, so she bit back her irritation. Priest could come back, Booker was a competent detective... It was just for a few more days. This was a situation where she could be the "team player" Briggs wanted her to be.

"Booker's fine."

"Good."

Riley hesitated at the door. "Are you okay, boss?"

Briggs smiled. "I guess it finally caught up with me a couple of nights ago. Demons, angels, Heaven, Hell. My best detective died and came back to life. A lot of the stuff I gave up a long time ago as myths and fairy tales is being thrown in my face as real. So I just need some time. Sorry if I was a little abrupt with you."

Riley shook her head. "Trust me, it's probably well-deserved. I'll keep you updated."

Briggs nodded her thanks as Riley left the office.

Riley used her computer to find a few addresses that she would have to visit and checked out Burt Woods' records. She tried calling Booker at home and let the phone ring twice before she gave up. She could be a team player, but sometimes it suited her better to be a lone wolf. She left a message for Booker with the service in case he came in and went looking for her, then went downstairs to the holding cells.

The main holding cell was a wide space with benches around the perimeter and four more benches lined up in the middle of the space. There was a metal toilet in the corner, the cinder block walls all around it colored by graffiti. About half the benches were full of people either sleeping or too lost inside their own misery to notice her arrival.

Muse was sprawled on the far bench, his feet up and his knees forming mountains in front of him. Riley whistled and he lifted his head. "Detective Parra, thank God." He half-rolled off the bench, getting his feet underneath him just in time to stop from falling. He launched himself at the bars and gripped them with both hands. "Tell me you'll get me out of here."

"The day is young, Muse. I just want to make sure you were treated okay last night. And see if you remembered anything since we spoke. Have you remembered anything about Burt Woods?"

"Not a thing. The name doesn't even ring a bell. And you know me, Detective. If he was someone from No Man's Land, I oughta at least have *heard* of the man."

"Yeah. That's pretty weird." She looked at her watch. "Sit tight. I'll see what I can find out today. This stuff takes time under the best circumstances, and my best source of information is currently sitting in a jail cell."

Muse looked around the cell and shook his head. "Easier said than done, lady."

Riley put her fist through the bars and Muse half-heartedly bumped it with his own.

Priest was in the kitchen loading the dishwasher when Riley got home. Riley glanced at the couch as she passed, noting the folded blanket and pillow on one end. Priest was dressed in a white blouse and slacks, and she smiled weakly when Riley joined her in the kitchen. "You're failing as a houseguest."

Priest's smile faded. "But I'm doing your chores and I cleaned~"

"Exactly. You're supposed to laze around on the couch and eat junk food and watch soap operas all day." She waved at the dishwasher. "Leave that for now. We're going for a ride."

"Where?"

Riley shrugged. "Field trip. You want to go out like that, or do you want to get all gussied up first?"

Priest adjusted the knot in her tie as she stepped out of Riley's car, smoothing her palm down the front of her vest as she shut the door. Riley noticed that she was holding herself straighter, her head higher. Priest looked at her. "What?"

"It's just nice to see you back. I missed you."

Priest smiled and looked at the place Riley had brought her. "War Pigs. It doesn't exactly sound like a family place."

"No. The name is from a Black Sabbath song, I think. C'mon."

The front door of the bar was open. When she walked inside, Riley could see that the alley entrance was also open to create a cross breeze and provide light. Everything in the bar looked dingy and flimsy in the harsh light of day. The room stunk of beer and other things Riley didn't particular want to identify. The man at the cash register behind the bar barely glanced up as they came in.

"We're closed."

"Kind of risky to have that money out in a neighborhood like this."

"You don't see what's being aimed at you under the bar."

Riley brushed aside the tail of her jacket to reveal the badge on her belt. "That's probably a good thing. Detective Riley Parra, this is Caitlin Priest. We have a few questions."

The man showed his hands. "Sorry. You can't be too careful. I'm Paul. What can I do for the police?"

Riley approached the bar. She leaned over it until she saw the butt of the sawed-off shotgun that comprised the War Pigs' security system. She took the gun and laid it on her side of the bar for the duration of their talk. "I need some information about a couple of guys who were in here last night. Markus Skaggs and another man, Milo."

"Milo Garvin?"

"Big hair, beard with no mustache?"

Paul nodded. "That's him. What did they do?"

"Why don't you tell us?"

He looked toward the pool table and shrugged. "They played a couple of games and then they had some drinks. Looked friendly enough."

"You know Mr. Garvin pretty well?"

"Well enough to know his usual. He comes around occasionally. Doesn't cause trouble. Tips well." He smiled. "I only know his name because he pays with a credit card. If you're hoping for an address, I'm afraid I can't help you."

"That's all right. Did he ever have access to both drinks when Markus wasn't around?"

Paul shook his head. "Maybe if the other guy went to the can or something once I handed the drinks over. Other than that, no way. A couple of years back, there were a bunch of GHB rapes in this area. The ladies got drinks from the bar and woke up the next morning with no idea what they'd done. None of 'em were from this bar, thank God, but I started taking precautions. People get their own drinks."

"Sounds like a hassle."

"Less of a hassle than knowing that a woman came to my bar and ended up raped."

Riley nodded. "That's one way to look at it. So Markus and Milo seemed friendly while they were here?"

"I don't think they knew each other before last night, but yeah. Friendly enough."

"What about a man named Burt Woods?"

Paul considered the question and then shook his head. "No, doesn't ring a bell."

Riley took a card from her pocket. "If you think of anything else that might be useful, give me a call?" He nodded and took the card. Riley picked up his shotgun and laid it on the bar. "Leave it there until we're outside, all right?"

"Of course."

Riley motioned for Priest to follow her outside. Despite the fact they'd only been inside for a few minutes, they both squinted against the sunlight. "How did that feel?"

Priest looked at her. "What do you mean?"

"I mean, questioning someone. Finding a clue. How does it feel to be back at work?"

"I don't know. It feels good to be out like this. To have a purpose."

"Well, get used to it. I talked to Briggs, and you're back starting Monday."

Priest's smile was wider than Riley had seen in a while. "Thank you, Riley. And I should thank her, too. That's great news."

They got back into the car. "You'll be on probation, which means you're my responsibility. Briggs isn't too thrilled about having you back after the whole Angel Maker situation. So we'll be walking on eggshells, but we'll get through it."

"Wait. Monday. So what am I doing here now?"

Riley shrugged. "I couldn't find my temporary partner, so I thought I'd bring you along as backup."

"This is how you walk on eggshells?"

"Well, you know. Eggshells. If they're on the ground, they're probably already broken anyway."

Burt Woods had lived in an apartment building near the waterfront. Riley parked in one of the empty lots that flanked the building and looked up at the crumbling façade it presented toward the street. She could smell the brine and sludge from the water even from a block away, and she wrinkled her nose as she climbed out of the car. "Waterfront property doesn't exactly have the same cachet here as it does in other towns."

Four teenage boys were sitting on the front steps of the apartment building and none of them moved as Riley and Priest approached. One of them, wearing a thick jacket that was far too much for the mild weather, looked down the street at nothing in particular. "Think you ladies stopped at the wrong place."

Riley held up her badge. "Anyone of you happens to know Burt Woods and is willing to answer some questions, my partner and I promise we won't run warrants on any of you."

The group quickly dispersed, and Riley started up the stairs.

"Yo. That guy you're looking for, Woods?" Riley and Priest turned to see one of the teenagers lingering on the sidewalk. He looked back to make sure his friends weren't watching him talk to the cops. "He got dead last night."

"We know. We're trying to figure out why."

The teen shrugged. "He made a lot of people mad by dying. He owed money to some really bad dudes."

"Sounds like motive to me."

"Not for those guys. Can't pay your debts if you're dead." He had already started backing away and, when he finished speaking, he turned and sprinted across the street to catch up with his fleeing friends.

"Looks like Burt Woods made friends everywhere he went," Riley muttered.

Woods' apartment was on the third floor, and Riley knocked before searching around the door for a key. She found it on top of the door jam and let herself into the apartment. Priest followed and closed the door behind her. The apartment was miniscule; the kitchen, living room and bedroom all shared a space. There was a small closet and bathroom right next to the front door. Take-out containers, dirty clothes, and various other pieces of garbage covered practically every horizontal surface.

Priest looked at the disarray. "Who says crime doesn't pay?"

"It pays, you just have to be good at it."

"You said he had a long rap sheet."

Riley nodded. "You only get one of those if you're caught. A lot." She pointed toward the coffee table. "You look over there. I'll take the bedroom."

"What exactly are we looking for?"

"Anything that ties him to me, Muse, or Marchosias. Anything that ties him to Milo Garvin, for that matter." She kicked aside a truly impressive stack of porn magazines so she could get to the nightstand. She dreaded what she would find there, but she had to at least look. She found a piece of notebook paper with phone numbers on it, as well as a map page taken from the phone book. Part of the map had been circled in red ink, and Riley noticed the circle included both War Pigs and the warehouse where Woods' body had been found.

"Hey, how do I call wings?"

"Wings? What do you mean?" Priest put down the book she'd just thumbed through.

"Wings, angels. You were always there when I needed you, but if I need to talk to Sariel, how would I do that? Spin in a circle and chant her name three times?"

While Riley was blinking, Sariel appeared in the small kitchenette. "That won't be necessary."

Priest nervously put down the book she had been going through and moved closer to Riley. Sariel looked at her before focusing on Riley. "I'm your guardian, Riley. I'm always near."

"That's... creepy." Riley pushed aside the invasion of privacy for the moment. "I need you to tell me if~"

"No."

Riley raised her eyebrows. "What?"

"I'm not your personal toy, Riley. I'm your guardian. I'm here to make sure that you don't become endangered during the regular course of your life." She glanced briefly in Priest's direction. "It's obvious you became a bit spoiled by my predecessor, but that won't be the case with us. I will not be a fixture in your life. If you summon me, I will come. But I won't perform like a trained seal."

"I didn't volunteer for this, okay? I didn't sign up to be the cop who has to clean up No Man's Land single-handed. If there's a crime where demons are involved, then I'm going to need to call in the big guns now and again."

Sariel was unmoved. "You signed up for it when you slew Samael. You took away this town's protection and laid it all upon your own shoulders. Zerachiel found it necessary to hold your hand. I do not. Best of luck with your case, Riley, but it's none of my concern."

Riley parted her lips to reply, but Sariel was gone. Riley looked at the empty space for a moment and turned in a circle to make sure she had really left. "What a bitch. And yeah, I know you can still hear me."

Priest cleared her throat. "I'm sorry I didn't help you."

"Nothing you said would have convinced her anyway."

"What did you want her to tell you?"

Riley gestured at the apartment. "I want to know if this place stinks of demons. If Burt Woods was just a patsy to get Muse arrested, then maybe the demon met with him here."

Priest shook her head. "I don't think so. Sariel was far too comfortable here. If a demon spent any amount of time in this apartment, her discomfort would have been hard to hide."

"So she answered my question just by showing up to say she wouldn't answer my question. Works for me. Did you find anything?"

"No. Not exactly an intrepid return to police work, is it?"

"You're doing fine. You can't find something if it's not there to find. C'mon, we have another stop to make."

Priest followed Riley out of the apartment. "Where to now?"

"Someplace I was sure I would never see."

Riley had met Muse on the streets and, in their subsequent meetings, he always chose neutral locations to lessen the risk of anyone seeing him meeting the cops once too many times. For the first few years Riley had no idea where he lived, but once day she stumbled over the address for an M. Skaggs in the course of another investigation. She kept the information to herself, just in case it would come in handy someday.

"You never told me how you met Muse."

"Sort of the same way I met Christine Lee, only reversed. These guys were robbing a convenience store and the silent alarm got tripped. I was still in uniform back then, so I responded to the call. Grabbed two guys with guns and their getaway driver. Muse was one of the guys with a gun. He told me that he was the one who tripped the alarm and the security cameras backed him up. He said he just wanted some quick cash, but the guys he was with were scaring him. So he ended things before someone got hurt. I told him that if he ever had information about No Man's Land that could help us out, I'd see what I could do about getting him some money."

"You saved him."

Riley shook her head. "Gave him an opportunity."

"That was more than anyone else had offered him."

"He's still out there with the same guys he robbed a convenience store with. The only difference is that now he's doing something about it."

Priest shrugged. "Maybe that's enough. You saved a life there, Riley."

"Yeah." She looked out the window at the decayed and denigrated buildings of No Man's Land she was driving past. "One down, a few thousand to go."

Riley was surprised when rundown apartment buildings and strip malls gave way to an actual neighborhood. The homes were just as dilapidated as the apartments, but they had yards and garages. Most of them were surrounded by chain-link fortifications that enclosed untended lawns. She checked the address she had for M. Skaggs again, suddenly wondering if she had made a mistake.

"This is where Muse lives?"

"I guess so." Riley got out of the car and looked down at the cracked sidewalk. The word MARCUS had been written in one segment before the concrete hardened, and a crack had developed through the ARC. The letters were drawn with the precise care of a child's hand, and it seemed old enough to have been written by Muse. The gate opened with a rusty squeal and Riley followed the weed-choked brick pathway to the cluttered porch.

The door opened before she could even look for a bell. A tall, slender black woman stood in front of them, leaning heavily on a cane that was attached to her right forearm. Her hair was long and straight, and actually appeared silver instead of white or gray. She was dressed in a flowing purple and black gown, a pair of reading glasses dangling down in front of her. She lifted the glasses with her free hand and peered through them. She ran her eyes down Riley's body, then craned her neck to do the same to Priest.

When she dropped her glasses, she settled her weight on the cane and rolled her shoulders back. "Well, you're not from the grocery store."

"No, ma'am. We're with the police. We need to talk with you

about your son, Marcus."

"He's in jail."

Riley frowned. "Uh, yes. He is. But we're trying to get him out."

The woman looked at Priest again. "Why?"

"We believe he's innocent," Priest said.

"No, I mean why now? Marcus has been in prison for goin' on five years now."

Riley looked at Priest and then forced a smile. "I think we should talk about this inside, Mrs. Skaggs."

Despite its outward appearance, the interior of the house was warm and inviting. The couch on which Riley been directed to sit was so plush that she feared she wouldn't be able to get up. Pictures of the boy who would grow up to be Muse decorated the walls, smiling down at her from ten, fifteen, and sometimes twenty years in the past.

Muriel Skaggs finished pouring the tea, and Priest helped her carry the tray back into the living room. Muriel settled herself in a well-loved armchair and adjusted the bodice of her gown with arthritic hands. She looked at Riley and suddenly smiled. "Oh, I remember where I saw you before. You're the police officer who was on television. You stopped that terrible man."

"That's right. I mean, I had some help."

"Well, isn't that nice. A celebrity right here in my home. And you want to do something to help my Marcus?"

Riley cleared her throat. "That's right. But we don't, ah, have all the facts. Maybe you could walk us through everything that happened five years ago."

Muriel sighed. "I don't much like reliving it. But if it'll help my boy, I'll do whatever it takes. Mark was in with the wrong crowd. It's not hard to do in No Man's Land, I'm sure you know. But I guess I looked the other way because they were the best of the bad boys. They might skateboard or graffiti or something but they weren't hurtin' people. So I let it be. But one night I get a call that Marcus got picked up for robbing some convenience store. My baby boy was in jail for possession of a deadly weapon during commission of a felony or something like that. He got some free lawyer and got put in jail."

"Did... you go to his trial, Mrs. Skaggs?"

She shook her head. "Not with this hip of mine. I can barely get down to the mailbox in the mornings. But Marcus called me every night and tol' me what was going on."

Riley was trying not to look as confused as she felt. It was like she was trapped in an alternate reality, seeing what would have happened if she hadn't helped Muse that day. "It must be difficult for you. Not seeing your son in five years."

Muriel smiled sadly and ducked her chin. "Hardest thing I've ever had to live with. Hip included. But I know he'll need me when he gets out, so I'm waiting. I'm waiting."

"Do you have any idea when that will be?"

"No. They always say good behavior and all of that, but then they keep delaying his hearings and..." She waved a hand as her voice trailed off. She composed herself and straightened her back. "Now. What on earth do you think you can do to help him? Marcus confessed, and I know - God help me - I know that he really did have that gun on him. It's not a matter of being in jail for the crime of bein' black. He's guilty."

Riley glanced at Priest. "Well, my partner and I think that he's served his time. He should be home."

"That's true enough, I suppose. How can I help?"

"Do the names Milo Garvin and Burt Woods ring any bells?"

"Burt... hm." She touched her chin with one finger and looked toward the thin yellow curtains. "No. I don't believe I know anyone by those names."

Priest said, "What about Muse?"

Riley looked at her, but Muriel's eyes lit up. "Oh, yes. Of course."

Riley raised an eyebrow. "You know Muse?"

"Of course. James Muse. Marcus' lawyer. At first I was horribly angry at him. I blamed him for my son going away. But then he sent me a wonderful letter apologizing, and promising to make it up to me if he could. I sent him a letter back, and we've been exchanging messages ever since. He's a wonderful man and... he's the reason I can be here instead of a nursing home. I mentioned how tight finances were and he started sending me money. A few twenties here and there, but enough to make a difference in a tight spot."

Riley closed her eyes, realizing she had discovered where Muse's CI money ended up.

"Mr. Muse hasn't mentioned anything about a detective reopening his case..."

"Mr. Muse doesn't know about it. We didn't want to get

Marcus' hopes up without a reason. I'm sorry that we have to leave so soon, Mrs. Skaggs, but we should probably talk to as many people as possible before the day is out."

Muriel rose slowly, using her cane. Priest offered a hand, but she politely refused the help. "The sooner you talk to everyone, the sooner my boy is home. I understand, Detective. I wish you luck."

Riley took the older woman's hand. "Thank you."

"Have... you spoken to my son? Is he well?"

"Yes, ma'am. He's very well. He's doing just fine."

Muriel smiled, tears shining in her eyes. "Well, I suppose that's all you can ask for in such situations. Tell him I'm thinking about him and that I'm praying for him every night."

"I'll be sure to tell him that." Riley glanced at Priest before extricating her hand. Muriel insisted on escorting them to the door, forcing Riley and Priest to move at her glacial pace. When they reached the door, Muriel gripped her cane tightly and looked out at the lawn. "When he was growing up, I thought we were so lucky. He came through so much. Losin' his daddy and living in a place like this... I guess maybe it was just waiting around the corner for us to stop paying attention."

Priest shook Muriel's hand. "Your luck hasn't run out yet, Mrs. Skaggs. Detective Riley Parra is standing in your living room telling you she's going to do everything in her power to free your boy. It might not be a lot, but in my book... that's pretty damn lucky."

Muriel smiled. "You have a good partner, Detective Parra."

"Let's hope she does, too. Good afternoon, Mrs. Skaggs."

Riley waited until she heard the door close behind them before she spoke. "What the hell was that?"

"Apparently Muse has been lying to his mother for five years. Why would he do that?"

Riley shrugged and walked to the car. "I don't know. Knee-jerk reaction is to say there's bad blood and he lied to cut ties with her. But why would he then invent a public defender to keep in contact? Why write the letters and send the money? If he just wanted a way out, why go to all that trouble to keep connected?"

"I don't know."

Riley fastened her seatbelt. "I think we need to talk to someone who does know."

"You talked to my mama?"

Riley ignored the anger in Muse's voice and waited for him to calm down before she spoke. "I did. The question is why you haven't spoken to her in five years."

Muse rested his head against the bars, eyes closed. "It's not important to what's going on now. It doesn't matter."

"I think it does matter. Someone set you up for a murder. Now I find out that there are people who think you're already in prison."

"Not people. Just my mom." He sighed and released the bars. "Marcus *is* in prison. Or he might as well be. On the streets, I'm Muse."

Priest softly spoke up. "It's a bit odd to keep using your last name if you want to stay hidden."

"Yeah, well, not a lot of people know my last name. Mom taught me right and wrong, and she told me that people should pay for their crimes. I figured she would think I was breaking the rules by turning on my friends." He smiled. "Weird, huh? It's more respectable to pretend I went into prison than explain how I stayed out."

Riley said, "Your mother wouldn't have cared. You became a CI. You're helping..."

"And staying in the same bars and hanging with the same people who led me down the wrong path. You think she'd let that go? You think she'd be okay with that?" He shook his head. "Better she think I'm paying a debt to society."

Riley rested her hands on the bars. "We need the whole truth from you on this, Marcus. Did you know Burt Woods?"

"I never even heard the name until you said it to me."

"Okay. Why were you were at War Pigs? Was there any reason you chose that particular bar to drink?"

Muse shrugged. "They got nice pool tables and they don't water down their drinks. I go in there every couple of weeks."

"So someone could have waited for you to show up. When you left, you said Milo had already been gone for a half hour. Are you sure you didn't see him again after your game?"

Muse scanned his memory. "It wasn't that crowded. I think I would have noticed him. I mean, he tried to hustle me and I hustled him back, but we kinda had a mutual respect thing going on, you know?"

Riley nodded. "What happened after you left? You said you lit a cigarette and thought about calling me. Do you remember why?"

"I don't know. Maybe I saw something. Or I heard something in the bar." He squeezed his eyes shut and rested his head against the cell door. "I don't know. The whole night between leaving the bar and when your pals showed up is real hazy."

Priest cleared her throat. "Riley, may I?"

Riley indicated that she should give it her best shot, stepping back to let Priest take her place at the cell doors.

"We haven't been properly introduced. I'm Riley's partner, Caitlin Priest."

"Yeah, how you doing?"

"I'd like to help you remember what happened, but you'll have to trust me. Can you do that?"

Muse glanced at Riley. "Hell, if she kept you around all this time, I guess you must be all right. I didn't think she'd let anyone partner with her after Sweet Kara. So if she trusts you..." He shrugged. "Do your worst."

Priest smiled. "Close your eyes. I want you to imagine the War Pig. It's a small place, but there aren't many people there. You can smell the beer and the chalk from the pool cue. Cigarette smoke is heavy in the air. You decide to leave the bar and walk to the corner. The weather is..."

Muse filled her silence. "Chilly, but I didn't really care."

"It's cold, but not enough to make you long for a coat. You take the cigarettes out of your pocket as you walk, and you stand on the street corner to light it. You take a drag and let the smoke fill your lungs. The street is..."

Muse said, "Empty. Not a lot of cars."

"But there are a few cars. You take the cigarette from your mouth and you think about Riley because..."

"There's some dudes watching me from a car."

Riley stepped forward. "Who?"

Muse had opened his eyes. "I don't know. Man, I can't believe I forgot about those dudes. There was a car sitting across the street from the bar, on the opposite corner. There were two guys sitting in the car."

"Did you get a good look at them?"

"No. But you know that feeling you get when someone's watching you? I had that, in spades. It was like they were trigger-locked on me. I thought about calling you to come and run 'em off for me. I'd have called it a down payment on our next exchange of information." He smiled, eyes twinkling. "Instead, I just turned and went the other way. In case they started following me."

"Did they?"

Muse scratched the back of his head, eyes closed, lips pressed together. "I don't know. I really don't know."

The desk sergeant opened the door and cleared his throat. "Detective Parra? The medical examiner would like to see you."

Riley frowned and nodded. "Sit tight, Muse. We're doing everything we can to get you out of here."

He nodded and stepped away from the bars, moving back to the bench he'd been perched upon when they arrived. When they reached the stairs, Riley turned to Priest. "Looks like you've got a bit of that angel mojo left in you after all."

"What are you talking about?"

"That little trick with Muse, helping him open up that memory. That was highly impressive stuff, Cait."

Priest shrugged. "I guess some of the tricks stayed with me."

They arrived at the morgue and Riley concluded the body covered on the center table was Burt Woods. Gillian was standing at the foot of the table and waved as they entered. "I'm glad they were able to grab you before you left. I found something interesting."

"In our dead body?"

Gillian shook her head. "In your friend, Muse. I was thinking about his symptoms. The amnesia, the blackout, his aggression in the interrogation room... I decided to test his blood. For a full work-up, I wouldn't have the results back yet. But I was looking for something in particular. And I found it." She took a piece of paper off the table and handed it to Riley.

She scanned the scientific jargon and focused on the result. "GHB?"

"The date rape drug," Gillian said. "It takes about a half hour to take effect, and the victims report amnesia and blackouts. Someone slipped Muse a roofie."

Priest shook her head. "But the bartender said that Muse's drink was never out of his sight."

"That only means that he was either mistaken or lying." She remembered something else the bartender had said. "There was a lot of GHB floating around a few years ago, and that was why he was so cautious. I think we need to have another discussion with Paul the bartender."

Riley found the War Pigs front door was still standing open when they arrived, and she knocked before entering. "Hands above the counter, Paul. It's the police again."

When her eyes adjusted to the darkness, she saw that Paul was across the room by the jukebox. He smiled and held his hands up. He had been loading discs into the jukebox; compact discs instead of vinyl. Riley felt a twinge of nostalgia for a period of time that she really had never lived through.

"Don't worry, Detective. I'm unarmed this time. What can I help you with?"

Riley moved closer. "I just had a few follow-up questions to our original interview. You said there were some GHB rapes in the area a few years back." Paul nodded. "Do you know if we caught whoever was doing it?"

"Uh, no."

"No you don't know, or no we didn't?"

Paul shrugged and smiled nervously. "It was a long time ago. I don't really remember. I mean, you must have. They stopped, right?"

"Or maybe something else happened to make them stop. You know, once you have someone's name, it's pretty easy to dig up a lot of stuff on them. There was a fellow named Paul Lodes. Nice enough guy. Maybe a little quiet or shy most nights. He spent some time in prison for assaulting a woman. She positively identified him as her attacker because she'd given him two black eyes and a split lip when she got away. Paul Logan, on the other hand, is an honest and upright citizen who is doing his job and trying to keep the women of the city safe from~"

Paul suddenly threw a handful of CDs at her, the discs winging through the air like tiny flat UFOs. Riley wasn't sure if the discs could cut her, but she wasn't going to take the chance. She swept them out of the air with her hand and they clattered to the ground as she drew her weapon. Paul was already on the move, pushing through the back door that had been standing open earlier.

"Paul Lodes, freeze!" Priest was blocking the end of the alley, her hand up and her other hand on her hip as if she was going for a weapon. Paul skidded to a stop and turned to see Riley coming out of the War Pigs' back door, blocking his only other way out of the alley. Paul saw that he was pinned and closed his eyes, holding his hands out to show he was surrendering.

"Why'd you run, Paul? I was just telling you a neat story."

"I'm not that guy anymore." Riley pulled his arm behind his back and fastened her handcuffs to his wrists. "I changed in prison, okay? Trust me, once you've been on the receiving end of a..." He pressed his lips together and hung his head. "I don't do that shit anymore."

"But you still had your little pills, right? You slipped one into Muse Skaggs' drink last night. But why would you do that? Maybe those nights in jail really did change you."

"No! It wasn't like that." Paul swallowed hard. "Someone told me to do it. I have a girlfriend now. I have this bar. He threatened to tell her everything about who I used to be. I'd worked so hard that I-I couldn't... I couldn't risk that."

Riley started walking him toward her car. "Who told you to put the pill in Muse's drink?"

"The guy he was drinking with. Milo Garvin. He's the one who set the whole thing up."

Riley considered it. Muse had pinpointed Milo as a hustler, but maybe he hadn't realized that Milo was playing to lose. The entire game was a set-up for the celebratory beer.

"Did Milo tell you why he was going after Muse?"

"I'm already in enough~"

Riley squeezed Paul's arm. "We're going to find him sooner or later. You need to stop worrying about what Milo is going to do and start thinking about how much time you want to spend in prison. You help us out, we'll help you out. I really believe you're reformed. I think enough people forced themselves on you that you finally wised up. So I'm willing to go to bat. But you have got to give me something to trade on. We're talking about a murder here."

"His name is really Milo Rowland. His family owns most of this area, the neighborhood."

Riley looked at Priest. "His family? He's not a member of the Rowland family, is he?"

"The heir apparent."

Riley groaned. "Of course he is."

Paul ignored her comment. "He comes around every now and again. Usually leaves me alone. But this time he threatened me, threatened to destroy everything I had unless I put a pill in his buddy's drink. He told me it was nothing important, just a prank. But I'm not going to question one of the Rowlands, you know? The choice... it wasn't even a choice. It was something I had to do to protect myself."

"I'm sure the jury will be sympathetic." She opened the car door and let Priest deposit him into the backseat. When the door was closed, Riley sighed and leaned against the trunk. "The Rowland family. Sweet baby J."

"Who is the Rowland family?"

Riley sighed and held out one hand. "Marchosias doesn't single-handedly run all crime in No Man's Land. Think of him as the CEO of a company. Underneath him, there's a man named Dupre. A long time ago, Dupre cut No Man's Land into five segments, and he chose men to govern those segments like... managers. The people who work for those five managers are called their family, so cops have been calling them the Five Families. There's Rowland, Hyde, Burke, McGowan and Pierce. Apparently the Rowland family is behind Muse's little dust-up."

Priest looked into the car. "So what are we going to do? If Milo Rowland is as connected as they say he is~"

"That doesn't matter. We need to talk to him about a murder, so we're going to talk to him no matter who he works for. Let's drop this guy off at the station before we go punching the hornet's nest."

They deposited Paul Lodes, also known as Paul Logan, to booking and Riley headed up to the office for a quick internet search. She printed her findings and then led Priest back to the car. Priest had remained silent while they were inside but she became more agitated once they were in the car.

Riley beat her to the punch. "You want to know why we haven't gone after the Five Families before."

"Actually, yes. They seem like a logical stepping stone to Marchosias."

Riley nodded. "Yeah, but they're powerful. Not every bad guy out there is a demon, but they can still pack a powerful punch. Going after any member of the Five Families is basically career suicide. Plus even if we managed to take one down, the others would take revenge out of solidarity. They're like squids, with tentacles going all over the city. Legitimate business interests tangled up with criminal interests, a cigar shared here and a golf game shared there... Liam Burke once ran for mayor, and he only lost because Alan Hyde convinced him to drop out in favor for the candidate he was backing."

Priest said, "Do they have influence over the police as well?"

"You know Commissioner Benedict? The guy who pinned the medal on my chest at that stupid ceremony after the Angel Maker crap?" Priest nodded. "He's married to one of the McGowans. Whether the McGowan family has any influence into his policy or the decisions he makes, that's a source of rampant speculation throughout the department."

"So now that we have evidence that Milo Rowland is involved in Muse's situation~"

"We have an excuse to mess up their evening. Probably not much more than that, but it'll make me feel good. And it'll look good in the papers."

Riley was amused to discover that even the "good" part of No Man's Land was hardly a step up from the decay and rot of the bad parts. The houses rose a little taller, and the lawns sprawled a bit more, but the sidewalks were still cracked and broken. Some houses had bars covertly placed on the windows, hardly visible from the street, and others were ringed by tall security walls with a security camera on each corner.

The Rowland manor was near the waterfront, a few miles away from the warehouse where Muse and his purported victim had been found. It was two stories, with every window on the top floor open to let in fresh air. For some reason that made the building seem more fragile to Riley, as if it was a dollhouse that could be blown over by a strong gust of wind.

They parked with the car blocking the gate. Riley got out of the car and held her badge up to the camera perched on the wall. "Detective Riley Parra. This is Caitlin Priest. We're here on official police business, and we'd appreciate it if you open the gate so we could have this conversation in person."

Priest looked at the house. "Do you think that will work?"

Riley shrugged. "Worth a shot. I don't think the car would survive ramming the gate, and I can't afford to get a new one right~"

She was cut off by a loud, metallic squeal as the gate swung inward.

"Look at that. Honesty really is the best policy."

They walked up the drive to the house. Two men were standing just outside the open front door, their hands hanging casually by the bulges in their sports coats. Riley tapped the butt of her gun. "Weapons where I can see them, gentlemen. This is just a conversation."

The men exchanged a look and then, very carefully, opened their jackets. They took their weapons out by the butts and bent at the waist to lay them on the ground. The older one, with a ring of white hair around a bald dome, straightened first. "May I ask your business here, Detective... Paris, was it?"

"Parra. We'd like to talk to you about Milo and his activities last night."

The man who hadn't spoken touched his ear and turned away from them. Riley could hear him muttering under his breath before he turned to face forward again. "Now isn't exactly convenient, Detective Parra. If you could perhaps call and~"

"No, now's good."

She stepped onto the porch, brushing between the two men. Priest followed a bit reluctantly and the men fell into step as the four of them entered the house. The quiet man was speaking into his jacket sleeve again and a sliding door to their right opened with a wooden rasp. The man was shorter than Riley, with thin white hair. He wore a sweater and had a book closed on his finger to mark his place.

"It's not often the police come around here."

"Consider it community outreach, Mr. Rowland."

He leaned forward. "You're the officer who was on television. You killed the Angel Maker."

Riley smiled. Having a reputation as a killer could only help her in this situation. Unless they decided to take her out before she could turn on them. She resisted the urge to touch her weapon.

"We'd like to speak to you about your son, Milo. Is he here?"

The man turned toward the stairs. "Milo, could you come down here please?" He faced Riley again. "My name is Theodore Rowland. You'll have to forgive me, I only remembered your face because it was so fetching. What was your name again?"

"Riley Parra."

"Yes, that's right." He glanced toward the two men who had escorted Riley in, and she knew calls would be made. She wondered who in the department would be fielding that call. A door opened upstairs and Riley heard footsteps before she saw the man. He fit Muse's description to a T.

"I did everything I could with your computer, Pop. You might just have to take it in to get..." He slowed as he saw the group gathered in the foyer. "Guests."

Theodore said, "This is Detective Riley Parra, and her partner, Caitlin Priest. They'd like to talk to you about something that happened last night."

Milo reached the bottom of the stairs. "Am I obliged to speak with them?"

Riley was about to admit he wasn't, but Theodore beat her to the punch. "Yes, you most certainly are."

Riley stepped forward. "Do you know a man by the name of Marcus, or Muse, Skaggs?"

"Yeah. We had a couple of drinks last night at the War Pigs. Nice guy. Excellent pool player. I left before he did, I think. Didn't see him again all night."

"What about a man named Burt Woods?"

Milo laughed. "I haven't seen Burt Woods in a dog's age. How is he doing?"

"Dead."

Milo's smile wavered, but not by much. "Well, that's a shame. He owed me quite a bit of money. Owed to a lot of people, as I understand it." He pretended to think. "Do you think that this Muse fellow I had drinks with was involved in Burt's death?"

Riley shook her head. "No, not really."

Milo was a bad actor. He blinked, and narrowed his eyes. "You don't. Then why bring them up together?"

"Because someone wanted us to believe Muse was the killer. See, Burt Woods owed a lot of people a lot of money. It would be very unusual for one of those people to kill Mr. Woods, because dead men can't pay their debts. But Muse didn't even know Woods. Never met him, never loaned him any money. Muse might be the only person in No Man's Land who would conceivably want Mr. Woods dead and be willing to make it happen."

"Sounds like you have the right man, then." Theodore was looking between Riley and his son, his expression unreadable.

"Yeah, except the thing that makes him look guilty also gives him an alibi. Why would Muse randomly kill someone? There's no violence in his rap sheet. He risked going to jail when he thought someone might get hurt, so why would he kill some stranger on the street? It didn't make sense. So I started thinking about the GHB rapes, and the fact that you seemed to tie Muse and Woods together."

"Pop..." Milo's voice was a warning.

Theodore Rowland was staring at Riley, his lips pressed together in a hard line. He waved at Milo to quiet him. "Let her talk. You know how I love detective stories."

Riley moved closer to Milo. "Woods owed everyone money. Everyone in No Man's Land had a vested interest in keeping him alive. That made me think... someone who owes that much money to that many people... we've gotta be talking thousands of dollars. Tens of thousands, maybe. So I decided to look up Mr. Woods' financials. He was heavy in debt. Made me wonder why people kept loaning him money.

"But then it dawned on me. Burt Woods didn't pay back his debts in cash. He paid them back by favors. Dirty work. Odd jobs here and there in order to have his debt wiped clean. Until the next time he needed to borrow money, of course. But there was something big on Burt Woods' financial records from last week. Seems his mother's house got paid off. Free and clear. I don't have an exact dollar figure, but it must have been pretty steep. So why don't you tell me, Milo?"

Theodore had his eyes locked on Milo. Milo was glaring at Riley, his casual attitude slipping the more Riley said.

"Why don't you tell us the price tag Burt Woods put on his life?"

Milo didn't turn away from Riley when he spoke. "Pop, are you gonna let this woman speak to me like this? In our own house?"

Theodore carefully put down his book and crossed his arms over his chest. "I believe we're waiting for your answer, son. How much did you ask to borrow from me two weeks ago? Fifty thousand dollars?"

"You had people follow Muse after he left the bar. You were waiting for the GHB you put into his drink to kick in. When it did, you drove him to the warehouse where Burt Woods was waiting. He let you kill him, and you made sure to get his blood on Muse's clothes."

Milo suddenly stepped forward. Riley brought her gun up as Theodore left his seat much faster than Riley would have thought possible. He put his hand on his son's shoulder and, despite his diminutive appearance, had enough strength to shove the younger man back. He pinned Milo against the banister, and Milo refused to fight off his father.

He glared at Riley over Theodore's head. "Muse is traitor. He plays like one of us, but he's no better than a stinking cop. He snoops, and he reports to his handlers. He turns on his friends. I should have killed *him*, but I wanted him to suffer. I wanted him to pay for what he did by seeing what it was like on the other side."

"And Burt Woods? He decided his life was only worth fifty grand?"

Milo growled. "Like you said, he had a lot of debts. He figured it was only a matter of time before someone decided he wasn't worth the effort. This way, he was able to do something good when he went."

Riley kept her eye on Milo but directed her next question to his father. "Mr. Rowland, are you going to let me take your son out of here?"

"I'll even hold the door for you, Detective."

Milo looked at his father, anger and betrayal vying for dominance on his face. "Dad, what the hell are you doing?"

"I covered for you. With those girls. You and the bartender, drugging those girls and this is how you repay me?" He shook his head. "You don't deserve this family."

Riley had holstered her weapon and took out her handcuffs. Theodore stepped away and motioned for Milo to turn around. He reluctantly obeyed his father's instruction and Riley fastened the cuffs around his wrists.

"Nice to know even you guys have standards. Milo Rowland, you are under arrest for the murder of Burt Woods. You have the right to remain silent. Anything you say can and will be used against you in a court of law. You have the right to an attorney. If you cannot afford an attorney, one will be appointed for you..."

"I can afford a damn~"

Theodore interrupted him. "No, you can't. *I* can afford an attorney, and this family can. But you... better hope for a good public defender."

Milo's eyes widened as Riley led him outside. The men who had been flanking the door moved aside to let Riley through, Priest following behind to make sure no one tried to free their crown prince. Theodore came out of the house and stood on the porch, hands in his pockets. Riley put Milo into the backseat and looked over the top of the car at the Rowland family patriarch. He turned and disappeared back inside, his men trailing behind him. The door closed with a definitive slam.

Once they were alone, Priest let go the breath she had been holding. "Looks like we got lucky."

"Yeah. I've been having a streak of that lately. Let's get out of here before it runs out on us."

"Riley... did the elder Mr. Rowland seem awfully strong and agile to you?"

"Almost supernaturally so. Yeah, I noticed that." She looked toward the house and, although the windows were all empty, she could feel they were being watched.

"One problem at a time. Let's take care of Milo and get Muse back where he belongs."

Somehow the press had already been alerted to the Rowland arrest by the time Riley and Priest arrived at the station. A pair of uniformed officers performed crowd control so that they could pull into the underground garage. Priest watched the crowd through her window. "I hope my presence doesn't become a problem for you. Seeing as I'm not officially a police detective."

"Don't worry about it."

She parked near the elevators and took out her cell phone. "This is Detective Riley Parra in the garage. I need a couple of officers down here to help me bring in a prisoner."

They got out of the car and removed Milo Rowland from the backseat. The elevator was already in motion, so Riley escorted him toward the doors. Just before it arrived, Riley heard the sound of footsteps approaching from deeper in the garage. Her instinct began sounding the alarm, and she tightened her grip on Milo's arm as her other hand went to her weapon.

"Detective Parra!" Gail Finney moved faster once she was sure she'd been spotted. Her blonde hair was pinned back, and she wore a red blazer and form-fitting blue jeans. Riley resisted the urge to shoot her. "I just have a few questions."

"They'll have to wait." The elevator arrived and Riley tried to rush Milo inside. Priest stepped back and to the side, putting herself between Milo and the reporter.

"It will just be a moment of your time."

"Not now."

Priest stayed out of the elevator, blocking Gail from following Riley into the car. "You still owe me an interview from the Angel Maker case, Riley. An exclusive, do you remember? I feel we have a lot to discuss about that case and what exactly happened inside Terrence Bishop's home."

Riley turned to face Gail. "You and I have absolutely nothing to discuss, Miss Finney. Now or ever." The doors closed on Gail's bemused expression.

Riley didn't want to think about how Gail got into the parking garage, or just what she knew about the way the Angel Maker case had really ended. Now all she cared about was putting Milo Rowland behind bars and getting Muse out.

It had been a long day, and she was looking forward to putting an end to it.

Riley walked to the store and returned to the car with a six-pack of soda and some chips. The sun was just starting to set, turning the sky a strange yellow and pink color. The shadows stretched long across the ground, the darkness moving farther with each passing minute. Riley tossed the chips to Muse, who was sitting on the back of her car, and leaned against the trunk beside him. "So." She took one of the cans and popped the top. "You're a free man."

"Thanks to you."

"Well, I'll probably call up the marker one of these days. You'll owe me one."

Muse smiled. "Look, Riley. The stuff you found out, about my mom and everything~"

"You don't have to explain, Muse. Your private life is just that. I'm just happy I was able to help. And my boss is pretty happy that I managed to bring down the future head of the Rowland family. Happy enough that she's going to overlook the fact I took an unauthorized partner along with me on the investigation."

Muse held out his soda can, and Riley tapped hers against the side.

"So what's the plan now?"

Muse exhaled. "Truth. Or something similar."

Riley looked down the street to Muse's childhood home. "She'll be happy to hear it."

"Yeah. Expect cookies in the mail. You got her boy out of the clink, she's gonna wanna reward you for it." He slipped off the trunk and finished his soda in one swallow. He handed the empty can to Riley. "Wish me luck."

"Good luck, Muse."

He started down the street and then stopped, turned, and smiled at Riley. "Next time you need information..."

"I'll find you."

He saluted her with two fingers. "Say hi to your girl for me. Make up for last night, y'hear?"

"You got it, Mr. Skaggs."

Riley waited until Muse was opening the gate to his mother's house before she gathered the chips and remaining sodas. She tossed them into the passenger seat as she heard a shriek of pure happiness coming from the direction of Muriel Skaggs' house. She fished her cell phone out of her pocket and dialed Gillian's number.

"Hey, it's me."

"I was just thinking about you. What's up?"

"I was thinking about you, too. Listen, Priest is already at the apartment, so why don't we find someplace a little less crowded tonight? Someplace without any interruptions."

Gillian chuckled. "Mm, I like the sound of that. Have any place in particular in mind?"

"I'm sure we can think of something before I get to the station and abduct you."

Gillian laughed. "I'll wrap up my paperwork. Can't wait to see you."

"Ditto. See you soon."

Riley hung up as she pulled away from the curb, leaving the long shadows of No Man's Land behind her.

FRIARS AND EREMITES

EVEN WITHOUT her divinity and faced with life as a mortal, Priest couldn't help but feel that the Sabbath should be kept holy. She spent the morning irked that Riley and Gillian's idea of worship was sleeping in and going out for a big breakfast at a nearby restaurant. She was invited, of course, but she chose to attend a church service instead. She dressed in her finest suit, put on a touch of makeup, and sat in the back pew just as the first hymns began.

By the end of the first round of songs, Priest was in tears. She felt nothing. The words were just lyrics, and the music was just sound. She thumbed through the Bible a woman loaned to her, but none of the words spoke to her. She felt trapped, isolated. It was as if one of her senses had been completely obliterated and she was left fumbling in the darkness.

Zerachiel had responded to worship with nearly sexual bliss. The sound of voices lifted to Heaven had been enough to make her swoon. Now there was just sound and fury, signifying nothing.

Priest left before the service was half over and returned home to Riley's empty apartment. She gratified herself, settling for a physical orgasm, but even that was a shadow of her former happiness and it left her more depressed than before.

Gillian noticed Priest's demeanor and tried to talk with her.

Priest thanked her, but assured her it was nothing that talking would help. Gillian kissed her cheek and reminded her that she and Riley were there if she needed anything. She suggested a movie, and Priest surrendered the couch so Riley and Gillian could sit together without being crowded.

Priest lost interest in the movie fairly quickly. The plot had something to do with war and battles in a gray and washed-out forest. People shouted at each other with fake accents, and other people threw themselves to the ground with fake wounds. She didn't see the appeal in fictions like that, so she ignored the plot and surreptitiously watched Riley and Gillian.

At work, they seemed to make a conscious effort to touch as little as possible. They kept their relationship professional, save for the occasional 'sweetheart' or 'dear.' At home it was a different story. Hardly five minutes went by without some sort of touch; Riley resting her hand on top of Gillian's, or Gillian brushing a hair out of Riley's face. Riley kept one arm around Gillian for almost the entire movie, her fingers occasionally stroking Gillian's neck in an almost unconscious caress.

They spent the rest of Sunday together, with Gillian reading and Riley watching whatever happened to be on television. Priest attempted a crossword puzzle and, when she missed some pop culture references, settled for reading about the current events. When the TV became boring, Riley talked Priest into joining her for a run. "You're not working with angel dust anymore," she had said. "You have to keep in shape. I'll make sure you don't get a spare tire."

They remained mostly silent during the run. Riley asked if Priest was worried about going back to work in the morning. "I'm fine. Excited, even. I look forward to making a difference again." The words were true, and she felt them, but she was worried she wouldn't live up to Riley's expectations. Despite working together on Riley's last case, she was afraid she wasn't up to par with Riley's expectations. It was her worst nightmare thinking Riley might get hurt because she wasn't ready to be back in the field.

They returned home and Riley let Priest take a shower first. She took the time to explore her human body; she'd never noticed how grimy and disgusting it could get in just the course of a few short hours. Had Zerachiel been doing maintenance on her human form? Or was Zerachiel just so powerful that she never broke into a sweat? Either way, she used as much soap as she could, scrubbing and washing every curve twice just to be certain she got them all. She put her hand between her legs and moaned as she felt the pleasure, leaning against the tile wall as she pushed a finger inside herself. Orgasm was the closest she could get to how she used to feel during worship. She stayed in the shower until Gillian politely knocked on the door to see if she was okay.

She changed into a pair of Riley's old sweats, gray drawstring pants and a Police Academy shirt, and apologized if she used all the hot water. She was only slightly surprised when Riley and Gillian headed for the bathroom together. Their shower was even longer than the one Priest had taken, although she doubted they spent the entire time bathing.

Dinner was tacos, which Riley and Gillian made together. Priest set the table, taking the opportunity to watch the two women interact. Riley chopped the tomatoes, showing Gillian "the proper way" to accent a taco shell. They experimented with a multitude of meals: hard and soft shell tacos, burritos, quesadillas, and Riley laughed more than Priest had heard her laugh in ages.

And, of course, the tight quarters of the kitchen provided ample opportunity for Riley and Gillian to touch and caress and collide with one another. Riley slipped past Gillian, letting a hand linger on her hip as she reached for a bowl. Gillian leaned against Riley, their hips touching, as they sprinkled cheese over the ground beef.

It was like watching two charged atoms with an undeniable attraction dancing around each other. She kept an eye on the microwave clock to time how long they went without at least a small touch, and she never got above three minutes.

After they ate, Riley decided she was going to bed early. Gillian agreed, and they bid Priest goodnight before heading down the hall. Priest resigned to the living room, to the television and her pile of blankets, and tried not to think about what tomorrow would bring. She watched several decades-old game shows - she appreciated them because they were real people, with real emotions, rather than actors following a script - and a few infomercials.

She could hear Riley and Gillian in their bedroom. They were good at being discrete, but sometimes Gillian lost a bit of control. She would moan, or cry out, and then Priest would hear the quiet, "shh shh," from Riley. Priest sometimes wondered what Riley could be doing to her, what possible moves she could be using to make the normally buttoned-down Gillian Hunt make such noises, but then she decided it was probably better not to know the details.

Priest curled up and left the TV on, hoping that Chuck Woolery's voice would be enough to tune out Riley and Gillian in the other room. She was preoccupied with thoughts of the next morning running through her mind, praying to anyone who was still listening that she would be capable of doing her job. Sometimes her thoughts strayed to darker territory, wondering what it meant to be human and the inevitable final chapter. She was going to die.

Even talking Sariel out of killing her was just a reprieve; she was dying at that very moment. She put a hand over her heart and counted the beats. She could get ill, suffer, and then she would die. Maybe tomorrow or in thirty years. It was enough to keep her awake until the rising sun started to brighten the living room window.

Priest was the first to wake in the morning due to only dozing throughout the night. She showered, dressed in a clean suit, and came out of the bathroom to find Gillian in the kitchen preparing breakfast. Her hair was up and she was still in her robe and pajamas, wearing her thick glasses instead of contacts. She had yet to put on any makeup, and her face looked pale and unfinished. But there was a subtle beauty to Gillian's features - the dusting of freckles across her nose and the slightly too-wide eyes - that made Priest think she could get away without makeup if she wanted to.

Gillian looked up at the sound of Priest's arrival and smiled. "Good morning, Caitlin. How'd you sleep?"

"Fitfully. And..." Priest had a flashback to the sounds Gillian had been making the night before. A year ago, she would have asked what exactly Riley had been doing to her. But mortality, and Riley's lessons, had given her a certain amount of tact. "Uh. How about yourself?"

Gillian adjusted her glasses. "Slept just fine. Want some pancakes?"

"No. My stomach is a bit... unusual."

"Does it feel like churning? Like your stomach is the water on a stormy day?" Priest nodded and Gillian smiled. "Ah. First day jitters."

"I've been a detective for two years."

"You and Zerachiel have been a detective for two years. Now it's just you. You're nervous about failing, about not measuring up." She smiled. "It's okay. It's *human*. Sit down and I'll make you some toast."

Riley came out of the bedroom as Priest took a seat. She wore a tank top and pajama pants, her hair hanging in a loose mess around her face. "Hey, Cait. Ready for today?"

"Hopefully."

"Do I have time to hop in the shower before breakfast?"

Gillian nodded. "Just don't take too long."

Riley waved over her shoulder as she went back down the hall. Gillian transferred the first batch of pancakes to a plate, started a second, and placed two pieces of bread in the toaster.

"Do you need a hand?"

"No, I like playing housewife." She smiled and went back to her preparations. She glanced toward the bathroom as the shower started running. "Caitlin, may I ask you something that might seem a little... uncomfortable?"

Priest nodded slowly. "Sure."

"Do you think Riley and I are having too much sex?"

"Oh." Priest looked toward the bathroom. "I don't think I know what the standard amount is. You are engaged, after all."

Gillian nodded. "Yeah, I know. But lately it seems like every time we're near a horizontal surface, we tear into each other. Not that I'm complaining, I'll take whatever I can get. But I don't want to become one of those couples who do all their bonding in the bedroom."

"I don't think you have to worry. You lived the nightmare of every cop's spouse. You saw your lover's dead body. And you got her back." She shrugged. "You're celebrating her life. You're expressing your gratitude for the gift you've been given in the simplest, most life-affirming way. This is the honeymoon phase. Things will return to normal soon, I'm sure."

Gillian smiled and put her hand on top of Priest's. "Thanks, Caitlin."

"I do what I can."

"And I'm sorry if the-the walls are a little thin."

"I don't know what you're talking about."

Gillian returned to the stove to finish making the pancakes. Riley returned from the bathroom a few minutes later in a maroon T-shirt and jeans. Her hair was wet and slicked back, tied by a string, and she draped her jacket over her seat as she joined Gillian at the stove. Priest noticed Riley's hand went to the small of Gillian's back as if magnetically drawn to that spot.

"Need any help with breakfast, hon?"

"You can pour the juice."

Riley kissed Gillian's cheek before she went to get the glasses.

Lieutenant Briggs was waiting by Riley's desk when they arrived. Riley slowed and spoke low enough that only Priest could hear. "Don't let her get to you. She's still pissed about everything that happened with the Angel Maker." She smiled and raised her hand in a friendly wave. "Hiya, boss. How are you? I hope you'll notice that I am efficiently partnered up, as you requested." She gestured at Priest like a game show model showing off a new car.

"I see." Briggs was staring at Priest. "You've proven yourself to her, Detective Priest. Since she has more reason to be pissed than I do - just barely - I'll cut you some slack. Has she explained that you're currently on probation?"

Priest nodded. "Yes, ma'am."

Briggs pushed off the edge of Riley's desk and revealed what she had been hiding; Priest's badge and gun were sitting in the middle of the blotter.

"Don't make me regret this. Either of you. And don't get comfortable." She held out a piece of paper. "The commissioner wants you on this personally, Riley. You're as close to a celebrity as this department has, and the case is high profile."

Riley took the paper. "Hargrave... Of *the* Hargraves?"

"The same. The Rowlands last week and now this case... looks like killing the Angel Maker has made you our highest profile detective. That was the plan, right?" She glanced at Priest. "Apparently one of the Hargraves has been murdered. Details were fuzzy as to which one. The unis are waiting for you at the scene. I assume you know where they live?"

"Yeah, I have a pretty good idea."

Briggs nodded and went back to her office. Riley gestured for Priest to follow her back to the stairs.

"Who are the Hargraves?" Priest asked.

"You know how the city neighborhoods get incrementally worse the farther out you get, right? No Man's Land runs along the outer edge of the city..."

Priest nodded. "And the inner city is the safest and cleanest."

"The Hargraves live one block from the city center. They own Hargrave Towers, which is where half the elite in the city lives. The commissioner, people who work for the mayor's office... anyone who is anyone and wants to ignore the fact that this city is going to

Hell in a hand basket lives there. The Hargraves are developers, and they got their money from doing shoddy work for a quick buck. They're a big part of the reason half of No Man's Land is falling down around us."

"Maybe someone decided to take their frustrations out on the family."

Riley shrugged. "Stranger things have happened."

Priest looked down at her badge, holding it so that the gold caught the light. The gun felt heavy against her side, in the shoulder holster that crossed her back where her wings had once emerged. Everything felt so strange, so slightly off center that she kept trying to adjust the collar of her shirt. She followed Riley out to the car and hooked the badge on her belt before she climbed into the passenger seat.

"Nice to have you back where you belong, partner. How does it feel?"

Priest inhaled and looked down at the badge. "It feels good to finally have a purpose again."

Riley nodded. "Buckle up."

Priest was more accustomed to driving into No Man's Land, so it was unusual to leave the station and drive into a nicer neighborhood. The buildings were clean, the sidewalks were swept, and no one lingered in doorways or passed merchandise to each other out of sight. A few blocks from Hargrave Towers, they passed a wide swath of greenery with shining playground equipment. A few kids were playing under the watchful eyes of nannies and babysitters.

"District Park." Riley barely looked over as she drove past it. "Where the Eloi let their children scamper and pretend the Morlocks don't exist."

Hargrave Towers wasn't as tall as Priest expected. It stood twelve stories including the lobby, but the exterior was extravagant enough that it earned the lofty title. Riley parked in front of the building behind two squad cars, and a uniformed officer approached their car with a doorman in tow.

"Detectives. I'm Officer Doucette, and this is~"

The doorman extended a hand. "Richard Lacey. I discovered the body this morning."

Doucette motioned for Riley and Priest to follow him inside. "Mr. Lacey found the body as he said and called us. The victim was positively identified as Achilles Hargrave, the current head of the household. He inherited it when his parents died fifteen years ago. He'd been shot twice in the chest from a distance; the window to the penthouse was broken, and my partner is checking out the possible shooting position on the neighboring buildings."

Riley was still stuck on one piece of information. "His name was Achilles?" Doucette shrugged and shook his head. "Okay. Do we have witnesses?"

"Just one. She's... not being very helpful."

The doorman used a card to access one of the elevators. "Access to the penthouse is restricted to a select list," he explained.

"We're going to need to be on the list for the duration of this investigation."

He nodded quickly. "Yes. Yes, of course."

They stepped into the elevator. The doors whispered shut and they began their ascent without as much as a lurch. Priest had an uneasy memory of taking flight and pushed it down before she could get bogged down in everything she had lost.

"Okay, so the victim was Achilles Hargrave?" Doucette nodded. "Then it stands to reason the witness is his sister."

Richard Lacey nodded. "Yes, Hippolita. Although she prefers Lita."

Priest watched the numbers above the door increase toward eleven. She was confused; the building was at least twelve stories on the outside.

"Who requested me?" Riley said.

The doorman answered again. "Lita did. She read about your exploits in the newspaper and wanted to meet you in person."

The doors parted and they stepped out directly into the living room of the penthouse. Priest was amazed at the side of it and quickly discovered where the missing floor had gone; the ceiling was at least twenty feet above them, the remaining floor space turned into a loft surrounded by a wrought-iron banister. Directly in front of them were three floor-to-ceiling windows that looked out over the city. The window on the far left had been shattered and was covered by plastic. She could see the decay of No Man's Land in the distance; it seemed so far away from this vantage point. The living room was decorated in shades of white and black, with a piano standing next to the broken window.

Doucette received a call on his radio and turned away to quietly answer it. He listened for a moment and then reported to Riley. "Medical examiner is on her way up."

"Thank you, Officer." She walked into the living room and saw the body laid out as it had been found. Achilles Hargrave was lying on his back in front of the couch, his chest covered with blood. He was wearing a dark blue dressing gown over a pair of matching pajamas, his head tilted at an unnatural angle with his mouth hanging open as if he was stunned to have these plebeians in his home.

"Where's the witness?"

"Upstairs in the loft. The other officers are with her."

The elevator dinged as Riley started across the room. Gillian stepped out and blinked in surprise. "Well, hi."

"Fancy meeting you on this side of the tracks. I have a witness."

"My body?"

"Great, as always. But the corpse is over there."

Gillian grinned and brushed her hand against Riley's as they crossed paths. Priest smiled at the sight; apparently they didn't keep things entirely professional when they were at work. Maybe she had just been blind to it before.

Priest followed Riley up the spiral staircase to where the witness was waiting. The loft was probably bigger than Riley's entire apartment, decorated to serve as a library, a living room, and a bedroom all in one. Two uniformed officers were standing on the far side of the space and they looked up as Riley appeared. One motioned her forward.

Hippolita 'Lita' Hargrave was sitting on the floor with her back against the wall, her legs extended in front of her. She was dressed in a robe similar to her brother's, but it was green. Her red hair was a mess and both her hands were covering her face. The officer who had motioned them over moved to intercept them.

"She's still pretty shaken up. She was dozing on the couch when it happened. The sound woke her up and she saw her brother falling. She passed out and called for help when she came to."

Riley nodded and thanked him. "Ms. Hargrave? I'm Detective Riley Parra, and this is Detective Priest."

The woman lifted her head and looked at her. She frowned, and then her lips curled into a difficult and weak smile. "You're the police detective from the news. It's so peculiar to see you in my home."

"Well. It's not exactly a social call."

"No. Of course not. No." She looked toward the banister. "Of course not."

Riley moved toward the banister and Lita looked up as if just realizing she was there. "I'm sorry. I'm still just trying to process what happened."

"Why don't you just tell us what you remember and we'll go from there?"

Lita took a deep breath as if bracing herself, closed her eyes, and began to speak. "We had both just woken up. Lee was talking about breakfast, and I had just brought in the newspaper. I was sitting on the couch, and Lee was in front of me, and then all of a sudden he... his chest..." She blinked back tears. "He fell backward and I saw so much blood. Everywhere. I just passed out."

"You didn't hear the gunshot or the breaking glass?"

Lita shook her head. "I was looking at him and suddenly he was falling. I just passed out."

Doucette appeared at the top of the stairs. Riley nodded at Priest, who walked over to get his report.

"My partner finished his search of the next-door roof. No sign of the shooter, but there is a clear line of sight into the living room of the apartment."

Priest nodded. "Okay. Seal off the roof and let forensics have a chance to go over it. Did you find the bullets?"

"Uh, no, ma'am. The wounds weren't through and through, so the bullets are still in the body. Dr. Hunt requested Detective Parra's presence when she had a moment."

"I'll tell her. Thanks, officer."

When Priest returned to the group, Lita looked up and met her eyes. Priest offered a smile, and Lita tried to return it before she looked down at her hands. "I don't know what I can do to help you. We didn't have any enemies. Well..." She held her hands out palm-up. "People hated us, of course. But they weren't really... real. I mean, we never saw any of them. My brother and I rarely left the apartment."

"Never?" Riley said. "You must have gone out sometimes."

Lita shrugged. "We had our groceries or whatever we needed delivered. Richard would bring it up to us, so there was no need. Lee did everything for the business over the internet."

"When was the last time you left the apartment?"

Lita pondered the question and then shook her head. "Two years, maybe. I don't know. Something like that. But Lee would occasionally leave, if there was something he had to sign in person or a business... thing he had to deal with." She waved her hand, indicating that Lee had most likely been in charge of the family's business.

Riley looked up and slightly widened her eyes in disbelief. "Unfortunately, all that tells us is how the killer knew where to find him. Had your brother discussed any business transactions that had gone sour, or anyone who might want to take their frustrations out on him?"

"He didn't talk about stuff like that to me. He seemed... angry lately, though." She ran her tongue over her lips and then searched the room. She closed her eyes and angrily shook her head. "I'm sorry. I wish I could help you, detective. I just can't wrap my head around it as something that really happened."

"I understand." She produced a card. "This is my number. You can call me if you think of anything else that might be important."

Lita nodded and took the card. She glanced at the front of it and then looked at Priest. "And... you said you were a detective priest? I don't know what that is. Did someone call the church for me?"

Riley hid her smile behind a brush of her hand. "No, ma'am. This is Detective Caitlin Priest. It's just her name."

"Oh." Lita's voice was quiet. "I'm sorry. Do you have a card?"

"No, I'm sorry. But if you call Riley, she can get hold of me."

Lita nodded and put her hands in her lap, staring at Riley's card.

"Is there anyone we can call for you?"

"No. To be honest, the policemen being here is... too much. I'll feel better when I'm alone." She smiled. "Alone used to include Lee. I don't know what I'm going to do without him."

Riley nodded, but Priest didn't think she understood.

"It can be hard to lose someone who means that much to you. Someone who is a part of you is suddenly gone, it can hurt more than you can explain with words." Lita was staring at Priest with something almost like reverence. "We'll do everything in our power to make sure whoever took him from you is brought to justice."

Riley told Lita they would be in touch and then led Priest back to the stairs. "Have you been watching reruns of *Dragnet*?"

"It seemed like the appropriate thing to say. Officer Doucette's partner didn't find any evidence of a shooter on the neighboring building, and Gillian wants to talk with you."

At the bottom of the stairs, Riley saw Gillian bent over Achilles' body. "Did you solve the case for me again? Because you know I hate that."

Gillian looked up and offered a meager smile. "We might have a problem."

"Big or little?" Riley pinched the knees of her trousers and pulled them up slightly as she knelt next to Achilles, on the opposite side from where Gillian was working.

"Depends. The story is that someone shot from next door, through the window, and hit him here?" Riley nodded. "No."

"What do you mean no?"

"A bullet that traveled that distance, through this glass, would be severely slowed by the time it hit the victim. But he got the full force of the shot. It wasn't point-blank range, but the gun was definitely fired inside this room." She glanced toward the loft. "If I had to put money on it, I would say it was from up there."

Priest said, "Shouldn't we smell the gunpowder?"

Riley shook her head. "A room this size, not necessarily. Not to mention the fact the wind blowing through that window would have cleared the air pretty quick. We only have Lita's word that everything happened the way she said it did. At least until Dr. Hunt gets a time of death."

"Judging from the body's condition, I'd say that part of the story is actually accurate. I'd wager he's only been dead for an hour, maybe two. Given that his sister passed out before making the call, it fits."

"Okay. Let's keep this between us until we know what it means." She stood up and looked toward the loft. "What do you think, Cait?"

"We don't know that Lita lied. She admitted she never heard the glass break, and everyone just assumed it came from outside because of the broken window."

Riley turned and looked at the window. "And how did that happen? Killer broke the window to throw us off?"

Priest looked toward the elevators. "Or to get rid of the gun. He couldn't be seen wandering through the lobby with a high-powered weapon, so he got rid of it before he left the scene."

Riley motioned for Officer Doucette to join them. "I want you and your partner to search the alley beneath this window for the weapon. Let me know if you find anything."

Priest watched him go and then turned to Riley. "What about Lita?"

"What about her?"

"If this is about the Hargraves and their business, then she might be in danger, too."

"Whoever killed Lee left her alone when she passed out."

Priest nodded and looked at the couch. "Unless that was why they left her alone. They may not have wanted to do it while she was defenseless."

"Murderers don't work that way," Riley said.

Gillian stood up. "Maybe the killer knew them personally. It's like a husband covering his wife's face before he shoots her. When Lita passed out, the killer couldn't bring themselves to finish her off in such a vulnerable state."

"Could be. Or we could be looking at it all wrong. We know the gun was most likely fired inside this room. And we know that there were probably only two people in this room at the time."

Priest was surprised. "You think Lita is a suspect?"

"I don't know what to think right now. We'll look into all the angles. For now, whether she's in danger or a suspect, she needs to have someone sitting on her. I'll get a couple of the uniforms to stay here and keep an eye on her."

"Actually..." Priest hesitated and looked up at the loft. "I'd like to volunteer."

"You?" Gillian glanced at Riley.

Riley was just as surprised. "Why you?"

Priest shook her head. "I don't know. I feel like this is where I need to be."

Riley shrugged. "If you're sure, I have no problem with it. I'll head back to the station and start running down some leads." She turned to Gillian. "Are you done here?"

"Yeah, I was just about to load him up and ship him out."

"Okay then. Cait, keep in touch with me. Let me know if anything comes up. See if you can get a little more from her about people that might have had it out for her and her brother."

Priest nodded.

Riley seemed reluctant to leave but, once Gillian and her assistants had the body loaded onto a gurney, she and the uniformed officers followed them into the elevator. Riley turned at the doors. "You're not doing this to hide out, are you?"

"No, of course not. I truly believe Lita is in danger and I want to be the one looking out for her."

Riley smiled. "Like old times?"

Priest smiled sadly. "I may not be Zerachiel anymore, but old habits die hard."

"Okay. You have my cell if you need it."

Priest stepped back and Riley stepped into the elevator. The door closed on her concerned expression, and Priest was left alone in the apartment. She went up the spiral staircase to the loft where Lita was still sitting on the floor with her arms wrapped around her legs, her head resting on her knees.

"Ms. Hargrave?" Her head rose quickly and she blinked bloodshot eyes. "We think that you may also be in danger, so I'm going to stay here to make sure you stay safe. If that's okay."

Lita nodded. "Yeah, it's... fine. Thank you."

Priest smiled. "My pleasure."

Lita asked if she could go to sleep, and Priest checked out her bedroom to make sure it was safe. The windows were small and shaded, and the only access was through the front room. She agreed and Lita thanked her in a meek, small voice. Once she was alone in the apartment, Priest decided to use her time to examine the crime scene. The broken window made no sense to her. If the shooting had occurred inside the apartment, then the killer must have broken the window. But the glass had fallen *in*. She had watched the crime scene unit photograph it and sweep it up.

Priest walked to the window and looked at the pieces of glass that remained in the sill. She could see yellow crime scene tape flapping in the breeze on the neighboring roof. She trusted Gillian's word that the shooter had been inside the Hargrave apartment, so why was the glass broken? She envisioned a demon standing on the roof across the street, launching itself through the window and... opening fire with a high-powered rifle? No. A demon wouldn't resort to such mundane methods.

She crossed to the couch where Lita had been sitting. Achilles' blood had seeped into the carpet and made an abstract shape. Achilles would have been standing directly in front of the window; a perfect target for the imaginary gunman across the street. But if Gillian was correct, then the killer had been standing... Priest turned and looked up at the loft. It was mostly open to the ground floor, the border marked by a thin black banister. A shooter could have stood there and leveled the weapon... maybe they'd even used the banister as a prop for the barrel of their weapon.

Priest was surprised when Lita suddenly appeared at the banister, breaking her reverie.

"Ms. Hargrave. Is anything wrong?"

"No. I just couldn't sleep. I know you're supposed to be protecting me, but I thought... m-maybe we could talk."

Priest nodded. "Yes. Of course."

Lita came downstairs and Priest saw that she had changed into a nightgown and robe. Her hair was a mess, indicating she had tried and failed to sleep. Lita self-consciously touched her hair when she saw Priest looking at it and her deathly pale complexion colored slightly. "I'll make us something to drink. Do you like tea?"

"Yes, I think so."

"You think so?"

Priest smiled. "I'm not exactly the person I was a few months ago."

Lita's smile faded slightly. "I know how that feels. I'll get us some cups and we can find out together, how's that?"

"Sounds great."

Lita disappeared into the kitchen and Priest wandered toward the stairs. She wondered at her reaction to Lita. Was it purely visceral? Subconscious? She had red hair and delicate features, like Gillian. She supposed it was possible she was just transferring her feelings about what she was hearing at night onto a woman who bore a passing resemblance to her partner's fiance. She was facing the windows when she heard a bell sound behind her.

Priest had one hand on the butt of her gun as the elevator doors parted. Richard Lacey stepped into the room and froze when he saw Priest. "Oh."

Lita came out of the kitchen carrying a tea service. Her feet stuttered on the carpet and she looked at Priest before she composed herself. "Mr. Lacey. What are you doing here?"

He covered his confusion well. "I thought the police had all left. I was coming to make sure you were okay, Ms. Hargrave."

"Detective Priest offered to stay here in case there were any further attempts. They think my brother may not have been the only target this morning."

His eyes widened. "Good heavens. Do you think this killer will strike again?"

"We doubt it, but it's better to be safe than sorry. Mr. Lacey, were there any unusual guests in the building this morning? They may not have necessarily been acting suspicious, but anyone out of the ordinary is of interest."

"The other detective asked that as well, as she was leaving. I couldn't think of anything then, and I've been wracking my brain trying to think. And I wish I could help you but, no. I can't think of anyone like that."

"Okay. Keep thinking about it and, if you come up with anything, please let us know."

He nodded as if his head was bobbing on water. "Yes, of course. Uh, now that I know Ms. Hargrave is in good hands, I shall return to my post. Ladies. Uh, detective."

Priest watched him go, and then turned to watch Lita place the tea cups on the coffee table. "That seemed unusual."

Lita made a wry noise of humor. "Mr. Lacey has had a bit of a crush on me since he started work here. He was just twenty-one, and I was seventeen, but it was love at first sight."

Priest did quick mental calculations. "So he has been carrying a torch for nearly twenty years."

"No, more like ten."

Priest blinked. "But you said he started working here when you were seventeen."

Lita looked pointedly at Priest. "Yes. Ten years ago." She arched an eyebrow and Priest realized she was enacting a social contract between two women. She didn't understand the need to lie about something as basic as age, but she went along with it.

"Right. I must have been mistaken."

Lita smiled and proceeded to pour their tea. Priest came around the edge of the couch, noticing that Lita had chosen the end of the table as far from Achilles' final resting place as possible. She had her body tilted at an awkward angle so she couldn't see it when she sat down. Priest looked past her to a small sitting area on the opposite side of the piano. "Ms. Hargrave, perhaps we should have our tea in there."

"Yes." Lita seemed relieved at the suggestion. "Yes, I think that would be a marvelous idea, Detective."

Priest helped Lita transfer the tea service from the living room table to the other small table, turning to look at the elevator before she took her tea cup. Innocent or not, twenty years was a long time to harbor an unrequited crush. After that much time, it could begin manifesting itself in dangerous ways.

"Riley Parra."

"Hello. It's me. You asked me to check in." Priest was standing by one of the two unbroken windows in the Hargrave's living room.

She had her cell phone to her ear with one hand, the other raised to shade her eyes from the sun. "I've been talking with Lita most of the morning, through lunch. I've been avoiding the murder directly, but I've addressed it surreptitiously." She looked through the glass at the sky, squinting at the sun.

"Find anything worth noting?"

"The windows. At about noon, the sun was shining through the window to the farthest right. That means at the time of the murder~"

"The sun would have been shining on the window our alleged sniper shot through. It would be like trying to shoot through a mirror. Nice catch, Cait."

Priest smiled proudly.

"The shooting from across the street was already looking pretty iffy. First Jill's evidence about the strength of the bullets, and then forensics found something odd on the glass."

"Odd how?"

"Tape residue. Certain pieces of the broken glass are sticky."

Priest frowned. "What does that mean?"

"Someone taped the window so they could break it would all the glass shattering outward. Then they used some kind of tool to pull the broken glass into the apartment. Then they just took off the tape and scattered the pieces for us to pick up."

Priest furrowed her brow. "That sounds very complicated."

"I guess whoever the killer is was dedicated to their cover story." She was silent for a long time before she spoke again. "How is Ms. Hargrave doing?"

"She's still in shock over what happened, but she's been talking more. Nothing substantive, but I think that she's becoming more comfortable with me. When I feel she's ready, I'll bring up the topic of the murder. How are things on your end?"

Riley said, "It's nice being back in the slums. Feels like home. Gillian is doing the autopsy as we speak, but there shouldn't be many surprises. She did confirm the bullets were fired from inside the apartment. There's no way they could have done the damage she's seeing after they traveled fifty yards and came through a sheet of glass."

"Detective Priest?" She turned and saw Lita standing at the foot of the stairs. She held up a finger to indicate she was almost done.

"I should go. I just wanted to fill you in. Talk to you soon."

"All right. Thanks for the pieces of the puzzle."

Priest said goodbye before she hung up and slipped the phone back into her pocket. Lita had finally decided to get dressed. She'd changed into a green blouse over a black skirt, her feet still bare as she entered the living room. She glanced toward the couch again, the area marked off as a crime scene, and shuddered almost imperceptibly. She gave the crime scene a wide berth and forced a smile as she approached Priest. "What shall we do with the rest of our afternoon? I don't entertain very often."

"I was thinking we could talk about your brother."

Lita shrugged and led the way into the sitting area. "He was the face of our little empire. He did the business transactions and I gathered my allowance." She smiled. "I didn't mind it, obviously. One who has never worked a day in her life doesn't look gift horses in the mouth. I should have realized it couldn't last forever. Now I don't know what I'll do without him."

"You'll do what he did when your parents passed away. You'll do whatever needs to be done."

"I suppose."

"How did your parents die?"

Lita sat down and tucked her legs under her. "Car accident. I'd lived my entire life cloistered and coddled, and I thought it was the end of the world. But Lee made sure that the shockwaves didn't hit me. He took control of everything and, after the funeral, I was able to live like everything was the same. I thought he was doing me a favor. Maybe if he hadn't done that, I would be prepared for this."

"Nothing can prepare you for this," Priest said. "You can just deal with it the best you can." She sat across from Lita. "I recently went through a pretty drastic change myself. I'm not really ready to discuss it, but it's like I told you earlier. I'm not the same person I was a year ago. For a while I thought I was going to die because everything was so... different. I retreated. But a friend found me and brought me back."

Lita smiled. "That's the problem. I don't have friends, and I don't have anywhere to retreat. I haven't left this apartment in years. Do you think I can't see what the city looks like out there? It gets worse every day. The thought of going outside scared the hell out of me. Lee handled it better, but I could see that it got to him, too. We didn't go outside unless it was absolutely necessary. And there's a garden on the roof where we can get fresh air."

Priest nodded. "I know how you feel, trust me. When the world changes, the hardest thing is to keep on going. You said you don't have anywhere to retreat. I think you already retreated. Here, to this apartment. You hid from the world with your brother. Maybe you should take this as an opportunity to stop running. Someone has to be the face of the Hargrave family, right?"

Lita sighed. "I don't know if I have it in me..."

The elevator began to hum, and both women looked back at it. "Are you expecting someone?"

"No..."

Priest took her gun from the holster as she stood. "Get on the floor, please." Lita dropped down and Priest moved around the couch. She skirted the edge of the crime scene as the elevator arrived and the doors slid open. Priest immediately recognized Riley's profile and dropped her weapon as Riley and two uniformed officers stepped out of the car. "Riley?"

"Where is she?"

"Lita, it's okay. It's safe."

Lita rose from behind the couch and eyed the officers. "What's going on?"

"Ms. Hargrave, do you own a hunting rifle?"

"Yes... I used to... I mean, my parents used to take my brother and me out on weekends. I never shot anything. It was just for fun."

"I hope that's true, ma'am. We have a warrant to search the apartment for any weapons you may own. Specifically a thirty-aught-six rifle."

Lita blinked. "I-I have two. They're upstairs in the closet."

Riley nodded to one of the officers, and he started up the stairs.

Priest crossed the room. "What are you doing, Riley?"

"We confirmed the killing shot came from inside the apartment. Specifically the loft. The entry wound was angled to confirm the shooter was elevated. We did a little research and discovered that Ms. Hargrave took shooting lessons when she was a teenager. We just want to ask her a few questions."

Priest lowered her voice. "You saw how shaken up she is. She's obviously in shock from seeing her brother killed."

"Or she's in shock because she pulled the trigger. We'll know more once we talk to her. Sorry, Cait, but this is how it has to be."

The officer returned with two shotguns. Riley acknowledged them and took a pair of handcuffs from her belt. "Hippolita Hargrave, you're under arrest for the murder of Achilles Hargrave. You have the right to remain silent..."

Lita looked completely confused. "Detective Priest..."

Priest shook her head. "I'm sorry, Lita. But you can trust Riley. If you didn't do it, she'll figure out who did. You just have to trust her."

Riley fastened the handcuffs on Lita's wrists and finished reciting the Miranda rights. Riley guided her toward the elevator and told the officers to continue their search of the apartment. "Cait, you coming?"

"Yes." She stepped into the elevator with Riley, meeting Lita's eyes as the doors closed on them. Riley pressed the button for the lobby and leaned against the wall.

Priest lowered her voice, even though it was pointless to whisper in such tight quarters. "Riley, you're making a mistake."

"The evidence is pointing toward her, Cait. I'm doing what I have to do."

"What about the broken window?" She turned to Lita. "The gunshot came from inside the apartment. Either you lied about being alone, or you're the only person who could have possibly murdered Achilles. Which is it?"

Lita shook her head. "I-I don't know what... what you're talking about..."

"Someone was in the loft," Riley said. "That's where the shot came from, not through the window. Either someone else was in the apartment, or you're the only possible suspect."

"But the window~"

"Broken from the inside. Someone went to a lot of trouble to make it look otherwise." Riley crossed her arms over her chest. "Any ideas who?"

Lita blinked rapidly and shook her head. She looked at Priest. "You have to help me."

"I don't know if I can, Lita. I'm sorry."

They arrived at the lobby. Richard Lacey was standing at his post, still obviously shaken by the arrival of Riley and the police officers. He stepped forward, thought better of it, and then nervously shifted his weight to his other foot. Riley guided Lita toward the door.

"What is going on here?"

Riley held up her hand as he tried to come around the desk. "Stay back please, Mr. Lacy. It's not your concern."

Priest remembered his sudden appearance in the Hargraves apartment and slowed down. She looked at Lita and Riley and then faced Richard. "She's being arrested for her brother's murder."

Riley stopped at the door. "Cait..."

Priest ignored her and approached the desk. "All the evidence is telling us that she killed her brother and covered it up. She apparently wanted his money."

Lita's eyes widened. "How can you say that?"

"Detective Priest, may I have a word with you?" Riley's voice was firm, angry.

Richard shook his head frantically. "No. N-no, that's... not what she would do. I know her. She would never~"

Priest ignored Riley's furious expression. "She was the only person in the apartment. She's the only one who could have done it. Unless you have any information that could help us..."

Richard looked at Lita and his expression wavered a bit. "She wasn't alone in the apartment this morning."

Riley looked at Priest and realized what she had just done. "And you would know this because?"

"Because I was there." He swallowed and shook his head. "I'm sorry, Lita. I know we said we would... but I didn't..." He closed his eyes and hung his head. "I shot Lee. She's innocent. Leave her out of this, please?"

Riley nodded for Priest to handcuff Richard as well. "I think we're going to sort this out downtown."

Riley deposited the two suspects in different interrogation rooms and then guided Priest back toward their desks. "What the hell was all that about?"

"Richard showed up at the apartment after he thought Lita was alone. I didn't think anything of it at the time. But his expression when he saw Lita in the handcuffs was very telling. I decided to gamble."

"It was a hell of a risk. The only information was can trust is that Lita and Lee were definitely not alone when the murder happened, but that's it. We still don't know for sure which of them pulled the trigger. He could be covering for her."

"But we are one step closer to finding the truth."

Riley sighed. "Yeah. We are." She looked toward Briggs' office and scoffed. "I guess it serves me right. All those years using my own playbook, and now I'm the one yelling at someone who doesn't follow the rules."

"Are you saying you rubbed off on me?"

"No offense."

Priest smiled. "I'd consider it a compliment. If I can be half the human you are~"

Riley held up one hand. "Don't get too mushy. We still have a murderer to catch. Which one do you want to talk to?"

"Lita."

"Let me know what you find out." She slapped Priest on the arm and they went into their respective interrogation rooms.

Lita was sitting with her head down on the table, her face pressed into the crook of her elbow. Priest closed the door and she looked up. "Oh."

"Hello, Lita." She put down her file and sat down. She turned on a tape recorder. "Interview with Hippolita Hargrave, conducted by Detective Caitlin Priest. Two-fourteen in the afternoon." With the formality dealt with, Priest looked across the table into Lita's red eyes. "I want to know what really happened this morning in your apartment. The whole truth, right now."

"I'm sorry I lied. He said... he said that the police would just accept whatever I said because I'm a Hargrave. I was scared. I didn't want to go to prison."

Priest nodded. "I understand. But we have to know what really happened."

Lita took a deep breath. "For two years, I've only really spent time with two people. My brother and Richard. He would bring up deliveries and Lee was always too busy to deal with it. So I was the one who would talk to him. I'd help him bring in the groceries, and he would help me put them away. After a while, I guess we struck up a mutual attraction. I suppose you'll find this hard to believe, but I'd never been with a man before. I simply didn't have the urge, I suppose, or I had spent too much time with my family members as my only company. But Richard made me feel like I had been missing something.

"We met furtively whenever we could. Kissing, and groping. Richard said he felt like a teenager again, and I could only think about all the fun I had missed out on. I wanted to experience everything. So last night, I asked Richard to come up to the apartment after Lee went to bed. I wanted to finally..." She pressed her lips together and dipped her chin. "I wanted to see what I'd been missing."

After a lengthy pause, Priest nodded. "Go on."

"Richard fell asleep. We planned for him to be gone by the

morning, but we woke up to hear Lee downstairs. We didn't know what to do, so I went down to prepare Lee. I thought that if I just told him, we could all be adults about it. Lee... apparently... thought otherwise. He called me names. He yelled at me. Then he started slapping me, and he threw me onto the couch. I think he was going to really hurt me." She closed her eyes and sniffled. "He said I deserved better than 'some doorman.' He said the Hargraves were better than trash like that.

"That's when Richard shot him."

"Using your gun?"

Lita nodded. "They weren't hidden or anything. He grabbed one and loaded it as soon as Lee raised his voice. I think he was just going to scare him. But then things got violent and he reacted. He was just doing it to protect me."

"And what about the fake shooter?"

"That was Richard's plan. He said that we could get away with it because of who I am. He said if we didn't give the police any suspects, the trail would go cold and the case would be put away in a drawer somewhere. I said that I passed out to give us time to stage the scene."

"How did you break the window?"

"Richard put an X on it, and used a hammer to crack the glass. Then he used the claw to pull the glass inward so it broke over the carpet. Then I just peeled off the tape." She licked her lips. "What happens now?"

Priest said, "That's for the DA to decide. Technically, what Richard Lacey did was self-defense. But then you tried to cover it up. I'm sorry, Lita, but you may have to face the consequences of your actions."

Lita closed her eyes and nodded. Priest stood up and went to the door, and Lita stopped her. "Detective. I'm sorry that I lied to you."

"I am, too. I wish you luck, Lita."

Priest left the interrogation room and leaned against the wall until Riley joined her. "Hey. Richard pulled the trigger because he loves her?"

Priest nodded. "That's the story I got, too."

Riley sighed and stood next to Priest. "Alternate ending to Romeo and Juliet. They kill their family instead of themselves. I guess it's better than a double suicide, but it's still a long way from a happy ending."

Priest smiled sadly. "What do you think will happen to them?"

"Hard to say. Technically self-defense, but they screwed everything up by lying to us and trying to cover it up. It depends on how forgiving the DA is."

"I'm sorry."

Riley glanced at her. "For?"

"I feel like I screwed up. I got too close to Lita and didn't see the obvious."

Riley laughed. "Priest, you closed the case. You found the doorman and you kept an eye on the suspect, even if we weren't certain she was a suspect at the time. You kept an open mind, and that is why we made two arrests today. You did great." She held out her hand. "Welcome back to the force, partner."

Priest looked at Riley's hand and then took it, squeezing gently.

Priest sat at her desk, staring at the far wall of the bullpen. After handing Lita and Richard over to a pair of uniforms who would take them down to holding, she and Riley had been doing the paperwork required to officially close the case. Technically, Riley was doing the lion's share of the paperwork. Priest couldn't clear her head long enough to keep a coherent thought.

She couldn't stop thinking about Briggs' update, the slap on the back and the "good job." It didn't feel like a good job. The DA had talked Lita and Richard into an agreement. Richard took a plea and accepted full blame for the cover-up, while Lita was released without charges. According to the DA, she was given a sweetheart deal because of who she was. "The city can't function without a Hargrave pulling the strings," was the official report.

Riley noticed her mood. "You okay?"

"Lita was as culpable as Richard. She should be punished, however lightly, for her role."

"She got scared. Happens all the time." Riley closed down her computer and stood up. "They got the guy who pulled the trigger. Screwing with a crime scene is a, a slap on the wrist. Even if they decided to pursue charges - which they would never do, not against a Hargrave - she would probably get a fine, maybe probation."

"It doesn't seem right that she's at home now just because of her last name."

"Welcome to the criminal justice system," Riley said. She put on her jacket and pushed her chair in. "Jill and I are going for Italian. You want to join us?"

"No. Thank you."

"All right. I'll see you at home. Try not to stay out too late."

Priest smiled and watched Riley go. She finally decided there was no reason for her to stay, so she packed up her things and left as well. She felt odd staying in the apartment when they weren't home, so she left them a note and went out for a long walk. That was something else she hated about being mortal; weariness. She was already exhausted from the long day and, after only a few hours of walking, her entire body ached. She was back in No Man's Land, the area she'd frequented during the first few unbalanced weeks after she became mortal.

She found a park bench in a wooded area that wasn't soiled by the homeless or staked out by drug dealers. The trees were thick around it, and the two streetlights spaced fifteen feet apart did little to combat the darkness. Still, she sat and listened to the sounds of the park, confident that she could hear trouble coming and slip away before it found her. Her legs were protesting her walk, and sitting felt wonderful. She would let her body rest and then seek out public transportation for the trip home.

"Running away again?"

Priest closed her eyes. She didn't have to turn around to know who the new arrival was. Sariel moved quietly despite the fallen leaves that littered the sidewalk. Her silence made Priest mad; she couldn't even cross a room without scuffing her feet or bumping into something. She announced her presence in thousands of little ways without even realizing it. She'd never known being mortal was so... clumsy.

When she finally looked, Sariel had taken a seat next to her. Her brown hair was pulled back, enhancing the almond shape of her blue eyes and her high cheekbones. She wore a leather jacket with the collar turned up, despite the fact she couldn't feel the cold. She was scanning the park with a haughty self-possession that Priest envied. She looked down at herself, wearing a thick coat she'd borrowed from Gillian, her hair whipped into wild shapes by the wind, and she couldn't help but feel inferior to the being sharing the bench with her.

"There are three drug deals underway within a block of this bench, and two men are fornicating in that restroom. This is hardly a place for someone like you, Caitlin."

"Yeah. Well. I'm not who I used to be."

Sariel lifted her chin. "I could have changed that. When you first became mortal, I gave you the option."

Priest nodded; she remembered it all too well. She had told Riley she needed time to adjust to her new existence, which was true. But she'd left out Sariel's offer. Divinity, but at a price: returning to Heaven.

"*Divinity can be spent, but it doesn't evaporate. Angels don't just disappear in a wisp of smoke. Zerachiel was a soldier in God's army for centuries. He wouldn't allow something so precious to just cease to be. With time, I could reunite the two of you.*"

Priest was sitting in her living room, grasping at the straws of hope Sariel was offering her. "*And then things would return to normal? I would be Riley's guardian again?*"

Sariel blinked. "*No. That's... not what I was offering. You and your divinity should never have parted. Caitlin Priest and Zerachiel were never two distinct entities. You should have perished when Zerachiel was spent. I'm offering to make things right by~*"

"*By killing me. We just went through this, and you told Riley that~*"

"*I wouldn't be killing you. You're a remnant. You're a shell that Zerachiel left behind. You don't belong here. You can't exist without Zerachiel's guidance.*"

Priest stood up. "*I'm not Zerachiel. I'm Caitlin Priest. Zerachiel couldn't have existed without me.*"

Sariel faced her down. "*Are you certain about that?*"

After that, Sariel's tests began. Attempts to prove that Caitlin Priest was just a vessel, an empty boat adrift on the waves. Sariel reluctantly admitted that Priest existed independently of her divinity when the tests were complete. But although she'd passed the test, they had left Priest shaken and confused about who she really was. So she'd run. She hid in No Man's Land, hungry and homeless, struggling to forget who she once was and replace the memory with the new truth. She had been spiraling out of control.

And then Riley found her and saved her.

"Why are you here?"

Sariel shrugged, one elbow bent on the back of the bench. "Because I am charged with the safety of Detective Parra. That extends to those close to her. Should something bad happen to you, she will be forced to come to this bad section of town and endanger herself. I am protecting her by protecting you."

"What if something bad happens where she is?"

"Then I'll be there in time to help her."

Priest breathed in the night air and closed her eyes. That was a plus; air smelled sweeter as a mortal. It was brisk and cold, and it burned her nostrils as she breathed it in. She thought of Lita hiding in her penthouse, ignoring the world outside for her own safety.

"I don't want to hide anymore."

Sariel looked at her. "What does that mean?"

"It means I don't want to be afraid. I don't want to keep thinking about what I lost. I didn't lose my divinity, I gave it away. I gave it to Riley, and to Gillian. No matter how painful things might get, I will never regret that choice."

"Even though it means your eventual death?"

"Yes. Although admittedly I hope that won't happen this evening."

Sariel looked around in the darkness. "There are creatures in the darkness."

"Then maybe I should have an angel escort me home. I mean, unless Riley needs you."

Sariel met Priest's gaze and then looked past her toward the streetlight on the corner. "Riley and Gillian seem to be doing well on their date. I suppose I can take you home."

Priest smiled. "Lead the way."

She and Sariel stood at the same time, Priest taking the time to brush off the seat of her pants before she started walking. She wasn't Zerachiel, and she would no longer think of herself as a "former angel."

She was Detective Caitlin Priest, and she was ready to stop hiding from the world.

THE KINGS OF NO MAN'S LAND

It was standing room only in the basement of The Cell. Riley, Priest and Lieutenant Briggs were standing in front of Markus' prison, while Sariel moved slowly around the perimeter of the cellar and examined the sigils Zerachiel had created before sacrificing herself. Gillian was standing by with a gurney at the bottom of the stairs, the closest she was willing to come inside. The room was dark save for the crossing beams of their flashlights. Briggs aimed her light at the unconscious body lying in the middle of the devil's trap.

"Are you sure he's alive?"

"Fairly sure." Riley stepped closer. The last time she'd seen Markus, she'd left him in a state of mid-exorcism. Now it seemed like the damage may have been too much for the human host to survive.

Sariel joined the group and looked down at the body. "The demon is still there. He's hoping you'll let down your guard enough for him to escape."

The body finally stirred. "Why must you angel pricks ruin all my fun?" He pushed himself up and turned to face the room. Briggs took a step back, her fingers clenching around the flashlight.

"It's okay." Riley's voice was calm. "He can't get out of there."

Markus smiled at Briggs. "Are you sure about that, Detective?

Maybe your little torture trick made me stronger." He lunged forward, his human mask fading to be replaced by a repugnant, spiked visage. Briggs stood her ground, but the tightening of her jaw indicated that he'd scared her.

Sariel ignored the exchange. "You misheard his name, Detective Parra. He is Malphus."

"You know each other?"

Malphus smiled, and Sariel narrowed her eyes. "We've met."

Sariel held up her right hand, her palm and fingers straight, and spoke calmly. "*Avertes ex titemus et labres immortae.*"

The demon recoiled as if he'd been hit by a shotgun. His body reached the far side of his prison and crumpled.

Sariel lowered her hand. "Now he is dead."

Briggs blinked. "What... where did he go?"

"The demon was returned to Hell. The host was dead long ago." She stepped forward and used the side of her shoe to scrape away part of the painted circle that made up the trap. There was an electric sizzle in the air for the briefest of moments and Sariel entered the circle. She knelt beside the man who had hosted Malphus, touched his skin, and turned to face the mortals in the room with her. "I doubt you'll want to leave him here."

"We'll take him in as a John Doe." Briggs turned to look at Gillian. "Will you be all right with the autopsy, Dr. Hunt?"

Gillian nodded. "I'll be fine now." She pulled the gurney forward to the cell.

Riley touched Gillian's arm as she passed, and Gillian reached up to brush Riley's fingers. It was Gillian's idea to come; Riley had wanted to keep her as far away as possible. Markus or Malphus may not have been the demon who did such horrible things to her two years earlier, but he'd held the power to do even worse. But she declared she had to face her demons, literally, or she would never be able to sleep soundly. With Priest's help, she loaded the body onto the gurney and began strapping it down.

Sariel and Briggs stood beside Riley. Sariel watched Gillian and Priest guide the gurney forward. They collapsed the wheels and then bore the weight as they carried it up the stairs to the van waiting outside. Sariel lowered her voice, despite the fact there was no one left to overhear them. "A place like this is dangerous."

Briggs said, "But necessary. We can't exactly drag a demon into central booking. And just automatically sending them back to Hell doesn't give us anything, either. We need a place where we can use the demons for our own benefit. Markus~"

"Malphus didn't give you anything," Sariel countered.

"So the next one might," Riley said. "The simple fact is that you said yourself that we can't count on you. We're going to be picking up demons from time to time, and we need a safe place to keep them. This is good enough for right now."

Sariel turned and looked at the now-empty trap. "And when the demons discover this place exists, do you truly believe they will let it stand?"

Riley shrugged. "That's where you come in. I want to make sure no demons can trespass on this property unless one of us escorts it."

"I can't do that. If I could, we would just erect one around the entire town and end this particular battle once and for all." Before Riley could argue, Sariel looked up at the roof. "I can possibly blind them to its existence. It wouldn't be the best security ever devised, but it would be better than nothing."

"Better than nothing," Riley muttered. "That's our whole battle plan. When can you~"

"It's done. No demon will be able to see this building."

Briggs turned in a slow circle. "Hey. Where did the building go?" Riley and Sariel tensed, and Briggs offered them a weak smile. "Joking."

Riley raised an eyebrow. "Funny."

"If there's nothing else, I'll go now." Sariel looked at Riley. "Do not become complacent. A trapped demon can still gain the upper hand if you allow it."

"Thanks for the~" Sariel was gone, without a puff of smoke or a slow fade, the area in front of Riley was just empty. "Tip."

"That was disconcerting," Briggs said.

Riley shook her head. "She does that disappearing act all the time."

"Well, that. And the..." She gestured toward the trap. "But thank you for showing me this. It's good to know you have a plan."

They went upstairs and found Gillian waiting beside the van. Priest was sitting in the front seat of Riley's car with the door open and her feet on the ground. Briggs said goodbye and walked to her car, and Riley walked through the calf-high weeds to meet Gillian on the sidewalk.

"Hey. How are you doing?"

Gillian took Riley's hands. "Another room with another

demon in it. I can handle it."

Riley kissed the corner of Gillian's mouth. "Tough chick."

"Don't you forget it." She looked back at Briggs' car. "I'm signed off for the day and my assistant will handle anything that comes in. I look forward to spending the day finding out what a body looks like once a demon is done playing in it."

Briggs car stopped at the intersection and, a few seconds later, began reversing toward Gillian's van. She rolled down her window and Riley stepped into the street. "Boss?"

"A call just came in from a place near here. Four dead bodies in the courtyard of the Scanlon Heights housing development. You want to take it?"

"Sure, it's a slow morning."

"I'll get the other ME on the phone, have him meet you there. I'll send you some back-up, too. Four bodies is nothing to sneeze at."

"Thanks, boss." She went back to Gillian. "Duty calls. Have fun with your science project."

"I'll try."

They kissed goodbye and Riley jogged to her car. Priest closed her door as Riley climbed behind the wheel. "What's going on?"

"Got a value-pack of bodies over at Scanlon Heights. Four people apparently found dead."

Priest fastened her seatbelt. "Four people plus Malphus' host? And I thought today would be slow."

Riley scoffed as she pulled away from the curb. "This is No Man's Land. Five corpses and an exorcised demon *is* slow."

The Scanlon Heights housing development was a large apartment building complex shaped like a horseshoe, the street-side of the building designed to look like a Roman archway. Being in No Man's Land, however, resulted in so much decay and neglect that it mostly looked like a child's building block project that had been abandoned halfway through. The sidewalk in front of the building was mostly blockaded by broken down wrecks, some of them missing tires or doors, and there were more windshields missing than intact.

Riley parked in the first available spot, behind a police cruiser. She glanced at Priest and noticed a look of concern. "Something wrong?"

"No. Well... A woman from my old church lives here, I think. I had no idea the neighborhood was this bad."

"It probably looks worse to us. To the people who live here, it's just home."

The entry arch led directly into the courtyard. Two uniformed police officers were finishing with the crime scene tape. Riley showed her badge and one of the officers made his way over. "Thank God. That was quick. I'm Officer Maier."

"Detectives Parra and Priest. We were in the neighborhood." She looked past him and saw four bodies laid on the cracked tile. "What happened here?"

"We have four bodies, but the crime scene is obviously staged." He motioned for the detectives to follow him. When they got closer, Riley saw that the bodies had been laid out straight with their feet together. Their heads all pointed toward a different cardinal direction. They were all dressed business casual, with dress shirts and dark slacks but no ties. Two of them had blood on their shirts, one was missing part of his head, and the last had his throat cut. The tile underneath them was mostly free of blood.

"Yeah, that would be staged, all right." Riley ducked under the tape to get a closer look. The man with the slit throat had died with his eyes open and no one had bothered to close them. "Caitlin, come here. Does this guy look familiar?"

"You think so, too?" the cop said. "We were trying to place him, but it's... not easy."

Priest joined Riley and looked down. "That's Finn Burke, Riley."

Maier whistled when he realized she was right. "Holy shit."

Riley was already moving to one of the bloody-shirted men. "Right. And this one is Billy McGowan. The others~"

Priest and Maier's partner confirmed the other two men's identities. "Donald Pierce and Troy Rowland."

Riley stepped away from the bodies and walked quickly toward the yellow tape. She motioned for Priest and the officers to follow her. "We're out of here."

Priest reluctantly caught up with Riley. "What? We're leaving?"

"Yeah. We're getting the hell out of here before these guys' families come looking for them. Officer Maier, you and your partner are leaving, too. We'll call for backup and get a SWAT team in here. I don't know what the hell is going on, but if~"

Through the archway, Riley saw a black sedan pull up in front of the building. Riley stopped and cursed under her breath. "Officer

Maier, call this in. Tell them to get as many cops here as they can possibly afford."

Maier complied with her order, speaking quietly into his shoulder-mounted radio. The other cop, Casini, had his hand on the butt of his gun. "What the hell is going on here, ma'am?"

The back doors of the sedan opened and Riley identified Liam Burke from his truncated campaign for mayor a few years earlier. He straightened his jacket and scanned the street before his gaze locked on her. "Shit. All right. Caitlin, you stay here with the officers. I'm going to go speak with Mr. Burke."

She continued on, and Burke stepped forward to wait for her on the sidewalk. Riley kept a few feet of distance between them, making sure he could see the badge on one side of her belt and the holster on the other. She nodded to him and then eyed the men he'd left standing by the car. Liam Burke was a rock of a man, with a broad chest and wide shoulders. His gray hair was cropped short, and his darker-haired beard was almost sculpted around his jaw. He took a long time examining Riley's badge before he met her gaze.

"Detective."

"Mr. Burke. This is a crime scene. You can't be here."

He looked past her. "Is that my son in here?"

Riley ignored the question. "Who told you to come here, sir? We've barely arrived on the scene ourselves."

Burke reached out to brush past her, but Riley moved back to stay in his path. "Sir, I can't let you compromise the crime scene. We'll identify the bodies as soon as we can, but until then~"

Burke grabbed a handful of Riley's T-shirt and pushed. She was dealing with the sudden shift in her balance when he pulled her suddenly forward. He stepped out of the way and released her, letting her own momentum carry her to the ground. Riley stumbled and rolled onto her hip, drew her weapon and aimed it at his broad back. "Liam Burke, you just assaulted a police officer. Put your hands on your head and~"

A fountain of blood erupted from a spot just above Burke's right eye, knocking him back on his heels before his weight carried his body to the concrete.

Riley pushed down her shock at what she'd just seen and scrambled to her feet, staying in a crouch as she ran back into the relative safety of the courtyard. Priest and the two officers had their weapons drawn. Riley pressed her back against the wall of the building and craned her neck to look back out onto the street.

Burke's men had taken cover behind the sedan. Another sedan was blocking off the north end of the street and she saw men in dark turtlenecks assuming firing positions. She assumed one of them was the shooter who had taken down Liam Burke. Priest joined her and crouched out of sight of the street.

"Who are they?"

"Representatives of the other four families," Riley said. "Biggest crime leaders in No Man's Land, and four of them just got found dead together."

"Who is missing?"

Riley closed her eyes. "The Five Families are Rowland, Burke, Pierce, McGowan. Hyde. Hyde's the one that's missing."

Priest looked outside. "And who is shooting at us?"

"I think it's the Pierce contingent." She heard sirens in the distance and felt a mixture of relief and surprise. "Backup in No Man's Land, arriving sooner than a pizza. Who'd have thought?"

For a moment, she remembered Briggs' promise to send the ME. Her panic was tempered when she remembered Gillian had handed off all her cases to her assistant. She would be safe at the morgue while her replacement was the one walking into a standoff. She felt like shit for being happy about that, but she didn't care as long as Gillian was safe.

Burke's men and Pierce's continued shooting at one another in the street. Riley looked around the courtyard and counted three alternate entrances. "We can't let anyone from any of those families get in here and foul up the scene. Any one of them could be responsible."

"Why would they kill their own man?"

Riley shrugged. "Let's say it was Pierce. He killed his right-hand man for whatever reason, and then killed three of his rivals to make it look like a gangland thing."

"What about Hyde?"

"Scapegoat. He's the only one left out, so of course the blame will fall solely on him. We can't trust anything right now." She whistled and motioned for Maier to join them. "Find whatever you can to block those entrances. No one comes in without a badge."

Maier nodded and motioned for Casini to help him out. Riley fished her cell phone from her pocket and flipped it open. Briggs' number was third on the speed dial, and she hit the button as the gunfire continued in the street. She put the phone on speaker when Briggs answered.

"Boss, we've got a little bit of a problem here."

"We know. We just started getting a crush of calls from that area about gunfire. What's your situation?"

"Liam Burke is dead. He was killed by one of Pierce's men, I think. We've got four members of the Five Families lying here dead. I think the surviving members are showing up for the wake, and things are going to get more violent if we don't do something. And I mean now."

Briggs paused as she considered their options. "I've already sent out backup, along with a SWAT team. They'll seal off the area, so all you'll have to do is make sure the Burkes and Pierces don't tear each other apart. SWAT will stop the McGowans and Rowlands from joining the party."

Riley exhaled. "Easier said than done, Boss. The Pierces shot right past me to hit Burke. I don't think they'll hold their fire just because I'm a cop."

"There are innocent people in Scanlon Heights, Riley. There are people all through that area who might get caught in the crossfire."

"Right. Right." She rested her head against the wall. "Stop a gang war from breaking out. Easy. Just another slow day in No Man's Land."

Priest smiled weakly as the sirens grew louder.

"The backup is almost here. I'm going to see if I can talk these morons into putting down their weapons."

"Good luck. Keep me updated."

Riley hung up and hooked her phone on her belt. "You ready?"

Priest said, "How did Briggs know the Hyde family wouldn't be coming to claim a body?"

Riley frowned at her and then remembered Briggs saying the SWAT team would stop the McGowan and Rowland families, with no mention of the Hydes. "We'll worry about that when we have fewer people trying to kill us. You ready?" Priest nodded and took Riley's extended hand to help her up. It sounded like the sirens were all around them now, so Riley risked a look around the corner as the gunfire died down slightly.

"Hold your fire!" she shouted. She stepped out of cover, leading with her weapon. Priest covered Riley's back as she stepped out of the arch and onto the sidewalk. Pierce's men were still huddled around their car at the head of the street, while Burke's were hiding behind their sedan. Men on both sides were sprawled on the asphalt with what appeared to be mortal wounds. Some of Pierce's men had turned their weapons on the advancing SWAT team.

Priest knelt next to Liam Burke and felt for a pulse. She shook her head.

"Pierce's men... Burke's men. I think you've both lost a few too many people today. Let's not compound our losses, okay? I'm Detective Riley Parra, and this is my partner Caitlin Priest. We're going to investigate these murders as thoroughly as we would any other. It doesn't matter who these people are or what they did, they didn't deserve to be killed like this. So why don't we all just put down our weapons and deal with this like reasonable~"

One of Burke's men was hit by a bullet. Before Riley could process what had happened, another volley of gunfire broke the windows in the Pierce contingent's car and several of their men were dropped. Priest put an arm around Riley's chest and half-tackled her back to the safety of the courtyard as both groups opened fire. This time the Pierce group was fighting on two fronts, against the Burke group and the SWAT team.

"Who the hell was shooting?"

Priest looked across the courtyard and saw the black uniform of a police officer sprawled on the tile. "Oh, no."

Riley got up and ran to the body. Casini had been shot in the chest, just above the neck of his Kevlar, and blood was pooling in the hollow of his throat as he tried to speak. Riley grabbed Priest's hand. "Put pressure on this. Casini, where is your partner?"

His eyes cut to the right, and Riley moved to let Priest deal with his wound. Riley left through one of the alternate entrances she had identified and saw Maier standing against the brick wall with a shotgun at his side. She took cover behind a stone bench and aimed at his head. "Officer Maier, what the hell are you doing?"

"Just taking care of a little business, Detective." He racked another round and twisted to line up his next shot. Riley pulled her trigger first, and her bullet cut a line across Maier's right bicep. He lowered the weapon and clapped his hand over the wound. "God damn it. I'm trying to clean up No Man's Land, you crazy bitch."

"By causing a massacre in the middle of an apartment building?"

"These apartments are practically empty. Most people moved out a few months ago, and the rest are at work. That's why he chose this place."

He?

"Your boss? Your boss wants you to save No Man's Land by shooting at a bunch of criminals?"

"Get rid of the head and the body will die. He knew the Five Families wouldn't stand for something like this. He knew they would come. We get rid of them, their people will spread like dust in the wind, and the whole thing will topple. Then we can finally get a foothold in this damn place."

Or the remaining criminals will consolidate and become something bigger and even harder to stop. Didn't think of that, did you?

"Officer Maier, you don't know what you're doing. You're not yourself." He looked up from his wound long enough to frown at her, hissing as he tightened his hand on his wound. "I know the voices you're hearing are convincing, but they're not telling you the truth. There's something in your head that wants you to think it's in charge, but~"

"What the fuck are you talking about?"

Riley furrowed her brow. "Your boss. The man who is making you do this. He's in your head, he's whispering in your ear~"

Maier laughed. "My boss is upstairs. He's watching this whole thing from an empty apartment."

"Put down your weapon, Officer Maier, and put your hands on the top of your head."

"That's not part of the plan, Detective."

Riley aimed center mass. "I'm not going to give you another warning."

Maier brought the shotgun up and aimed it at her one-handed. Riley fired and Maier toppled back against the wall. He left a spray of blood behind him as he fell, and Riley closed the distance between them at a run. She kicked the shotgun out of his hand and knelt beside him. The bullet had hit him in the chest but, as she'd suspected when she saw how his uniform blouse was draping, he had taken off his vest.

Maier smiled up at her. "Just another cop on the Five Families tally. You think SWAT will let any of 'em walk out of here alive after this?"

Riley momentarily considered the choice of letting Maier bleed out and going to find his so-called boss. She took the shotgun from him and ran back to the courtyard where Priest was still kneeling beside Casini. "Anything?"

"He's gone. Maier?"

"He did it. I had to take him out."

Priest nodded. "So it's just the two of us against everyone out there."

"Fun times. Maier mentioned he had a boss upstairs. Someone who came up with this shitty plan. I don't want to leave the courtyard unprotected, but I don't want to risk whoever is up there getting away."

"We need someone else here."

"Right, but no one is getting past that cordon."

"Where do you need me?" Sariel asked.

Riley spun to face her, bringing the shotgun up out of instinct. Sariel looked at the weapon, looked at Riley, and raised an eyebrow. She was still in the long-sleeved white blouse and black jeans she'd been wearing that morning, but her brown hair was now braided.

"Do not... sneak up on someone as tightly wound as I am right now."

"Duly noted. Where do you need me? Searching or protecting the ground level?"

Priest said, "You can repel anyone from crossing the threshold of this building for a limited amount of time. Keep the bad guys out while Riley and I search for the mastermind upstairs."

"Move quickly."

Riley nodded and started moving toward the stairs. "We intend to. C'mon, Cait."

Sariel looked toward the apartments. "Detective Parra. The third floor, apartment three. I'm sensing something there."

"Thanks."

There were stairs on all but the front wall, and Riley chose the nearest one for their ascent. Priest lowered her voice as she followed Riley up to the third floor. "We have to prepare ourselves for the worst, Riley."

"What are you talking about?"

"Lieutenant Briggs knew that Hyde wasn't one of the victims. Maier was a cop. We have to be prepared for the possibility."

"That Briggs is the person who put all of this together? She was with us all morning."

"So she had her associate Maier do the dirty work and the heavy lifting. She could have taken an alternate route from the Cell and beaten us here so she would be in place while everything went down."

"I called Briggs at her office to tell her what happened."

"She couldn't have gotten back to the station that quickly. So she must have had her office calls forwarded to her cell, which means she could have answered from anywhere, Riley."

"Hey, where did the building go?"

Riley pushed the thought from her head. It was just a bad joke, nothing more. "Let's not speculate. Third floor, third apartment." She took the far side of the door, and Priest stayed on the near side. Riley tested the knob slowly, careful not to make too much noise. The door was locked so she withdrew her hand. "This is the po~"

The door exploded out of its frame, causing Riley and Priest both to dive and cover their heads. Riley remained in a crouch as she spun and aimed her gun at the open door, the shotgun lying fallen just out of her reach. The demon strode out of the apartment and looked down at her before turning at the waist to look at Priest behind him. He was tall, at least seven feet, and wore a red uniform shirt with shining gold buttons. His skin was deathly pale, most of his face hidden by the limp strands of his light brown hair.

"Hm. Funny." He held his hand out palm-down, pushed the air, and the landing underneath Riley trembled violently. She was thrown down onto her back, tightening her grip on her weapon to keep it from flying over the edge. The demon turned and faced Priest. "Former angel. Interesting."

He grabbed Priest by the throat and lifted her, letting her feet dangle as he turned and shoved her over the banister. Priest choked, grabbing his arm with both hands to support her weight as she was held in empty air. Riley got to her feet and picked up the shotgun.

"Don't do it, you son of a bitch."

"Raum."

Riley moved close enough to press the gun against the demon's side. "What?"

"The thing that is about to kill your partner is named Raum." He looked at her and smiled. "Pleasure to meet you."

He opened his hand and released Priest's throat. She dropped, but her hands held onto his arm so that she only dropped a few feet. Riley pressed the barrel of the gun against Raum's side, burying it into the soft flesh before she pulled the trigger. The force of the blast was enough to throw him violently to the side, and Priest was roughly pulled back onto the landing with him. Riley put an arm around Priest's waist and dragged her back, retreating toward the stairs.

"Ank oo," Priest managed.

"Fighting kind of sucks without that instant healing divinity thing, huh?"

"Very true."

Riley looked back and saw Raum examining the gory mess of his midsection. "What do you know about this fella?"

"He... I don't... I don't know."

"All right. Don't worry about it right now."

Sariel met them at the bottom of the stairs. She looked at Priest and furrowed her brow. "What happened to her?"

"What is that, concern?"

Sariel composed herself and looked up at the third floor landing. "What is its name?"

"Raum."

"A thief who destroys cities and reputations." She turned and looked at the four bodies lying in the middle of the courtyard. "He's attempting to do both with this tableau. By turning the Five Families against one another, No Man's Land will erupt in chaos."

Priest coughed and rubbed her throat. "Why would Marchosias allow that? Why would he let his lieutenants be slaughtered this way?"

"Marchosias doesn't care about any member of the Five Families. They are a means to an end. If this gambit fails, he'll simply bring together new lieutenants. The question is how did you become involved in this?"

Priest averted her gaze, and Riley refused to believe Briggs was involved. "One thing at a time. I messed Raum up pretty bad, but I don't think he's down for the count. How are things going outside?"

"The McGowan family has arrived and has taken up a position on the north side of the building, and I believe the Rowland family is approaching from the northwest."

"So much for SWAT stopping them," Priest whispered.

Riley ignored the implications. "If we give them the bodies, will they put an end to all of this?"

Priest said, "Will Raum let us hand over the bodies? If this is part of his grand plan, I don't see him standing by while we let those people inside."

"And there's the little matter of the SWAT team," Riley said. "We can't just explain to them that this is all a plot by a demon. They have half the criminal masterminds in No Man's Land standing in the same square mile, and they've all shot at cops today.

There's no way they'll just step aside and let the families walk away."

Above them, Raum gave a furious cry that shook the staircase. Riley and Priest both cringed. Sariel squared her shoulders. "Go. You'll both be able to pass through the barrier I put up, and anyone you bring back will be allowed passage as well. I'm going to ensure Raum doesn't interfere with your business."

"Right." Riley looked at Priest. "What business would that be, exactly?"

"Go out and bring representatives of the families back to reclaim the bodies of their people. Then they will go peacefully."

Priest looked past Sariel to the arch that led out into the street. "You mean we're going to go out there. Where the shooting is happening."

"You'll be fine~" Riley started, but she stopped when Sariel cupped Priest's face. "Caitlin."

They both ignored Riley. Sariel looked into Priest's eyes. "You are stronger than you know. Stronger than I gave you credit for when first we met. You will be fine."

Priest nodded, and Sariel released her.

"You gonna be okay, Cait?"

"I'll be fine." She stopped leaning on Riley and stood under her own power. "I don't get the feeling the families will take very kindly to a police detective approaching them. What's to stop them from killing us the moment they see us coming?"

Sariel thought for a moment and then reached up and touched the shoulder of her blouse. She used two fingers to work the seam, and then tugged. The sleeve tore and slithered down her arm to the wrist. She repeated the move with the other sleeve and then held them out. "White flags. They won't shoot at someone bearing these. They may not understand why, but they won't."

Riley took the sleeve and tied it around her neck like a bandana. Priest did the same.

Sariel backed away from them and tilted her head up. "Hurry."

A moment later, she was slammed to the ground by the impact of Raum's seven-foot bulk, which he had thrown over the railing of the third floor. He fell like a dart, and Sariel's body lay crumpled underneath him as he got to his feet again. The tile underneath them was splintered and cracked, and Riley and Priest turned away from the cloud of thick white dust produced by the force of his fall. Riley moved forward to help, but Priest pulled her back. "Don't. She'll be fine, but we would be slaughtered if we tried to help. Let's go get the families."

Riley nodded. "Okay, Burke is out front, and Pierce is at the southeast corner. What did Sariel say about the other two?"

"The Rowlands are coming from the northwest."

Sariel pulled herself from the rubble of the tile floor with a grunt of pain and a skittering of broken stone. She had her arms wrapped around Raum's midsection, squeezing tightly as he pounded her head with both fists. Blood trailed down her face, and Riley tried to ignore the brawl as she continued laying out her plan.

"But they're not here yet. Okay. You go to the north and get someone from the McGowans. I'll take care of the Burkes. They saw me talking with Liam, so hopefully they'll be less willing to open fire on me. Then I'll get the Pierces and you~"

"The Rowlands."

Riley nodded. "Keep in contact. You have your phone?"

Priest held it up.

"Call me if you get into trouble, I'll come running. Go, let's go."

They gave Sariel and Raum a wide berth, heading in opposite directions. Riley went back to the front of the building and crouched next to one leg of the arch, assessing the situation before she ran out blind. There were a few more bodies in the street but not as many as she would have expected. She wiped the back of her hand across her forehead, touched the knot she'd made in Sariel's sleeve, and took a few steadying breaths before she ran out into the melee.

Liam Burke was still lying face down on the pavement, the blood from his wound spreading in a wide oval around his head. Riley stepped past him and off the curb, staying low just in case Sariel's sartorial voodoo didn't work at long range. She crossed the street and one of Burke's men spotted her coming. He spun on his heel and aimed his gun at her but, true to Sariel's word, he didn't fire. Riley held her gun up, indicating she wasn't planning to use it, and continued forward.

The man kept his gun on her and nudged the person beside him. He turned, and Riley crouched a few feet from him. "I'm Detective Riley Parra."

One of the other men said, "She was with the boss when he got hit."

"Right. Hopefully you won't think that was my fault."

The man who'd spoken shook his head. "We saw them Pierce

pricks. They were shooting at you, too. What do you want, cop? We have a little business to take care of, if you hadn't noticed."

"No, I noticed," Riley said. "Look, you have a man lying dead inside that courtyard and your boss is on the sidewalk outside. I'm willing to escort you inside to retrieve them, but you have to swear to me you'll leave peacefully once you have them. And if you run into anyone inside, it's détente."

"No way."

The second man slapped the first's arm. "It's Finn and Mr. Burke."

"This is a one time offer. Either you go in with me, or those bodies go to our morgue. And judging by the way things are going out here, a lot of your friends will be going with 'em."

The first man finally nodded. "Okay."

"Leave the guns here. I'm not taking any chances." They reluctantly put down their weapons, and the second man turned to let someone else know where they were going.

When they were ready, Riley rose into a crouch and motioned for the two men to lead the way. They crossed the street with Riley bringing up the rear, rising slightly above the men's hunched back in the hopes that Sariel's sleeve would act as a shield for all three of them. She could practically feel the crosshairs lining up on her back, the countless bullets ready to be fired toward her. They entered the courtyard and Riley saw Priest arriving with a representative of the McGowan family.

"Son of a..."

"Détente," Riley reminded him. She stepped in front of the Burke men and held her hands out. "You're all just here to get your dead, all right? So let's do that peacefully and get outta here."

The front door of an apartment on the second floor exploded outward, and everyone in the courtyard ducked as Sariel was expelled from within like a missile. She crossed the open air in a wide arc, crashed into the tile of the courtyard, and tumbled end over end before slamming into an apartment door. She rose, her shirt torn and her skin red with blood, and watched as Raum stepped off the second floor landing as casually as a person would take a step.

Sariel's wings extended from her back, stretching to either side before the feathers ruffled in the gentle breeze. Sariel launched, and Raum howled at her until she slammed into his midsection and shoved him through the wall of an apartment.

Burke's men were frozen in place. "What... the..."

"Yeah, trippy shit," Riley said. "There was a methylone leak and we've been seeing all kinds of weird things. Cait..."

Priest nodded and the groups converged on the display in the middle of the courtyard. Burke's men were obviously affected by the sight of their friend, one of them pressing his fist against his mouth and turning his back on the sight to compose himself. The other knelt beside the corpse, took off his own necktie, and used it to bind the wound in Finn Burke's throat. One of the McGowan people covered Billy McGowan's face with his coat.

"No one did this," Riley said. "It wasn't a member of the Hyde family, it was no member of the Five Families. Think about it. Would any of you do something this insane? Just for the~"

Sariel shouted within a nearby apartment. A flame lit several windows before dying out. Priest looked toward the disturbance with concern and then focused on Riley again.

"None of you did this, because none of you *would* do this. It's counterintuitive to your goals. So just take your dead, give them a respectable wake, and put them to rest. Let's all just let this nonsense end here. Today. Got it?"

One of McGowan's men looked at her. "What did you say your name was?"

"Riley Parra."

He nodded as if that confirmed something. He looked at his cohort and then focused on the Burke men. "This wasn't us, and it wasn't you. We walk away with our people and this whole mess gets settled."

"Fine by us."

They picked up their men and carried them back to their respective exits. Riley escorted the Burkes out of the courtyard and waited while one of them stopped to pick up Liam as well. The Pierce group watched the developments with interest, holding their fire as Riley escorted the Burke men back to their barricade. Once they were in place, Riley caught the eye of a Pierce man and motioned coming over. He hesitated, conferred with someone, and then reluctantly motioned her forward with two fingers.

Sariel leaned against the wall of an empty apartment, blood bubbling over her lips every time she tried to draw a breath. Her ribcage was crushed, and she had two breaks in her right arm. She closed her eyes and breathed as deeply as she could, felt the pieces of her shattered body knit together once more, and moaned at the surcease of pain. Her body still ached, and her blood was still wet on her skin, but she was back in the fight.

She pushed herself up and looked down at her hands. Idly, she thought about Caitlin Priest. Who would choose to remain in a body so fragile? Who would want to continue on knowing that the slightest injury could prove fatal? That Priest had made the choice to remain alive in such an inferior form only proved there was something truly wrong with her.

Or something definitely right.

She had no more time to ponder Priest, for at that moment Raum found her. He swung one stone fist toward her face and she ducked just before it made contact. Sariel shifted her weight from her front foot to the back and, when Raum lunged at her, she launched herself into his chest with all the force as she could muster.

"You have heart. I'll enjoy ripping it from your chest."

"Worse foes than you have tried."

Raum closed one large fist around Sariel's head. His thumb dug into one temple, his ring finger into the other. He laughed and lifted her off the ground. "I do like these human shells. They have such interesting features. Like blunt fingers. What a quaint idea, don't you think? Of course, there are many who think that talons..." His fingers began to grow sharper, breaking the skin. "...are just absolutely necessary."

Sariel felt the blood trickling down her face, down her neck. He was holding her too far away for her to do anything with her arms or legs. Her only hope was to break his fingers. She reached up and gripped his thumb.

It sounded like the entire apartment exploded at that moment, leaving Sariel's ears ringing as Raum released her. She fell to the ground, her skull throbbing even as her divinity began knitting the wounds. Priest entered the apartment, still aiming the shotgun at the ruin of Raum's upper body, and held out her hand. "Sariel... even that wound won't take him long to recover."

Sariel placed her hand in Priest's and let herself be pulled up. She grunted as she put weight on her crushed foot.

"Are you all right?"

"I'll be fine. I'm an angel."

"That doesn't mean invincible. Trust me, I know." She put Sariel's arm around her neck and carried her from the apartment.

Behind them, Sariel heard Raum pulling himself from the rubble as the shattered ruin of his chest reconstructed itself.

Riley watched as Priest helped Sariel down the stairs. The angel was bloody, listing heavily to her right, but she grew stronger with every step. Her clothing was torn so much that she was practically naked, her right breast and most of her left thigh revealed. Riley shed her jacket and handed it over, and Sariel took it without comment. Sariel scanned the courtyard and saw that all the bodies had been removed. The air was still full of sirens, but the gunfire had stopped.

"You succeeded."

"With step one," Riley said. "We need to get out of here now. You can't hold Raum off forever."

"I'm feeling better."

"You need to heal," Priest said. "You need to find a place of worship and~"

Sariel pushed away from Priest. "I will be fine. I can hold Raum off as long as necessary."

"The more you heal yourself without worship, the weaker you will be. It's only a matter of time before he kills you."

"If it protects Riley, then I am willing. I am certain you understand that, Caitlin."

Priest closed her eyes.

Riley growled in frustration. "It's not going to come to that, okay. God, all these angels throwing themselves on the sword for me. It's enough to give me a complex." She took out her phone and dialed Lieutenant Briggs' number. She put it on speaker. "Boss."

"Riley, I have reports that you and Detective Priest were seen escorting members of each family into Scanlon Heights to retrieve the bodies."

"Yeah. That was us. We didn't have a choice; it was the only way to end this thing right now. You have to understand."

There was silence on the other end of the line, and then a sad laugh. "Yeah, I think I do. What do you need on this end?"

Riley chewed her bottom lip. "I need you to call off the SWAT team and all the backup you sent in."

"No. No way, Riley. We have members of the five biggest crime families in this city surrounded, and we have *all* of them on charges of shooting at police officers."

"Four." Riley closed her eyes and looked up at the second

floor. She could hear Raum stirring again.

"Pardon?"

"We have *four* of the biggest crime families in this city surrounded. The Hyde family isn't here. You knew that, didn't you?"

Briggs was quiet for a long moment. "Right. But be that as it may, we have them all on irrefutable charges. And those charges will just be the tip of the iceberg once we have them in custody. We'll execute search warrants. We'll offer deals. We will get~"

"You'll get a lot more cops killed, and for nothing. You remove, what, half the hierarchy of the Five Families, and they'll just be replaced by tomorrow. None of this means anything without Marchosias, and there's no way you'll get him through this. This was all a game, Lieutenant. Cops versus the Five Families. The ones who don't get killed will be tossed into the system and the whole thing starts over again. It's not going to make a damn bit of difference."

Briggs was silent.

"You saw what we were up against this morning. It's not just crime families, it's demons. It's angels. It's No Man's Land, boss. We're not going to take it down this way."

"Damn you, Riley."

"I'm sorry, boss, but it's the only way we're going to end this. Boss, I haven't had time to update you yet. Maier was working with this demon. He killed Casini and he was shooting at the Pierce family to further agitate things. If he was sent in to escalate the situation, who knows who else on the force has instructions to make sure this ends in bloodshed?" *And please, tell me that's not why you sent me and Priest into this hell hole.*

"Fine. All right, fine. I'll tell the SWAT team to pull back. They won't stop the families from leaving."

Riley sighed with relief. "Thank you, boss."

"I want to talk to you when this is all over."

"Right. I figured you would." She looked at Priest. "I want to talk with you, too."

When Riley hung up, Sariel said, "We can't just leave Raum. Or I should say that he won't just let us leave. Caitlin, get Riley out of here. I'll~"

"And who will stop Raum after he slaughters you?" Priest said. "We're not leaving. I've watched Riley go into enough stupid, suicidal situations to know that it doesn't always prove fatal. I trust her to get us out of this alive."

Riley chuckled. "Thanks. I think."

There was an explosion on the second floor, and Raum appeared again. He jumped from the second floor landing to the courtyard.

"We need to get him to the Cell."

Sariel shook her head. "If I can just regain a little of my strength, I can exorcise him. Deal with him another day."

Priest cleared her throat. "Amazing... grace. How sweet the sound. That saved a wretch like me..."

Sariel frowned. "What are you doing?"

"Praise. Worship." Priest put her arm around Sariel again. "It works. Trust me, it's saved my life on more than one occasion. Riley..."

Riley grimaced. "Oh, hell. I once was lost. But now am found. Was..."

"Blind..."

"Blind but now I see. I... was... a whore." Priest stared daggers at her and Riley shrugged. "What? It's not on Gillian's iPod."

"T'was grace that taught my heart to fear," Priest continued, and Riley began humming the melody.

Raum lifted one hand and pressed a finger to his ear. "Please. Stop. You're killing me."

Sariel tightened her arm around Priest's shoulders. "I think I feel it working. Keep singing."

Priest continued the verse, with Riley mumbling along as best she could. Sariel stood under her own power again and advanced on Raum. He advanced as well, his lips curling into a smile.

"One thing the mortals did get right. Entertainment. I've watched a great many films. Westerns. The showdown between the hero and the~"

Sariel held up her hands and sent forth a burst of energy. Raum was lifted off his feet by the force of the blast, thrown across the courtyard, and landed on a stone bench hard enough to snap the legs clean in half. While he was still lying on his back in shock, Sariel advanced on him. The jacket she'd borrowed from Riley, draped loosely on her shoulders, flapped in a breeze that seemed centered on her and her alone.

She stepped onto Raum's chest, holding him down with her weight while she locked eyes with him. He sneered, and she held a hand out over his head.

"Avertes ex titemus~"

"Winged bitch."

"*~et labres immortae.*"

Raum convulsed as she finished the incantation, his jaw widening and his eyes churning with alternating waves of fire and darkness.

"Go home, little demon," Sariel growled. She stepped off his body as the smoke rising from him began to dissolve. His corpse steamed like a block of ice left on a sidewalk in the middle of summer. She pulled Riley's coat closed and held the lapels with one hand, extending her arm until Priest took it and supported her weight again.

Priest looked at Riley. "Now what?"

"Briggs is pulling back the SWAT team so the families can retreat. Everyone saves face, and no one else has to die. So we just wait until the street is cleared out to bring in the ME to take Raum's shell away, and then we head back to the station."

"So today was a wash?"

Riley's face revealed how conflicted she was. "No. I think we all learned some very valuable information today."

Sariel looked at Priest and nodded her thanks. Riley led the two of them back to the arch so they could observe the retreat.

They sat in the very back pew, having slipped in after the service already started. Priest made sure to choose a church she had never before visited; she didn't want to deal with anyone welcoming her back to the flock. Sariel looked like a battered woman, with bruises lining her forehead and cheek. Her lip was busted, dark with dried blood. She had managed to change clothes into something more presentable, but she still wore Riley's jacket.

Priest felt uneasy in the church. It was like wearing a scuba suit in the shower; she could feel the power of the worship, but it left her untouched. The pain made her want to cry, but instead she put her arm around Sariel's shoulders and drew her close. Touching her during a hymn was like touching a charging battery. She was warm and seemed to thrum with power.

"I suppose you were right about this," Sariel whispered. "I feel better already."

"Zerachiel chose to live over a church for this very reason. I think that is why she was so powerful, and why she was strong enough to bring Riley back."

Sariel nodded. After a moment of swaying to the music, Sariel spoke again. "I have a confession to make. I considered you a failure. When I was told to come in, I assumed it was because you had failed. But now I know the truth. You succeeded. You did what so many guardian angels never even consider, and for that... you will always have my respect."

Priest closed her eyes and a tear fell free.

Something soft brushed her lips and Priest pulled back from it. She opened her eyes and saw that Sariel's face was inches from hers.

Priest kept her voice at a whisper despite her shock. "What are you doing?"

"I'm sorry. Is that what mortals do to convey affection and gratitude?"

Priest thought about explaining it, thought about telling Sariel how she had things so wrong. Instead, she cupped Sariel's cheek and brushed her thumb over Sariel's bottom lip. "Yes. That is what they do." She leaned in and returned Sariel's kiss as the rest of the congregation continued their song.

Gillian was the most beautiful thing in the world. Riley felt filthy, dragged through the mud, sweaty and dingy, as she stood in the morgue doorway and stared at her lover. Gillian in her green scrubs with her hair tied back, her face veiled by a surgical mask as she worked. She soon realized she was being observed and twisted at the waist. "Riley." She hurried across the room, peeling off her bloody gloves as she came.

"Hey, darling." She pulled down Gillian's mask and leaned in to kiss her. "I know you heard about today."

"I wasn't worried." Gillian's smile betrayed her lie, but Riley expected it. "I would hug you, but~"

"Yeah. Mid-autopsy hugs aren't really big in my world."

Gillian laughed. "I'll keep that in mind. Where's Caitlin?"

"She took Sariel to church."

"Wow. Has she been to church since~"

Riley shook her head. "I don't know. I don't think so. Sariel got pretty banged up during this whole mess, but she didn't cotton to the whole faith healing thing. Priest is going to show her how it can be."

"Nice of her."

"Almost saintly." She kissed Gillian again. "So, what did you find out from Markus?"

Gillian sighed. "Interesting things. Come."

Riley followed Gillian across the room to the body lain out on the table. "Mostly his body is as to be expected. All the organs right where they belong, et cetera. But this guy basically had a parasite living inside of him. As we all know, demons can physically manipulate their human hosts. It affects their strength, their stamina, and even their facial features." She picked up a scalpel and indicated something inside of the chest cavity. "His heart basically exploded after Malphus left his body. All his muscles have atrophied, and it looks like there were a series of tumors left behind in his brain."

"Jesus. Any indication of how long he was possessed?"

"No." She leaned against the table and stared at the body. "If the Duchess had~"

"Hey."

"~been in me for any longer..."

"Don't go there." Riley turned Gillian around and hugged her. You survived that because Priest exorcised the demon in the right way. All that matters, the only thing that matters, is that you survived. A hundred percent, completely survived." She pulled back and kissed her softly.

"Thanks. It's been bugging me all afternoon. Thinking about what might have happened."

"Don't go there. Just focus on your survival. Nothing else matters."

Gillian nodded. "And now we know that once demons have been inside of you for long enough~"

"Yeah. Kind of a depressing thought. But we can't always save the host from being injured, so maybe this will make it easier to walk away from them. Their death is as much a blessing as we can offer them."

"Yes." Gillian sighed and slipped out of Riley's embrace. "I need to finish up a few things here. Will you be all right?"

Riley nodded. "I have some stuff I need to talk to Briggs about. I'll meet you in the locker room."

"Mm. I'll wait until you show up to start showering."

Riley smiled. "I can't wait. See you then."

Riley reluctantly released Gillian and left the morgue without looking back. Looking back would just make her want to stay, make her postpone the conversation she knew was coming. But Briggs was upstairs, and they definitely had to talk before another day went by.

The bullpen was empty, lit by only by the lamps on a handful of desks. Briggs' office door was open, and her overhead light was off. She was sitting in the light of a single lamp, looking at the pictures hanging on the wall. Riley knocked on the glass beside the door before she stepped inside.

"Detective. Close the door, please."

Riley did as she was asked and leaned against it. "You wanted to talk to me?"

"Yes, I did." She was holding a glass with amber liquid inside. "How much have you figured out already? I want to save as much exposition as I can."

Riley looked down at her feet. "You know, a while back, the papers did a story about the department. Not one of those Gail Finney witch hunts, but an honest to goodness article. They put out a statistic that claimed one in every three cops employed by this city is corrupt. I don't know where they got that number. I don't remember being sent a survey. 'Are you corrupt? Check Yes or No.' Maybe, I don't know, maybe I was sick that day. But today I've been thinking a lot about that number. One in three cops. There's me. Priest. And you."

Briggs raised an eyebrow. "Good deductive reasoning."

"Well, I am a detective."

Briggs leaned back in her chair and took a bottle from the drawer of her desk. "Want a drink? We're both off-duty right now."

"No, thanks."

"Suit yourself." She poured herself a glass, took a drink, and then topped it off. "I was a kid. A stupid kid in a uniform. I fell in love with a man. That's all it really boils down to. Stupid decisions I made that can't just be erased." She exhaled and rubbed the bridge of her nose. "It turns out that the man I loved was Sean Hyde. He introduced me to his parents. They told me that they could do things for me. Money, favors, whatever I wanted was at my fingertips."

Riley gestured at the office.

"This job, no. At least not that I know of." She sighed. "I rose through the ranks on my own, as far as I know. But it was because of their help that I was such a rising star. If a Hyde family member came up in an investigation, I would let them know. And then a member of another family would end up in the target. My work as a detective led to the arrest of several members of the Burke family, and the Pierces. Some people claimed I would single-handedly take down the Five Families. But no one ever noticed that I never brought in a member of the Hyde family. Not one."

Riley couldn't stand anymore. She moved to a chair and dropped into it. "Still?"

"Not as much anymore. Sean and I are divorced, but it was amicable." She ran her finger along the lip of her glass. "Sometimes I'll get a call. I got a call this morning. Alan Hyde heard that the other four leaders of the families were getting anonymous calls about missing people. They'd been told where to find them, and the call heavily suggested Hyde was responsible."

"So you had me check it out. That was the call you got, not something from dispatch."

"I knew something big was happening, and I knew I couldn't trust anyone else with it. I'm sorry, Riley. I had no idea how bad things would~"

"Save it." She stood up and, unsure what to do next, stuffed her hands into her pockets. "There's only one side, boss. You can either work with me and Priest, or you can stay in the Hyde family's pocket. This thing we're doing? There's no gray area. There's no fence to straddle. You have to choose."

Briggs nodded. "I choose this. But if my body ends up washing up on the waterfront~"

"Priest and I will take the Hyde family down for you."

Briggs smiled ruefully. "Thanks, Riley."

"We're not done with this, boss. You've been working with criminals. But if I turn you in, you'll get fired and who knows what kind of monster they would put in your place."

"Yeah." She looked up. "So you kind of own me now."

Riley suddenly hated the darkness of the office, the oppressive atmosphere. They should have done this on neutral ground, where it would come off as less of a threat.

"I need to be able to do my job. And you know that my job doesn't exactly coincide with... what I do for a living. When you took this job, you told me that I'd be on a leash. You expected me to play by the rules without exception. Now you know the truth and you know the rules don't always work."

"Right."

"From now on, my game plan is my own. I'll do what I have to do in order to protect this city. In exchange, I keep quiet about what you just told me."

Briggs lifted her glass. "We have a deal, Detective Parra."

Riley nodded and turned to leave.

"Riley. I'll do my best to earn your trust again. The things you and Priest are doing are the only real shot this town has at surviving. I want to be a part of that no matter what the consequences are."

She opened the door and left without answering. She took the elevator down to the morgue, unable to summon the strength to use the stairs. When she reached the locker room, she saw Gillian had kept her promise: she was sitting on a bench, her back to the wall and her feet out in front of her, a bag of toiletries resting on the floor next to her. She frowned at Riley's stricken expression and stood, taking Riley in her arms. She touched Riley's cheek, her hair, and whispered to her. Riley shook her head and whispered back, and then they kissed silently.

Gillian undressed Riley, and Riley undressed Gillian, and the two of them stepped into the farthest stall in a row of public showers and washed off the day.

ANTHEMUSA

RILEY KISSED Gillian as she slipped out of bed. Gillian murmured and lifted her head from the pillow, eyes barely open as she forced herself out of slumber. "Jog?"

"Yeah. Go back to sleep." She kissed Gillian again and smoothed down the wild cowlicks of her hair. "I'll wake you up when I get back. Want me to pick up breakfast?"

"No, I'll make something here. I'm craving waffles."

"Okay. Go back to sleep, pretty lady."

Gillian grinned drowsily as she put her head back down, already slipping back to sleep as Riley quietly dressed. She chose sweats and an old T-shirt, tying her hair back in a ponytail as she left the bedroom. She took a bottle of water from the fridge and unlocked the apartment door. She saw the person sitting in the hall, but it wasn't until she looked again until she recognized her partner.

"Cait? What are you doing out here?"

Priest was sitting with her arms wrapped around her knees, back against the wall. "I'm just thinking."

Riley sat down next to her. "About what?"

"I think I..." She reached up and rubbed her face. "I'm thinking about losing my virginity."

Riley laughed. She caught the stricken expression on Priest's face and patted her arm while she got herself under control. "Sorry. I didn't mean to laugh. What brought this on?"

Priest ran a hand through her hair. "I kissed someone tonight."

"Hey, way to go." She nudged Priest with her elbow. "Anyone I know? Kenzie?"

"That's not important. We kissed, and I felt... desire. It was strange. Even when I was experimenting with Kenzie and Chelsea last year, I was fine with just watching. It was an observation and nothing else. But now that I'm mortal I have these..." She closed her eyes and shook her head. "I don't even know if I'm really interested in women or if that's just because you and Gillian and Kenzie and Chelsea are the only couples I'm around. I only know a handful of men."

"This person you kissed. Was it a woman?" Priest nodded. "And it aroused you. I think at the very least that would mean you're bisexual. Hell, I'm no expert."

"Why did you choose women?"

Riley smiled. "I didn't choose anything. I fell in love with a woman. And then I fell in love with another woman. In between I never felt half as strongly for any man, so I decided that my interests didn't lie there. If you're attracted to someone enough to kiss them, and if that kiss makes you want to do more, then don't think about it in terms of gender. Just be with that person."

"I can't be with that person."

"Is she married?"

"It's complicated."

Riley winced. "It's not Gillian, right?"

Priest smiled. "No."

"I just had to check. Look, don't let anyone tell you what's right or wrong, and don't overthink things. And don't jump into anything. Take it slow. You're still pretty young, don't forget."

"Thank you, Riley."

"My pleasure. I love giving relationship advice in the hallway at half past four in the morning." She smiled and pushed herself up. "You want to come for a run with me?"

"No, I'm tired. I've been walking around all night since I left Sari~" She tried to stop herself, but there were only a handful of ways she could have finished the word. "Sariel. That's who I kissed."

Riley groaned and let her shoulders sag. "Oh, God, your replacement? She's such a..." She cleared her throat and caught herself before she insulted Priest's potential love interest. "Such a nice angel."

"It's all right. It was just a response to what had happened and the fact she put herself on the line for the both of us yesterday. I was caught up in the emotions."

"Well, congratulations. You're definitely human." She held out her hand to help Priest up. "Get some rest and we'll talk about it later, all right?"

Priest nodded and Riley unlocked the door to let her back into the apartment. Once she was alone in the hall she thought about Priest and Sariel locking lips. The image gave her an unpleasant shudder, and she pushed it aside as she turned and headed for the stairs. She hoped she could clear it from her mind during the run so it didn't linger for the entire day.

She envied the people who had parks to run in. Even outside of No Man's Land, the parks were best avoided after dark. Riley instead jogged through the maze of streets around her building, using alleys and side streets to create a more unique path. She would have preferred running on a dirt track, but the truth was that any running she would have to do at work would be on concrete. It made sense to condition herself on the same sort of surface.

She ran for forty-five minutes, stopping only to rehydrate at the halfway point. As she approached the front of her building, she spotted a blonde woman loitering near the front door. A lot of people waited there for the bus or to take their morning smoke, so she didn't think much of it until she was close enough to recognize who it was. She stifled the curse that threatened to rise up from within her, bracing herself for a confrontation.

The blonde woman turned and offered Riley a tight smile. "Good morning."

Riley slowed down, wishing she wasn't drenched with sweat and wearing a dingy T-shirt. "Gail Finney. I didn't know your keepers let you out of the cage this early."

Gail smiled. "Oh, Detective Parra. What I wouldn't give to have ridden the school bus with you. I'm sure you were just chock full of nasty rhymes and mean nicknames for the nerdy kids."

Riley brushed her eyebrow. "What do you want?"

"A conversation."

"A word that, in your terms, means 'interview.'"

Gail shrugged. "A woman has to make a living, doesn't she? You're the big draw around these parts, and it would be a coup for any reporter--"

"Great. Give me the name of your biggest competitor and I'll make their day."

"Funny. Look, you promised me an interview after the Angel Maker case ended. You *promised*."

"Now who is in elementary school?"

Gail's smile wavered. "Look, Detective. You don't like what I write about your department, but you refuse to do an interview to defend yourself. If I'm not given anything to work with, I can't be blamed for what I write."

Riley practically sneered. "Oh, you can be blamed. Believe me. Now if you'll excuse me, you're blocking the entrance to my building."

"I don't want to badmouth you or the department, Detective. I just write what is available to me."

"You want a quote? Fine. The police of this fine city are doing everything we can to make sure No Man's Land becomes a thing of the past, but it's not easy. It's not going to happen overnight. And vultures like you make it all the harder to make progress because we're expected to perform miracles every damn day. It doesn't work that way, and the sooner you realize it, the better. Is that a good enough quote for you?"

"Oh, it'll do. Thank you, Detective."

Riley flung open the door, nearly colliding with another resident as she stormed inside. She murmured an apology as she moved directly toward the stairs. She was shaking with anger, mostly at herself for taking Gail's bait so easily. The calming effect of her run had been shattered, and she didn't have time for another jog before work. She barely had time for breakfast and a shower, and even then she'd still probably get the stink-eye from Briggs. Her thoughts hit a brick wall when she got to Briggs, a lieutenant she and trusted and who she now knew was a dirty cop. That would make things *so* much easier around the office.

She all but slammed the apartment door as she went inside. Gillian came out of the kitchen, her brow furrowed. "Hey!"

"Sorry. Gail Finney was waiting for me outside."

Gillian went to the couch, picked up Priest's pillow, and carried it to Riley. "Let it out."

Riley took the pillow and buried her face in it just as she released the scream. Her knees bent slightly with the force of her noise, and she felt Gillian's hand like an anchor on her back. She screamed until the oxygen ran out and then lowered the pillow. She closed her eyes and pinched the bridge of her nose as she caught her breath.

"Better?"

"Much." She kissed the corner of Gillian's mouth. "Love you."

"Love you, too. Now go shower and I'll have breakfast ready when you get out."

Riley slipped her arms around Gillian's waist. "How'd I get this lucky?"

Gillian kissed Riley. "I threw a penny in a wishing well and asked for someone who would appreciate me."

Riley smiled and kissed Gillian again. "I'm going to shower."

"Okay. I'll head downstairs and hose off the sidewalk so you don't have to step over any trash on your way out."

"Bless you."

An hour later, Riley and Priest arrived at work a mere fifteen minutes after the morning briefing. As soon as they arrived in the bullpen, Riley could sense the somber mood and half the heads in the room turned toward her with pissed-off expressions. Briggs came out of her office and stormed directly toward Riley. Riley sighed and braced herself. "Oh, boy. What happened now?"

Briggs' voice was loud enough that everyone in the room could hear. "What the hell did you say to Gail Finney?"

"Nothing she could have printed this fast."

Ken Booker cleared his throat and tapped the side of his computer monitor. "Webcast."

"A what?"

Booker turned his monitor around so she could see that he was on Gail Finney's website. "It's like a talk radio program that's on the internet, grandma."

Riley glared at him. "We don't know each other well enough for that, Bookie." He held his hands up in apology and then hit a key. Briggs walked up, arms crossed as Gail's unmistakably haughty voice came through the speakers.

"Guess what, folks? Police work isn't easy! It's really hard, and they wish that we would just leave them alone so they can figure out how to do their jobs on their own without all the pressure. So, you see, it's *our* fault that No Man's Land seems to grow with every passing day. We're distracting the police by expecting them to do their jobs. These aren't my words; these are the words of one

Detective... Riley Parra. Well! My, my, my. The woman of the hour and the woman who 'cleaned up the streets' after the Angel Maker made them unsafe."

Briggs reached down and jabbed the keyboard. Gail was mercifully silenced. She stepped away from the desk. "My office. *Now.*"

Riley followed Briggs like a prisoner on her way to be executed. Once she was in the office, Briggs slammed the door. "What the hell were you thinking?"

"She caught me off-guard. She was waiting by my building's door when I got back from my jog and I wasn't thinking."

"You're damn right. What did you say? Exactly?"

"Exactly? I don't remember."

Briggs muttered a curse under her breath. "I'm going to have to issue a statement. The commissioner is not happy. No one between me and him in the chain of command is happy. I got one person requesting your resignation. They said we could write it off as PTSD following the whole Angel Maker ordeal."

"Are you asking me to do that?"

"God, no. Maybe I'd consider it if I didn't know the truth about this whole..." She waved her hand vaguely toward the window. "But this is not a free pass, Riley. What you know about me? I won't let you own me."

Riley nodded. "I wouldn't try. I just want the leeway you promised and I'll be happy."

"The next time you see Gail Finney, you don't say a word. You mow her down to get to a door, you pull your jacket over your head and crouch in the corner until she gets bored and leaves. You do not talk to her or the press ever again, on the record or not. Am I understood?"

"Yes, ma'am."

"And you're not leaving the building today. Catch up on your paperwork, send Priest out for whatever you need, but your ass is in that chair until quitting time. Got it?"

Riley fought the urge to protest but, with Gail Finney's little web show, she agreed it would be best to stay out of the public eye. "Sure. I've been meaning to catch up on some things."

Briggs looked relieved, as if she had been expecting a fight. "Good. You can even go hang out in the morgue if it's not too busy."

"You mean if it's dead down there?"

Briggs almost managed to hide her smile. "Go to your desk, Detective."

Riley left the office to find Priest waiting by her desk. "Get comfortable, Caitlin. Mom grounded us."

"Oh." She pulled her chair out and sat down. "It'll be nice to have a day off from violence and No Man's Land."

"Yeah. Last time we stuck around the office, the place nearly got blown up and Gillian got possessed for a few minutes."

"I did say a day off. Not an *easy* day."

Riley sighed. "True. Not a lot of easy days going around." She turned on her computer and tried to remember which case she'd last done paperwork on.

It was barely ten before Riley realized why being chained to a desk was a punishment, and Priest didn't even make it until eleven before she was looking for an escape route. She offered to buy lunch for the detectives who remained in the office - three, including Booker - and took Riley's money downstairs. The consensus was for sub sandwiches, and she stood on the street and tried to remember where the nearest shop was.

"Need a little help?"

Priest turned. The woman had just exited the building behind her, leaning forward slightly to close the distance between them without fully invading Priest's space. Her dark brown hair formed a widow's peak on her forehead, the long strands pulled back into a braid. She wore a white turtleneck and a leather vest, her floor-length red dress still swaying around her legs from exiting the building.

"I'm trying to find the sub shop."

"Super Heros? It's just down here about two blocks. I'm walking that way if you'd like an escort."

"Uh. Uh, sure. Thank you."

"My pleasure." She held out her hand. "You can call me Al."

Priest shook her hand as they started walking. "Caitlin Priest."

"No Paul Simon joke?"

"Hm?"

"The... song. Never mind. I just need to clear my head. Police station, ick." She gave a theatrical shudder. "I had to give a statement because I saw my coworker's car get hit on my way to work. So I gave up my entire morning to write one page about how I didn't really see anything. I saw maybe two letters on the license plate and that's it." She looked at Priest. "What were you in there for?"

Priest hesitated; if this woman didn't like cops... "I'm a homicide detective, actually."

Al's eyes widened. "That is amazing. You really go out and look at dead bodies and all that?"

"Pretty much."

"I thought stuff like that only happened on TV and in books. It's kind of weird thinking about real detectives. Although, if I may say so, you don't exactly look like the typical detective from TV. They usually don't cast such pretty women in those shows."

Priest tilted her head. "I thought there were a lot of pretty cops on television. At least that's what my partner is always complaining about. She says that nothing on those shows is real, and even the people~"

Al held up a hand. "Sorry. I-I was just trying to compliment you."

"What?"

"I was saying you were very pretty."

Priest blushed. "Thank you. You are, too."

Al grinned. "You're kind of a funny woman, Caitlin Priest."

"Sorry. I've been trying to stop."

Al threw back her head and laughed. She gestured across the street. There was a narrow storefront with a red and yellow sign that announced it was called SUPER HEROS! with the misspelling to indicate it was a sandwich shop. "Well, here we are. Safe and sound."

Priest nodded and then faced Al fully. "Can I buy you lunch?"

Riley looked up as Priest appeared at the top of the stairs. She was carrying a bag with the sandwiches. "Finally. Where did you go, Clemente's?"

"No, Super Heros."

"That's only five minutes away. What the hell took you so long?"

Priest placed the sandwich on Riley's desk and leaned down to whisper in Riley's ear. "I think I met someone."

The irritation melted away from Riley's face, replaced by surprise. "That quick? I'm impressed, Cait. So that's where you were?"

"I bought her lunch. I... I owe you ten dollars next payday."

"Don't worry about it. Call it a belated birthday present, and repay me by telling me about this woman."

Priest smiled. "Her name is Alyssa Graham. She said I could call her Al."

"Are you going to be her bodyguard?" Priest tilted her head in confusion. "Paul Simon?"

"Oh. That's what she said, but I didn't understand." She sat on the edge of Riley's desk and crossed her arms. "She had to give a statement about her coworker's car being hit. We left the building at the same time, and she showed me where the sub shop was. She's very pretty, and funny. And I think she likes me."

Riley nudged Priest's leg. "Of course she likes you, Cait. Well done."

"We're going out to dinner tonight. I have her phone number to let her know about reservations."

"Wow, that's quick."

"Is it too quick? I wasn't sure." She chewed her bottom lip. "I'd really like to have sex with someone tonight, if I can."

Riley heard Booker choke on his sandwich and regretted not taking the conversation somewhere more private. "No, it's all right. I understand. But you also can't just jump into this blind. You don't really know anything about this woman."

"About that... I mentioned to her that it would kind of be a... group... thing."

"You want me and Gillian to go on the date with you." Priest nodded. "Yeah. Sure. That would give us a chance to keep an eye on you in case something comes up."

Priest looked relieved. "You're not mad that I invited you?"

"Absolutely not. It'll be fun." She started to unwrap her sandwich. "You looked out for me, now it's time for me to return the favor. It'll be fun."

Gillian closed her office door. "What the hell did you say to Gail Finney this morning?"

"God. Has it ruined your day, too?"

"No, I'm just getting dirty looks from every cop who comes through here. I think they paint us with the same brush."

"Sorry."

"Don't be. Fuck 'em." She kissed Riley. "If they're mad at you, then they're mad at me, too. It's a package deal."

Riley smiled and laced her fingers in the small of Gillian's back. "About that. Priest went out for lunch today and she actually met someone. They're going to dinner tonight."

"That's amazing. And irritating. She's on the market one day and she gets a date?"

Riley shrugged. "Well, you've seen her. That body was sculpted by Heaven to host an actual angelic being. She might not literally glow anymore, but she's still an angel."

"I'm getting jealous over here."

"*You* put all the angels in the heavens to shame, you're the reason the sun gives up and shuts itself away at night, you~"

"Okay, shush."

Riley smiled. "Anyway, Priest kind of told this woman that it was a double-date."

"Oh?"

Riley licked her lips and shifted her weight from one foot to the other. "Yeah, so... um. I was wondering, if you weren't busy, maybe you'd, I don't know, want to go out to dinner with me tonight, if you're not busy." She bit her bottom lip and widened her eyes.

Gillian leaned in and whispered in Riley's ear. "I'm washing my hair."

Riley grinned and whispered in Gillian's ear. "What if I promised you'd get lucky?"

"In this scenario, shouldn't I be the one deciding if anyone gets lucky?"

Riley chuckled. "Depends on who you ask. So are you in?"

"I'll get all dolled up. And I'll take off a little early to take Priest shopping for something date-appropriate." She smiled and toyed with the collar of Riley's shirt. "I like going on dates with you, Riley. You're quite the closet romantic."

"Don't tell anyone. I should get back upstairs. Paperwork tends to pile up."

Gillian looked at her desk. "Tell me about it. I'll see you after work." They separated and Riley went to the door. Gillian sat down. "You know, it'll be fun. It's been a long time since I had a foursome."

Riley stopped and turned to face her. "Wait, long time. You mean you've~"

"Paperwork, Riley."

"You can't expect me to concentrate on my work after~"

"See you tonight, Riley."

Riley groaned. "You're a tease."

Gillian blew her a kiss as Riley left her office.

Riley came home to an empty apartment, showered, and changed into a dress shirt and slacks. She put on a touch of makeup, just enough so that Gillian couldn't complain she wasn't wearing any, and finished getting ready as Gillian and Priest returned from their shopping excursion. "Hey, we're back." She stopped as soon as she saw Riley, her eyes running from head to toe and back again. "Wow. Hot stuff."

"Did you find something?"

"Hm?" Gillian's eyes were on Riley's outfit, but they snapped back up to her face.

"For Priest." Riley smiled at her fiance's distraction. "Did you find something for her?"

Gillian cleared her throat. "Caitlin?"

Priest stepped in from the hallway. They'd done more than shop for a dress; Priest's hair was styled, a blonde wave of finger curls cascading down the right side of her face. She wore a sleeveless blue dress that had nothing special about its design other than the fact it was draped over a beautiful woman's body.

"I thought with a figure like hers, the dress shouldn't be that distracting."

Riley raised an eyebrow. "I almost feel sorry for the woman you're meeting."

Priest blushed and looked down at herself. "I feel silly."

"That's how you know you're a woman going on a date. I'm going to go get ready." Gillian kissed Riley's cheek and dipped her head to sniff Riley's neck. "Mm. Scrumptious."

Riley brushed her arm as she went by and then turned to Priest. "So what's the plan with this 'Al' woman? Are we picking her up?"

"No, we'll meet at the restaurant." Priest reached up to touch her hair and then dropped her hand. "I'm terrified, Riley."

"That's to be expected. It's your first real date. Just breathe through it. Just remember that whatever else happens, this woman agreed to go out for a meal with you. That's the very least it has to be, and anything else is bonus. Just relax."

"I'll try. Thank you for agreeing to go, Riley."

Riley shrugged. "It's a slow day, right? No demons, no crimes, just boring paperwork and mundane domesticity. We've earned a day like this, right?" She winked and smiled, even as she prayed she hadn't just jinxed them.

She gave Priest some more tips on how to behave during the date, troubleshooting any potential problems so they wouldn't have to solve them on the fly. She was about to go see what was taking Gillian so long when the bedroom door open and she came out. She wore a little black dress that ended just above the knee, high heels with straps that wrapped around her ankles, and her hair was up in a loose bun.

Riley immediately rose to her feet, not blinking, and tried for a full ten seconds to speak. Finally, she cleared her throat and forced herself to look away. "Caitlin?"

"Yes?"

"Thank you for making us go with you tonight. Otherwise I might not have seen this."

Gillian smiled bashfully, dipping her chin. "I think we're all ready to go."

"Yeah." Riley cleared her throat. She put out her elbow and Gillian put her arm around it before they walked Priest to the door.

The restaurant Priest had chosen was about as nice as they could hope for this close to No Man's Land. It had a small ante room where people could wait on padded benches for a table, separated from the dining area by an aquarium of tinted glass. Priest led the way in, with Riley and Gillian following. Priest nervously scanned the people waiting on the benches, her unease finally showing when she turned to face Riley. "She's not here. She didn't come. We should probably just go... it was a bad idea."

Riley put a hand on Priest's shoulder. "Just wait a second, okay? We're a little early." She guided Priest to the hostess stand. "Excuse me. It should be Priest, party of four?"

"Yes, I have it right here. Would you like to be seated while you await your other guest?"

Riley was about to answer when she felt Priest stiffen beside her. She turned and saw a gorgeous brunette standing in the doorway of the restaurant. The woman was smiling at Priest, and Riley turned back to the hostess. "No need. I think she just arrived."

Gillian was the closest to the new arrival and was the first to greet her. "Alyssa? Hi, Gillian Hunt."

"Oh, hello." She folded her hand around Gillian's and squeezed. Gillian's shoulders jerked slightly, and her smile wavered before she corrected it. "Alyssa Graham. Please, call me Al."

The introductions continued with Riley, and then Al faced Priest. "Hi. I wasn't sure if I should expect to see you here tonight. I thought you seemed kind of nervous at lunch and... well. I'm just glad you're here."

Riley said, "You'll have to forgive Cait. She just got out of a pretty... intense... relationship and she's still a little gun shy."

"I understand that."

The hostess tried to unobtrusively get their attention. "If you're all here, I can show you to your table."

Gillian smiled. "Shall we?"

They started toward the table, and Riley fell back to walk with Gillian. "What was that shudder when you shook her hand?"

"Nothing. Her hands are really cold."

Riley chuckled. "Maybe Priest can warm them up before the night is out."

Gillian's face was flush, and she nodded before she slipped her arm around Riley's.

During appetizers, Al explained what she did for a living - something to do with the mail room of a law firm- and where she had grown up - somewhere in the south - but Riley found it increasingly difficult to focus on what she was saying. She sipped her water and tea when the waitress brought it over, but her mind kept drifting to Gillian's dress. She pressed her back against the chair, leaning back as casually as she could, and glanced down. Gillian's hand was resting on her lap, just below the spot where her thigh and crotch met, and Riley stifled a groan by pressing her napkin against her lips.

"After I moved here, I just... I don't know. The crime really gets to me after a while. Not that I'm laying the blame on you guys. You get enough of that from the newspapers and that lady on the radio."

Riley wondered if Gillian would lift her dress so she could see her thighs.

"Right?"

Riley looked up and realized she'd been spoken to. "Sorry?"

Al looked embarrassed. "I... I was just saying that I'd seen you on television. You were involved in that Angel Maker thing a few months back."

"Oh. Right, yeah, that was us. Me and Priest, really. Both of us. Were involved." She cleared her throat. "Priest was hurt."

That turned Al's attention back on her date. "Oh, my God. Seriously? I remember hearing about someone being injured, but I didn't connect it with you. How badly were you hurt?"

"It was more mental than anything, I guess." Priest had noticed Riley's odd behavior and watched her as she answered. "I needed some time to recover from everything that happened."

Al put her hand on top of Priest's and squeezed. "Well, may I say on behalf of this town, thank you. You guys probably get sick of going out and making a difference only to have people say you should do more."

Riley emptied her water glass with one long draught. "Yeah. 'Scuse me." She pushed away from the table and walked quickly toward the bathroom.

"Did I say something wrong?" She heard Al's question, but didn't want to stop long enough to address it. Gillian excused herself and gave chase.

The bathrooms were in a narrow corridor blocked from view by a trellis. Plastic vines trailed up and down the wooden diamonds and made the alcove feel like a forest trail. Riley rested against the wall and, a moment later, Gillian appeared. Riley shook her head before she could say anything. "I'm sorry. I don't know what's gotten into me, but I cannot stop thinking about~"

"You." Gillian's voice was a primal growl. She grabbed Riley's face and kissed her hard, thrusting her tongue into Riley's mouth.

All the questions about why this was happening flew from Riley's mind as she pulled Gillian to her. They both moaned, Gillian's hands sliding over the material of Riley's shirt to caress her breasts. Riley pulled Gillian to the right, pushing the women's room door open and kicking it shut behind them. They twisted until Gillian's back was against the cool tile of the wall and Riley began kissing down her neck.

Gillian groaned and pawed at Riley's body. "I kept thinking about reaching over and opening your fly. Fingering you. God, I could hardly stop myself from~"

"You shouldn't have even tried. Stopping yourself, I mean." Riley licked Gillian's neck and then kissed her chin before their lips met again. Their teeth clacked together, but neither noticed. Riley pushed up Gillian's dress and rubbed the back of her thigh through her pantyhose. She pulled back, sucking Gillian's bottom lip for a moment. "You should have worn stockings."

"I shouldn't have worn anything. Then you'd feel me..." She

took Riley's hand and pressed it between her legs. "Feel that?"

Riley groaned and kissed Gillian's neck again. She stroked with her tongue, sucking hard enough that she knew she would most likely create a hickey. Gillian didn't seem to mind; her fingernails were raking Riley's back hard enough that she was afraid the nails would rip the material.

"Need to fuck you." Riley was surprised by the desire in her own voice, hands trembling as they searched for an opening in the clothes. She was even more surprised by Gillian's reply.

"Then do it."

Riley managed to push herself away. "Not here... we can excuse~"

"No. Here. Right here. Out on the goddamn table. Show Priest how to fuck a woman, huh? Show her how you make me... m-make me moan. Every night. You know she hears. Probably touches herself, makes herself come. We should show her what to do with her tongue with the whole restaurant watching."

Riley moaned and chuckled at the same time, nuzzling Gillian's neck. "You are so nasty tonight, baby." Something was wrong with what Gillian was saying, but Riley couldn't make herself care as they kissed again.

Something clicked behind them and Riley twisted, using her body to block Gillian's. A woman was standing at the sink facing them, eyes wide, lips parted in a silent gasp. She was clutching a purse to her stomach and, when she realized she'd been seen, she swallowed. "Do-don't stop on my account."

Riley looked at Gillian and saw a flush rising in her cheeks. She smiled and whispered just low enough for Gillian to hear it. "Guess all that 'on the table' stuff was just talk, huh?"

"Tell her to take off her clothes." Gillian licked the shell of Riley's ear.

"What?"

Gillian bit Riley's ear almost hard enough to hurt. "Tell her... to take off her clothes. Tell her to masturbate for us. I want to see her get off because of us."

Riley swallowed and pulled the hem of Gillian's dress down over her thighs. "You should go back to your table, ma'am. Sorry about... sorry."

The woman seemed reluctant, but she pushed away from the sink and left the bathroom in a hurry. Once they were alone again, Riley pulled back and looked at Gillian. "Are you sure you're all right?"

"I'm fine. I'm just horny." She pawed at Riley's clothes again. "Want you."

Riley felt her resolve weaken again and she kissed Gillian hard. "I want you, too. But... home. At home." She nodded and, after a moment, Gillian nodded as well. Riley brushed Gillian's cheek with her thumb. "I don't want to share you with anyone."

Gillian took Riley's thumb into her mouth and sucked it. Riley moaned and sagged against her. Her resolve was slipping.

"Take me home right now."

"Priest is~"

"I don't fucking care about Priest. Take me home, Riley. I'll fuck you all night long if you take me home right now."

Riley had heard worse offers. She took Gillian's hand and led her out of the bathroom. The air of the restaurant seemed freezing on her skin, and Riley wondered how deeply she was blushing. Gillian followed after her at a trot, and only then did Riley realize that she was practically running. She saw their bathroom voyeur at a table with an older man, and the woman dipped her chin and smiled nervously when Riley hurried past.

Priest looked up with relief as Riley and Gillian returned, but her expression turned confused at their demeanor.

"Caitlin. Sorry. We have to go. It's a matter of~" Gillian suddenly grabbed Riley's ass and Riley squeaked. "~it's very important." She took out her wallet and dropped a pair of twenties onto the table. "That should cover dinner. We're... really sorry, but we really have to go. Sorry."

She and Gillian fled before Priest could even vocalize a complaint. They breezed past the hostess stand, and out into the frigid night air. Riley relished the cold, closing her eyes as her breath plumed around her head like a cloud. She remembered the night she and Gillian had stood waiting for a light in the crosswalk to change, their cheeks together and watching their breath mingle in a frozen cloud in front of them.

Gillian was openly groping her now, and Riley was finding it harder and harder to swat her hands away. "What the hell has gotten into you?"

"Two of your fingers." Gillian kissed her hard. "Three of your fingers." She bit Riley's bottom lip. "Your fucking fist."

Riley shivered and clutched Gillian around the waist. She knew she couldn't even try driving, so she guided Gillian to the curb and tried to look for a cab as Gillian kissed and sucked her neck. Riley finally shoved Gillian away, spinning her with the same movement. She got an arm around Gillian's waist and pulled her back against her. Gillian's body seemed to mold to the shape of Riley's, and Riley pressed her palm against the front of Gillian's dress.

"You wanna know what I'm going to do when I get you home? Little princess?" She licked Gillian's ear, wondering where the pet name had come from.

"Tell me..."

"I'm going to rip this dress off of you. I'm going to make you naked, lay you down on the floor, and then I'm going to lick you. I'm going to lick your feet, your ankles. I'm going to nip and nibble on your calves." Gillian squirmed against Riley, and Riley thrust her hips forward against the curve of Gillian's ass. "I'm going to suck the back of your knees. I'm going to brush my hair on your body like a paintbrush. Tickle you." Gillian purred and writhed. "I'm going to~"

A horn bleated, and Riley lifted her head, suddenly furious at the interruption. A cab was in front of them, the female driver in a hounds-tooth cap making a point of looking at the road ahead. "You, uh, ladies going somewhere, or is this where the party is?"

Riley guided Gillian to the cab's back door and opened it. "Crawl inside." Gillian smiled and placed her hands on the backseat, making sure Riley got a good look at her ass as she crawled into the car. Riley climbed in behind her and managed to remember her address well enough to tell the driver where to go.

Gillian put her legs in Riley's lap, and Riley put a hand between her thighs. Gillian put an arm around Riley's neck and pulled her close.

"What else would you do?"

Riley licked Gillian's cheek. "First the fingers. I know you love how I use my fingers on you. Then the toys. You know your favorite one, the one with the flared tip that opens you up so... so wide when I push it all the way in?"

Gillian squirmed as Riley's hand pushed higher.

"Then my tongue. Because I want to taste you when you finally come."

The cabbie cleared her throat.

"I want my tongue in you when you come for the first time. Make you squirt for me. I want to lick it all up, and then I want to spread it on my breasts so you can suck them~"

The cabbie coughed.

"~dry." Riley met the driver's eyes in the rearview mirror. "Either watch, or kick us the fuck out. Either way, I'll need you to shut up."

No more sounds issued from the front seat as Riley turned back to Gillian and kissed her. Gillian undid a button on Riley's blouse and pushed her hand inside, cupping her breast through the bra. Riley arched her back as her nipple hardened at Gillian's touch, groaning as Gillian pinched and kneaded and plucked her nipple while their tongues parried for dominance.

Something was wrong, Riley was clear-headed enough to realize that. Gillian, shy Gillian who sometimes covered her mouth when she came so the neighbors wouldn't hear, had wanted someone to watch them make love. And Riley, who ordinarily wouldn't want to share Gillian with anyone, had just invited the cabbie to watch them. And 'make love'? This wasn't making love, not by a long shot. This was animalistic, primal. This was the kind of fucking Riley did with her one night stands before she had chanced upon the best relationship that ever happened to her.

Maybe every couple needs to fuck once in a while, she thought. She cupped Gillian, feeling the wetness through her panties as she stroked.

"I think the cab driver is masturbating."

Riley looked and, sure enough, the cabbie only had one hand on the wheel. Riley felt her ears burning at the sight and turned back to Gillian.

"What are we doing?"

"I want you. I always want you."

Riley kissed Gillian and decided she had a point. She always wanted Gillian, too. Day and night, when they were together and especially when they were apart. The only time her desire for Gillian was sated was when they were in bed together, right after making love, but her satisfaction never lasted long. She always wanted more, more, again.

"But I can usually focus. God... why can't I focus?" Riley kissed Gillian's cheek again.

"You're not saying naughty things," Gillian whined. "Make me wet, baby."

The cab rolled to a stop and the cab driver cleared her throat. "W-we're... here." She didn't turn around. "You guys need, uh, any help getting up to your apartment?"

"Let her come with us," Gillian whispered excitedly against Riley's ear. "We can have so much fun with her. Look at her. She's gorgeous."

Riley fished some money out of her wallet and handed it over the seat. "Here... s-sorry about... everything."

She pulled Gillian from the cab, clinging tightly to her as they walked into the building. It was like trying to get a drunk up the stairs, only with more kissing and groping. Riley succumbed a few times herself, dipping her head to kiss Gillian's collarbone when the strap of her dress fell. When they got to the door, Riley took Gillian's purse to find the keys.

"No, no. Fuck me in the hallway."

"Jill..."

"Call me little princess."

Riley's resolve wavered. She lifted her head, her face inches from Gillian's. "Little princess. My little princess." She slid her hand down Gillian's body. "You're being so damn bad tonight, little princess."

Gillian whimpered. Riley smacked her ass, and Gillian yelped and squirmed. Riley took a handful of Gillian's ass, squeezed, and spanked her again. They'd never introduced spanking into their bedroom, so what was it about right now that made her hand swing out and impact again. Gillian cooed, smiled, and rolled her hips. "My queen."

Riley found the keys and unlocked the door. They practically fell into the apartment, separating just long enough for Riley to slam the door shut and turn to face Gillian.

They faced each other from a few inches apart, maybe the furthest apart they had been since Riley excused herself from the restaurant table. Gillian's hair, so perfectly coiffed when the night began, had fallen loose and wild. She was breathing hard as she closed the distance between them and put her arms around Riley.

"Something happened to us," Riley said between kisses. Gillian lifted one leg and Riley grabbed it, hooking it against her hip and massaging the back of Gillian's thigh.

"Mm, I know. It's fucking wonderful." She chuckled. "And leads to wonderful fucking."

Riley pushed away from the wall, carrying Gillian with her over to the couch. They dropped onto the carefully folded pile of Priest's bedding and clawed at each other, Gillian pulling her legs together just long enough for Riley to tug her panties down to her ankles.

Gillian kicked them away and then untucked Riley's shirt from her pants. When she lay back, she turned her head and inhaled the scent off the pillow. She laughed and ran her hands over Riley's stomach. "Hey... *we* should fuck Priest."

That was shocking enough to break through the fog. "Gillian, that's..."

"Brilliant? Hot? Does it make you wet?" She moved her hand to the crotch of Riley's trousers and rubbed her. "Mm, something made you wet..."

"You," Riley admitted. "But Priest is..."

"Gorgeous!" Gillian's groan was full of longing.

"Yes... she~ she's my partner. Jill... something is very wrong with us."

Gillian tugged on Riley's blouse and popped a button. "Yes! All of these clothes..."

Riley let Gillian take off her blouse and toss it aside, cradling her head when Gillian sat up to kiss her chest. Riley shifted her weight and pressed her thigh between Gillian's legs. Gillian gasped. "Oh! Yeah, yeah, yeah, do that. Here." She wrapped her legs around Riley's and began to grind, both of them moaning at the contact.

Riley closed her eyes and clung to Gillian. Was this what their life was going to be from now on? Non-stop love-making? Since her resurrection, it seemed like they couldn't go one day without having sex at least once. Had it gotten to the point where it was like a drug? But why would it have happened so suddenly? She remembered being in Gillian's office that afternoon, how close they had been. Surely they could have torn each other's clothes off then, but something stopped them.

"Oh, Riley..."

Riley stroked Gillian's hair as she came. She felt the warm flow of Gillian's tears on her chest, calming her as she trembled and bucked in her arms. When she relaxed, Riley lowered Gillian to the couch and carefully stretched out on top of her. The thigh of her trousers was wet; Gillian had ejaculated. Riley closed her eyes and tried to catch her breath. At least it was over...

"Dildo..."

"What?"

"Fuck me with a dildo now. C'mon. They're in the bedroom..."

Riley sat up and looked down at her. "Baby, you just came."

"I know. I want to come *again*." She was almost pouting. "Strap-on? You can wear the strap-on and fuck me from behind..."

"No." It was the hardest thing Riley had ever said. She pulled away. "Jill, something–"

Gillian slapped her, hard, and Riley reeled away from her. Gillian sat up, eyes flashing anger. "Are you fucking Priest?"

"What?!"

"Is it Kenzie? Is it Briggs? Who are you fucking?" Gillian scrambled to her feet and stood next to the couch. "Maybe I'll go fuck someone else. Maybe I'll–"

Riley got to her feet and grabbed Gillian by the shoulders. "Jill–"

"Either fuck me or let me go find someone who will." Gillian slapped Riley again, this time leaving a stinging remnant on Riley's skin.

Riley bit the inside of her cheek. Something inside of her was angry, was trying to make her return Gillian's slap. She never would. Never. But her arm actually ached from holding it back. Instead, she cupped Gillian's face and tenderly kissed her. No tongue, no intention for anything else. Gillian reached for Riley's crotch and Riley slapped her hand away. Gillian whimpered.

"Kiss me." Riley's mouth moved against Gillian's. "Just kiss me."

Gillian returned Riley's kiss. Reluctantly at first, eager to move on to the next step. But then her hands came up and rested on Riley's shoulders and she began contributing to the kiss. Riley put her arms around Gillian's waist, loosely, keeping a sliver of air between them as Riley broke the kiss to change the angle of her head.

Slowly, their breathing returned to normal. Gillian's hands were no longer trembling. Riley kissed the corners of Gillian's mouth and her chin before she guided Gillian's head to her shoulder. Gillian suddenly sobbed, and her hands curled into fists. "Oh, God, Riley, I *hit* you..."

"Sh."

"What the hell was that all about?"

The fog had cleared and Riley was more concerned than ever. "I don't know. But I think we better find out."

"You should go."

"Do you want me to go?"

Gillian started to answer and then lifted her head. "I never *want* you to go. But I think Priest is in a lot of danger. If whatever whammy that was hit us like that, then I can only imagine how it would hit her. She's still very naive and innocent. So, yeah, I want you to go because I'm worried about Caitlin. Not because I want you gone."

Riley stroked Gillian's arm. "I just thought after what happened..."

Gillian smiled. "I've had rough sex before, Riley. And sure, that was kind of like rough sex on steroids, but it was with you. I'm fine with it. I'm even a little excited by how far we went. We do need to talk, but... about the things that happened tonight that are very, very okay."

"Really? Like what?"

Gillian shrugged shyly. "I kind of liked when you spanked me."

"You did?"

"Well. Yeah. And little princess. Where'd that come from?"

Riley chuckled. "That one I've been holding onto. It never seemed right to pull it out."

"Feel free. Not at work, but in the bedroom..." She stopped stroking Riley's stomach and reluctantly pushed away from her. "Something obviously happened to us tonight. It was scary, like letting someone else pull the puppet strings, but I'm not sorry it happened. I was mostly in my right mind until the end, when you tried to stop me. It was like my common sense got turned off. There was no filter."

"Same here. The desire wasn't new, but losing control of it like that..." She touched Gillian's chin. "I'm usually much better at keeping my libido in check, even when it comes to you. It's the fact that I lost control so completely that confuses me."

"Right. It was us, but with all the inhibitions eliminated."

Riley considered that. "So if it came from us, then all of those women you said could join us..."

Gillian blushed.

"I'll keep that in mind, Dr. Hunt." She smiled and leaned forward to kiss her.

"I love you, Riley. But you really should go."

"Yeah. I know." She looked down at herself. "But I should probably change."

Gillian looked at Riley's pants. "Right. Sorry about that. I've never~"

"I've never made anyone do that before. So... yeah. Something to aim for next time." She kissed Gillian again, cupping her blushing cheek, and reluctantly stood up to change her clothes.

The hostess looked up as the door opened, her professional posture changing slightly when she recognized who the new arrival was. "*Oh*. Welcome back."

Riley added the restaurant to the list of places she would never show her face again. "Hi. The couple we were with, are they still here?"

"No. They left not long after you and your... friend did."

Riley looked at her watch. Almost an hour had passed since their mad dash from the restaurant. "Did they drive?"

"No, they took a cab. I called it for them."

"Which company?"

"We're not allowed to give out that sort of infor~" Riley pulled out her badge and held it in front of the girl's face. "Do you have a warrant?"

Riley sighed. "The blonde woman we left behind here is my partner, and I have reason to believe she might be in danger. So if you want to wait around for me to wake up a judge and get a warrant - and I definitely could get one if you want to take the time - while my partner is raped, then by all means..."

The girl's eyes widened and she picked up the phone behind her podium. She dialed a number and kept an eye on Riley as it rang. "Hello, this is Mae again. I called a little earlier for a cab. I have a detective here who needs information about it." She listened and then turned her attention to Riley. "The cab was 1J7R."

"Tell them to send it back here."

The girl relayed the information and told Riley it would be there in about six minutes. Riley left the restaurant and waited on the curb, looking up and down the street for signs of the yellow cab. Now that her head had been cleared by the night air, she was humiliated that she'd let herself get so distracted. It was a little easier to deal with since it had been Gillian distracting her. She could ignore a bomb blast so long as Gillian was in her arms. But she'd walked out and left Priest in a very dangerous situation.

The cab rounded the corner and Riley was suddenly afraid it would be the voyeuristic driver who had taken them home. She hid her relief as she saw the thick-beard of the driver through the windshield, his thick hands gripping the steering wheel as he pulled to the curb and she ran to meet him. She bent down and showed her badge through the open passenger side window.

"I need to know where you took the two women you picked up here earlier tonight."

"Down near the waterfront. I can take you there if you want, no charge."

"Thank you." Riley opened the back door and climbed inside. "How were they acting?"

The cabbie whistled and shook his head as he pulled back onto the road. "If I had a security camera in this thing, I'd put that thing on YouTube so fast your head would have spun. Still, nothing compared to what my pal Ingrid saw in her cab tonight. Couple of ladies nearly tore each other's clothes off right in front of her. Some kinda town after dark, huh?"

Riley clenched her teeth and looked out the window.

Her anxiety over Priest's situation grew as the cab drove deeper into No Man's Land. Maybe they had decided to go to Al's place, and maybe Al lived in a really bad part of town. She tried not to worry, tried to prepare herself for bursting in on Priest's first time. That would go over real well; no mental trauma to worry about there.

The cab pulled to a stop, and the driver looked over the seat at her. "Here we are."

Riley stared at the abandoned warehouse. "You're kidding me. Are you sure?"

"Lady, when two well-dressed women get in my cab, maul each other, and then ask to come to a place like this in the middle of the night? It sticks in my mind."

"Right." She opened the door and started to get out. "Thanks for the ride."

He held up a hand. "Look, I warned them, too. Not that they were listening. But you want to go someplace else. Anyplace else. This is a very bad part of town and once I go, you're not gonna get another cab to come pick you up."

"I'll be fine. Thanks for the warning, though."

He shrugged, his due diligence done, and waited for Riley to step away before he drove off. The sidewalk was cracked and choked with weeds, and the chain link fence had long ago ceased to be a barrier to trespassers. It sagged dramatically, with gaps wide enough to drive through. The building beyond was a mess of broken windows. Riley stepped through the remnants of the fence and tried very hard not to think about the last warehouse she'd broken into in the middle of the night.

"Riley, my job is to keep you alive. Even at the cost of my own life. You'll get a new angel to protect you. This is what I was sent to do. So run, Riley, please."

She'd almost lost Priest that night, too. She shuddered at the thought and looked toward the sky. "I could really use some backup right now, if you've got any available."

"All you have to do is ask." Sariel was standing beside her, examining the building with a critical eye. "This is a bad place."

"Nice of you to show up. Where were you earlier tonight?"

Sariel looked at her. "Away. What happened?"

"Not entirely sure. Gillian and I got a little... randy at the restaurant, and I think we left Priest in a dangerous situation."

"So that's why you reek of sex."

Riley tried not to blush; she'd been doing far too much of that tonight. "I put on perfume. There's only so much I can do. Deal with it. Is Priest still in there?"

"I don't know. But there's a presence casting a shadow over this place."

"Yeah, you mentioned that. Bad place. Do you have my back or not?"

"It's my mission."

"Kudos to you." Riley advanced, and Sariel spread her wings and followed Riley to the nearest entrance. The door was hanging loose on its hinges and Riley pushed it to one side as she swept the interior with her weapon. She didn't hear anything, couldn't see anything but vague ghostly shapes of white sheets covering machinery. She entered cautiously, turning to examine the metal stairs that led to a catwalk overhead.

She motioned for Sariel to go right, and she went left. Sariel's wings provided a subtle glow, just enough light to see by, but Riley still moved cautiously. She didn't want to alert anyone to their presence. As she followed the wall toward a row of offices, she thought about the sequence of events. Something had hit her and Gillian with some kind of pheromones at the exact same moment. It was a good plan; desire for Gillian was the one distraction that wouldn't raise any alarms in Riley's mind. It was the one thing that could make her run out on Priest.

The office doors and windows had all been removed long ago. Riley paused in the cavities of the doorways just long enough to ensure the room was empty before she moved on to the next one. She was starting to get the very bad feeling that Al and Priest had only told the cabbie to stop at this address and then moved on to a different place. The only places within walking distance were hardly places Riley wanted to explore in the dark.

The last office in the row was filled with discarded furniture. Riley stepped inside the room and realized there was a rudimentary path through the garbage and followed it toward the back corner of the room. She braced herself to find a body, the worst case scenario, but what she saw instead made her blood run cold. She tensed and called for Sariel over her shoulder. She kept her weapon drawn but dropped into a crouch as the angel appeared behind her.

"I don't believe Caitlin Priest is in this building."

"No, she's not." She pointed at the hole in the floor.

"What is that?"

"That's an access point to the Underground. It's a section of the city that was condemned after a big fire, and the city rebuilt a few stories up. It was supposed to be sealed. Damn it." She rubbed her face and stood up. "Priest is down there."

"I need you to tell me exactly what happened."

Riley turned to her. "Caitlin got all hot and bothered after your kiss - yeah, she told me - and she decided she needed to lose her virginity. So we were on a double date with her and her new friend and~"

"Who was her new friend?"

"Some woman she met outside the police station. Al. Uh, Alyssa, I think, Graham." Sariel's eyes widened subtly. "What?"

Sariel shook her head angrily. "I should never have allowed... This is my fault. If I had been paying attention, none of this would have happened."

"What's really going on here?"

"You and Gillian left Caitlin behind because you became incredibly and undeniably aroused, am I right? You felt an uncontrollable urge to fornicate?"

Riley nodded.

"And this urge developed after Caitlin's date touched you?"

Riley almost said no, but then she thought back to the sequence of events. She'd desired Gillian from the moment they met, and she'd felt a low burning as soon as she saw Gillian's outfit. But she didn't become uncontrollably horny until after she and Al shook hands. "Yeah. I guess that's right."

"Her name is not Alyssa Graham. It's Gremory. She's a succubus."

Riley stepped closer to Sariel, away from the hole. "And what does that mean to Priest?"

"Gremory is powerful. She feeds off lust and love, desire and sexuality. You and Gillian making love probably fed her enough to make her extremely powerful. She used the two of you like a battery. Now that she has Caitlin, she's going to focus all of that energy on her."

"Because Priest is a virgin."

"She's a *maiden*," Sariel corrected. "Her sexuality remains untapped. You've heard of virgin sacrifices. If she succeeds, Caitlin will be killed and Gremory will be nigh unstoppable for a time."

"How long of a time?"

"It doesn't matter."

"Considering I'm the protector of this city~"

"I mean that it's so far beyond the human life span that it won't be your concern."

Riley looked at the hole. "I'm going to stop her before that happens. Are you coming?" She didn't wait for an answer. There was a set of wooden stairs leading down, and Riley had to duck down to fit into the tunnel. She had just started wishing for a flashlight when Sariel joined her in the darkness. The glow from her wings intensified and filled the space until Riley could see the tool marks on the curved dirt walls to either side of the stairs.

"Once we're in the Underground, I may be able to track Gremory's presence and find where she has taken Priest."

"May be able?"

"I have to find the trail in order to follow it. As I understand it, the Underground is quite vast."

They reached the bottom, where someone had laid down planks of wood to serve as sidewalks. They were standing in front of a blank-faced storefront with obvious fire damage. Riley recalled the last time she had been in the Underground; it seemed like every criminal and demon in the joint knew she was there the moment she set foot on the subterranean surface.

"Gremory. Alyssa Graham. Whatever you're calling yourself. We're here and we're not going anywhere until we get our friend. So come and get us."

Sariel was glaring at her. "Why did you do that?"

"You want to search this entire place and hope we get lucky, or do you want to bring the mountain to Mohammed?"

Sariel started to respond but was suddenly thrown backward.

The light from her wings dimmed and Riley was forced to rely on the dim light of the lanterns hanging at random intervals along the "street". She brought up her gun as Gremory appeared, her date clothes replaced by a dark red gown. Riley brought the gun up even as she ran her eyes down Gremory's body. She fought an urgent desire to drop to her knees and offer to lick the demon's high heels. Her skin was several degrees more pale than it had been at dinner, and her widow's peak was more pronounced. Her eyes were black with a red tint, and she pulled her lips back over pointed teeth when she saw who her prey was.

"You interrupted my dinner."

"Well, I guess we're even. I was looking forward to trying that place out." She ignored the sweat currently beading on her forehead and focused on holding her weapon steady. "Where's Priest?"

Gremory hissed and closed her eyes. "Mm. Do you know how long I have waited for a virgin? I nearly lost hope. I nearly began staking out high school chess clubs. But then fate dropped a former angel in my lap. Pristine, untouched..."

"So I guess masturbation doesn't count." Riley licked her lips as the comment made her imagine Priest touching herself. She forced the thought out of her head and replaced it with Gillian's face. Gillian in bed, eyelids heavy, smiling after they made love. The image gave her the strength to push through whatever Gremory was sending out. "So how do you want to play this? A big battle?"

In the corridors branching out to either side, howls began to echo like dogs responding to a passing siren. Riley ignored it.

"No. I'm hungering for a maiden. You... well, you haven't qualified for a good many years, have you, Detective Parra?"

Riley recoiled as her mind was suddenly filled with the image of every person she'd ever slept with, shuffled like a deck of cards. Her gun was knocked aside and Gremory grabbed Riley's throat. She lifted Riley off the ground, carrying her almost effortlessly to the ruined store. She hit hard enough to force the air from her lungs and she grabbed Gremory's arm with both hands to try and loosen her hold.

"Maybe I'll fuck you anyway... an aperitif for my grand feast." She leaned in and kissed Riley's lips. Her breath was nauseating, and the feel of her mouth was like kissing a corpse. Riley was utterly sickened by the contact, gasping when Gremory pulled away and smiled. "Good. Fight. I like that."

"You wanna know what my plan was?"

Gremory laughed. "It's a little late to worry about rescue now, Detective Parra."

"Oh, I wouldn't be so sure about that. You forgot about my angel after you knocked her down." Gremory twisted at the waist, her free hand up to ward off an attack that didn't come. The area behind her was empty; Sariel had vanished. She snarled and faced Riley again. "What are you doing?"

"I'm staying still." She turned her head and spit the taste of Gremory's kiss out of her mouth. "Last time I was here, my angel told me to keep moving. Demons are thick down here, and they can sense me. So the absolute worst thing I could do in the Underground is stay in the same spot."

"You..."

"I think you're about to lose your exclusive rights to killing me."

Gremory dropped her and spun around as a trio of demons appeared at the mouth of the tunnel. "Riley Parra!" One of them lunged forward and grabbed Gremory's outstretched arm. "She's mine!" He opened his mouth wider than any human being could have and sank his pointed teeth into Gremory's flesh. The second demon jumped into the air, brushing the vaulted roof of the Underground, and slammed into Gremory. His weight knocked her and the biter to the ground while the third joined the fray with flashing claws and gnashing teeth.

Riley ran to the stairs, scrambling up as more demons flooded into the clearing. The majority were focused on Gremory, fighting for their right to a prize that was currently making her escape. But a few came after her, and Riley was forced to turn and ascend the stairs backwards as she fought them off. Her bullets wouldn't kill them, but demons in human form still adhered to the laws of physics. A bullet to the head would tilt their balance and send them tumbling, while crushing the butt of her gun against a hand would make the fingers release their grip. Her pant legs were torn, razor sharp claws drew stinging red lines on the flesh underneath. Riley smashed the heel of her shoe in a demon's face, twisted and dove through the opening into the office of the abandoned warehouse.

She lay face down on the dirty floor, bleeding and trying to catch her breath before she rolled onto her back and aimed her gun at the access point. A demon's head rose over the edge and Riley fired into it. The demon cried out as it fell, and Riley remained on the floor as she shoved the nearest piece of furniture - a desk - over the gaping hole.

She heard claws and fists trying to dislodge the item as she pushed herself up and applied her weight to the next desk. It inched across the floor, groaning the entire way, and then the load became lighter as someone started helping her. She turned and saw Priest, her new dress torn and her hair a mess, standing at the corner and straining against the weight of the desk.

Together they managed to get it into place, and the clawing eventually ceased. They leaned against their makeshift blockade, and Sariel placed her hand atop it. The room hummed with energy and Riley could almost feel the demons falling away down the dark stairs. When she lifted her hand, silence fell on the tiny office.

"You came for me."

Riley blinked at Priest. "Of course I did."

Priest pushed away from the desk and wrapped her arms around Riley. Riley awkwardly returned the hug and patted Priest on the back. "You would've done the same for me. In fact you have. Multiple times."

Sariel said, "That was a stupid plan, Riley. But it worked. When you called Gremory, it was easy for me to find the path she had taken. I followed it back to Priest. We interrupted Gremory in the midst of her preparations. Fortunately that was as far as the demon had gotten. Caitlin is still..."

"Still a virgin." Sariel pointedly looked away and Priest smiled with a mixture of embarrassment and excitement. "We both did a fair amount of... exploring, but we never crossed that final line. After this experience, I may just decide that it's all for the best."

Riley put a hand on Priest's shoulder. "I don't know. I hardly remember being a virgin, so how great could it be?"

Priest looked at the blocked Underground entrance. "What now?"

"Now we get out of here." Sariel went to the door and motioned for Riley and Priest to follow her. Riley thought about the cabbie's warning and hoped Sariel had a plan. They left the warehouse and saw a checker cab waiting outside the fence with the engine running, the headlights surprisingly bright against the darkness. Riley put an arm around Priest's shoulders to support her as they crossed the cracked parking lot of the warehouse.

"You don't have to worry, Riley. I've been educated in the evils of intercourse. After tonight, I don't think I could even think about having sex with anyone."

"Don't count it out yet. This isn't an after-school special, darling." She smiled and followed Sariel to the waiting cab.

Priest wrapped her arms around herself, looking up and down the street while they waited for an answer. "I don't know about this, Riley."

"You don't have to do anything. They may not *want* you to do anything. But I think being here would be better for you than coming home with me and Jill." She nudged Priest's arm. "Sex isn't bad, okay? You're a human now. Humans need sex. It's a biological fact. You don't have to feel ashamed about it, you don't~"

She heard the locks being thrown and turned to face the door as it opened. Kenzie was wearing a T-shirt and shorts, her hair mussed but still combed forward to obscure the scarred part of her face. "One of these days, Rye, I'm going to see you in sunlight. Count on it."

"Sorry about waking you up, Kenzie. How's your head?"

"Recovering." She looked past her at Priest. "Hey, Caitlin. Are you okay?"

Riley said, "Priest had a really rough night. We thought it would help her if she could spend the night with you and Chelsea."

Kenzie looked at Riley and intuited her meaning. "Spend the night like..."

Priest put her hand on Riley's arm. "Riley, we should go."

"No." Kenzie pushed away from the door and took Priest's hand. She ran her thumb over the knuckles. "Chelsea and I have a spare bed. And anything beyond that, we can discuss. If you want to."

Priest sighed. "I'm not sure what I'm sure about."

"We can talk about that, too."

Riley stepped back so Priest could move closer to the door. "I'll call you in the morning. You'll be okay."

"Thank you, Riley." She leaned in and kissed Riley's cheek. "I'm sorry. Apologize to Gillian for me, too."

"There's no need to apologize. Good night, Priest. And Kenzie."

"See you in the morning, Rye."

Riley stepped back as Kenzie put an arm around Priest and led her inside. She waved as the door closed and locked again, and Riley went back to the waiting cab.

The driver looked over his shoulder as she got into the

backseat. "Just you?"

"Yeah, just me." She gave him the address of the restaurant so she could finally retrieve her car before going home, slumped against the seat and watching the city roll by her window.

"I know that look," the cabbie said. "Long day?"

Riley smiled. "Nice and slow day. I earned it. Now I'm going to go home, crawl into bed with my girlfriend, and fall asleep with her in my arms."

"That's the life, right there."

Riley smiled. "You don't have to tell me."

Gremory was torn, slashed, tattered. She was covered with blood, her own and not, and her clothing had been shredded. Her ear had been missing when she first rose from the melee and she kept reaching up to touch the empty space. She hated the restraints of a human host, the frailty, the recovery time required when it became damaged. The angels had the right idea. The manufacturing of bodies that could heal automatically. Demons tried to do the same, but their bodies always ended up being hideous and misshapen.

She pushed the door open without unlocking it, breaking the strike plate. The door bounced off the wall and hit her arm as she entered the apartment, dragging her left foot behind her. The lights were off except for one lamp in the living room.

"Where are you?"

Gail Finney rose from the couch and gasped at the sight. "Alyssa?" She had changed into her pajamas and she ran to her lover. She cupped Gremory's face, blood smearing her palms. "Did Riley do this to you? The bitch. I'll kill her."

"No. Our plan didn't work. We need a new one." She winced as her human body, the shell, sent another wave of pain through her. "But I'll need to recover."

"What can I do?"

Gremory cupped the back of Gail's head and pulled her forward, kissing her hard. Gail sagged forward and Gremory guided her to the floor. Gremory's dark fingernails turned into talons, and she ran it down the front of Gail's pajamas. The clothes were torn, the two halves falling apart to reveal the naked flesh underneath. Gremory was panting, and Gail was almost whimpering with each exhale. Gremory began tearing her clothing off as she positioned herself between Gail's legs.

"It's going to be a very long night."

Gail whimpered as Gremory began to use her.

Gillian was in a nightgown. Riley put on a tank top and shorts, trying and failing to climb into bed without disturbing her partner. Gillian murmured and Riley put a calming hand on her shoulder. "Don't wake up... I'm just going to spoon you."

"Mm. Are you okay?"

"I'll be fine." She had tended to her leg wounds in the bathroom, wrapping them in gauze. She hoped that if Gillian felt them, she would assume they were just socks. "You?"

"Still a little sore. Nicely sore. But please don't touch me."

"I'll try very hard." She kissed Gillian's ear, exhausted and grateful that they could just sleep. She pressed herself against Gillian, their bodies fitting together perfectly under the blankets. She rested one hand on Gillian's stomach and stuck the other under her pillow.

They were both falling asleep when Riley kissed the back of Gillian's neck and whispered, "Good night, little princess."

Gillian kept her eyes closed, but she giggled and rubbed Riley's arm. "My queen, my queen."

Riley laughed and buried her face in Gillian's hair, breathing deeply as finally slipped into sleep.

THAT OLD FAMILIAR STING

LESSONS WERE hard-won in No Man's Land and only became lessons if you lived until the next time.

The little girl, slender but tall for her age, was desperately trying to turn "never steal from someone with more friends than you" from a bad mistake into a life lesson. She used a trash can to get enough height to grab the highest point of the chain link fence, but her weight made it sag too much for her to climb. She attempted it anyway, and the brackets holding up the top part of the fence pulled from the brick wall in a shower of brick dust.

She was forced to let go and hit her knees, scrambling up just as the three-card monte players stormed the mouth of the alley.

There were three of them; the dealer, the lookout and the plant. All of them were older than her, all of them heavier than her, and all of them had weapons. The girl considered her options and took the folded money from the pocket of her hoodie. "Fine, you want the money so bad? Here, take it."

"Oh, it ain't about money anymore." The dealer moved closer. "We're gonna use you to teach the entire street a lesson. A lesson 'bout what happens when you try and steal from us." He began to unfasten his belt.

"Aw, come on. If I'm not scared of your switchblade, I'm not gonna be scared of *that* little thing."

"Tommy, hold 'er down. We'll show her what to be scared of."

The lookout stepped around the dealer, advancing toward the girl. She retreated from him, subtly trying to find another exit route. The fence was still sagging and, with a little bit of a running start, she could probably get over it. These numbskulls were nowhere near nimble enough to follow her. She considered running for it when the lookout, Tommy, suddenly lunged at her. She tried to get a way, but he stepped forward and slipped his arm under hers. He reached around her back, grabbed the other arm, and twisted until she had both arms pinned against his chest.

"Get your hands off of me!"

"Ain't the hands you need to be worried about." The dealer had his jeans open now and the girl could see the material of his briefs. Her bravado faded slightly and she bucked against Tommy. "Just hold still and it'll be over quick. Maybe."

From the mouth of the alley, one of the kids made a 'huh-huh-huh' laughing sound. He twisted to make sure no one was going to interrupt them at just the right time for a chunk of brick to bounce off the front of his face. His nose spouted blood, and when he dropped to one knee, he spit out two teeth. "Thon of a bith! Rick!"

The dealer turned just as the squat, redheaded boy raced into the alley. He had a baseball bat in his left hand, swinging it like a propeller as his sneakers pounded the pavement. "Babe Ruth, Mickey Mantle, Hank Aaron, Jackie Robinson!" His shouts echoed off the walls of the alley as he swung the bat up from the ground and planted it between the dealer's legs.

The dealer howled in pain and both hands went to his groin. The new arrival took the bat and thrust it forward like a battering ram, slamming the blunt head into the center of the dealer's chest. He folded in on himself and tumbled like a felled tree.

The lookout had been watching with dumb shock, but he finally released the girl's arms. He pushed her out of the way to get to the bat boy, and the girl stuck out her leg. The lookout tripped over it, and the boy swung his bat and hit the lookout in the chin. His trajectory changed, rapidly and completely, and he crumpled limply on a pile of black trash bags.

The boy looked at his bat, frowned at the blood on it, and then looked at the girl. "You okay? Can you run?"

"It's what I'm best at."

The boy held out his hand and the girl took it. They ran together, not taking the risk to look back until they were several blocks and a few jumped fences away from the aching card cheats. The boy sagged against the wall, hands on his thighs and bat lying at his feet. He exhaled and pushed his red bangs out of his face. "Phew. That was a rush."

The girl took the card players' money out of her pocket. She thought about counting it and then just held it all out. "Here. Take it."

"I don't want your money."

"I would'a given it to them to get away. Here. Take it. You earned it."

The kid sniffled, rubbed his nose and the sleeve of his jacket, and took the money. He peeled off two tens and handed the rest back. "That's all I really need. You keep the rest. Maybe it'll keep ya from robbing anyone else tonight."

The girl took the money back. "Thanks."

He waved it off, pushed away from the wall, and picked up his bat.

"If you want to wash that off, I know a place. They have a faucet on the back wall, and you can use as much as you want."

"Can I use it to take a bath?"

The girl shrugged.

"Show me?"

"Sure."

They started walking together, a few feet between them as they left the alley. The boy swung the bat by his side, letting it swing like a pendulum in time with their steps.

"I'm Eddie Cashion." The girl looked at him and he smiled. "You don't gotta tell me your name if you don't want."

The girl considered staying quiet for a moment, but she couldn't stop thinking about what he had prevented. The least she could do was tell him her name. "Riley Parra."

He laughed. "That's a boy's name."

She blushed furiously.

"I'll call you Parra."

"Whatever."

Riley stuck her hands in the back pockets of her torn jeans, leading Eddie to the restaurant with a working faucet where he could wash his bat and take a bath.

Present Day

Riley crouched against the brick wall of the bar, hands clasped between her knees in an effort to keep her fingers warm. There was a crack, barely noticeable, where the heat from inside was filtering out. It was a small window of warmth but it was enough to make her stake it out until her legs fell asleep. People coming out of the bar didn't notice her and walked to their cars oblivious to her presence. She brought her hands up and blew into her fists, looking up and down the alley before she decided she had to get moving.

She walked to the end of the alley and walked north. She was halfway to the stairs leading up to the el station when she became aware of someone walking a few steps behind her. She turned her head just a fraction and looked into the reflection off a parked car's window. A woman was walking down the sidewalk toward her. Riley moved toward the latticework of the el tracks, letting the thick supports block the wind however briefly.

The pedestrian who had been following her stopped, looked toward the street, and then faced Riley fully. The woman raised her voice to be heard without moving closer. "Do you have enough money for a coffee?"

Riley shrugged and shook her head. "I'm good. I'm fine. I'm not panhandling."

"It's very cold tonight. I'd hate to think about you freezing to death out here. And it's not panhandling if I buy the coffee for you, right?" The woman gestured down the street. "There's a diner right over there. Come with me and get some coffee. You can warm up a little bit at least."

Riley shuffled her feet, hugging herself as she looked toward the diner. It *did* look very inviting.

"Just a coffee."

"Yeah."

Riley left the shelter of the el tracks and started walking. The woman started walking as well, the two of them separated by a few feet that Riley slowly and subtly closed. She moved her hand and brushed the back of her hand against the other woman's. The woman smiled and bumped her back, still scanning the street as she tugged on the lapels of her coat and held them together with her free hand.

"That was good," Riley whispered. "How many homeless women do you generally pick up in a week?"

Gillian sighed. "Oh, who keeps count?"

Riley smiled and let Gillian lead the way into the diner. The warmth was like a revelation, and Riley paused in the doorway to let it wash over her before continuing on. She and Gillian took seats at the counter, as far away from the door as possible to avoid the gusts of other customers entering. Riley unfastened her coat and let it hang open so that she could capture some heat inside when she buttoned it again. Her hair was down and unwashed, and she was wearing a pair of Gillian's old glasses to further obscure her familiar face. She took off the glasses and set them on the table so her vision wouldn't be hindered when she looked at Gillian.

Gillian put her hand on top of Riley's and squeezed it through the glove. "You are *freezing*."

"I've had worse nights." The waitress made her way over and Riley ordered coffee for the both of them.

"That was a giveaway," Gillian said. "You shouldn't know how I take my coffee."

"Sorry. Force of habit. Wanda is one of ours, though. I'm more careful in public."

"Good." Gillian tugged her necklace out from under her shirt and idly toyed with it. Riley's engagement ring hung from the chain, kept there for safe-keeping until Riley was out of No Man's Land.

Riley stared at the ring, admiring how it looked around Gillian's neck, and dropped her hand under the counter. She rubbed Gillian's thigh. "Missed you."

"You know when I went to Georgia, and you chose to sleep in the on-call room at the station instead of going home to an empty bed?" Riley nodded. "I know how you feel now. The first two days I didn't get any sleep at all, so I finally just moved to the couch."

"I take it Priest is still spending her nights with Kenzie and Priest?"

Gillian shook her head. "No, she came home. We just hook up to keep my mind off missing you." Riley squeezed Gillian's thigh playfully. "Do you have any idea how much longer this will be?"

"It's hard to guess. If I don't find something, Briggs has okayed the operation lasting one more week, so maybe that long." Gillian whimpered. "I know."

Riley had always been ambivalent about undercover work, but it was different now that she had someone to come home to. The undercover assignment was Briggs' idea, a way to keep Riley busy without feeding her to the wolves after Gail Finney's article. Three homeless people had been found murdered in the past two weeks, and the commissioner wanted it stopped. Riley volunteered, sick of being deskbound or digging through cold case files just to fill her days. She hadn't realized at the time that her commitment would require separation from Gillian for this long. She swung her leg out so that their knees bumped.

"You want to spend the night in a shelter with me? That could be my cover. I could be a prostitute to get my food."

Gillian laughed. "Role play? That's actually kind of appealing. But no. You should focus on your work."

"Speaking of work, how is Priest doing?"

"She and Booker are actually a decent team. I don't think Priest likes taking the lead, but she's managing it well. I think she'll be happier than I am when you come back."

"Has she talked to you about Kenzie and Chelsea?"

Gillian shook her head. "She smiles and blushes whenever I bring them up. I assume that's a good sign." The bell over the door rang as another customer entered and Gillian reluctantly turned so that Riley's hand fell off her thigh. She took out her pocketbook and placed ten dollars on the counter. "Buy yourself something hot to eat, too. Promise me."

"I promise. Thank you, ma'am. God bless you."

Gillian looked toward the other customer, obviously debating whether she could get away with a goodbye kiss. She slid off the stool and rested her hand on Riley's shoulder.

"I hope you find someplace safe to stay tonight." She leaned in and kissed Riley's cheek, letting her lips linger just a fraction longer than necessary.

"Thank you. And thank you for the meal."

Gillian nodded, waved goodbye to the waitress, and hurried out of the diner before she could give herself away by crying. Riley watched her go and then watched the steam rise from her coffee until it was cool enough to drink. When the waitress returned, Riley used Gillian's money to buy a burger and fries.

She ate slowly, not eager to return to the cold night. Briggs had offered her backup, cops who would trail her and be ready at a moment's notice. As comforting as that would have been, Riley knew No Man's Land didn't work that way. Help was either right beside you or completely useless. Not to mention the fact that a tail would be almost immediately discovered and give away her true identity.

She wasn't prepared for the mental regression being all by

herself would cause. She felt sixteen again, completely cut off and without options. She'd been flashing back to moments she hadn't thought about in years. She remembered learning to pick pockets with just her index and middle finger so that her thumb wouldn't brush the mark's side. It was like riding a bike. Once she learned how to evade and disappear, she had never forgotten the basics.

When the food and coffee were both gone, Riley put her gloves back on and reluctantly replaced Gillian's eyeglasses. "My girlfriend is freaking blind," she muttered, blinking behind the thick lenses before pushing them down her nose so she could look over the frames. She waved goodbye to Wanda and left the warmth of the diner for the blowing cold night.

It was three blocks to the shelter that she'd chosen for that night. She turned up the collar of her pea coat and started walking. The wind was blowing across the waterfront, adding an extra bite to the chill as it buffeted her. She crossed the mouth of an alley just as someone cried out for help. The word was cut off, a strangled "Hel-" that immediately put Riley on edge. Her mind snapped into a horrible fiction about Gillian taking a shortcut to the el and being grabbed by muggers or worse.

Riley ran down the alley, not caring about her cover, suddenly certain that the woman in danger was in fact Gillian. She saw vague, dark shapes struggling at the far side of the dead end alley. Two men were grunting, and the woman's voice had faded to muted whimpers. Riley hit one of the men in the back at full speed, throwing her weight against him. He was unbalanced and easily toppled, and Riley hit the ground with one knee before spinning to face him.

The man swung at her. It was too dark in the alley to determine if he was armed, so Riley assumed he was. She stepped back out of his reach. He was forced to shift his weight, and Riley dropped and lunged at him. She hit him in the stomach and knocked the wind out of him as they both fell backward.

Riley was grabbed from behind. "You picked the wrong night to play hero, asshole. This is a private party." He was much stronger than Riley and managed to toss her aside like she was a pile of laundry. "Puny little punk. C'mon. Let's take the bitch somewhere more private."

She realized they thought she was a man, so she stayed quiet as she got back to her feet. She swung out and slapped the back of the first man's jacket. He sighed angrily and spun on her. Riley punched him in the face before he could get his hands up and he rocked back on his feet.

"Son of a bitch!"

Riley lifted her leg, twisted, and brought her foot down on the back of the first man's knee. He went down and Riley kicked downward. His knee cracked against the pavement and he cried out in pain as Riley focused on his friend. His roundhouse punch caught her on the chin and knocked her back and she sprawled against the brick wall.

"I would've let you walk away, buddy." He moved closer, the distinctive sound of a switchblade coming from the vicinity of his hand. Riley could smell the rotten stink of his breath as he loomed forward.

Riley swung her knee up into the knife-man's crotch. As he howled, Riley palmed the front of his skull like a basketball and shoved it backward. He tripped over his own feet as he went down, hitting his now-crippled partner. Riley stepped over them and found the woman they had been assaulting. "It's okay," she whispered. "Come with me."

"You're dead, asshole..."

From the strain in his voice, Riley knew it was the man she had kicked. Her eyes had adjusted to the darkness enough that she could see the vague outlines of their bodies. She reached into the pocket of her coat and palmed a small black box. She squeezed the hand of the woman she'd rescued.

"Close your eyes," she muttered. Aloud, she said, "Hey, asshole. Want to see something neat?" She closed her own eyes and turned on her flashlight. She'd aimed it right at the attempted rapist's head, and both men howled as their eyes were burned by the sudden brightness. Riley tightened her grip on the woman's hand and pulled her forward as they ran from the alley.

They only stopped running when they were in a well-lit portion of a neighboring block. Riley stopped and put a hand on the woman's shoulder while she caught her breath. "It's okay. You're fine now. Are you hurt?"

Fortunately the woman seemed to have made it through the ordeal unscathed. She was shaking, and several buttons were missing from her coat. She tucked the loose strands of hair behind her ears and shook her head. "No, I'm... th-they didn't get that... f-far. You shouldn't have done that."

"I thought you were my girlfriend. Even though you weren't,

I'm sure there's someone who would have wanted me to step in."

"Don't be so sure." The woman took a shuddering breath and looked around to determine where they were. "Will you walk with me to Taft Street?"

"Sure. I'm going that direction anyway."

"I'm Anita."

Riley held out her hand and gave her cover name. "RJ."

Anita shook Riley's hand, pulled the front of her coat together, and led the way down the street. As they walked, Riley kept an eye out for pursuers. She doubted the men who attacked Anita would be up for a chase given their condition, but they were far from the only two vultures in No Man's Land that night.

"You know, you really shouldn't be out by yourself at night."

"Not a lot of options. I need to find a second job, and I can't exactly take time off from the first to interview. I thought I could take care of one and get home before the beasts came out to play. I'm just glad you were there."

Taft Street was a row of tenements all crowded together to make the most of available space. One building was just a shell, all that remained after a fire, and there had been no attempt to repair it. They reached the ornate stone steps of Anita's building and she turned to Riley. "You can stay with us tonight if you don't have anywhere else. It's not much, but it's probably better than a shelter." She paused and then winced. "Well, at least it won't be as crowded as a shelter."

Riley knew that anyone who was really in her position would take the invitation, but she needed to be at the shelter to keep an eye out. She debated a flat refusal and a compromise, and settled on the latter. "I'd love a cup of coffee, just to warm up and stay awake. But after that, I should go."

"Cup of coffee. Least I can do." She smiled and motioned for Riley to follow her upstairs.

The walls of the lobby were covered with several layers of graffiti. Their footsteps sounded hollow as they headed upstairs, Anita's hand resting lightly on the railing as she led the way up. On the third floor, she produced a key and unlocked her apartment.

"Here we go. Home sweet home, for the time being." She invited Riley inside with the wave of a hand. The main space of the apartment was a living room. Anita and her partner had attempted to form a bedroom by putting up a three-framed privacy screen. Riley saw the foot of an unmade bed beyond the screen. The couch was only a few steps inside the front door and was covered by laundry in various stages of folding. Anita nervously swept a hand through her hair. "Sorry about the mess. It's not really, I mean..."

"It's fine."

"I'll get you the coffee. Ed? We have a guest..."

Riley heard movement at the back of the apartment. A bare-chested man came around the privacy screen in a pair of ill-fitting jeans. He was tall and lean, his head shaved, and he looked at Anita before noticing the stranger standing in the doorway. He froze briefly, obviously debating whether he should retreat to put on a shirt or act like it was no big deal. He settled on the second option and nodded to her. "Hey."

Riley frowned and took off her glasses. His face was thinner and she'd never seen him bald, but there was little doubt about those eyes. "Eddie?"

Anita paused in the entrance of the kitchen. "Oh. Do you two know each other?"

He kept looking at Riley until realization dawned on him. "Riley?"

She stepped around the couch and Eddie scooped her up in his arms. She was only a little smaller than him now, but he still managed to get her feet off the floor. He crushed her briefly with his hug before he released her. His eyes were wide with shock and disbelief as he stepped back. "Where the hell did you come from?"

"I ran into Anita outside. She offered me coffee."

Anita cleared her throat and Riley realized that she was embracing Anita's half-naked partner. She stepped back and nervously turned around. "Sorry about that. Uh, we... knew each other. A really long time ago."

"Lifetime ago." He furrowed his brow. "I thought you got out of No Man's Land a long time ago, Riley."

"It's a long story. Complicated."

Anita said, "You can tell us over coffee. How do you take it?"

"You know, I really... should be going."

"Where are you staying these days?"

Riley knew how he'd react, but she was too thrown to come up with a lie. "The, uh, Women's Shelter on Morton Ave."

"A shelter?" She could see the invitation to stay forming on his lips and she started shaking her head. "Come on, Riley. We have a couch."

"It's fine. I want to stay there."

Eddie didn't seem convinced, but he wasn't willing to fight. "At least stay long enough that we can catch up."

"That I can promise," Riley said.

He smiled and crossed the room to Anita. He looked down at her coat and reached out to touch the spot where the buttons had been torn away. "What...?"

"It's nothing. I'm fine."

Eddie turned and looked at Riley. "Just ran into each other outside?"

Riley cleared her throat. "More or less."

Anita had to lift herself up on her toes to kiss Eddie's cheek. "It's fine. Everything is fine. Go put on a shirt and we'll get to know each other better over coffee. Okay?"

Eddie nodded and left the living room. Riley heard him rummaging in the back room and moved closer to Anita so she could speak quietly. "I'm gay, and I'm in a committed relationship. Besides, Eddie and I were never... I just don't want you to worry that I'm~"

"Thank God. I mean, I wasn't... I didn't think you would try... but..."

Riley went past Anita into the kitchen. "Where do you keep your coffee pot?"

"Let me show you."

Riley was only dimly aware of the conversation over coffee. She absorbed the information provided as if through osmosis: Anita and Eddie had met almost fifteen years earlier, not long after Riley made her escape from No Man's Land in the back of Christine Lee's cruiser. They dated off and on before they ended up moving in together because Anita lost her apartment, and they had stayed together long enough to become common-law husband and wife.

The main portion of Riley's mind was filled with renewed memories. The scrape of pavement on her belly as she slipped under a chain link fence. Sitting on the roof of an apartment building and separating a bag of jelly beans into two equal piles. She smiled and remembered about arguments over whether the black ones were disgusting or the best of the bunch. The taste of blood and tears on her lips, and someone sitting beside her and telling her it would be okay.

Somehow she made it through her cup of coffee and insisted she had to be on her way. She rinsed out their cups in the tiny sink, since Anita had made the coffee, and began bundling herself up for the walk.

"Let me walk you to the shelter," Eddie said. "It's the least I can do. It's not exactly a safe neighborhood."

Riley wanted to refuse him, but that wasn't something she had ever been good at. "Okay. If Anita doesn't mind..."

"Hey, I saw her moves. She'll be protecting *you*." She kissed Eddie goodbye and told him she'd be waiting up for him. Eddie put on his coat and a knit cap before escorting Riley outside. He waited until he heard Anita turn all the locks before he started down the stairs. They were both silent until they were outside the building and standing together on the sidewalk.

Eddie put his hands in his pockets. "Answers."

Riley shook her head. "Too long."

He hunched his shoulders against the cold and looked down the street. "You okay?"

"Perfect." Riley nodded. "I'm not lying to you. I wouldn't trade my life now for anything. I'm happy. I have someone I'm crazy about who, for some reason, feels the same way about me."

"Sure?"

"Positive."

They started walking, their elbows bumping in a companionable way. Eddie kept his head down, watching their feet on the cracked pavement.

"Do you still see Farrah?"

Eddie laughed and shook his head. "No. I haven't seen her around in a long time. I think she finally wised up and moved somewhere more lucrative. That's sorta what I thought you did."

Riley buried her hands in the pockets of her coat, giving off body language that the question was off-limits.

"Can't go into it?"

"I'm sorry, Eddie. The specifics are... sensitive. I can't talk about it. Not even with you."

"All right. How about I tell you what I know?" She nodded. "You left without saying goodbye to me when you were sixteen. Went back to school, started hanging out with a cop. Then one day you were just... not there anymore. I never saw you on the streets or at the usual hangouts. I thought you'd gone back home, but I broke into your Dad's apartment and you weren't there. So I figured you'd gotten out.

"Then I started hearing stories about this cop who actually

patrolled in No Man's Land. She took down the bad guys. A cop who actually cared about the people down here. A couple of people had heard her name. You never forgot about us."

Riley shook her head. "I never really got out of here. No Man's Land is a part of me no matter where I go."

Eddie nodded. "And now here you are, and you're giving up a nice warm apartment so you can spend the night in a women's shelter. That only makes sense one way. You're going to the shelter 'cause you have to. That's where you need to be tonight or else someone's gonna get hurt."

She smiled and shook her head. "You always were the better detective, ironically."

"Nah. I can just read you like a book." Eddie put a hand on her arm to stop her from walking on. "Is there anything I can do to help?"

"No. But I'm going to be in No Man's Land for a couple more days. I'd like it if you, me and Anita could meet up again. Maybe we could grab some dinner."

"I'd like that. Just... promise me you have someone to take care of you. You act tough, and you *are* one of the toughest people I've ever met. But you don't do well on your own."

Riley smiled. "Yeah. I have some angels on my shoulder. I'm... getting married."

Eddie's eyes widened. "Who the hell would marry you?"

Riley slugged him in the shoulder.

"Ow. I mean, who is the lucky guy?"

"The lucky gal is named Gillian."

"Oh. So that wasn't a phase, huh?" He winked. "Good to know it wasn't just me."

Riley smiled and continued walking. Eddie trailed behind her. "Trust me, Eddie, if any guy had any shot at all, it would have been you. And I did feel bad that I never came back to get you out of here."

He snorted. "Yeah. No, it's good you didn't. Some people can make it in the real world, but I'm not one of them. And if I hadn't been here, who would 'Nita have? I belong here in No Man's Land with her. But I'm glad you're doing well. I thought about you a lot and I really hoped that you were the cop everyone was talking about."

"Do you ever watch the news?"

"Hell no. It's depressing enough looking out the window."

"I've kind of been on it a lot lately. I investigated a serial killer last year."

Eddie smiled. "Catch him?"

"Yeah."

"That's my girl. Nice to see you don't need my help anymore."

They reached Morton Avenue, and Riley saw that the lights over the front door were still burning. "Looks like we made it. Thanks for the escort."

"Old habit." Riley was amused by how he echoed her own words to Gillian earlier. "Whatever you're doing here, I know it's important. I may not be a kid anymore, but I'm willing to lend a hand if it comes to that."

"I'll keep that in mind, Eddie." She extended her hand and he took it, squeezing until she squeezed back. Riley clenched her teeth and shifted her thumb, and Eddie grunted and torqued his wrist to apply extra pressure. Riley smiled, a pained rictus, and put her shoulder into it. Eddie finally gasped and let go, and Riley relaxed. "I always could outlast you."

"I hurt you more, you just ignored it better." He rubbed his hand. "That's not always the way to win, Riley."

She nodded. "Thanks, Eddie. I can't tell you how good it was to see you again."

"You too. This was a nice reunion. I'll see you in another twenty years?"

"Better not wait that long." He looked toward the shelter. "You should go before they shut the doors on you."

"Right."

"Hey. The thing with Anita. How bad was it?"

Riley hesitated. She didn't want him to panic unnecessarily, but she also thought he should be aware of the truth. "It was pretty bad. One of them had a knife, and the other one might have had something worse."

Eddie shook his head. "I told her it was too dangerous to go out alone. She's more stubborn than you used to be."

"Hey," Riley snapped. "I'm still more stubborn than anyone you'll ever meet."

Eddie laughed. "I apologize if I offended you, milady. Stay safe tonight."

"Same to you."

She watched him turn and walk back down the street, occasionally lit up by the streetlights he passed under. Riley exhaled and shook her head, trying to free her mind of the memories their reunion had unearthed. She jogged across the street to the shelter. The manager Mary Luttrell was standing in the vestibule with her arms crossed and her lips pursed. She pushed the door open, clutching the neck of her sweater closed as Riley rushed in.

"Cutting it close tonight, RJ."

"I know. I'm sorry."

Mary pulled the door shut and twisted the lock. "It's okay. We would have let you in even if you showed up late. But don't make a habit of it."

Riley went into the main room of the shelter, a basketball court that doubled as a cafeteria and meeting room. The tables were still set up for dinner, but the window to the kitchen was closed. Mary came up behind Riley and touched her shoulder. "Did you eat tonight?"

"Yes, I had a burger. A... a very beautiful woman bought me a hamburger."

"Well, I don't know which one is luckier, the woman or the meal." She smiled and patted Riley's arm. "We have a few rooms open, so you have your pick tonight."

"Okay. Thank you, Mary."

Mary shuffled off to take care of another of her myriad responsibilities while Riley took off her coat and scanned the room. There were a few other women in the room, lingering over their meals or having conversations. A foursome of women in one corner had a deck of cards, and a woman Riley vaguely recognized waved her over.

"Hey, RJ. Up for a little stud before bed?"

Riley took a seat. "Never. But I'll play cards."

That prompted laughter from the others, as the woman with the card began dealing.

The white rotary phone was in the small office next to the kitchen. There was no door, but it offered a bit of privacy if one of the residents wanted to make a call. Riley sat in the overstuffed armchair and twisted the cord around her fingers as she waited for an answer. She was about to give up when the ringing stopped and Gillian spoke after a moment of fumbling. "This is Dr. Hunt. I can be ready in fifteen~"

"Baby, it's me."

"Riley?" She heard bedclothes rustling and closed her eyes to form a mental image of their bedroom. "What's wrong?"

"Nothing's wrong. I just needed to talk. I didn't mean to wake you~"

"Don't be silly. What's wrong?"

Riley rested her head against the wall. "Nothing's wrong. I ran into someone I used to know. Eddie Cashion." She smiled saying his name. "I don't think I've ever mentioned him to you, but he saved my life a long time ago."

"Well, then I owe him a beer."

"Ditto for me. He taught me everything I needed to know to survive in No Man's Land. Without him, I would have died ten times over before Christine finally pulled me out of there. I could tell you a hundred stories about how he saved me."

Gillian said, "Well, how about we start with just one?"

A story came to mind immediately. "The first night I decided I couldn't face going back home, I went to find Eddie. He was the first person I let see me cry. And he didn't try to make it better, he just sat with me. And then when it got dark, he broke into this sporting goods store and stole a sleeping bag. Then we found this brick alcove, and he made a sort of... this nest thing for us. We fell asleep together."

"Was he your first?"

Riley remembered a succession of men in her room, friends of her father, the sound of her father laughing in the other room while strangers pushed down her pajamas.

"Yeah. He was." She cleared her throat. "He didn't want to at first, and I just thought it was what people did. It wasn't great, but I didn't think it could be great. I don't think Eddie liked it either. He never asked me to do it again, anyway."

"Are you sure he's not gay?"

Riley laughed.

"Seriously, babe, you're the Lays potato chip of sex. Can't have just one."

"Jill, you're..." She rubbed her temple. "I'd rather let a killer go free than be away from you for one more night."

"Don't act on those feelings. But the fact that you want to is good to know."

"I'll catch him as soon as I can. And I'll make him pay for taking me away from you."

Gillian laughed. "Good. Be careful, baby."

"I'll be back before you know it."

"Mm. Too late."

Riley closed her eyes and imagined she was in bed with Gillian. "Goodnight, little princess."

"Mm. Goodnight."

Riley reluctantly hung up and freed her hand from the curled wire. She wiped her eyes and put her glasses back on before she left the office. She was startled by a woman standing next to the door, stringy gray hair hanging on either side of her face like unwashed curtains. She furrowed her brow and leaned close, examining Riley closely before she backed up a step.

"Evening."

The woman flinched slightly. "You look strange."

Riley touched her glasses. "Uh, I'm... I'm sorry."

"I don't... think I had my medication today. I need to go lay down."

"Okay," Riley said. "Do you need help finding your bed?"

The woman laughed and patted Riley's arm. "No, no. No, I'll be fine. You'll look right in the morning."

"I sure hope so. Goodnight."

The woman had turned her back and was shuffling toward the rooms. She waved over her shoulder. "Goodnight, Jackie."

Riley almost ignored the woman, but then the name triggered something in the back of her mind. She froze, eyes wide behind her glasses. Mary came out of the kitchen, smiled, and then sensed something was amiss.

"RJ? Is everything all right?"

"That woman who was just standing here..."

"Bess?"

Riley nodded. "Who is she?"

"Oh, she's one of the old guard." Mary sighed. "She's been coming here for as long as I can remember. That was when I was still a teenager, if you can believe that." She chuckled and, when Riley didn't join her, tilted her head to one side. "RJ? Are you all right?"

Riley shook her head. "I think Bess knew my mother."

Mary had a small apartment at the front of the shelter, segregated from the rest of the population by the kitchen and Mary's office. She led Riley through the empty rooms and turned on a lamp so they could sit comfortably and talk without fear of being overheard. Mary settled in an armchair while Riley sat on the overstuffed couch that almost seemed determined to swallow her whole. She scooted forward to perch on the slightly more firm edge of the cushion. "Do you know the woman Bess has me confused for?"

"Oh, yes. I remember her very well. Jackie and Bess were inseparable, and most of our guests left them alone. Bess was never exactly all there and Jackie..." She hesitated and looked at Riley.

"I know my mother had problems. She tried to drown me in the bathtub when I was a baby. That's why she left. Please, anything you can tell me would be wonderful."

Mary toyed with the hem of her sweater. "Jackie could be a very frightening person. Most of the time she was normal and sweet, quiet and funny. She helped in the kitchen when she could, and sometimes she was there to help when women decided they could go back to whoever had been beating them. She would go weeks at a time without an episode. But then when you let your guard down she would snap."

"Snap how?"

"It depended on the night. She once broke every tray in the kitchen by hitting them on the floor. She was screaming the entire time, and she wasn't even slowed down by the pieces of plastic cutting her hands. Sometimes she would attack other women. She was schizophrenic. Pills didn't help, not that we could convince her to see a doctor for a prescription. We slipped her some pills we took from junkies, but they didn't do anything but make her sleepy. I think Bess was less frightened of her because she could forget the outbursts. Jackie was just her friend."

Riley nodded. "How long was she here?"

"Off and on for a few years. There would be a few weeks when she wouldn't be around and then she'd show up out of the blue. I think she could sense when it was going to be a bad night and she tried to avoid other people." She ran her hand through her white hair and looked over her shoulder as if she could see through walls. "Then she just disappeared."

Riley closed her eyes as the memories of that night washed over her again.

A huddled mass of dirty laundry in the alley. The air so cold that everything looked blue, as if even light had iced over. Her shoulders hunched as she stepped over the outstretched legs. She could still hear...

"Help..."

Riley had stepped to one side, out of reach in case the woman tried to grab her. "There's a shelter about two blocks to the east. They'll take care of you."

An angel had finally revealed what Riley had truly done that night. She'd turned her back on her own mother, left her to freeze to death in a filthy alley.

"Are you all right?"

Riley looked up and saw Mary watching her. "I could have helped her. My mother. I was... there. She was following me the night she died. She wanted to be sure I was safe, even though she was sick."

"You've been on the streets that long? I'm surprised I never saw you before this week."

Riley shook her head. "I'm not... exactly who you think I am. I'm a police detective. I'm here undercover because three homeless people have been found dead in the past few weeks. They want me here to look for anything suspicious and maybe put a stop to it."

Mary's eyes widened while Riley spoke, and she leaned back in her chair. "My God. The police have actually arrived. I stopped calling you folks about twenty years ago."

"Yeah. The one problem No Man's Land doesn't have is an excess of police. But I'm trying to change that."

Mary shook her head in disbelief. "Well. Well..."

"Do you think it would be possible to speak with Mary?"

"Speak with her? That would be possible. But if you're hoping for a coherent conversation, I'm afraid you'll be disappointed."

Riley looked down at her hands. "I've spent my whole life hearing second-hand lies about my mother. If Bess was her friend, I want to hear what she has to say."

Mary hesitated and then made a 'why not' gesture with one hand. "I suppose it couldn't hurt. Bess doesn't have a lot of people willing to talk to her since Jackie left. Sometimes it's strange, even after all these years, to look out there and see Bess sitting by herself. I'll introduce you so that Bess won't think you're a social worker."

"Thank you. And for now, if we could keep who I really am between the two of us..."

"Of course, of course. I wouldn't want to dissuade the police from coming down here. Please." She stood up and motioned for Riley to lead the way out.

The women Riley had played cards with were gone, and most of the lights had been turned out as guests went to bed. Bess was sitting alone at a table with a bulwark of knitted material in front of her. She was emptying out a large handbag, muttering to herself as she placed several items on the table only to put them back in the bag. She was oblivious to Riley and Mary's approach until Mary spoke.

"Bess?" The woman grabbed her things, protecting them with her hands as she looked up at the interlopers. "It's all right. This woman would just like to talk with you for a minute. Is that okay?"

Bess twisted to see who Mary meant, and her face lit up. "Jackie! Sit, sit. I haven't seen you in so long! You look so young!"

"Yeah, I suppose I do. Thanks, Mary."

"Call me if you need anything else, RJ."

Riley watched Mary go and then stepped over the bench seat of the table. She sat down and smiled at Bess. "I'm sorry, but I'm not who you think I am. I'm not Jackie."

"Ahh." Bess waved her hand dismissively and went back to unloading her purse.

"Do you remember Riley?"

Bess didn't look up. "Your little girl?"

Riley hadn't known what to expect, but the knowledge her mother had spoken about her was a surprise. She pushed down the emotion and forced herself to focus. "Yeah, my girl. Do you remember anything I might have told you about her?"

"You said she was very important. And you said that you didn't know if leaving was the right thing to do to save her because it left her with *that man*." She finally looked up. "Did something happen to your little girl?"

"No. She's doing just fine." Riley blinked back tears. "Tell me something about *me*."

"You're Jackie."

"That's right."

Bess finally stopped fidgeting with her purse and picked up her knitting needles. "You're very nice to me even though I don't know why. You like to sing sometimes, especially when you're doing a chore. I like when you sing."

Riley smiled at the thought of her mother singing. "Do you know what my favorite song is?"

"Mm-hmm." She hummed a melody as she began to knit. "*Arrorró mi niña, arrorro mi amor...*"

On the second line, Riley began to sing along. "*...arrorro pedazo, de mi corazón, Este niña lindo, que nació de día.*"

Bess smiled. "Yes, that was the song."

Riley closed her eyes. "She used to sing that to me when I was a baby."

"Who did, Jackie?"

"My mother." Riley looked at Bess again. "Thank you for telling me these things, Bess. It really meant a lot to me."

"I don't mind. Tell me something about me now."

Riley glanced over her shoulder to see if Mary was nearby. She reached out and touched Bess' wrist to make her stop knitting, and then squeezed her hand. "You are Jacqueline Parra's best friend in the entire world."

Bess smiled brightly and bent down to kiss the back of Riley's hand. "You're a sweet lady."

"I'm going to let you finish your knitting. I'm going to see if they need any help in the kitchen. Will you be all right out here?"

"Oh, sure, sure."

Riley smiled and stood up, leaving Bess to whatever massive object she was creating. Mary was standing in the door to the kitchen and she brightened with hope when she saw Riley. "RJ. There's something you need to see."

"What's wrong?"

"There's a man lurking outside. A lot of women are here because it's not safe to go home, and I just... I thought with what you said about the..." She lowered her voice to a whisper. "...the murders."

"Right. Where is he?"

"He's out in the alley."

Riley tried not to get her hopes up. There was a chance it was just Eddie coming back to make sure she was okay. She zipped up her coat as she followed Mary down the hall to the back door that led out into the alley. The thick chain that usually held the door shut had been removed, so Riley leaned on the push bar and stepped out into the freezing wind. She was forced to squint against the crystals of sleet that pelted her face like little needles as she searched around the black shapes of trash cans for the lurker. The alley leading to the street was empty, and Riley looked toward the dead end of the fence. "I think he's~"

Something hit Riley hard from behind, knocking her off her feet. She tried to get up, but the object swung down again and clipped her on the side of the head. Riley's arms refused to support her weight, and she fell to the pavement. She had just enough time to acknowledge the ground was beginning to ice over and the fact that there was only one person with her in the alley before she blacked out.

She came to as her dead weight was manhandled into a sitting position. She realized her arms were being chained a fraction of a second too late, pulling away just as the links were secured by a padlock. She twisted at the waist and saw that she'd been chained to the thick metal railing of the stairs that led down to the neighboring building's basement. Worse than the chain was the fact that her coat had been taken off. The wind cut through the thin material of her triple-layered shirts and chilled her to the bone.

Mary tugged on the padlock to make sure it was secure before she stepped away from Riley. She was still holding the chunk of brick she had used to knock Riley out, and she tossed it underhand down the alley before she pulled her gloves back on. Her eyes were puffy with unshed tears. Riley saw her coat draped over the trash can next to the door.

"Mary, what the fuck... unlock this."

"I can't. I won't." She sniffled and looked toward the shelter. "Of all the times for a cop to actually show up. I should have known. I should have *known*." She bit back a sob. "Why did you suddenly decide to care? They're just homeless people in No Man's Land, right? That's what you cops always thought when I called before."

"Y-you... killed them?"

"I showed mercy." Mary was shuddering despite her coat, and Riley was finding it difficult to speak through her chattering teeth. "Those people were sick. Terribly ill and in pain, and they kept coming here. I couldn't turn them away. But bringing them in meant that we didn't have room for other people. People who could have been helped. So I made them comfortable, and I let them pass peacefully. I showed them mercy so I could continue to help the others who came to me."

Riley tugged on the chains, but she was wrapped too tightly to move. "We c-c-can ta... talk about this. Mary. Don't do this, you're... not a c-cold-blooded killer." She inwardly groaned at the pun, but kept her gaze locked on Mary's.

"I can't. Because you're *here*. You would have found out, and you would have taken me away, and this place would close. You can't just look the other way, right? So all these women would have to go out on the street, and back to their abusive husbands, and who knows how many of them wouldn't survive that. Do you even know what it's like to be abused, Detective?"

"I was raped by... by f-four of my father's friends. Repeatedly. I lived on... the streets... for three years. I know h-how important... these places are. What you're doing is wrong."

"I did it for the women who needed a haven. I helped those who were in pain. And because of that, you want to throw the rest of the women out on the street to die. I won't let you. I won't." She refolded Riley's coat. "You gave your coat to Bess. The kitchen staff saw the two of you talking, and I'll support it. Bess won't remember come morning. And then you very unwisely got locked out because you thought you saw someone suspicious. We'll find your body in the morning."

Riley pressed her feet flat against the ground and pushed. "Don't do this, Mary. Don't do this." She had to rush all the words together to get them said without stuttering. Her teeth felt like pieces of porcelain rattling in a china cabinet, caught in an earthquake and given a life of their own. Her heart thudded against her ribs as she tried to force the chains free.

"I'm sorry. I'm sorry this is happening to you just because you cared." She reached for Riley's mouth, and Riley tried to bite her. It was a spiteful move, and exactly what Mary had been hoping for. She placed a wooden peg between Riley's teeth and then pressed a piece of tape across her lips. With the peg in her mouth, Riley couldn't work her lips to twist the tape off.

"You have to believe me. I really am sorry."

Riley glared at the woman, who still looked like a sweet grandmother despite what she'd just done, and watched as she disappeared into the warm glow of the shelter. The door swung shut behind her, cutting off the soothing yellow light. Another gust of wind swept down the alley and Riley tensed as it hit her like an ocean wave.

She told herself that it wasn't extremely cold. It was just a few degrees below freezing, but the wind was making it feel worse. She could survive in that for a lot longer than if it was really cold. She tried to relax and twisted so she could get a look at the chains holding her to the rail. All she had to do was break the padlock. If it was colder, the metal would freeze and she could break it with a little tap.

Make up your mind, Parra. Want it colder or not?

She almost laughed at the contradiction, but her body wouldn't cooperate. She turned her wrist so she could get her hand around the padlock and hissed at the cold metal touching her bare fingers. *Don't freeze. Don't freeze. Don't freeze.*

She tugged on the small square, but it didn't budge. She looked to the sky, the swirls of blue and violet clouds blocking out all the stars. *Come on, Sariel, you winged bitch. Earn your paycheck. Human in danger down here.* She waited for a response she knew wouldn't come, and then she closed her eyes.

Gillian turned on the lights in the morgue. She hummed a song - "*Arrorró mi niña, arrorro mi amor*" - as she crossed to the sink. She washed her hands and pulled on a pair of gloves before she walked to where Riley was lying, thawed, on an examination bed. Gillian sighed and clucked her tongue. "Here we are again. I guess you have to be pretty stupid to die twice in one year, huh? To be honest, I'm not even sad anymore. I'm just embarrassed. To think I was going to *marry* you. What was I thinking?

"I mean, really. Look at you. One of the most pathetic displays I have ever seen. You had demons after you, Riley. You had supernatural nightmares from Hell out for your blood. And how do you get killed? A little old lady in a *fucking* pair of orthopedic shoes? That is just humiliating. So you need to wake up. Right now." She lowered her lips to Riley's ear and shouted. "*Wake up!*"

Riley jerked as much as the chain would allow her. Someone was walking down the alley and she struggled to make her lips work. She struggled against the wooden peg, the tape still tight across her cheeks. She managed to grunt a single syllable as the phantom got close enough for Riley to see that it was a woman wearing a uniform.

The officer didn't have a face, but Riley recognized her nonetheless. She hooked her thumb over her shoulder and didn't bother to break stride as she walked past. "There's a shelter right around the corner. They'll take care of you."

Riley fought the urge to cry as the cop walked on. The last thing she needed was a sheet of ice frozen on her cheeks. The cop faded in a sweep of blown snow, either obscured from sight or proving herself to be a figment of Riley's imagination.

I'm sorry, Mommy. I'm sorry I didn't stop. I'm sorry I didn't help you.

Riley woke suddenly from her second dream, wondering how

long she had been out. Her skin felt numb and she couldn't feel her hands. Eddie and Christine and Kenzie and Priest and Sariel... she couldn't count on any of her protectors now. All the people she had gone to in the past for help. She remembered the sagging fence that had prevented her escape the first time she met Eddie and looked at the sides of the railing that was holding her hostage.

Worth a shot... She managed to get her feet underneath her and pushed up. The chain rattled on the cold metal pipe of the railing and Riley found herself crouched with her upper body twisted back like a crab. She breathed deeply through her nose, and the cold air burnt as it went in, but she needed as much oxygen as she could get. She kept her feet shoulder-width apart and then threw her body upward with as much strength as she could muster.

Her back and shoulders immediately protested the move, but she didn't let up. Her face contorted into a grimace behind the tape and one corner of it popped loose. She just needed one rusty bolt, a weak connection somewhere in the railing, and she would be home free. Her body seemed to be under more strain than the pipe, but she couldn't let up. If this worked, she would have time to heal. If it didn't, well, it didn't matter how much damage she did before the end.

Finally, when her reserves were finally depleted, Riley sagged and dropped back onto her butt. Her breath plumed in front of her as stars appeared before her eyes.

This is really it. No demons, no vengeful angels or spirits of the damned. Just me and a little old lady.

In a sick way, it made sense to her. She had escaped No Man's Land, but in the end, she came back to die. She had always been fated to die in an alley here, so it was perfect symmetry.

She closed her eyes. *I'm sorry, Gillian. I wish I could see your first gray hair. Your first wrinkle. I wish I could have put a ring on your finger. My biggest regret is that I made you sleep alone this week. I'm sorry that-*

Her eyes snapped open. She hadn't said I love you. In the diner, Gillian had left because someone had come inside, and neither of them had said it before parting ways. They'd been too busy trying to protect the cover that they'd neglected to make sure they said it. Had they said it on the phone? She couldn't remember. Riley pulled on the chain with a renewed vigor. She couldn't leave it that way, and if there was any chance of escape, she wouldn't. She pushed up with her left hip and down with her left shoulder. She arched her back and leaned forward.

The chain slipped against her right arm. It was just a centimeter at most, but it was slippage. Riley relaxed, took a breath, and twisted again. *C'mon. C'mon.* She pulled her lips back under the tape, feeling it give slightly. She pursed her lips and rolled her jaw and one corner of her mouth was freed. She panted around the blockage of the wooden peg, her head throbbing and sweat trickling down her face despite the cold.

She thought, *It won't work* as her right arm suddenly leapt up. Her shoulder hit her in the ear and the chain was now loose around her right elbow. She caught her breath and tried to repeat the move with her left side. She pulled and twisted, muttering a prayer as she tugged. The chain fell to her elbow on that side as well. Riley bent her arms and used the new slack to rearrange herself. She sat on her knees and used her hands to try and untangle the thick links of chain.

Her right arm came free and Riley shouted in triumph. The tape fell away from her mouth and she spit the wooden peg away.

She realized she was sobbing as she pulled both arms free of the chain. She got to her feet, tripping on her first step but quickly recovering as she ran to the mouth of the alley. She felt like there was a thin layer of ice over her entire body, rubbing her arms frantically as she burst out onto the sidewalk and looked for signs of life. All that she saw was a broken payphone, the dangling cord visible even from where she was standing.

She exhaled and said, "Sariel! Bring me some fucking backup."

Mary unlocked the back door with tears in her eyes. She'd been crying all night, forcing herself to stay away from windows so she couldn't look outside and see the detective freezing to death. It was bad enough she would have to take away the chains and the tape in order to sell her story about Riley Parra accidentally dying of exposure. If she'd actually witnessed it, she would have stopped it from happening no matter the consequences.

She pulled the door open and stepped into the alley. She gasped when she saw the chains hanging limp around the railing. She turned to run back inside and she saw three people standing at the mouth of the alley. Her blood ran cold, and it had nothing to do with the temperature. The people stepped forward and Mary identified them as detectives despite their thick winter clothes. Riley Parra was with them, still shivering but bundled in a thick jacket and a knit cap with POLICE emblazoned on both.

"Mary Luttrell?"

"Yes. That's me."

"My name is Detective Caitlin Priest, and this is Detective Ken Booker. We'd like to have a word with you."

Riley stepped forward. "And I want my coat back."

Mary released the door handle and lowered her head as the detectives came forward.

Mary confessed to her crimes. Priest let Booker take her statement and escorted Riley back to the unmarked sedan. "Are you sure you're warm enough?"

"I'll be fine now." Riley was still clutching her thermos of steaming coffee like it was the Holy Grail. "What's going to happen to the shelter?"

"A... former associate of mine, Pravuil, will watch over them tonight and until a permanent guardian is found."

Riley looked down the street as they got into the car. Priest was behind the wheel, which caused Riley a bit of apprehension, but she wasn't in the right mind to drive herself. "There's a woman who lives nearby named Anita. She lives with a man named Eddie Cashion. She needs a job and, most likely, a place to stay when their landlord finally kicks them out. I think they'd be a good fit."

"Eddie? Your Eddie."

Riley frowned. "How do you know Eddie?"

"I was your guardian angel from birth, Riley. I saw... I saw everything."

Riley looked at her. "Everything?"

Priest closed her eyes and nodded. "You have to understand that sometimes the hardest part of being a guardian angel is to do nothing. To allow bad things to happen."

"Like when you're a parent and you let the kid stick a fork in the toaster. 'She won't do that again!'"

"It's not the same thing, Riley."

She rubbed her forehead. "I know. I'm just..." She surprised them both by suddenly sobbing. She fought back her tears and straightened in the seat. "It's been a bad night. Memory Lane isn't exactly a fun road for me."

"I understand."

She watched the streets pass by the window. "If you're taking me to the police station, I'm really not in the mood to give my statement. I'm sore and~"

"I'm taking you where you need to be."

Riley fell silent and remained that way for the rest of the ride. When Priest finally pulled to the curb, Riley looked out and smiled at the sight of her home.

"Thanks."

"My pleasure. I wish I could have been there for you when you needed me."

Riley held out her hand. "You were."

Priest shook Riley's hand. "I'll see you tomorrow afternoon sometime."

"Heh. Yeah. Maybe." She got out of the car and headed inside. The walk from the curb to the lobby was bearable, which meant the night was beginning to warm up however incrementally. She shook the cold off as she headed upstairs. She unlocked the apartment door and, with appropriate reverence, went into her home and shut the door behind her.

Gillian hadn't been lying; she was stretched out on the couch under a thin white blanket. Riley quietly took off her coat and hat, keeping her eyes on Gillian's slumbering face as she undressed. When she was down to her underwear, she padded barefoot across the room and lifted the blanket. She had just lowered herself to the couch when Gillian began to stir.

"Mm... what..."

"Sh. It's just me."

Gillian touched Riley's face in the darkness. "This is a nice dream."

"Let me take you to bed."

Gillian nodded, and Riley lifted her. The effort caused her back and shoulders to scream in protest, but she ignored them both. She put Gillian down on the bed, kissed her lips, and then stretched out next to her. Gillian kept touching Riley's face and body, her eyes half-lidded as if she was still mostly asleep. Her thumb dipped into Riley's navel and she ran the backs of her fingers up Riley's stomach to her breasts.

"You look sad."

Riley blinked away her tears and nodded. "Yeah. I had a lot of memories brought back tonight."

"Eddie?"

She had forgotten about calling Gillian about her encounter. "Eddie, and... I met a woman who knew Mom. She's not entirely there, but she remembered things. She remembered her. Thought *I* was her. It's the closest I've gotten to knowing Mom in a really long time."

"I can see how that would hit you like a ton of bricks. Wanna talk about it?"

"Yeah. But not now." She settled against Gillian's warmth. "Am I too cold?"

"Mm. I'll warm you up soon enough."

Riley stroked Gillian's hair. "I'm never going to get out of there, am I?"

"Where?"

"No Man's Land. I was born there, and that's where I belong. It's only a matter of time before I get pulled back there for good."

Gillian shook her head. She reached behind her neck with both hands and unfastened her necklace. Riley watched as she gathered the chain and then slipped the engagement ring off of it. She'd been wearing it for the duration of Riley's assignment to keep it safe. She lifted Riley's left hand and slid the ring onto it.

"There's your anchor. Keeping you where you belong: right here. With me. Forever."

Riley bent down and kissed Gillian's hand. "If you ever realize how little I deserve you, give me some warning. Don't just up and leave in the middle of the night. Okay?"

Gillian laughed. "It's a deal."

"You're supposed to deny you'll ever realize that."

"Oh." She leaned in and kissed Riley. "If you spoon me, you'll get warmer faster."

"I'm willing put that theory to the test. Roll over." Gillian rolled over, and Riley spooned her from behind. She wrapped her arms around Gillian, her head on Gillian's shoulder, and closed her eyes. She was asleep long before she got fully warm, and Gillian's theory went unconfirmed.

PERMANENT SCARS

THE DETECTIVE thrust the door open, knowing that his sudden arrival would be shocking in the silent room. He pushed the door shut with his fingers for the same reason, the resulting slam echoing off the walls as he moved toward his seat. The chair legs scraped on the floor and he grunted as he lowered his bulk into it. He barely acknowledged the woman sitting on the business side of the table. She looked barely awake, cuffed hands in her lap, leaning slightly forward so that her hair hung in her face.

He placed an old fashioned tape recorder on the table, pressed down play and record, and set it on the table between them. He looked at his watch and opened the file that was sitting on the table. "Three-fourteen in the morning, Detective Charles Timbale conducting interrogation of suspect. Please state your name and occupation for the record."

The woman across from him lifted her head as if she'd just realized he was there. She looked at the tape recorder. "Jesus, you're still using that."

"Whatever works." He tapped the table. "Your name and occupation, please."

She sighed. "Mackenzie Crowe. I'm a private investigator."

"Where were you this evening between the hours of ten and midnight?"

"I was on a stakeout on Elbridge Gerry Street, where it meets the waterfront. I got there at eight, and I was there until you guys came and got me at a little past twelve-thirty."

Timbale nodded. "And where was your partner during all of this?"

"Hasn't she told you that already?"

He finally made eye contact with her. "Your partner isn't talking very much, so we thought we'd give you a chance to fill in the blanks. Even if she had told us something, we'd like to make sure your stories match up. So if you please, for the record, where was Chelsea Stanton during the hours of ten and midnight?"

Kenzie took a deep breath. "I'd like a lawyer, please."

Timbale smiled sadly. "Is that the way we're going to handle this?"

"Lawyer, please."

Timbale shut off the tape recorder and stood up. He scratched the side of his nose. "No one wants this, you know. We all know how this needs to go, and we all know what you need to say to get out of here. So why don't you just say it and save us all some trouble?"

Kenzie kept her eyes on the mirror. "Lawyer."

Timbale shook his head and carried the tape recorder away from the table. He paused with his hand on the knob and suddenly turned to face her. "Why the hell are you doing this, Kenzie? We know that you know what she did. You were around back then. Chelsea Stanton has this coming. So just tell us that you don't know where she was tonight and end this right now."

"Go to hell, Timbale."

The detective closed his eyes and shoved away from the table. "You'll both go down for it. It's either her, or both of you. No one wants that."

Kenzie took a breath and let it out slowly through her nostrils. She stared at the mirror until Timbale cursed and stormed out of the interrogation room.

Once he was gone, Kenzie put her cuffed hands onto the table. She put her head down, resting her forehead on her thumbs, and squeezed her eyes shut.

Two Years Earlier

The original plan was to hang around for a while and try to figure out what secret Riley was keeping from her. Another reason was that Riley was technically single again; her girlfriend was on an indefinite vacation and, if she knew Riley, it was only a matter of time before she got sick of waiting. Kenzie kept her hotel room and woke up refreshed the morning after they saved Radio from the Underground. It was amazing what a few days of running around with Riley Parra could do for her psyche.

She spent the day touring some of her old haunts, revisiting a few old friends to let them know she was back in town. She kept her hair combed forward to cover her scarred face, but unless she wanted to be partially blind, it wasn't the best solution in the world. So she let some of the scar tissue show. She hadn't realized how self-conscious she was about it until she felt the relief that no one mentioned it.

The sign jumped out at her, half-glimpsed from the corner of her eye and forcing a double-take. Stanton Investigations. The smaller print underneath the name identified the owner and operator as Chelsea Stanton.

A multitude of emotions ran through her. Anger won out over confusion and irritation, and she jerked the door open and stormed inside.

The aroma of flowers was dominant in the small space, and Kenzie followed it through the waiting area. Both desks in the main office were empty. The entire back wall was glass, and she saw a complete greenhouse full of white roses on the other side. She was momentarily taken aback by the unusual sight, and she moved closer to make sure she was really seeing them. They were definitely white roses, and they were perfectly real. Small beads of water glistened on their petals. She stood in the doorway of the greenhouse and breathed deep, attempting to let the scent soothe her anger.

"Can I help you?"

The voice pulled the anger back, and she spun on her heel. Chelsea Stanton looked almost exactly the same as she had the last time Kenzie saw her. Dark hair cut short, an elfin face with high cheekbones and a pointed chin. She was tall and slender, dressed in a sleeveless white blouse and black slacks instead of the detective's suit that Kenzie always pictured her in. Her eyes were still the same unbelievable pale blue, but now they were focused just slightly off-center.

"You have a lot of damn nerve staying in this town, Stanton."

She dipped her chin and smiled sadly. "Well, you're obviously a cop who was on the force when I was. Officer Parra was a little taller, so you must be Officer Crowe. Would it help if I said I was sorry?" She asked it like a question she already knew the answer to.

Kenzie advanced on the disgraced cop. "You tried to throw the entire department under the bus to save your own druggie ass. You confirmed every damn lie they were telling about female cops, and you made it that much harder for the women who came after you. I left the department because of what you did. Went to Afghanistan and got a really nice parting gift." She pushed her hair out of the way so Chelsea could get the full effect.

Chelsea lost the wry smile, but didn't look at the burn. "What kind of parting gift?"

"You know, fuck you." Kenzie dropped her hair and stormed toward the door. Chelsea stopped her by grabbing her arm.

"I'm asking honestly. I was shot when I left prison and I can't see much. I can see the shapes of things, but not..." She blinked away tears, her eyes still focused vaguely on Kenzie's forehead. "Please. Tell me what happened."

"A roadside bomb. A member of my platoon knocked me out of the way, but it got part of my face. It's scarred."

"May I feel?"

Kenzie was completely still. No one touched her scar, not even Riley. It was like letting someone touch her breast or cup her between the legs. It was far too intimate. But her guard was weakened by her anger and the shock at Chelsea's admission. There was also a part of her that wanted Chelsea to know exactly what she had to live with. She licked her lips and turned to face Chelsea fully. "Fine."

Chelsea lifted her hand and gently placed it on Kenzie's face. Kenzie fought the instinct to pull back and closed her eyes. Chelsea carefully examined the terrain of Kenzie's scars, over the remnant of her right eyebrow. Kenzie could only barely feel the caress, but Chelsea's touch was light. Two fingers moved down her cheek, and then her thumb brushed over Kenzie's undamaged bottom lip before retreating. The damage was much lighter on her jaw, and Chelsea dropped her hand away.

"I'm sorry for my part in what happened, Officer Crowe."

Kenzie found that she had lost a lot of her anger in the last couple of seconds. She looked down at her feet. "Why did you do it? Why did you take the drugs, and do such a fucking stupid thing?"

Chelsea sighed and walked over to one of the empty desks. "I didn't want to be the first. I hesitated to take my detective's exam. I was willing to just float. But then my lieutenant told me that stagnation was almost as bad as just quitting outright. He told me I would be a damn good detective, an asset to the force. So I took the test and passed it the first time. I became the city's first female homicide detective. I became a statistic. A blurb in the newspaper. What I was doing wasn't nearly as important as what I was. Sometimes it seemed like every woman I met wanted me to succeed, and every man I worked with wanted me to fail. And the brass was so determined to make an example of me that every move I made was scrutinized. The pressure got to me. When my confidential informant told me to take drugs to earn his trust, I was eager for a way to shut down for a little bit. Once I started, I couldn't stop."

"When did you decide to sacrifice every other cop you worked with? You stole the drugs from that bust, and when someone did the right thing and turned you in, you said the men were just trying to make you look bad. And the brass was so eager for you to succeed they turned it into a witch hunt. If no one had suggested drug tests, would you have still come forward? Or would you have let someone else get fired to cover it up?"

Chelsea looked at the floor. "Now, I would have. But the person I was then... strung out and desperate to be what everyone wanted me to be? I don't know. I highly doubt that version of me would have done the right thing."

"What's so different about the person you are now?"

"Why don't you have dinner with me and find out?"

Kenzie was stunned by her boldness, and by her reluctance to turn down the invitation outright. She remembered the feel of Chelsea's hand on her face, the gentle caress. How it hadn't felt like the violation she expected it to be.

"Whatever," Kenzie finally said. "Girl's gotta eat, right?"

Now

Riley followed Priest into the main bullpen, still wearing her heavy coat and scarf. Lieutenant Briggs wasn't in yet, but Detective Timbale was sitting at his desk typing out his report. Timbale was a cop from back in the day, months from his pension, and he mostly liked to just sit at his desk and stay out of trouble. Out of respect for his seniority, he got mostly easy cases to deal with. What he was doing on a case like this, Riley had no idea.

He glanced up as Riley approached his desk, and he smiled. He seemed to have gained a couple dozen pounds since the last time Riley noticed him, his white hair a bit thinner on top.

"You're here early, detectives. Come to watch justice served?"

"Did you arrest Chelsea Stanton and Mackenzie Crowe?"

He smiled proudly. "I sure did. It's just a matter of time before I get Crowe to turn on her partner. And then Chelsea Stanton can go right back where she belongs."

"Where are they?"

"Interrogation 2 and 3." He frowned at her. "You're not going to take this bust from me, Parra. I don't care if you're the new hotshot~"

"Kenzie isn't going to flip on Chelsea. So you're either going to end up arresting them both on false charges, or letting them go. Let me deal with this, and maybe you won't be a laughingstock tomorrow morning. Okay, Charlie?"

Timbale pressed his lips together and turned to face his computer. "Stanton was a bad cop. She needs to be in jail to draw the line between cops and criminals."

"Yeah, because that would be such an easy line to draw." Riley left Timbale behind and went to the interrogation room. Priest tagged along behind her.

"Thank you..."

"You said that nine times in the car, Priest. It's fine." She opened the door to interrogation room 3, and Kenzie sat up and looked at her. "It better be a damned good story, Kenzie."

Kenzie shook her head as Riley shut the door. She and Priest sat down opposite her, and Priest extended her hand across the table. Kenzie took it and squeezed, brushing her thumb across the knuckles. Priest held the pose awkwardly and then pulled her hand away. Riley watched them for a moment, taking in the sight before she spoke.

"From the beginning."

"Riley... I asked for a lawyer. I shouldn't be talking to you."

"Come off it, Kenzie. It's me. We're not here as cops. Just tell us what happened."

Kenzie leaned back in her seat. "I was on a stakeout. It was a nothing case. Someone was breaking into furniture stores every night and bedding down. They'd take blankets and pillows off the beds and make a nest in the middle of the storeroom floor. The owners wanted to catch whoever it was in the act, and find out how they were getting in. So I got to sit in my car for six hours freezing my ass off. I was about to head home when a cop car pulled up behind me and I got dragged in here."

"What do they think you did?"

"Not me. They're just accusing me so I'll get scared and flip on Chelsea." She looked down at her hands. "They think she killed someone tonight."

Riley nodded. "And since you were alone on the stakeout, you can't verify her whereabouts."

"Yeah. They know that. They just need me to say the words so they can drag her down to processing. And once she's down there..." She closed her eyes and shook her head, unwilling to even consider the possibilities.

"Okay, you may not know exactly where she was or what she was doing, but I'm sure you could make an educated guess."

Kenzie shook her head. "That's just it. Usually when I'm on stakeout, I have a Bluetooth so she can call and check on my progress. A lot of times she'll just keep me company. Tonight, nothing. No calls, no texts, just radio silence from her."

"Did you think that was odd?"

Kenzie shrugged. "I assumed she was tired and went to bed early." She glanced toward Priest and looked away quickly. "That's what's got me so concerned about this whole mess. I have no idea where Chelsea was tonight."

Riley rubbed the back of her neck. "Okay. I'll see what I can find out from Timbale. Sit tight."

"I don't really have much of an option, do I? Cait, could you stay? It'll be nice to have a friendly face."

Riley nodded to Priest that it was okay, patted her on the shoulder, and left the room. Timbale was looming outside, his arms crossed over his thick chest. "She tell you anything important?"

"Doesn't matter. It's not my case. I need to know why you brought them in."

"I'm not sure you have the authority to make me tell you anything."

Riley tried a softer approach. "I'm *asking*, Timbale. If you want to take down someone as infamous as Chelsea Stanton, you better get used to telling your story and getting the facts straight."

Timbale considered the argument and brushed a hand over the

bottom of his face. "Okay, fine. A couple of uniforms responded to a silent alarm at an office a little past ten last night. When they showed up, they found a man lying in the lobby with two gunshot wounds in his chest. The officers did a sweep of the premises and found Ms. Stanton's car parked in the building's underground garage."

Riley raised an eyebrow. "Chelsea *drove* there? You know that~"

"Her eyes, yeah. But the car was registered in her name, and it's common knowledge she has *some* sight. She could easily have driven three miles on late night streets. She could use the headlights of other cars to make sure she stayed in her own lane. I'm not saying it'd be easy, but she could do it."

"So she abandoned her car at the scene. Where was she when you found her?"

"She wasn't on the premises. I was called in and shown the evidence, so I went to Ms. Stanton's place of business. It was just past eleven, so she was still awake, sitting in the main office with a bottle of Scotch. She seemed unsurprised to see us when we showed up, so we asked her how her car had gotten to our crime scene. She asked for a lawyer."

Riley nodded. "How did Kenzie come into all of this?"

"We knew the two of them were working together, so we asked where she was. Ms. Stanton told us where we could find former officer Crowe."

"Was there any evidence beyond Chelsea's car being at the scene?"

Timbale smiled. "The gun."

Riley was thrown by that. "You found the gun?"

"It was on the front seat of the car. Prints were wiped off, but in and of itself..."

Priest stepped in. "You found her car at the crime scene, but she was at her office? How far apart are the two scenes?"

Timbale wavered a bit. "It's about three miles."

Riley picked up on Priest's train of thought. "The silent alarm went off around ten, and you arrived at Chelsea's office at eleven. It takes about an hour to walk three miles, right? Did Chelsea show any signs that she had just walked that distance? Or was she, as you said, sitting at her desk with a bottle of Scotch?"

"I don't know why you're doing this. This is a good bust."

"I'm not asking anything the DA won't ask, and I'm coming up with them while half-asleep. You'll want to get these answers before you formally press charges."

Timbale growled and looked toward the window. "She could have taken a cab from the scene."

"She could have. Although why she bothered to put the gun in her car and then leave it behind is a bit confusing."

"Go to hell, Parra. You and your partner both." He brushed between them and went into Kenzie's interrogation room. He slammed the door behind him.

Priest leaned against the nearest desk. "This is very bad, isn't it?"

"Pretty damn bad." Riley looked around to make sure they were alone. "So how do you fit into all of this?"

"What do you mean?"

"Don't play dumb. You weren't home tonight, and you weren't working. If you can give Chelsea an alibi, even if you have to admit sleeping with her~"

"I wasn't with Chelsea. We don't..." She ducked her chin and summoned the courage to finish her thought. "We don't pair off that way. Chelsea and Kenzie are a couple, and I'm the third. I don't do anything alone with either of them. That was the deal."

"What, did you guys hash out a contract?"

"Basically."

Riley smiled and shook her head. "So how did you get involved?"

"They let Kenzie make a phone call when they brought her in. She called me first because she knew I'd be aw~"

"And why would she know that?" Riley stepped closer and lowered her voice. "It's really starting to worry me that you won't answer, Caitlin. Where were you tonight?"

Priest closed her eyes and gave in. "I was with Kenzie and Chelsea before Kenzie went on her stakeout. We had... sex, and then Kenzie went to work while Chelsea and I had dinner. Over dinner, Chelsea and I had a fight."

Riley was surprised to discover that hearing Priest talk about sex was uncomfortable. It was like hearing her little sister talk about getting laid. She pushed aside the awkwardness and stayed on topic. "What did you fight about?"

"Chelsea wanted me to move in with them permanently. She and Kenzie had talked about it, and they wanted to make me a part of their relationship."

Riley shrugged. "You're basically living there full-time now.

What would be the difference?"

"Commitment. I'm not ready for that level of commitment with one person, let alone two. I was concerned that I would destroy their relationship just by trying to wedge myself into their lives. We argued about it. It ended with my decision that we shouldn't... do what we had been doing anymore."

"You broke up with them."

Priest nodded. "Then I went to Kenzie to tell her what had happened."

Riley was still reeling from the information, but she forced herself to focus on the case. "What time did all this happen?"

"My fight with Chelsea was around nine. I was with Kenzie from a quarter to ten until ten thirty. I left Chelsea in a very agitated state. An hour later, the police believe she murdered someone."

"Do we know who she supposedly murdered yet?"

"The police haven't identified him yet, but... I saw the photograph. I know who it is. And I'm afraid once Timbale knows the full details he'll be even more convinced of her guilt. It was a man named Jon Casady. He was originally a file clerk here at the station. But if the name sounds familiar it's because~"

"Goddamn it, Priest. I know who he is."

Priest nodded.

"You're withholding information from the police. If they find out you knew... Come on." She grabbed Priest's arm and dragged her toward the interrogation room. She knocked and stepped to one side when Timbale came out.

"What the hell do you want now?"

"Priest identified the victim."

Timbale turned his attention to her. "Oh, really? Pray tell."

"His name is Jon Casady. A few years ago he wrote a true-crime book about Chelsea."

Timbale's expression softened with surprise. "You're kidding. Our victim is the guy who made Chelsea Stanton the modern-day Eva Braun?"

Riley didn't know how Chelsea was supposed to be Eva Braun, but asking would give her far too much insight into Timbale's thought processes. "Yes."

Riley slumped against the wall, Priest looked chagrined, and Timbale looked positively gleeful. He grinned and clapped Priest on the shoulder. "I'd say you just gave me the final nail in Chelsea Stanton's coffin. Thanks a lot."

Timbale went back into the interrogation room, more ammunition to try and turn Kenzie, and Priest leaned against the wall beside Riley.

"Bad night," Riley said.

Priest closed her eyes and knocked her head against the wall a few times in agreement. "Why would Chelsea tell them where to find Kenzie? Didn't she know they were just going to arrest her?"

"She probably was trying to give Kenzie an alibi. Proving she had been on the stakeout all night. Blame Timbale for turning it into a witch hunt."

Priest sighed. "Have you ever read Casady's book?"

"Yeah. My reaction was... different then that it would be now."

Three years earlier
"You're looking at that damn book like it's pornography."

Riley glanced up as Kara got back into the car. She closed the book on her thumb to mark her place. "Hey, I was there for most of this. This bitch could have ruined my entire career." She looked at the cover image of Chelsea Stanton. It was a terrible picture, her mug shot taken the night she finally admitted to taking the drugs. Her normally beautiful eyes were bloodshot, her hair unwashed and pulled back into a ponytail. She was holding up an identification card, but the title - "DETECTIVE SNOW WHITE" - was spelled out instead of her personal information.

"You transferred in after she was already gone so you don't know what it was like."

Kara nodded and tapped her cigarette on the edge of her open window. "Kind of a crazy time back then, huh?"

"She accused the male cops in the department of trying to railroad her. And the brass believed it. Kenzie and I stood up with the guys so that we wouldn't be painted with the same brush once Chelsea was gone, but Kenzie... she couldn't imagine sticking around for the aftermath. She hightailed it, and I blame that entirely on..." She thumped the cover with her middle finger.

"But her leaving led to you becoming a detective. And meeting me." Kara smiled and winked. "So some good came from it."

"I do like being a detective. You, I tolerate." Kara slugged Riley in the arm. "I guess I just hope the book will explain why she did what she did."

Kara looked at the remaining stub of her cigarette and considered tossing it out the window. "How many cigarettes do I have left?"

"Two." Riley tossed the book onto the dashboard. "And if you're serious about quitting, don't buy another pack. I'm sick of holding them for you."

"I have to ease out of it. It's not just the addiction, it's the habit."

"Right. I'm not giving you any more cigarettes until..." She looked at her watch. "Three o'clock."

Kara looked at her watch and sucked a breath through her teeth. "You bitch." She took another drag, savoring it this time. "So gaining any insight?"

"Not a lot."

"Why is it called 'Detective Snow White'?"

Riley picked up the book again and thumbed to the picture section. "Because she stole cocaine, and she looked like... this." She held the book open to a picture of Chelsea Stanton's official police ID. She wore her uniform phenomenally well, her chin held high and her dark hair slicked back against her skull. She looked regal, like someone should be bowing to her. Her eyes were like shards of ice.

Kara whistled. "Heigh-ho."

"You got the ho part right." She checked her watch again. "Okay, the bastard has to be in his office now. You want to go bother him again?"

"Let's." They got out of the car. "Let me know how the book ends."

Riley laughed. "It ends with Chelsea Stanton in jail. My definition of a happy ending."

Now

There were only three voices Riley found it acceptable to be woken by, and none of them were male. Two men were speaking extremely close to her, and her back ached. She stifled a yawn as she realized she'd fallen asleep at her desk, starting to sit up before she heard what the men were talking about.

"I don't know what the hell the situation is. I thought Detective Priest was sleeping with her partner and that ME. They were all shacked up together, I know that."

"Well, Timbale's implying that Priest is biased because she's sleeping with Stanton and her girlfriend."

The first guy scoffed and whistled. "I guess you never know, huh?"

Riley sat up without warning, and the conversation stopped suddenly. Riley stretched her arms over her head, yawned, and pushed her chair back.

"Timbale doesn't know what he's talking about. Where is he?"

"Uh, talking with Briggs."

Riley left without further comment on their conversation. She knocked on Briggs' door and waited for acknowledgement before she stepped inside. Timbale was sitting in one of the chairs, and he rolled his eyes when he saw her.

"Detective Parra. I was just about to call you in. Please, sit down."

"Great." Timbale spoke under his breath, but it was loud enough that both Riley and Briggs couldn't help but hear him.

Briggs folded her hands together. "Riley, Charles tells me that you and Detective Priest insinuated yourselves into his investigation early this morning, and now it comes to my attention that there may be a conflict of interest. I'm inclined to agree with him, given what I know about your relationship with Ms. Crowe and Ms. Stanton. And am I to understand Detective Priest is now in a relationship with one of them?"

"Both of them, actually." Riley took the seat next to Timbale. "But they broke up last night. Cait and I may be biased, but not more than Timbale or the rest of the department. Chelsea Stanton is no longer the woman who turned her back on the department. She's made amends."

"She was a cop in jail who made a deal to get out early," Timbale muttered.

Riley smiled. "Yeah, I'm sure if you went to jail you'd serve your entire sentence. You'd have a great time, locked up with all those criminals you sent away."

Briggs held up her hand. "All right. While I do believe Detectives Parra and Priest have a bias, I'm not going to discount the possibility that Detective Timbale has one as well. So, Riley, since your personal relationship with Kenzie Crowe is in the past, I'm going to temporarily assign you to work with Charles on this case. I expect you to keep each other honest."

Timbale sighed heavily and shook his head. "I haven't needed a partner in five years, Lieutenant."

"That was an arrangement you made with Lieutenant Hathaway. It's a one-time thing, Timbale. When and if this goes to trial, I want the DA to be able to say we gave this thing a professional investigation. Deal with it. Both of you." She waved them toward the door. "Get to work, please."

Riley stood and held the door open for Timbale. He grudgingly led the way out and Riley followed him into the bullpen.

"How did Priest's relationship with the suspects become common knowledge?"

"I was escorting Ms. Crowe's lawyer into the interrogation room and witnessed her kissing your partner. Normally I gotta pay a couple bucks for action like that. Anyway, I confronted her and she told me everything."

"All right, but it goes no further. It's not pertinent to the investigation." Timbale averted his gaze and Riley's shoulders sagged. "You already told everyone you could find. Great. Where are they now?"

"We placed Stanton under arrest when Briggs got here." He held up his hands before Riley could argue. "She saw the evidence, and I even admitted your three mile thing. She thinks Stanton could have hopped on the el or borrowed Crowe's car. We're holding her until those things can be explained away."

Riley groaned. "Just wonderful. Priest and Kenzie?"

"Downstairs. Once Stanton gets processed, they want to talk with her."

"I'd like a chance to speak with her myself." She brushed past Timbale and walked to the stairs. He started out following her but, due to the difference in their age, quickly fell behind. When Riley got to the holding area, she saw Priest and Kenzie sitting in the orange plastic chairs holding hands.

Priest saw them first and let go of Kenzie's hand. "Riley. I was going to wake you, but~"

"Don't worry about it. How is she holding up?"

Kenzie looked more afraid than Riley had ever seen her. "She's afraid. She doesn't want to go back to prison, Rye. She would never do anything that would cause her to go back to that place."

"All right. Briggs put me on the case with Timbale, so I'm going to see what I can do. Sit tight." She looked at Timbale. "I want to talk with Chelsea alone. Is that going to be a problem?"

He faked a smile. "It's your case too, Detective."

"Thanks." She turned and left him with Priest and Kenzie. The sergeant on duty looked up as Riley approached. "I need to speak with a prisoner. Chelsea Stanton. I'm on the case with Detective

Timbale."

The sergeant shrugged and motioned for Riley to follow him. They went down a short, dimly lit hallway a separate holding area. She was led to a small door away from the main cells to a solitary confinement cell. He unlocked the door and pushed it open as he stepped to one side. "I'm sure I don't have to tell you the rules, Detective."

"I'll be fine. Thank you." She waited until he was gone to step inside and close the door.

Chelsea was sitting on the foot of the room's single cot, her arms resting on her knees. She had been given a pale blue jumpsuit and her hair was pulled back. She looked like she hadn't slept at all, not that Riley could blame her if she hadn't. She looked toward the door and smiled. "Riley Parra. I was sitting here and thinking about how much things had changed since I last sat in this room. For one thing I could *see* the room. And you were probably upstairs popping champagne."

Riley pulled a chair across the floor and sat down. "I need to know what happened last night, Chelsea. First of all, can you drive?"

"In certain emergency situations, yes. My eyes are terrible, and I'm legally blind, but I can see headlights and streetlights. You probably wouldn't want to ride with me, but yes. The fact my car is at the scene is pretty bad."

"Were you there?"

Chelsea dipped her chin once. "Earlier in the evening. Before Caitlin came over. Kenzie didn't know about it. I just told her I was doing errands. You know who the victim is, right?"

"Jon Casady. Priest told me."

"He emailed me to let me know that he was going to re-release 'Detective Snow White.' He was adding chapters to deal with my injury, my blindness, and... somehow he had found out about Kenzie and Caitlin. He made it out to be some kind of harem, like I was corrupting other cops. I went to beg him to leave Cait out of it. Her career could be destroyed by an allegation like that, even if it is just in a dumb book."

Riley agreed. "What did he say?"

"He laughed in my face. He told me that he could put whatever he wanted in the new book, lie or not, because it was no worse than what Gail Finney was saying on the radio every day. The only difference was that he was dealing with specifics. So I left and, before you ask, yes. He was alive when I left. I was too pissed off to attempt driving, even on the side streets, so I walked home."

"What time did all of that happen?"

"Around five in the afternoon. His office was empty. No secretary or anyone who could confirm that he was alive when I left."

"Well, maybe there's a Rolodex or a day planner that can tell us whether he had any meetings after you. Maybe he left a note about your visit. We can hope. The gun~"

Chelsea shook her head. "I don't know if it's mine or not. I have a gun. I'm a blind former cop working in No Man's Land, I have *several* guns."

Riley stood up. "Okay. I'll see what I can do. Hold tight."

She was almost out the door when Chelsea spoke again. "Riley. You should have been the first female detective in this department. You would have been the role model they deserved. This is probably far too late, but I am truly sorry I screwed things up for you and Kenzie."

"Water under the bridge. I'll get you out of here this time, Chelsea."

She shut the door and saw the sergeant waiting at the other end of the hall. She took a deep breath before she started walking, hoping she had the ability to keep her promise.

Timbale rested his elbow in the open window, two fingers extended under his bottom lip as Riley drove. He finally sucked in a breath and turned to face her. "So which rumor is true?"

She kept her eyes on the road. "You'll have to be more specific than that."

"You know, the ones going around about your partner. I mean, it's pretty clear she's hooking up with Crowe. But a couple other people said she was with you and your girl before that. So I'm just wondering if she~"

Riley whistled shrilly, and Timbale winced. "I'm not discussing my partner's sex life with you, Timbale. Nor my own. So just drop the conversation right there."

He held up his hands as if she was out of line for not answering, but he didn't pursue the question further. They arrived at the office Jon Casady was keeping and parked in front of the main entrance. "Where is Chelsea's car?"

"Got towed to impound after I got done going through it."

"I want to take a look at it."

"Be my guest. It is your case too."

Riley rolled her eyes as she went into the building. Timbale pointed at the black board of the building directory, small white letters indicating who was where.

"Casady is on the third floor. Elevators are over here."

"Stairs are right there."

Timbale ignored her and jabbed the up button for the elevator. Riley changed her course and joined him in waiting for the doors to part. Timbale's waistline suddenly made a little more sense to her.

She watched the numbers above the door, displayed in a half-circle with an arrow fluidly moving from one to the next. She finally asked the question that had been on her mind all night. "Since when do writers have offices? I thought the whole point of writing was that you could do it at home."

"Maybe he likes keeping his work space and his private space separate. You know, don't bring your work home with you."

The doors parted and Riley stepped into the elevator. "I guess. Just seems like a waste. Wake up, get dressed, drive downtown, sit in an office and just stare at a screen all day. Why bother with the commute?"

Timbale shrugged. He'd obviously lost interest in the conversation.

They arrived at the third floor and Riley quickly found Casady's office. The upper part of the door was smoked glass, with the name J. CASADY written in arcing letters. She took down the yellow crime scene tape, used her key to slice through the sticker that spanned the door and its jamb. She pushed the door open and scanned the office before she stepped over the threshold. Timbale, who'd been there that morning, brushed past her and went in without hesitation.

The walls were papered with Post-it notes covered with dark chicken scratch handwriting. The desk was against the far wall and facing away from the door so that Casady could look out the window while he wrote. Waist-high bookshelves lined the walls, crammed with textbooks and biographies with even more books and binders stacked on top of it. Loose papers were shoved haphazardly into books as placeholders. Riley was surprised to see an old-fashioned typewriter on the desk with a stack of blank paper standing neatly next to it.

Timbale stopped in the middle of the area, just behind the wheeled chair that was parked under the desk. "Body was here."

"Really? Right where the bloodstains are? That's odd."

Timbale made a face.

Riley walked to the wall and read a handful of the notes. From what she could decipher, it was a timeline of Chelsea's life. The ink changed from blue to red and began to detail crime in No Man's Land. Riley had to admit that would make a highly interesting read. He had listed the five crime families and all known members, and then another list that showed people who worked for the Dupre family.

One uniquely unfilled note simply read "March? Mark Otis?"

"The guy did his research."

"Neighbors said it was almost obsessive. Guy on the north is an appraiser and sometimes he was at work until ten at night. He said Casady was almost always in here, jabbering away on his phone or tapping at that keyboard."

Riley gestured at the desk. "Did he have a computer?"

"Some of the tech geeks took it. They're tearing it apart right now, probably."

Riley looked into the guts of the typewriter. "Why didn't they take the ribbon, too?"

Timbale laughed. "Nice catch. I didn't know kids your age knew about typewriters. The ribbon is fresh. He hadn't written anything with it. Made me think maybe Stanton took the old one, just to cover her ass."

Riley scanned notes Casady had made for a story on the Angel Maker. She cringed at how often her name had come up. "You said the neighbor works late. Did he hear anything?"

"Murder happened after ten. None of the neighbors stay much later than that."

Riley continued her circuit of the room, eyeing the notes. She paused and backtracked. "Huh. This is a little weird."

Timbale looked at the spot she was examining. "Hm?"

"He uses different colored ink for each subject. Right here is green for research he was doing on the Angel Maker case. And here, it goes to red for a biography of someone I've never heard of. But right in the middle, there are two rows with black ink..." She turned and pointed at the other wall. "The blue ink is for a book he's writing on the city's mayors."

"Who the hell would read any of these crappy books?"

"Literates," Riley muttered. "Look at these notes. They're all kept in perfect order. So why did a row of these end up over there?"

"Maybe he ran out of room over there and he had some extra space. Look at this place. I'm surprised he didn't have crap on the ceiling."

Riley went to the incongruous area. She used her gloves to take the notes down and examined the empty space. Either someone had taken the last bit of research on the Angel Maker book or the first part of the biography. Knowing her luck, it was the former. "We need to get these dusted for prints. Odds are whoever switched these out also took the notes that were already here."

"You really think Stanton is innocent of this?"

"Chelsea was never a murderer. After everything she's done and everything she's been through, I can't comprehend her doing something that will send her back to jail. Did forensics find any prints besides Chelsea's?"

"Some, but it's an office. I mean, he did interviews and stuff here. Probably all kinds of people came and went. Lab is going to run them all, but we found Stanton's. It's gonna be a waste of time."

"Maybe, maybe not."

Timbale shook his head. "I don't understand you. This lady made it nearly impossible for women to be taken seriously on the force. I would think you'd be dancing on top of your desk that she was going back to jail."

"It's complicated. Last year, there was some very bad stuff happening. Chelsea went into No Man's Land with me, without hesitation, and put her life on the line to save people who mean a lot to me. That earned her a lot of points in my book. And then she came through again during the Angel Maker case. She's more than paid her dues."

Timbale snorted. "Depends on what you think she owes. You just had to forgive her for betraying lady cops. I have to forgive her for trying to hang every man with a badge for her crimes. It's gonna take a lot more than making an assist to get me to forgive her."

"Forgiving is one thing. But are you willing to send an innocent woman to prison and let a killer go free?"

"I guess that's why you're here, Detective. To make sure I don't do that."

They rode the elevator down again, past the lobby to the private garage. As they stepped out, Riley looked up toward the ceiling. "Security cameras?"

"Dummies."

"Of course they are."

Timbale pointed with two fingers. "She was parked right there. Just a few steps from the elevator. Even if there were cameras, she might have been able to sneak in before they saw her."

The entrance was about a hundred yards ahead of them, and Riley looked at the ceiling to see the metal grill that got lowered to block entrance during off hours. "Was that gate down when you guys showed up?"

Timbale stared, and Riley turned to look at him.

"Detective Timbale. Was the gate~"

"I don't know. I don't remember."

Riley started across the garage with Timbale trailing behind. "It doesn't matter. If it was down, maybe that explains why Stanton left the car behind when she left."

"It matters if they put it down before ten. Chelsea admits she was here during the afternoon. She walked home and left her car behind. If the gate was down while Jon Casady was still alive, then we have proof Chelsea couldn't have driven here."

There was a small office behind the gate, unmanned but with a small intercom. Riley pressed the button and waited only a few seconds before there was a buzz.

"Building manager."

"This is Detective Parra with Detective Timbale. We're investigating Jon Casady's death. We just had a question about the gate on the garage."

Another burst of static. "Go 'head."

"What time do you close it at night?"

They waited and Riley glanced at Timbale. She knew that the response would vindicate one of them.

Static. "Business hours are eight in the morning until seven at night. Unless one of the occupants requests it remain open a little longer, we close it every night at a quarter after eight."

"Were there any requests to keep it open last night?"

"Nope. Night attendant's report says it got closed at... let's see. Eight-seventeen last night."

Riley thanked him and turned to Timbale. "Chelsea was with Caitlin Priest at eight o'clock last night. She couldn't have driven here any later than that." She walked past Timbale. "Your one and only suspect is innocent, Timbale."

"This doesn't prove that for sure."

"Then let's go see what else we can find."

Kenzie and Priest waited outside the holding area with Riley. Riley had convinced the lieutenant that the closed gate supported Chelsea's version of events, and that was enough to release of her on recognizance. The door opened, and the sergeant escorted Chelsea out. Her cuffs had been removed and she was wearing her own clothes again. Kenzie was the first to step forward. "Chels."

Chelsea smiled and held out her hands, letting Kenzie come to her. They kissed softly, whispered to one another, and then Chelsea said, "Is Cait~"

"I'm here." Priest stepped forward and, to Riley's surprise, also kissed Chelsea. Instinct told her to look away, but it was shocking to see her partner kissing someone like that. When they parted, Chelsea turned her head slightly until she spotted Riley.

"The woman of the hour."

"Don't start the parade yet. There's still a killer out there."

Chelsea nodded. "If I could help you, I would."

"I know. Don't worry about that, just get yourself home. You've had a hell of a night."

Chelsea put her arm around Kenzie and then tilted her head toward Priest. "Cait..."

Priest leaned against Chelsea's side. "Riley, if you can spare me, I think I should~"

Riley cut her off. "Go. Go on. You guys have a lot to talk about."

Priest nodded her thanks and followed Kenzie and Chelsea out of the room. Riley took the stairs up to Homicide, where Timbale was stewing at his desk.

"Congratulations on taking the investigation backwards. We now have absolutely no suspects and no clues in this murder."

"We have clues. Those Post-its..."

"For crying out loud. The guy's pen ran out of ink. He put them there so they'd be in his line of sight. It's a damn row of Post-it notes."

Riley shrugged and held her hands out. "You want off the case, I'll tell Briggs. I gave the notes to forensics and they'll tell us if anyone besides Casady touched them."

"And you think that will lead us to the killer."

Riley shrugged. "It's better than what we have now. I'm going down to the morgue to see if they found anything on Casady's body. Wanna come along?"

Timbale made a noise of disinterest and went to his desk. Riley was grateful he opted out; she hated to have guests when she visited Gillian.

She took the stairs down, trying to keep her pace professional. When she arrived, Gillian was in the midst of her autopsy and barely looked up.

"Rile E. Coyote."

"That's me. *Querulous Detectivus.* What do you have for me, Roadrunner?"

Gillian looked up. Her eyes were magnified by her work goggles, and the bottom half of her face was covered by her mask. "Querulous? What are you complaining about?"

"No, it means full of questions."

Gillian thought for a second. "Inquisitive detectivus?"

"Doesn't work as well." Gillian shrugged and let it go. "What do you have on the body?"

"Two forty caliber Smith and Wesson bullets taken from the chest cavity. I sent them down to forensics to find out what gun they came from. He had way too much coffee the day he died. And he received oral sex within minutes of being shot."

"Please tell me you mean minutes *before* he got shot."

"Yep. He came before he went."

Riley winced. "Poor bastard."

"I know some guys who would pay to go out like that. I swabbed the saliva for DNA~"

"Sent it down."

Gillian made a gun with her finger and shot Riley with it. "So what's new with you?"

"I got Chelsea Stanton released."

"Good girl."

Riley shrugged. "I'm working with Charlie Timbale."

Gillian wrinkled her nose. "Ugh. I don't like him. He still calls me 'miss' every time he comes down here."

"He's a product of another age."

"Hm. He's living in this age now, so he should catch up. I'm about done here. Do you want to grab a late lunch?"

"I'll probably work through lunch. Bring me something?"

"Tuna sandwich."

Riley nodded. "Thanks." She blew a kiss so she wouldn't

contaminate Gillian's ensemble. "Let me know when you're ready to go home. I'll give you a ride. Sorry you had to take a cab this morning."

"Hey, Priest needed your help. I understand."

"How did I get blessed with you?"

Gillian lifted a shoulder. "I'm balancing out all the other shit you have to deal with in your life. I'm your prize."

"Worth it." Riley smiled. "See you later."

Gillian waved goodbye and went back to her corpse.

Riley drove back to Casady's office so she could get a feel for it without Timbale looming over her shoulder. She took the stairs up and opened Casady's office again. She had taken a look at the crime scene unit's file before she left, so she knew what had been taken as evidence. The laptop, several drafts of a book taken from the desk drawers, and cigarettes taken from the ashtray. Riley started on the row of Post-it notes nearest the door and began reading them. She didn't know what she hoped to find, but there was so much content that she hoped there was some clue.

She reached the section on Chelsea's story and almost skipped over it. She went ahead and looked, reading snippets about Chelsea's childhood and her home life. Toward the bottom of the row was a note that said, "3some sexual relationship? Det. C. Priest, M. Crowe. VARIFY. Source - GF;G."

Riley reached for that note just as there was a knock on the door. The man was tall enough that the top of his cap was obscured by the doorframe, but Riley recognized the uniform for Over Night Parcel Delivery Service. He was carrying a thick envelope. "ONP for a Jon Casady?"

Riley showed him her badge. "I'll sign for it."

"What happened here?"

"Someone got killed last night."

The deliveryman whistled as she signed his clipboard. "I guess sometimes even overnight isn't fast enough, huh?"

"Yeah, sometimes." She took the envelope from him and carried it to Casady's desk. The address had been written in the same handwriting as all the Post-its she had just been reading. She ripped the package open and reached inside to find a typewritten manuscript. The cover page gave the title as *Wings of Blood: The True Story of the Angel Maker, His Capture, and the Police Cover-Up*.

"Shit." Riley put the book down and thumbed through it.

There was a fairly accurate accounting of the crime scenes, and she and Priest were, naturally, prominently mentioned. She went to the back of the book, to the chapters detailing the Angel Maker's capture.

"A motley crew of crime fighters - including a medical examiner, a police lieutenant, a former detective, and a former police officer - converged on Terrence Charles Bishop's house in the early hours of Friday morning. Witnesses on the scene the following morning revealed that this strange assortment carried an even stranger armory: water guns."

Riley thumbed ahead to the next part.

"My own examination of the house further confused the situation. A large amount of blood was discovered in the upstairs room where Bishop met his end. This blood was separate from the position of Bishop's body and can only be explained by the mysterious 'injured officer' reported in the original radio calls from Lieutenant Zoe Briggs. The facts in the case are these: Caitlin Priest, purported to be the detective injured in the assault, was *not even present* at the scene. There were no witnesses who could place her at Bishop's house before or after the call went out.

"Most damningly, emergency medical technicians who responded to the call reported a second dead body in the room with Bishop. This body was identified as a Hispanic female in her mid-thirties. She was pronounced dead at the scene and taken to the morgue in a body bag."

Riley was almost trembling. She shoved the book back into the envelope and turned to leave, only to discover the doorway blocked by the demon Gremory, also known as Priest's first romantic interest, Alyssa Graham.

The succubus didn't carry any lingering reminders of the assault in No Man's Land. Her porcelain skin was unflawed, and she wore a silky black blouse and trousers that billowed around her legs as she took a step forward. She smiled and gestured at the package.

"You're welcome, Detective."

"You did this?"

Gremory smiled, showing teeth filed to dangerously sharp points. Riley felt an undeniable pull, an urge to drop onto her hands and knees and let the demon do whatever she wanted. It was easier to fight back now that she knew what it was, but the draw was still there. She braced her shoulders and focused on Gremory's dark eyes.

"I did it for you, Riley. I'm sure you wouldn't want this book hitting the shelves. Mr. Casady didn't quite make the leap from water guns and mysterious resurrections, but he would have. Or, if he didn't, someone else would have made the leap for him. When this book came out, you would be exposed. The war between Heaven and Hell would be on the bestseller list. And you would have to reveal you died, and your sweet little partner gave up being an angel to save your life. And, oh, the panic in the streets when people find out that demons are real and Heaven just doesn't give a shit."

Riley held up the envelope. "So why did you cover this up? Seems like a riot would be right up your alley."

"There are other things, other truths, that Mr. Casady was close to uncovering. It was in our best interest to keep those quiet for the time being. But keeping the truth about the Angel Maker case covered up, well... that's just icing on the cake."

Riley's hand strayed toward her gun. "How is this going to go?"

Gremory held up her hands. "I'm not here for a fight. I just wanted to let you know that you now owe me, Detective Parra. The angels would praise my name if they knew what I had prevented last night."

"You framed Chelsea Stanton for Casady's murder."

"I needed *someone* to blame. She was convenient. Plus it ensured your involvement on the case. Imagine if Detective Timbale had been here, if he had discovered the manuscript currently in your hands. You and Lieutenant Briggs would have had a lot to explain about."

"How'd you find out about it?"

Gremory chuckled. "Oh, I have my sources. Farewell, Detective Parra. We'll be in touch." She blew Riley a kiss and stepped back through the doorway. Riley blinked, and the demon in woman's clothing had vanished.

Riley looked at the envelope again. If Gremory had killed Casady, he would have died with a smile on his face instead of two slugs in his body. She remembered the evidence of oral sex Gillian had uncovered. Gremory had lowered Casady's guard, but someone else actually pulled the trigger. There was a mortal involved, and Riley had a good idea who it might have been. If she had an angel watching her back, then why wouldn't Gail Finney have a demon watching hers?

She looked at the Post-its on the wall. *Source - GF;G.*

Gail Finney and Gremory.

She took out her cell phone and dialed the precinct as she went back downstairs. "This is Detective Riley Parra. I need you to run a registry check. I need to know if Gail Finney has any weapons other than her poisoned pen."

Gillian brought Riley a cup of tea and then sat next to her on the sofa. Riley had just finished telling Gillian what had happened at Casady's office. Gillian rested her elbow on the back of the sofa, her hand under her chin as she watched Riley. Finally, she broke the silence. "What do you want to do?"

"My options are limited. I can either let Gail Finney get away with murder, or I can bring her in and let this book come to light."

Gillian looked down at the manuscript. "You have to decide which option is the lesser evil. Do you think Gremory was right? That the people of this city would riot if they learned the truth about angels and demons?"

"I think people have rioted for less, and in cities with fewer reasons to riot than No Man's Land. Releasing this book would play right into Marchosias' hands. But if I leave the case open, the public opinion will always be that Stanton really was guilty and we just let her go. We can't have this case go unsolved. Gail owns the gun that killed Casady. I don't have to give it to forensics to know that. Gremory gave her the access and Gail pulled the trigger. If I turned her in, I would finally have her off my back."

"And yet, the motive..."

Riley picked up the manuscript. "If the book wasn't around, it would just be Gail's word for what was in it."

"You'd destroy evidence?"

"I don't know." Riley sighed. "I've been thinking it would be easier if everyone just knew about angels and demons and the whole damn mess."

"But you know they're not ready for it." She leaned in and kissed Riley's cheek. Riley turned her head until their lips touched. "I'm going to bed. Are you going to stay up for a while?"

"Yeah, at least a few minutes."

Gillian nodded. "I'll keep the bed warm for you."

"Thanks." Riley watched Gillian walk out of the living room and then looked down at the pages in her hands. Every possible solution came wrapped up in a package of other problems. Would people even believe what the book said? A detective resurrected by her angelic partner? Demons and angels running rampant through No Man's Land? She could say that Casady was delusional and Gail was insane for believing him.

But Casady only put down the cold, hard facts. Riley's blood, the testimony of the EMTs who were on the scene. If the book came out and if anyone else followed the evidence, they would arrive at the right conclusions.

Riley looked at her watch and thought about calling Priest for her opinion. She hoped the fact that Priest was still not there meant she had worked things out with Kenzie and Chelsea. She couldn't begin to understand the dynamics of that relationship, but they seemed to be happy with it. Anything that made Priest and Kenzie being happy was okay in Riley's book.

The decision was ultimately hers, so she moved to the far side of the couch and picked up the receiver of Gillian's phone. She hated the rotary dial on the phone, but it gave her the time to consider what she was going to say when the person she was calling answered.

"Hm. Yeah, what?"

"Detective Timbale. I have a new suspect in the Casady case."

She heard a shuffle of papers on the other side of the phone. "Give it to me."

Riley put the manuscript on the coffee table. "Her name is Alyssa Graham. Alias Al Graham, alias Alyssa Gremory. She's to be considered armed and dangerous, and should only be approached with the utmost caution."

"Spell the last name." Riley spelled the whole name, and Timbale paused while he wrote it down. "You think this lady's the one who killed Casady, huh?"

"I think she played a big part in his death, yeah."

"I'll send it down to dispatch. Hey. Uh." He cleared his throat and finally got the words to come. "Good work today, Detective Parra."

She resisted the urge to scoff. "Thanks. I'll see you around the office, Timbale."

She hung up and slid down until she could rest her head against the back of the couch. She had no doubt Gremory would never allow herself to be arrested, but maybe she would go to ground if all the cops in the city were looking for her. At the very least it might make things difficult for Gail Finney, at least for a few weeks.

"Ahem."

Riley opened her eyes and twisted to see Gillian standing at the entry to the short hall that led to the bedroom. She had changed into a short, dark green nightie and her makeup had been washed off. Her face shined, and Riley felt a tug in her chest.

Gillian flipped her hair over her shoulder and rested one hand on her hip. "I know I said I would wait up for you, but I wondered if you had an ETA."

"Yeah." Riley pushed herself off the couch and went to her fiancé. She put an arm around Gillian's waist and guided her back down the hall to their bedroom.

MORTAL COIL

Riley woke to the sound of murmuring in the bedroom. She opened her eyes and looked at the ceiling, one arm loosely wrapped around Gillian as she waited for the sound to repeat itself. The moonlight through the window indicated it was still too early for anyone in the building to be watching TV or preparing for work. She was about to write it off as a dream noise when Gillian suddenly spoke.

"Where're you?"

Riley looked at Gillian's face. She was fast asleep, her lips slightly parted. Her face was slack. She pressed her lips together, making a quiet smacking noise, and then shifted her position on the mattress. She lifted her head, placed it on a different part of Riley's arm, and sighed sleepily. "Where are you?"

Her hand was on Riley's stomach, the fingers relaxed. Riley covered it with her own hand and stroked the fingers. "I'm right here, babe." She kissed Gillian's forehead.

"M'kay."

Riley smiled and let herself fall back to sleep.

Gillian left the shower running as she stepped out of the tub.

Riley brushed her hand over Gillian's hip as she stepped into the tub and pulled the curtain closed again. She cupped her hands under the water and let the warmth wake her. As the water poured over her, she remembered the brief interlude in the night. She craned her neck, tilting her head forward so that the spray would wash over her hair and down her back.

"Hey. What were you dreaming about last night?"

"I was in a laundromat, and I didn't have enough quarters."

"Did you think I had some?"

Gillian laughed. "You never have any change. Why?"

Riley ran her hand over her head. "You kept asking where I was. 'Where are you, where are you?'"

"Huh. I don't remember that part."

Riley finished showering and turned off the shower. She toweled off while Gillian finished putting on her makeup and doing her hair in underwear and a T-shirt. Riley watched her, and Gillian glanced at Riley's reflection in the mirror and hid her smile.

"Stop it. I feel like a museum attraction."

"I'm just soaking it up. Saving it for a later date. Who knows when I'll see you again?"

Gillian scoffed. "Monday. You'll see me Monday. I just need to go down there and deal with being the family's newest bride. Plus I'm going to ask my best friend Maureen to come up and be my maid of honor. I'll be homesick in two hours and clawing at the door after one day. So you don't have to worry."

Riley shrugged. "Still, Monday? There's a lot of time between now and then. That gives me a whole weekend where I could forget what you look like and fall madly in bed with any number of women."

"Hm. Well, in that case, maybe you should come with me. I can show you off to my family and let them see how lucky I am." She glanced over her shoulder at Riley. "Has that ever been... you know, discussed? *Can* you leave town? I know you came down to Georgia to get me that one time, but that was kind of special circumstances. Could you just take a vacation?"

"I don't know. To be honest, I never really thought about leaving town even before I got the tattoo and became champion. Now I don't know what would happen if I left, especially with Finney and her little demon running around." She stepped forward and put her hands on Gillian's hips. "I do wish I was coming with you, though."

"Grammy and Mama wouldn't leave you alone. And when you did get a moment to yourself, you'd be bored to death."

"After the past couple of years, I could do with boring. I could really, really enjoy boring." She brushed aside Gillian's still-wet hair and kissed her neck.

Gillian turned her head to the side and closed her eyes. "Unless you have some masochistic desire to hear a septuagenarian complain about her bridge group, and a woman in her fifties worry that I'm not eating enough, then I think you're better off with the demons and murderers. The only person I want you to meet is Maureen, and she's coming up here anyway. Besides, maybe it'll be a slow weekend and no one will kill anyone."

Riley laughed. "Yeah, maybe."

Gillian pressed back against Riley's naked body. "What's the clothes situation? Am I putting on or taking off?"

Riley sighed. "Your plane leaves at noon, so I guess you should put some on. But I'm making that decision under duress."

"I know you are."

Riley reluctantly pulled away from Gillian and went into the bedroom to get dressed. She had gotten as far as her underwear when her cell phone rang. She sighed and flipped it open without checking the Caller ID. "Detective Parra."

"Where are you?"

The voice was barely a whisper, but it froze Riley where she stood. "Who is this?"

"Where *are* you?"

Riley disconnected the call and looked at her received call list. The last recorded call was from Priest the night before, with no memory of the call she'd just answered.

Gillian came out of the bathroom. "Who was on the phone?"

"I really have no idea."

"What's that supposed to mean?"

Riley thought about the flight Gillian was about to board, the fact she would be away and unable to do anything to help for three days. Putting worry in her mind was the last thing Riley wanted to do. It would fester and ruin her trip home. So she tossed her phone onto the bed and shrugged.

"It was just a wrong number."

"Phone calls should be illegal before nine in the morning, unless you use the speed dial. How hard is it to click the right name on a list?"

Riley smiled and took a shirt from the closet. "Sorry, hon. I didn't mean to send you off on a tangent."

"You just wanted to distract me so I'd miss my flight. Well, I'll make you a promise. If I spend three days down in Georgia~" She lengthened the name of the state into an overly Southern drawl. "~ Ah promise Ah'll come back heah with a verah, verah sexy accent."

"Mm. Might almost be worth it in that case."

Gillian smiled and kissed Riley. "Get dressed. You'll be late for work."

"I called Briggs and let her know I'd be in late today. I'm driving you to the airport."

"You don't have to do that."

Riley shrugged as she buttoned her shirt. "You'll be gone for seventy-two hours. I'm not going to let you spend your last hour in town with some cab or shuttle driver."

"Thank you." Gillian pulled on a turtleneck and flipped her hair over the collar. "You know, if this was a cop show, you and I would get caught up in a murder investigation at the airport and my flight would be delayed. Then we'd have to wait for the next flight together in the first-class lounge. You know, because they upgraded our seats for catching the dastardly villain."

Riley smiled. "Yeah?"

"Mm-hmm. The episode would be called 'Layover.'"

Riley laughed. "Whatever gets me more time with you, I'm all for. Are your bags by the door?" Gillian nodded. "Then let's get dressed and get this murder mystery on the road."

Riley draped her jacket over the back of her chair. "My life isn't a cop show."

Priest looked up at Riley's despondent tone. "Pardon?"

"Nothing. Never mind." She sat down, turned on her computer, and looked at the notes on her desk. She and Priest were back on the regular shift after Riley's punishment for her Gail Finney sound bite. It appeared all the overnight murders had already been assigned to other detectives and there wasn't much for Riley and Priest to do except for busywork.

"Did Gillian get out okay?"

"Yeah. Hey, if I need your help with something over lunch, would you be free?"

Priest nodded. "What do you need?"

"Just another set of eyes and someone with better taste than my own." She tapped the keyboard and the document for writing a report came up. It was supposed to be blank, but the first line was filled with one repeated phrase:

WHERE ARE YOU?

Riley stared at the words and then turned the monitor around so Priest could see it. "Cait, what do you see here?"

Priest looked up. "A blank report document?"

Riley turned the monitor around again. It was, as Priest said, blank. "Yeah. That's what it is, all right."

"Are you okay, Riley?"

She rubbed her face and nodded. "I'm just going into withdrawal from Jill not being here. I'll be fine. It's only three days." She cleared her throat and picked up the file so she could read her chicken scratch notes as she typed them up.

The slight, stoop-shouldered Middle Eastern man smiled as Riley moved down the glass case. His shop was cramped and narrow, with only a few feet of space for the customers to move around. The clerk himself had an equally-cramped area for him to move about behind the counter. Priest was on the other side of the store gazing through the glass at the diamonds and other gems while Riley shopped and tried to avoid the hopeful gaze of the shopkeeper.

Priest made her way around to where Riley had stalled. Riley looked up as Priest approached and shook her head in disbelief. "Would it kill them to put a price on something?"

The jeweler finally made his move. "Perhaps I could help you find something?"

"Yeah." She reached up and scratched her neck. "I'm looking for a, uh... a wedding ring. I didn't exactly put a lot of thought into her engagement ring, and I want to make up for it, but I'm... not very good at this sort of thing."

"Ah, yes." He gestured at Priest. "Your fiancé?"

"No, she's just—" She didn't want to use the term 'partner' and further complicate the issue. "She's helping me out. I figure my price range is about... uh..." She took a slip of paper from the counter and wrote a number on it, including both her bank account and savings before sliding it over.

The clerk picked it up and then raised his eyebrows at her. "It's customary to spend two to three months' salary on a ring."

"I am. I'm a cop."

He smiled again and dipped his chin, simultaneously an acknowledgement and an apology. "Do you have any idea on, perhaps, what sort of diamond you would like?"

"Ah... she said something once about how her favorite word was opalescence. She said it was one of very few words that sounded as beautiful as what it was describing." She smiled self-consciously. "So I was thinking maybe an opal with diamond accents."

"Let me see what I have for you." He held up one finger and went into the back of the store. Riley turned to see Priest was smiling at her.

"I've never seen you like this. Nervous and awkward."

"This guy is going to rob me blind and, because it's for Gillian, I'm going to let him. It makes me feel weird."

The bell over the door sounded and they both turned to see who the new arrival was. Priest tensed and Riley straightened as Sariel closed the space between them. She reached out as if she was going to grab Riley's arm.

"We need to go somewhere. Now."

Riley twisted at the waist. "I'm in the middle of something. It can wait."

Sariel glanced at Priest and then quickly looked away. "There's been a development. I've been trying to find you~"

"That was you?"

Sariel blinked. "What was me?"

Riley glanced at Priest and then shook her head. "Nothing. Whatever the problem is, it can wait until we're done here."

Sariel grabbed Riley's arm. She felt as if she'd been jerked violently forward, and the room went dark. Once she regained her bearings she saw the truth; the room hadn't gone dark, it had changed. They were standing in a tenement corridor, the only light coming from the window at the top of the stairs far to their right. Riley reeled at the sudden switch in venue, the smells and sights inherent in a low-income building like this at war with her memory of the shop she had just left. She grabbed the lapels of Sariel's blouse - an airy seamless garment that couldn't have been made by any Earth-bound manufacturer - and shoved her back against the wall.

"If you ever do that again, so help me I will~"

Sariel brought her hand up and placed it under Riley's throat. She flicked her fingers and Riley was thrown backward. Sariel followed Riley's movement and grabbed the front of her shirt as soon as she hit the ground. She lifted Riley off her feet with all the exertion of a soccer mom picking up a bag of groceries.

"You will what, Detective Parra?"

"Fine. Didn't think the threat through. Put me down."

Sariel hesitated, but then lowered Riley to the ground. "This is a matter of the utmost importance. I don't require wasting time traveling by mortal means and, in this instance, it was imperative that I get you here as soon as possible. There has been an incident." She turned and started down the corridor.

"You and I need to have a long talk about respecting personal space." Riley was still a bit wobbly on her legs, as if she'd just stepped off a boat on a stormy sea. "Priest would never have just grabbed me like that."

Sariel kept her face turned forward, but Riley could see that her lips were pressed together in a firm line. "Zerachiel was a... failure to you in many ways. It's my hope that I can undo the damage she did."

Though Sariel seemed to be a slight brunette, she was much more powerful than any human Riley had ever subdued. So she had to use her dirty takedown methods. Riley swung her right leg out and hooked Sariel's ankle with her foot. Sariel started to go down and Riley slammed into her from behind. They hit the floor and Riley pinned the angel in the way that she'd been taught in the Academy.

Sariel shoved up, and Riley put her arm across the angel's neck and slammed her back down. Sariel shouted angrily as Riley spread across the top of her body.

"Zerachiel gave her life to save mine. She was there for me, and the best parts of her live on in Caitlin Priest. Zerachiel was twice the angel you are, and I would take her back in half a second even if I had to sacrifice your sorry ass to get her. So if you ever badmouth that woman again, you and I will have issues. If I only get in one punch before you tear me into little bloody pieces, rest assured I am going to make that hit count. Apologize."

To Riley's surprise, Sariel seemed grateful for being knocked down. She closed her eyes and nodded. "I apologize. I misspoke."

Riley let her weight pin Sariel for a moment longer before she got up. She held her hand out and, after staring at it a moment, Sariel took it to help her stand up. Her bottom lip was bloody and she touched her finger to it in confusion.

"You might be an angel, but you've got a fragile little human shell to worry about. Sucks, doesn't it?" She brushed past Sariel and continued down the hall. "Where the hell are we going? You brought me all this way through the magic of fairy dust, why didn't you just take me directly there?"

"There's a matter of witnesses. The corridor was empty so we could arrive unseen. The scene is in the lobby."

They walked the rest of the way in silence. Riley saw that the lobby was the center of activity, but it wasn't until they reached the foot of the stairs that she saw why. Four patrolmen were blocking the front entrance of the building, and five women were standing against the wall next to the building manager's office. Riley approached one of the men in uniform and showed her badge. "Riley Parra with the four-ten. What's going on?"

"How did you get in here?" He decided his question didn't matter and motioned her away from the crowd. He looked at Sariel and focused his attention on Riley. "Are you from the Sexual Offenses Unit?"

"No, Homicide."

"Then it's not your problem. Count your blessings, 'cause this is a fucking bad one. Pardon my language. Those five ladies all called the police this morning because they'd been raped. Dispatcher let us know we were all headed to the same place. At first we thought it was a mistake, a duplicate call or something. But the apartment numbers were all different. We talked to the girls and all the descriptions match up. Same guy. Bastard had a busy night."

"Did he force his way in?"

"We didn't find any evidence of that. The women think he drugged them. They remember the incident clearly and they feel like they didn't have a choice but to comply with him. They had a sudden inexplicable desire to have sex with this guy they'd never seen before."

"None of them had seen him before? He just picked five women at random?"

The cop shrugged. "None of the ladies seemed to recognize him. We have the sketches if you'd like."

"Yeah, please." He went off to retrieve them and Riley turned to Sariel. "Okay, yeah, this is a terrible thing. But I don't know what it has to do with me."

Sariel reached into her pocket and then brushed the back of her closed hand against Riley's cheek. "Slap yourself."

Riley brought her hand sharply across her own face, the sting blooming even as she frowned in confusion. "What was that about? Why did I just do that?"

"Because I asked you to." Sariel unfolded her fingers to reveal a single white feather in her palm. It was slightly curved, with a tuft of down near the shaft. Riley reached out and stroked it without knowing why she was doing it, then withdrew her hand.

"What is that?"

"It's a feather from one of my wings."

"How powerful is it?"

The uniformed cop returned with the sketches. Sariel pressed the feather against his forehead. "Sleep." His legs went limp and he collapsed into Sariel's arms. She said, "Wake," and he straightened.

"Sor-sorry. I don't know what~"

"I think you tripped." Sariel helped him back onto his feet. "It's quite all right."

The cop handed the sketches over to Riley and began looking at the rug around his feet to see what had tripped him. Riley looked over the sketches. There were slight differences, like the distance between his eyes or the length of his nose, but they were all definitely of the same man. Or, she supposed, maybe a pair of brothers who had decided on a reprehensible bonding method.

"Get these out, see if anyone ran into him or saw him last night between his trysts."

"Yes, ma'am. Ah... someone from SOU is on the way. Should I tell them you're taking the case, or...?"

Riley started to shake her head, but Sariel stepped in. "Yes. Detectives Parra and Priest will be taking the lead on this."

"I think they'll be glad to hand this one over, to be honest."

When the cop was gone, Riley turned to Sariel. "Great. When Briggs finds out, she's going to kill me just so there will be a homicide associated with this case."

"Would you rather another detective uncover the connection to angels?"

Riley sighed. "Don't throw logic at me, okay? I'm just pissed that you're right." She took her car keys from her pocket and handed them to Sariel. "Give these to Priest and tell her where I am. I'm going to talk to these young ladies and see what they can tell me. Just so I'm clear, it's not an angel we're looking for, right? There's not a seraphic rapist running around."

"No. Whoever is responsible is simply using the feather to get what he desires. Caitlin will be here soon."

Sariel nodded.

"And you're welcome." Sariel tilted her head. "For this. You dragged me away from what I was doing, pointed me at it, and said 'Go.' I could have just walked away and let SOU deal with it." Sariel's face remained blank. "A thank you wouldn't be out of line."

"I'm helping you with your duty to protect the streets of No Man's Land, and keeping the war between Heaven and Hell a secret by bringing you in to conceal the angelic aspects of this crime. A thank you would not be out of line from you, either."

With that, Sariel turned and walked away so she could vanish without witnesses. Riley flipped her off behind her back, sighed, and walked over to where the women were waiting.

"Hello. I'm Detective Riley Parra. I know you've already been through a lot already today, but I was hoping you could answer just a few more questions for me."

Riley was just finishing with the last victim when Priest arrived. She looked anxious and annoyed, and much more human than Riley had ever seen her. She swept her hair out of her face and exhaled sharply as she came into the lobby, rolling her eyes when she spotted Riley. "I told the jeweler that you had to step out for an emergency."

"Thanks. Did Sariel brief you on what's happening?"

"Yes. Angel feathers. I don't know how anyone would have gotten their hands on a pair."

Riley moved Priest to one side of the lobby so they could speak without being overheard. "Do they decompose? I mean, obviously they're not your run of the mill attachments. Is there a chance these are Ridwan's wings? We never did recover them."

"It's not possible," Priest said. "Our... *their* wings don't decompose in the manner you're suggesting, but Ridwan's would never have survived this long in the mortal realm. Unattached from divinity, their power would fade and their feathers would be normal. After a time they would simply fade away. Wherever this feather came from, it's... fresh." She looked disgusted by the prospect.

"Is there any way Sariel can track it down? Maybe get an angelic bloodhound?"

"She's attempting to find it now. Presumably, an angel couldn't go undetected in the city without being sensed by the others. Sariel hasn't felt an unexplained presence, and all the angels she knows about are accounted for. The explanation for that is a binding circle. Zerachiel was placed in one by Kimaris last year. The circle completely negates an angel's power and cuts them off from the other seraphim that might be in the area."

"Like the trap we use to hold demons in the Cell."

"Exactly. Someone is holding an angel hostage and taking feathers from its wings."

"How would someone even do that? Was the angel summoned?"

Priest shrugged. "We'll have to ask this rapist when he's found." She gestured over Riley's shoulder and Riley turned. One of the victims, Eleanor Judd, had approached but was keeping a respectful distance.

"Ms. Judd, did you remember something?"

"I don't... know. I think I might have. The man you're looking for. When he knocked, he said he was from Tichino's. It's an Italian place not far from here. I told him that he had the wrong apartment, but he told me it was a coupon offer." She blinked tears from her eyes and looked away. Riley respectfully gave her a moment to compose herself. "I order from there all the time, so I just assumed it was some kind of loyalty program or something. Anyway, um, I think I believed him because maybe I recognized his voice. Like maybe he had really answered the phone when I called down there. I talked to the others, and they order from there all the time, too. It might not mean anything. I mean, it's right down the street, so..."

"It's still a possible connection. We'll definitely check that out. Thank you, Ms. Judd."

She nodded and went back to where she and the other four women had created a sort of support group. They'd pulled chairs out of the apartment manager's office and were sitting in a semi-circle to speak quietly.

"Come on. Let's give the girls some space."

Priest followed Riley outside, and Riley took a moment to get her bearings. Sariel had taken her halfway across town, over the border into No Man's Land. No wonder it had taken Priest so long to drive from the jewelry store. She snapped her fingers and made a grabbing motion, and Priest tossed her the car keys.

"Do you have any idea where this Tichino's place is?"

"I passed it on the way. It's about two blocks to the south."

They got into the car and Priest put up her hand before Riley could start the engine. "I had a little time between Sariel taking you away and when she came back to tell me where you were. I hope you're not offended, but I took the time to speak with the jeweler." She reached into the inner pocket of her suit jacket and withdrew a ring box. She handed it to Riley.

Inside was a beautiful opal ring, with diamond accents at the four corners. The band was white gold.

"Caitlin..."

"I know you're uncomfortable buying jewelry, and I thought buying something so meaningful for Gillian might make you freeze. I really hope I didn't overstep my bounds~"

"This is amazing, Caitlin. Thank you so much for doing this. I... this can't be in my price range."

"No. It was in mine." Riley looked up. "You can reimburse me what you can afford. The rest will be my wedding gift to you and Gillian. The two of you have done more for me in the past few months than I... I ever... You gave me a home when I'd lost everything I knew. I don't know the etiquette about buying a ring for your partner and her fiancé. I just wanted you to be able to give Gillian the ring you truly wanted her to have. Money shouldn't be an issue in that instance."

"I'm speechless, Cait. Thank you. And Gillian thanks you."

"It's selfish. You didn't register anywhere and I was close to being forced to buy you a toaster oven."

Riley laughed. "Was that a joke?"

"Did I do it wrong?"

"No. You did it just right." She looked at the ring one more time before she placed it in the glove box. She made sure the box locked before she started the engine. "I'll let you know what Gillian thinks of it when she gets back."

Riley drove them to Tichino's. It was in a square brick building that had been painted white at some point in the previous century, the layers peeling off to reveal the gray and brown underneath. Riley parked in a narrow alley alongside the building and climbed out of the car into a solid wall of cooking smells. She suddenly regretted skipping lunch.

She pointed toward the back entrance. "Stay here. Kid might try to run."

"Right. Be careful."

Riley nodded and went around to the front of the building. There were two customers sitting together near the front door. The dining area was separated from the kitchen by a long, high counter and she could see four or five people moving about around the ovens. She unhooked her badge and palmed it as she crossed the black and white tile floor to the front counter. A boulder-shaped man with a thick mustache was at the cash register and he smiled when he looked up, his facial hair twisting around his lips.

"Afternoon. Can I he'p ya?"

Riley held up her badge just high enough that only he could see. "Yes, I need to arrange pizzas for a party I'm having this weekend. I'll need about eight pies." She unfolded the sketch of the rapist and raised her eyebrows. "Do you think you could help me out?"

The man straightened slightly at the sight of her badge. "Oh. Oh, sure... uh, do you want to come into the back so we can talk about payment?"

"Of course." He stepped aside and led Riley into the kitchen. "Hey, Jo-Jo."

One of the kids working the oven, a twenty-something with limp black hair, turned at the sound of the manager's voice. He wiped his arm across his forehead and then noticed the woman walking behind the mustachioed manager. He immediately twisted at the waist and broke into a run, his sneakers slapping noisily against the tile as he headed for the back door.

"I'm sorry! I didn't think he~"

Riley ignored the manager's protests as she took off after him. The kid slammed through the back exit without slowing down, and Riley slipped through before it shut behind him. She saw Priest move to the middle of the alley with her arms extended as the kid raced toward her. The kid didn't even hesitate as he threw his weight into Priest and sent her sprawling. She hit the brick wall and went down hard on the alley floor, giving a sharp cry of pain as she rolled onto her side.

"Caitlin?"

"Go! I'm fine, go!"

Riley hated ignoring how Priest was cradling her left arm, but the kid was younger and faster than she was. She ran out of the alley and took only a brief second to spot him again. The few people on the street stepped out of the way to let him pass, like cars pulling over for the sound of a siren. Riley put on an extra burst of speed and kept the kid in her sights as she headed down the street.

"Police! Freeze!"

An Indian man washing down the product in front of his grocery story looked up at Riley's shout. He took stock of the situation, turned slightly at the waist, and aimed his hose at the fleeing kid. The spray hit the kid directly in the face and his body went rigid at the unexpected impact. He spluttered and put his hands up, suddenly worried more about drowning than his pursuer. The distraction was enough for Riley to close the distance between them. She tackled the kid from behind and knocked him face-first onto the sidewalk, pinning him as she had Sariel earlier in the day.

She got her cuffs off her belt and twisted his arm to get them onto his wrists. "What's the matter, Jo-Jo? You see a woman in full possession of her faculties and it made you shit your pants? Get your ass up." She hauled him up and looked at the shopkeeper. "That was an incredibly stupid thing for you to do. But thanks."

He waved his hand in the air. "Too many of these punks around. Good riddance to him!"

"You'll get yours, old man. Just you wait until I'm out."

Riley clucked her tongue and jerked on the kid's arm to make him walk. "Now, see, what you did there? No judge is going to let you have bail after that. So that makes what you just said a very, very stupid thing. C'mon, walk. Or I'll drag you back to my car facedown over the pavement."

She got back to the alley and found Priest sitting up against the wall with the restaurant manager kneeling next to her. She had a cold compress on her left elbow.

"Caitlin, you okay?"

"My elbow is really killing me."

The manager looked up at the kid with murder in his eyes. "That's evading arrest and assaulting a police officer, Joey. On top of whatever the hell else they were comin' here for. What the hell were you thinkin'?"

Joey kept his mouth shut and looked away.

The manager waved his hands in the air palm-out, symbolically washing his hands of the kid. "Whatever you need, detectives, anything I can do for you, just let me know."

"Yeah. Do you have this douche bag's address?"

The manager nodded. "It's inside. I'll get it for you."

Riley put Joey into the back of her car and used the radio to call one of the units from the crime scene to come pick him up. With Joey secured, Riley went back to where Priest was sitting and staring down at her arm. She crouched and looked at the ice pack.

"How bad is it?"

"I think it may be fractured."

Riley winced and looked over her shoulder to make sure Joey was staying put. "That's no fun. I guess you underestimated his strength."

"No, I overestimated mine." She met Riley's eyes. "You know exactly what happened, Riley. I'm not the cop I used to be."

"You made a mistake. It happens to the best of us."

Priest sighed and winced. "If I can't be an effective partner to you, then maybe it would be best~"

"Hey. I used to be partnered with a guy who was basically twice my age, had a beer gut, and was just barely in shape enough to walk from his bed to the car to come into work. He had to stop in the middle of an elevator ride to catch his breath." Priest smiled weakly at the joke. "Whatever else you are, or whatever you aren't, you'll always be my partner. Until I decide otherwise."

"Oh, until *you* decide?"

"Yeah. That's how it works. I'm the senior partner."

"I'm much older than you."

"You're three years old, and I've been a cop longer. So suck it, you're the baby."

The manager returned as Riley was examining Priest's elbow to make sure it wasn't too bad of a fracture. "His name is Joseph Bertram. We call him Jo-Jo. This is his address. As far as I know, he lives alone." He handed over a slip of paper. He sighed and, when he spoke again, his tone implied he didn't really want to know the answer. "What did he do, anyway?"

"He raped five women last night."

"Oh, Jesus. Take him the hell out of here, and tell 'im he's got no job to look forward to when he comes back."

"Will do."

A squad car arrived and parked behind Riley's car. "I'll hand Jo-Jo over to these guys and fill them in. They can hold onto him until we get a chance to ask him some questions. Meantime, I'll take you to get that X-Rayed and then we can head over to his apartment and see where he got the feather."

"You would wait for me before you go solve your mystery?"

Riley shrugged and held out her hand. Priest took it and let Riley carefully help her up. "Jill's out of town. I have to take care of *someone* just so I won't get rusty."

At the hospital it was determined that Priest fractured her ulna. The doctor splinted the injury and instructed her to take things easy for a few weeks. It was mid-afternoon before they left the hospital. Priest tugged on the shoulder strap of her sling and looked distraughtly at her bent arm. "I'll hardly be any use to you like this."

"Don't talk like that. Briggs will give you a little time off, I'll probably get stuck with Booker again, and you'll be back at work in no time. You're mortal now, Cait. Like it or not, you have to learn to take care of yourself. But until then, you want to check out this kid's apartment and see where he got his angel feather?"

"Sure."

Once in the car, Priest brightened ever so slightly. Joseph Bertram's apartment wasn't far from Tichino's, just inside walking distance of both work and the building where he'd assaulted the women. It was another nail in the kid's coffin.

They explained the situation to the building manager and, like Bertram's boss at the restaurant, he was more than happy to help them. He explained his distaste as he led them up the stairs. "Little punk is always banging up and down the stairs, all hours of the night. Hasn't paid rent in I dunno how long."

"Then why don't you kick him out?"

"I was all ready to, couple months ago. Then..." He looked away as he reached the door and fumbled with the key. "I don't know. Maybe it was just a burst of compassion for the dumbass."

Priest mouthed 'feather,' and Riley nodded. The manager pushed the apartment door open and indicated for them to be at liberty.

"Leave the door open when you leave. It'd serve the punk right."

Riley led the way inside. The living room was tiny and cramped, stuffed full of rummage sale furniture and stacks of old magazines and empty pizza boxes. The aroma of old Chinese food mixed with cold pizza and the stink of spilled beer and general maleness. Riley wrinkled her nose at the mixture of odors.

"And this is why I date girls."

Priest moved across the room, stepping over piles of dirty clothes, and examined the bookshelf. Bertram used it to store

DVDs instead of books, big surprise, and Priest tilted her head to scan the titles.

"He has porn."

"Gillian has porn. That doesn't prove anything."

Priest showed her one of the cases. "*Hold Her Down Until She Likes It?*"

Riley made an involuntary grunting noise of disgust. "Okay, yeah, maybe it proves more than I thought."

Priest turned. "What kind of porn does Gillian have?"

Riley smiled and continued down the hall to the back rooms. The bathroom door was open, revealing Joseph Bertram's hygiene was no better than his living conditions, and the bedroom door was standing slightly ajar. Between the two was what she assumed to be a closet. She nudged the bedroom door open with her foot to confirm it was empty and then tested the knob on the closet. It was unlocked. She pulled the door open and the stink of decay immediately wafted out. She dropped her hand to the butt of her gun as she took a step back and opened the door wider.

It took her a moment to process what she saw within. She swallowed a lump that felt like it was the size of a fist. "Cait... come here."

Priest came down the hall and froze when she saw what was in the closet. "Oh My Father."

The man inside the closet gave them a weak smile. "Our Father didn't have anything to do with this, Zerachiel."

To say he was just skin and bones would be an overstatement. His skin was parchment, clearly showing the lines of his ribs. His stomach was distended, his bony legs folded underneath him. His eyes were sunken into his skull, but still maintained a glow that rivaled most people Riley encountered during her day. But the truly impressive feature, the only thing about him that looked vital, were his wings.

They spread out from his back in a wide arc, curving around the confines of his small prison so that the tips overlapped the door like curtains. The vanes seemed to glow with a light from within, illuminating the small space and throwing shadows over the angel's emaciated form.

The angel smiled at her, a death's-head rictus. "I guess you finally heard me."

Where are you?

"That was you."

He nodded slightly. "I've been trying to get the message out for weeks now. I could only affect the quiet mind. Your partner in her sleep, or your idle phone. I wasn't sure I'd even managed to get through, but here you are. Hello, Detective. My name is Selaphiel. I've been waiting for you for quite some time."

"Actually, I didn't know what to make of those messages. We're here on a case. Joseph Bertram has been doing some very bad things with your feathers."

"Oh, yes. I used everything in my power to prevent him from discovering what they could do, but he eventually uncovered the truth. That's when I redoubled my efforts to contact you."

"Riley." Priest's voice was quiet and Riley turned to see what she was pointing at. A circle had been cut into the floor using some sort of knife, encompassing the closet entirely. Looking closer, she could see small designs inside the curved line. She could also see a thin layer of pale blue powder inside the crack.

"Flax," Selaphiel explained. "He burns it when he's home to add an extra barrier between us. I don't think he trusts the carvings very much." He smiled and shrugged. "Not that I would be much trouble if I did get out."

"How did he capture you in the first place?" Riley said.

Selaphiel cleared his throat and pointed at Priest. "That... was inadvertently your fault, Detective Priest. Do you have any idea what sort of upheaval you created when you brought Detective Parra back to life?"

Priest's face blanched. "I didn't... I-I just~"

He waved her off. "It's no matter. The Father was pleased with your decision. It was the ultimate sacrifice of Love. Or it... it would have been, had I not gotten in the way."

"Tea."

Priest and Selaphiel both looked at Riley. She blinked, realized she had spoken aloud, and then pointed at Selaphiel. "You were there."

Selaphiel smiled and nodded.

Then

Riley was on the floor in the Angel Maker's upstairs room, the room where she was going to die. She accepted that now. Lieutenant Briggs was kneeling beside her. She felt like it had been hours, days, since she looked down and saw the blade sticking out of her side. She was getting weaker with each heartbeat, and she was sure she could feel the blood pumping out of the wound. The only thing that wasn't right was her company.

"Get Gillian."

Briggs looked on the edge of breaking. "She's coming, Riley."

She wished she had the strength to get up, to go find her. It seemed *right*, somehow, that she had chosen Gillian for this mission. Ordinarily she would want Gillian as far away as possible from this place. But she'd let her come, and now she knew why. Gillian had to be there to say goodbye.

"You have to get Gillian. I want..." Her voice trailed off as she saw Gillian step into the room. She was dressed in white, and her hair was down. Riley smiled at the sight of her. "Hey, Jill."

"Hello, Riley. I'm not Gillian, but I am someone who has been very close to her for her entire life."

"Her guardian angel?"

The woman who looked like Gillian nodded. "Zerachiel felt she wouldn't be welcomed, so she asked someone to watch over you. I was here anyway. I chose to look like this to make things easier for you."

"Good job."

The angel reached out and touched Riley's face, and Riley realized she didn't hurt anymore. She sighed with relief and turned her head toward the caress. She was lifted from her position on the floor and Gillian's angel slipped one arm around Riley's. They walked, and Riley had the impression of being led through an archway and into a field. The grass was high enough to brush the legs of her trousers as she walked forward. Gillian's angel disappeared and Riley wished her luck in her mission to protect Gillian in the future.

She saw a two-story Victorian house in the distance and walked toward it. As she grew closer she heard the sound of hammering.

The side yard had a table set up with two chairs on either side. The hammering stopped and a man appeared on the roof. He waved to her and walked to the ladder leaning against one side of the porch's overhang. Riley stood next to the table and waited for him to arrive. He was an average sized man with dark skin and light hair. He wiped his hands on a cloth as he joined her at the table, and then he sat down.

"Hello, Riley."

"Where are we?"

"It's polite to say hello back when someone greets you. Hello,

Riley."

"Hello, God."

He straightened in his chair and laughed.

"What, you're not God?"

He waved her off. "The names amuse me. There have been so many over the years. Gods are gods, and people call me God. It's like naming your cat Kitten, isn't it? Just capitalizing it. My favorite name was Loki, but you can call me whatever you like."

Riley eased down into the other seat. "Maybe I'll call you Kitten."

He laughed again. "Fair enough. Do you want some tea?" He twisted in the seat and another man came out of the house. He was tall, fair-haired, and he wore his wings folded against his back. He was bare-chested and barefoot, wearing only a simple pair of brown trousers. He placed a tea service on the table and stepped back. Her host leaned forward. "I love tea. Thank you, Selaphiel."

He poured himself a cup, added sugar, and then looked up at her.

"I would feel self-conscious if I was the only person at the table drinking the tea. So I would refrain if you refused. However, if you would simply take a cup, I could enjoy a beverage."

Riley shrugged. "Fine."

"Good! Thank you. I appreciate it." She heard the sound of tea pouring into the porcelain cups like it was the only sound that existed. "We don't have long. What would you like to discuss?"

"Why me?"

A bellowing laugh. "Oh, you get straight to the heart of the matter, don't you? Well, Detective Parra. Why *not* you?" He took a sip of tea, and then placed His cup back onto the table. "Now our time runs short. What do you really wish to ask me?"

Questions began to form in Riley's mind. "Why *now*? Gail Finney is still down there causing trouble. I only just started this job, and now... I'm done?"

"You've done a lot of good in your short time on the job, as it were. You should be happy. A lot of champions die in horrible, unthinkable ways."

Riley looked into her teacup. "I don't feel lucky."

The ground trembled. Selaphiel and her host looked at one another. Her Host raised an eyebrow and His lips curled into a surprised smile.

"Well." He carefully lowered His cup to the table. "That is

certainly unexpected..."

"What's happening?"

Selaphiel looked alarmed and then focused on the Host. "You can't allow her to do this."

The Man seated across from Riley held His hands out, palm-up. "I can't stop her, if it is her free choice."

Selaphiel looked at Riley as if he was judging her.

Riley felt like her entire body was tingling. She held up her hands and looked at the palms, and they were coated in a thin white glow. "What's going on?"

Her Host finished his drink and placed the cup back on the table. "It would appear that your guardian angel is preparing to make the ultimate sacrifice. It was always possible, but only one has ever actually done it. Ridwan gave up a sizable amount of his divinity in order to save you all those years ago. It looks like you inspire great sacrifice, Riley. Your Zerachiel must be a truly special individual. I would like to meet her." His gaze shifted away from her briefly. "Selaphiel, will you see her back?"

Riley leaned forward. "Wait, that's it? A little tea and now... what? I just got here."

Her Host smiled and stood up. "No, you didn't. You've been here for quite a while, but you won't remember this conversation. Well, not the vast majority of it. Time is different here, as is memory. We have been talking for quite some time. Rest assured it was quite a conversation for us both." He winked. "But the time has come to make our goodbyes."

Riley felt something tugging on her, like the first tug of gravity when she started to roll off the bed. It almost felt as if she was hovering. She closed her eyes to focus against the sensation and she felt a hand on her arm.

"Just remember, Riley. You're getting a second chance. Don't waste it."

The next sensation was one of falling sideways, being thrown horizontally along a wide and dark room. The darkness coalesced into the familiar surroundings of the morgue. She saw Gillian and Priest in a swirl of light and movement. For a moment, she felt what they felt - pain and anguish and heartache. The world closed around her and she felt Priest's hands on her body. The energy coursing through her fingers was~

Selaphiel hovered over her. In a flash of energy, he was blown sideways until he vanished in a blinding flash of~

Priest was thrown back and Riley heard a rending in the back of her mind as~

Riley came back to life.

Now

Riley said, "You brought me back."

"I simply escorted you back to your flesh. Zerachiel brought you back. The energy dispersed by the act caused me to become bewildered and lost. I wandered for a time until I was found by a disillusioned former priest. It was he who knew how to bind me. He didn't want to keep me in the church or his home, so he brought me to his son's home." He indicated the closet. "I've been here ever since. Joseph has spent the intervening time attempting to find ways to use me to his advantage."

Priest turned and walked away. Riley watched her go and then faced Selaphiel again. "Bertram's father. Where can we find him?"

"There's an establishment not far from here called the Rubber Inn." His nose wrinkled as he said the name. "Their alcohol is cheap, and women disrobe for the entertainment of men. He is often there to satisfy one vice or the other."

Priest returned gripping a football helmet by the facemask. She lifted it into the air and then drove it straight down with all her strength on the closet's threshold. The floor cracked and Riley jumped to one side in shock.

"Jesus, Cait!"

Priest stepped into the closet and crouched. "Can you stand?"

Selaphiel put his hands on her shoulders. Priest put her right hand underneath his left arm. "Riley, could you..." Riley stepped into the closet, which was just barely large enough for the three of them, and together they eased the angel into a standing position. Riley stepped out of the closet first and watched as Selaphiel stepped over the line of the trap. "You broke the circle."

Priest nodded. "It only takes the smallest crack and the circle will be broken."

"By and by, Lord, by and by," Riley muttered.

Selaphiel leaned against the wall and sighed with relief. "Thank you. Both of you. But I fear that all you have done is ensuring I will not die as a prisoner."

"There's hope," Priest said. "If we can get you to a church, the worship~"

"No. The evil that Bertram and his son have done weigh upon

my soul. I can feel the harm they caused with the pieces they took from me. I look forward to the peace that passing on will afford me. But I have felt other things since my arrival on this plane. Things connected to you, Detective Parra. At our first encounter, I doubted the chance you were given. But now I see the truth. You love purely and platonically. Your devotion to Caitlin, even after what she had done to you in the past, proved you worthy."

Selaphiel closed his eyes and groaned. Riley put a hand on his shoulder, near the base of his wings.

"Do you need to lie down?"

"No. It would... not... help..."

Priest straightened suddenly, her eyes wide. "Riley, you have to get out of here."

Riley started toward the door. "What? He's in trouble. If~"

"There's nothing you can do. You need to leave here right this instant or things could get... strange." Priest looked at Riley with fear in her eyes, mixed with something that Riley thought might be hope. "Please, Riley, trust me."

Riley stepped back, letting Priest take Selaphiel's weight. She hesitated, but then she turned and ran for apartment's door. As she ran, she became aware of the fact that everything in the room was subtly vibrating. It felt like an aftershock was centered in the hallway behind her. She could feel the increasing vibrato of the pulse growing stronger with each step.

She ducked into the corridor and pulled the door shut behind her. She had expected the hallway to be empty, but Sariel was standing a few feet to her right. Sariel grabbed the lapels of Riley's shirt and spun her around, pinning her to the wall.

"What have you two done?"

Before Riley could respond, the shockwave hit. It was a mixture of light and sound, a cacophonous explosion that knocked both Riley and Sariel off their feet. Riley brought both arms up to protect her head in her certainty that the building was about to collapse all around them. Her heart was pounding in a slightly irregular pattern when the tremors finally ceased, and she dropped her arms to find the hall was miraculously untouched.

Riley pushed herself up on her hands and shook her head to clear the ringing. "What in the blue fuck...?" Riley got to her feet as the apartment door swung open and Priest stepped out. She had taken off her sling, her arm hanging by her side in its splint. Her hair veiled her face, and she seemed to be having trouble catching her breath. Her face was streaked with blood.

"Cait...?"

Priest suddenly screamed and dropped to her knees. Riley moved forward, but Sariel put up a hand to hold her back. "Wait."

"Let me go, damn~"

Wings burst through the material of Priest's shirt, long curved barbs that spread out to either side, the feathers spreading out in a gilded fan. The wings flapped once and filled the hallway with a brilliant golden light that almost burned their eyes, but Riley couldn't look away. Each feather seemed to be ruffled by a separate breeze, and Riley felt the warmth coming off of them even from a few feet away. Priest extended both arms and the splint fell away. Her fractured arm gave her no problems as she flexed her shoulders to make the wings sweep in wide arcs.

Kneeling in the middle of the hall, Priest looked down into her palms and then tilted her face toward the ceiling. Her eyes shone with tears, and her smile was the most pure Riley had ever seen. Light seemed to pour from Priest's body, her skin radiant and her hair lifted by air currents Riley couldn't feel. Finally she spoke one, single word in utter reverence.

"Father."

"What happened?" Sariel whispered. Her voice was strained.

Priest lowered her gaze until she found Sariel.

"Selaphiel retained part of Zerachiel. A portion of the energy expelled when she resurrected Riley was absorbed by him. At first he merely intended to keep her safe. But when he was imprisoned by the Bertrams, Zerachiel kept him alive. Her spark sustained Seraphiel long enough for us to find him. When he allowed himself to return to the Father, he released Zerachiel's essence. It went to the only living person in the room. Me." The tears were flowing freely down her face now. "I am Zerachiel again. I live."

Riley cautiously moved closer and dropped to one knee. "Cait? Are you still in there?"

Priest laughed. "I'm the same person I was before, Riley." She caught herself. "No. I'm... better. I've lived as a mortal. I've been Caitlin Priest and nothing more, and I know the importance of keeping her close to my heart." She cupped Riley's face and leaned in to lightly kiss her lips. "I love you, Riley. What you have done for me these past few months I can never hope to repay. But I will try with every moment I draw breath."

Riley stood, and Priest stood with her. She sighed and flexed her wings before drawing them back in. The holes in the back of Priest's blouse sagged, empty.

Priest took a steadying breath and then looked at Riley again. "I believe Selaphiel told us something about where we can find the elder Bertram."

Riley cleared her throat. "Yeah. Sariel, you~" She turned and saw the corridor behind her was empty. "Great."

"She had to leave. What just happened was hardly a... sanctioned activity." She rolled her shoulders, rubbed her left elbow, and widened her eyes slightly. "Don't worry, Riley. I believe that my time as a mortal has opened my eyes. Caitlin Priest is more than a shell, and she must be treated as such. From now on I will endeavor to let her guide my decisions when necessary. During the Angel Maker fiasco, I decided that I wasn't on Heaven's side anymore. I was on your side. Whatever that entails, you can count on me and you can trust me."

Riley held out her hand. "Good enough. Nice to have you back, Z."

Priest smiled. "Let's go catch a bad guy."

She could still hear the sound of Depeche Mode playing through the walls of the strip club. Riley stood in the open door, holding it open with her shoulder as she stared at her partner's back. "Hey. You want to be alone?"

Priest turned around to reveal she was smiling. "I want to be alone or with you. I don't care which."

Riley let the door swing shut behind her and joined Priest. They'd called in SOU and handed over the two Bertram men. Riley's story was that Joseph Bertram had put together a bizarre new form of date rape drug that he wore on his clothing. The women were exposed as soon as they opened their doors and took a whiff. When Riley took the father into custody, in the midst of a lap dance, she informed him of what it would sound like if he and his son tried to explain they were using feathers from an angel's wing to rape women.

She rested her elbows on the railing next to Priest. "Are you okay?"

"I'm fantastic. I finally feel like myself again." She looked at her palms. "But it's not the same as before, was it? Before I was pretending to be mortal. Now I've experienced life as a mortal. I've felt pain and pleasure~"

"Shit. What are you going to do about Chelsea and Kenzie?"

Priest shook her head. "I don't know. But I do know that I can tell the difference between love and lust. And I know that I still feel lust for both of them."

"And love?"

"Of course I love them. I love you and Gillian as well. It's a different sort of love than what you mean." She chuckled. "But there's a chance it could grow into that sort of love."

"I wish you nothing but the best, Priest. Have you talked to Sariel since this all went down?"

"I think she's avoiding me."

"Yeah, I can see how this sort of thing would be weird to her. Angel to mortal to back again."

"That's not why she's avoiding me." She picked at the cuticle of one finger before she realized it wasn't an issue anymore. "She feels lust for me, and it frightens her. We kissed, and she enjoyed it. It was a bigger deal for her at the time because she was an angel."

"And now that you're both angels?"

Priest shrugged. "I don't have any idea."

Riley looked down at her shoes. "Well, one thing is for sure. The sex would be earth-shattering."

Priest laughed and shook her head.

"Come on. You want to see Pa and Bertram Junior get carted off to the pokey?"

"Yes."

Riley pushed away from the railing and led Priest back inside.

Three days later

Riley leaned against the trunk of her car, scraping her shoe on the asphalt. The transit cops had tried to get her to move three different times, but she just flashed her badge and intimated she was on official police business. Her arms were crossed over her chest and she was trying her level best to stay calm. She focused on the reasons why she was nervous. Gillian had already said yes. They were engaged. This was just a ring. She wasn't even sure if presenting the wedding ring was something she was supposed to do. Was it supposed to be a surprise at the ceremony, like the dresses? Riley didn't want to do that. She wanted Gillian to see the ring and get her disappointment out of the way in private.

Of course, with Priest's input, the ring wasn't half bad.

Riley happened to look up the moment Gillian appeared

through the crowd. Her heart leapt into her throat and she abandoned her car, going through the wide sliding glass doors to the glass and plastic antiseptic world of the terminal. Gillian saw her as she came inside and her face brightened. She held out one arm in anticipation of Riley's running embrace, and she laughed as Riley pressed her face into her shoulder.

"That was a long seventy-two hours."

"It's only three days."

"But my way sounds a lot longer, so it's more accurate."

Gillian laughed and pushed Riley away just enough to see her. She smiled, kissed Riley hello, and let their contact linger before she pulled away.

"I can't believe I went over forty-three hundred minutes without a Riley kiss."

"God, how did we survive going cold turkey like that?" They kissed again. When they parted, they spoke at the same time.

"I have something to show you."

Riley smirked. "At the car?"

"Yeah."

Riley looked past Gillian. "Where is your friend? Maureen?"

"She's coming out soon. She has work, so she'll come up once we have an official date. Take me to the car."

Riley slid her hand into Gillian's, wondering when she had become such a sop. Gillian dragged her suitcase behind her, the wheels bouncing along the smooth tile with a steady growl. Gillian flexed her hand in Riley's, apparently appreciating how well they fit together. "So did anything exciting happen while I was gone?"

"They painted new stripes in the apartment's garage over the weekend."

"Oh, that'll be nice. Yellow?"

"White."

"Ah."

They took another few steps before Riley spoke.

"Priest is an angel again."

Gillian stopped walking. Riley continued until her arm was fully extended, then turned back to see what the delay was.

"Back up."

"The stripes? They're mostly at forty-five degree angles, I think, but I~"

Gillian closed the distance between them. "She's... back?"

"It's a long story, but yeah. This weekend has been the Priest and Zerachiel, reunion tour. I'll tell you about it over dinner." She leaned in and kissed Gillian's cheek just in front of her ear. "After we get reacquainted."

Gillian shuddered. "How is she handling it?"

"Pretty well. I think she's viewing her time as a mortal as a sabbatical. Or maybe a prison sentence, I don't know. She's back, but she's different. I really believe it'll be a stronger combination of Caitlin and Zerachiel this time around."

Gillian shook her head and let Riley load her bags into the trunk. "I leave for a weekend and things go haywire."

"Could have been worse. Priest told me that if I hadn't left the room when I did, I might have gotten the divinity instead of her. So you could have come home to find out you're engaged to an angel."

"I'm glad you left, then. I'd much rather have the heathen. Hey..." She tugged on Riley's jacket and made her turn around. "I want to show you what I brought back. I don't want to wait."

"Okay."

Gillian cleared her throat. "I told my mother and grandmother about you. That I'd finally found the person I had been waiting for my entire life. I told them all about how you make me feel, and how you're the person I want to spend the rest of my life with. I asked if I could have Grammy's ring."

She took the case out of her pocket and flipped open the top. Riley was dazzled by the shine of the diamond.

"Jill. I can't~"

"Sh. A man bought this ring almost seventy years ago. He gave it to my Grammy as a promise when he got sent to war. He said it belonged on love's finger. He died in the war, and Grammy never found anyone else worthy of it. She wore it every day in memory of him. She was going to give it to Mama, but Daddy wanted to buy her a ring himself so it stayed in Grammy's treasure chest. When I went back there this weekend, I told... Grammy that I had found the finger the ring had been waiting for all this time. I told them that I'd found the most selfless, beautiful, caring, and wonderful person I'd ever met, and that you asked me to spend the rest of my life with her. This ring has been waiting for you, Riley, and I think it's high time you put it on."

Riley let Gillian lift her hand, stunned by the speech. The ring was slipped onto the third finger of her left hand, and Gillian bent down to kiss it before she let go of Riley's hand.

"I don't know what to say after that."

"Don't say anything. Just show me what you wanted to show me earlier."

Riley panicked. "No. I can't, not..." She looked down at her ring.

Gillian caught the look and inferred its meaning. "Did you get me a ring?"

"I... I don't have a story. I don't have a family. I just have a ring."

"No, you have a ring from you. That's all I need." She smiled. "Show me."

Riley reached into her pocket. "Priest helped with the price. It was a little out of my range, so she made it a wedding present to me." She took out the ring case and, after a moment of regret, opened it.

Gillian stared, closed her eyes, and let her smile grow. "Riley... I never wanted a diamond ring. I thought..." A tear rolled down her cheek and dropped from her chin. "I didn't say anything. But I always thought the woman who gave me a non-diamond ring would be who I was meant to be with forever."

"Priest didn't pick it out. She just helped me pay for it." Gillian laughed. "I thought about you and... opalescent."

Gillian wiped her cheek. "Opalescent. My God, Riley. Put it on me."

Riley eagerly agreed, sliding the ring onto Gillian's finger.

"I can wait until the end of the month."

"What?"

Gillian blinked away her tears, but a few drops were caught on her eyelashes. "We haven't set a date, and I can wait until the end of this month. I understand we need a couple of weeks to get everything set up. But I really think we should get married before next month."

Riley smiled. "I think I can make that work."

They kissed, and someone passing by gave a catcall. Riley ignored them, her arms around Gillian, fighting the urge to cry even as she felt Gillian's tears on her lips. There would be time to exchange stories about their three days apart, for Riley to tell Gillian about how Priest regained her divinity. But that could all wait for later.

They had three whole days to make up for.

THIS HELL BOUND TOWN

THE IDENTIFICATION process was more like a theatre production than she cared to admit, but they put up with it for the family's benefit.

Gillian made sure that the other bodies were carefully put away in the cooler before she changed into a fresh set of scrubs. Her hair was tied back out of her face and she took her position by the head of the table to wait for her part in this little performance to begin. The body on the table was a Jane Doe, picked up at the waterfront that morning. There were rope burns on her wrists and her initial examination had found pieces of cloth caught in her teeth as if she'd been biting down on something at the time of death. Gillian's examination had revealed the victim had been held prisoner, and apparently beaten, before she was dumped by the water like garbage.

Gillian had done her best to clean up the body for this moment, but it would still be a shocking sight.

The door opened and Riley entered, pausing to make sure the woman with her was okay before they continued on into the room. Riley had one hand on the woman's shoulder, but the woman's gaze was focused on the sheet-covered body in the middle of the room. She lowered the Kleenex from her face and pointed before quickly looking away.

"Is that... h-her?"

"That's what we're trying to find out, Mrs. Tucker. This is Dr. Hunt. She's the medical examiner."

Gillian nodded solemnly. "Hello."

Riley stopped a few feet from the table and met Gillian's gaze. Neither of them enjoyed this part, but Riley knew that it ate at Gillian more than her. "Just let us know when you're ready. You can take as~"

Ann Tucker made a noise halfway between a sob and a groan. "Please. I just want to... to know. I have to..."

Riley nodded to Gillian, who pulled the sheet down just far enough to reveal the Jane Doe's head and upper chest. Her skin was the color of marble, her black hair combed away from her face and forming a starburst around her head. Ann's face twisted in confusion, and she moved a step closer. For a moment, Riley saw hope blooming in her expression and prepared herself for the unwelcome job of smashing it down. Sometimes death could change a person's face. Not a lot, but just enough to confuse someone used to seeing it in life.

"Oh, God." She immediately retreated, bumping Riley's arm before she turned away. "It's her. It's Abigail."

Riley put her arm around Ann's shoulders as Gillian covered the body back up. Riley resisted the urge to sigh. Their missing person case had just officially become a homicide.

Ann Tucker only looked up when she smelled the coffee Riley was offering her. She whispered her thanks and took the cup, cradling it with both hands as Riley sat in the plastic chair beside her. They were in the corridor outside the morgue, as far as Ann could go before she requested they sit for just a minute so she could regain her faculties. Riley sat in silence, hands clasped between her knees as she waited for Ann to break the silence.

"She used to call me Fanny." She smiled sadly. "When we were growing up. I hated it. She'd run up behind me and smack me, and she'd say, 'Gotta work on that fanny, Annie!'" She brought the coffee to her mouth but lowered it again without drinking. "This whole time I kept thinking she was being a stupid... selfish bitch. I was mad at her all week for running off without telling us where she was going. And now th~" She cut herself off mid-word by pressing her fingers to her mouth.

"It's all right. Mrs. Tucker, I'm sorry about this, but I do have to ask you a few questions about your sister."

She nodded. "Anything I can do to help."

"Your sister was missing for three days before you contacted us. Why did you wait so long?"

"Because it was *Abby*. She would get up to go to the bathroom and realize she had never seen Maine in the fall. So she would walk out and hop a plane to watch the leaves change color. We wouldn't know where she was until she came home with souvenirs. Two or three days was usually her limit, so I didn't get concerned until it had been forty-eight hours without a word. I went to her apartment and I found it... well, you know how I found it."

Riley remembered the mess they'd found in the apartment. Piles of clothes tossed around, DVDs and CDs spilled onto the floor, a lamp that had fallen and cracked a window. No blood, but they were fairly sure nothing had been stolen. Riley and Priest had secured the scene before handing the case over to Missing Persons. They had worked the case concurrently until a body matching Abigail Shelby's description had been found dumped near the waterfront.

"Do you know anyone who might have wanted to harm your sister?"

Ann laughed. "My sister was a photographer. She paid her bills with family portraits and graduation photos and, otherwise, she was in some nature preserve taking pictures of acorns. My sister inspired protectiveness. Even when she was being a twerp, you just wanted to wrap her up and... k-keep her safe."

Ann hung her head as another round of tears started. The elevators opened and Priest stepped out. She slowed her steps when she saw Riley and Ann. Riley motioned her forward and Ann looked up. "Oh. Detective Priest."

"Excuse us." Riley stood and led Priest out of Ann's earshot.

"I take it the viewing went..." She trailed off, and Riley couldn't help her. Could a viewing be said to go well?

Riley said, "It was definitely Abigail Shelby. What did you find out?"

"A couple of joggers saw the body this morning at around five, but they thought it was just debris washed in from the water. It wasn't until the man with his dog showed up that anyone bothered to look closer. She could have been dumped there any time during the night."

"Any cameras in that strip mall near the scene?"

Priest shook her head. "I can ask around and see if anyone was in the area and might have seen something. Both mortal and... upstairs."

Riley smiled. "You like being back in with the big boys, huh?"

It was meant as a joke, but Priest didn't return the smile. "I don't know. I'm not entirely sure I'm back in their good graces. It's been a week and I've hardly seen or heard from anyone, including Sariel."

"I'm sure they're just trying to figure out what it means for you to be back. Just chill and let them come to you. Speaking of which, I'll offer to drive Mrs. Tucker home and then we can swing by the crime scene. I'll help you canvas."

Priest nodded and Riley went back to where Ann was waiting.

"Mrs. Tucker, do you have someone to stay with you?"

"Mm. My husband is going to take the day off work when I told him I was coming down here. He's at home now." She stood up and looked down to make sure she wasn't forgetting anything. When she looked at Riley again, her face cracked slightly. "Will you find out who did this to her?"

"We'll do everything in our power to make sure they pay."

"I've been having odd dreams."

Riley glanced at Priest before turning her attention back to the red light. They had dropped Ann Tucker off at her home. Ann's husband Robert had promised to keep an eye on her. Ann said she just wanted to sleep and remember her sister. "What kind of dreams? Do they involve Kenzie in a French maid outfit? Because I think she plants those subconsciously when you date her."

Priest chuckled. "No. They're disjointed and confusing. There are two men, each of them backed by a large army, and they face each other across a narrow strip of dirt. The sky is dark and the men debate without speaking."

The light changed and Riley rolled forward. She could see the waterfront up ahead, but the crime scene was a half mile to the north. "What else?"

"Nothing. That's the entire dream."

"Well, I'm no Dr. Fraud, but I think it means you've watched *Lord of the Rings* too many times."

"I've never seen that once. Who is Dr. Fraud?"

"I don't know. I was mocking either Dr. Phil or Freud. Either one works. Next time we see her, we can ask Gillian. She's good with dreams."

Priest looked at her. "Really? I didn't know that."

"Yep. Apparently all of my dreams indicate I'm madly in love with her."

Priest grinned. "It must have been nice to figure that out."

Riley nodded. "Saved me some time. How long have the dreams been going on?"

"They started about a week ago. After the situation with Selaphiel and the Bertram men. Do you think it has anything to do with Zerachiel being rediscovered?"

"Doesn't Zerachiel have an opinion on that?"

"I wouldn't know." Priest looked out the window. "She's being stubborn."

Riley was surprised by the anger in Priest's voice. "Trouble in paradise?"

Priest sighed wearily and pressed back against her seat. "I learned to live without her. I learned to appreciate what she had done, but I was doing fine as a mortal. I had just started to come into my own, and now she's back. I don't want her gone, but I find myself reluctant to welcome her back with open arms."

"I can understand that. How does Z feel about it?"

"She's been adrift and unanchored from existence since the incident in the morgue. She thought that was what death was, so she didn't realize the truth. Selaphiel rescued her and held onto her until such time as he could take her back to where she belonged. He thought that meant Heaven, but fortunately..." She pushed her hair out of her face. "I feel like things are back to normal, but I also feel like I've taken an unwanted step backward."

Riley pulled to the curb. "Well, next time I get into a life threatening situation, you can sacrifice her again and go back to the way things were."

Priest didn't laugh. "I would."

"I know you would, Cait." The businesses along the waterfront were all that remained of an ill-fated attempt to create a boardwalk for tourists and beachgoers. Unfortunately, the beach had never evolved out of the rocky, garbage-strewn ribbon of dirty sand between land and water, and the buildings became revolving doors of low-rent small businesses. "You start on the north side of the street, I'll take the south, and we'll meet in the middle. Sound good?"

"It's as good a plan as any."

They climbed out of the car and Priest started down the street. Riley went the opposite direction, checking the time on her cell phone as she approached the first business. She looked to the right, out over the waterfront, and thought about the moment almost three years earlier when she and Kara had been called to investigate a body found in a drainage pipe. If she'd only known where that night would lead, she might have just stayed in bed.

She thought about her relationship with Gillian, partnering with Priest, reuniting with Kenzie, everything good and bad that had happened to her since that night, and reconsidered.

If she had it to do all over, even knowing what she knew now, she would probably have still gone out on the call.

"Lady, trust me. I been here eight years. I see anything out there after dark, you can bet I forget it pretty much immediately, awright?"

"Sorry, I didn't see anything. Even if I did, I don't really want the trouble. Sorry."

"You see the sign on the door, Detective? Nine in the morning until five in the afternoon. The sun goes down, so does the grate on the front of this building. I'm safe at home by dusk every night, no exceptions. Wish I could help."

Riley was leaning against the side of her car with a flatbread sandwich when Priest returned. "Did you get one for me?"

Riley picked up the sack off the roof of the car. "I got you chicken and ranch. I wasn't sure if you still... you know, appreciated food." Priest leaned against the car next to Riley and unwrapped her sandwich. "I'm not blaming you, but this whole thing is kind of weird for me. I got used to thinking of you as an angel, and you became a mortal. I get used to that, and now you're an angel again."

"I'm a mystery."

"You're a pain in the ass."

Priest smiled. "For the record, I do still enjoy food. Maybe not as much as I did two weeks ago, but I've learned to appreciate the ceremony of breaking bread with those you love. And certain foods do have an exquisite taste."

Riley wiped a speck of dressing away from her lip with one

finger. "You get anything out of your guys?"

"Nobuddy saw nuthin'," Priest said with a think guttural accent. "It's as if they believe that by keeping silent they're protecting themselves from having the badness fall upon them."

"Some of them do believe that. They think that the bad things that happen here, even in No Man's Land, are someone else's problem. It won't, and can't, happen to them. I've tried to appeal to them with the old 'wouldn't you want someone to come forward if it was your wife or sister' argument, but it doesn't hold much water."

"People are scared."

"It's my job to make them less scared. Both my jobs." Riley finished her sandwich and wadded up the wrapper. "Sometimes I think I'm failing at both of them."

She started to push away from the car, but Priest grabbed her arm. "Christine Lee was afraid. I wasn't directly involved with her when she was champion, but I was around. I walked No Man's Land when she served as champion. Do you know how many demons she faced? None. Do you know how many times she fought Marchosias directly? None. She was a cop first, and nothing else second. The champion before her committed suicide immediately after passing on the tattoo. You're the best champion this city has ever seen. For either side."

"The best ever? How do you know that?"

Priest furrowed her brow. "Because..." She looked away, closed her eyes, and then looked back. "I don't know. But take my word for it, Riley. You've already done so much more than anyone could have asked of you. Remember that."

"I will, Cait. Thanks." She turned around to look at the water. "Gillian said that Abigail was killed around eleven last night. That means the killer kept her alive for almost a week before he finished the job and tried to get rid of the evidence. There was no sign of sexual assault, but there's evidence she did have a lot of sex in that last week. Gillian claims it was consensual, but she was definitely restrained. What happened during the week she was gone?"

Priest considered the question, but she still had the confused expression on her face. She was obviously stuck on her comment that Riley was the best champion the city had ever seen. Riley decided to let her off the hook and walked around the front of the car.

"C'mon. You can finish your lunch in the car on the way back to the station."

They fastened their seatbelts and Priest suddenly turned to Riley with a look of fascination and fear on her face.

"We need to make a stop on the way."

"This isn't exactly on the way." Riley wasn't complaining, just pointing out the fact they had passed the station about ten minutes earlier. She was now slowly rolling through the affluent city center while Priest examined every white-brick building and fancy water feature they passed. "What exactly are we looking for? I could be an extra set of eyes."

"I wish you could. But I'm not entirely sure what I'm looking for. I'll know it when I... when I..."

"See it?"

"Feel it, is more accurate. It's very difficult to explain." She drummed her hands on her thighs as Riley made another turn. She spent so much time in No Man's Land that it was sometimes hard for her to remember just how different it was from the main body of the city. Here the sidewalks were frequently swept and the windows were cleaned. Buildings were fronted by courtyards decorated with abstract sculptures instead of trash piles and junkies shooting up. It felt wrong, like makeup on a corpse. It felt like it was trying to be something it really wasn't.

Priest shot out her hand and clasped it on Riley's forearm. "Stop. Stop."

Riley checked traffic and pulled to the curb. Priest was out of the car while it was still rolling, halfway down the sidewalk before Riley caught up with her. She went through a stone archway into a building's enclosed courtyard, pausing before she rounded the dry fountain to the front door. Riley trailed reluctantly behind, looking up at the blank windows of the building while Priest examined the ground floor.

The front door was blocked by a piece of plywood, as were the windows that stretched to either side. Priest tugged on the door and confirmed it was locked.

"That's strange." Riley took Priest's spot at the door and tried the handle herself.

"It's an abandoned building. There are many in No Man's Land."

"Yeah, in No Man's Land. This is the bright and shining center of town, where nothing bad happens ever." She stepped back and looked up at the building. "Why would this place be empty? No one would just let it sit, not on this block." There was a small golden plaque next to the door and Riley bent down to read it. "Bethel Luz."

Priest turned around quickly. "What did you say?"

Riley pointed. "A lot of buildings have these. They commemorate important events or just make the building look important. What does Bethel Luz mean?"

"I'm not sure."

Her face indicated she at least had a very good idea of its meaning. But if she wasn't willing to share, Riley wasn't going to press it.

"All right. Well, we're not getting in here right now. Let's get back to the Shelby case and we'll come back when we have time to dig around." Priest nodded and they started back to the car. "Are you sure you're okay? The dreams and the whole comment about me being the best ever, now this? I'm starting to worry about you."

Priest smiled and shook her head. "Just getting acclimated to being more than mortal again. I'm sure I'll be fine."

"Just let me know if that changes. The trip back to the station will take us right by Abigail Shelby's photo studio. Why don't we swing by and see if we can find anything we didn't notice Wednesday."

Priest nodded as she climbed into the car. Riley looked back at the mysteriously abandoned building and decided to leave the mystery for another day.

The front entrance of Shelby's Family Photography was flanked on either side by display windows that showed off her work. It was mostly family portraits and children wedged into their Sunday best just long enough to get the photo taken. Riley unlocked the door and broke the seal she herself had put up two days earlier the last time they had searched the office. Of course, at that time, they'd been looking for a missing person.

The front room was a combination waiting and play area for the kids. The actual photography took place in a large space on the other side of a waist-high barrier.

"Maybe she took a picture someone wanted covered up."

Riley thought about Jon Casady and his Angel Maker book. "Not likely. People posed for her and, otherwise, she was taking picture of nature."

"Maybe she was out in the woods and someone saw her with

the camera. They just assumed she had seen something."

"And then held her for a week, determined she didn't know anything, and killed her anyway?"

Priest considered that. "Maybe they let her see their face. By the time they realized she didn't see anything, she knew too much."

"That would be ironic. You're getting good at this cop stuff."

Priest smiled proudly as Riley walked past her into Abigail's private office. She turned on the lights and immediately locked onto the framed photo of Ann and her children. The room was filled with pictures of children, but that photo hung on the wall where Abigail could clearly see it from anywhere in the room.

Riley went to the desk and pulled out the chair, lowering herself into it as she scanned the desktop again. She'd been through the objects on the desk so often that she knew it better than she knew her own. She flipped through the date book and confirmed what Ann had said. There were no areas marked off for vacations, but there were entries on the date she returned. "Back from Canada!" or "Road trip over" with a colon and parenthesis sad face. She did plan ahead for visits with her niece and nephew, circling the date and marking times for baseball games and soapbox derbies.

Riley's cell phone rang and she answered it with a quick glance at the ID. It was the morgue's phone, not Gillian's personal cell number. "Detective Parra."

"I have a cause of death for you," Gillian said. "She died of a skull fracture from blunt force trauma, and she has eight broken ribs. Two on her left side, six on the right. I also noticed there were bruises on her right shoulder and hip. Combine all of that~"

"Car accident. She was a passenger."

"Seems the most likely explanation for all of these injuries. The fracture was on the right side of her skull, so I think it impacted the window. It had to be a hell of a wreck."

"And that means someone, somewhere, made a report about it."

"We can only hope. There's one other thing. There are signs of rough sexual activity, and a considerable amount of it to be honest, but I'm still not prepared to call it rape."

"You can tell the difference?"

"Yeah. Sometimes it subtle, sometimes it's obvious. Either way, I'm leaning toward the possibility that she had rough, consensual sex at some point during the week she was missing."

Riley drummed her thumb against the arm of Abigail's chair.

"Is it possible that the signs of restraint we saw were also consensual? Maybe part of the rough sex was that she liked to be tied up."

"It's possible."

"Okay. I'll keep that in mind. Thanks, Jill. Love you."

"Love you, too."

Riley disconnected the call and dialed dispatch. "This is Detective Riley Parra. I need a list of all traffic accidents from last night between eight and two. Let me know as soon as possible. Thanks." She hung up as Priest came into the office. "Anything?"

"Nothing that would explain who killed her. There were some notes under the cash register that we missed before. Sales stubs marked 'balance to be paid on' such and such date." She held them out to Riley.

Most of the receipts concerned unpaid debts less than thirty or forty dollars.

"You never know what could come in handy. Bag 'em. That was Jill on the phone. Abby died in a car accident. I have dispatch looking for any that happened around the estimated time of death." She started going through the desk drawers for anything else they might have missed. Between her own search, the detectives from Missing Persons, and the crime scene unit, she felt like anything of use would have been already found.

She looked up and saw the picture of Ann and her children again. Before it had been just another family portrait among all the others. Riley walked around the desk and took the picture down from the wall. She put it face down on the desk, flipped up the tabs holding the back in place, and lifted it away. There was a small manila envelope that Riley removed and opened to peer inside. "More pictures," she muttered. They were wallet sized, maybe a little smaller, and the envelope held about ten shots.

"Why were they hidden?" Priest said.

Riley looked at the first few and raised her eyebrows. "Because they're not exactly family photography." She turned around the least risqué example and Priest's eyes widened slightly. The picture showed Abigail Shelby wearing a small Harlequin mask that left her features recognizable. It was designed with a red and white checkerboard pattern that matched the red teddy and white gloves she was wearing. In the other pictures, the teddy was gone and Abigail had assumed a variety of sexual poses.

A few of them revealed Abigail posing with a variety of sex toys, sometimes wearing them, sometimes applying them to a person whose body was mostly out of the shot. They weren't the dirtiest pictures Riley had ever seen, but they were definitely worse than what was advertised on the walls.

Riley considered the pictures. "There's a chance we won't have a bad guy with this one."

"What do you mean?"

"Abigail frequently went missing. We got that from her sister and the people who work here with her. She would jump up and leave at a moment's notice without telling anyone. Jill thinks she died in a car accident. The only evidence we have that she was held prisoner are the rope burns and the fact she was gagged." She held up one of the dirtier pictures. "I'm not sure this is a woman who would say no to being tied up and gagged during sex."

"She was still dumped like a bag of trash."

Riley nodded. "And we'll get the person who did that. Unlawful disposal of a body is still a felony, but it has a maximum six-month jail sentence."

Priest took the photos and held them facedown as she returned them to the envelope. "Just because Abigail Shelby liked rough sexual relations doesn't mean she wanted it this time. She still had the right to say no."

"You're right. I'm not saying I've already made up my mind, but we should be open to the possibility that there was no malice intended."

"Okay."

Riley took an evidence bag from her pocket and placed the pictures, envelope and all, inside. As she sealed it, she looked around the office. "We should take a look around and see if she had anything else tucked away."

"You want to look behind all these frames?"

"Don't want to." Riley took down one picture and began to remove the backing. "But I think we probably should."

Priest reluctantly agreed and started on the opposite wall. They worked in silence, finding nothing but the occasional release form that gave her permission to use the picture for advertising purposes. It was Priest who eventually broke the silence.

"I don't understand."

"What?"

"Rough sexual intercourse." She placed another picture on the table, having determined it wasn't hiding anything incriminating.

"Do you and Gillian...?"

"No." She was uncomfortable, but she knew Priest was just curious. "Sometimes there might be the occasional swat on the rear end, but nothing major."

"But some people do engage in acts that, to an outside observer, might seem painful and wrong. So much so that the effects on the body are indistinguishable from rape. Why do people want that?"

"Different strokes for different folks."

"What?"

"It's a platitude designed to make people stop asking hard questions." Priest started to apologize but Riley waved her off. "It's fine. I can't really say, since it's not my cup of tea. I think it's about control, either taking it or giving it away. They turn it into a game. There are safe words. I really don't know the details, Cait."

"Hm."

Riley glanced over and decided turnabout was fair play. "So, Kenzie and Chelsea never tie you up? Make you watch them without touching?"

"No." She blushed at the thought. "That... definitely sounds like torture."

"Yeah. But imagine how fun it'll be when they finally let you go."

Priest looked into the distance for a second and then shuddered. Riley laughed.

"That's another reason people get into it."

"I see. Delayed gratification." Priest took another photo off the wall and removed the back. "Riley."

Riley looked at what she had found. It was a small plastic ID card with only the word "RIGHT" written on the front. There was a magnetic strip on the back and the number 61424 printed underneath it. "Any ideas?"

Priest shook her head. "It feels dark. When I touched it, I felt like there was a lot of lust and degradation attached to it. It makes my hand feel dirty." She rubbed her fingers when Riley took the card from her.

Riley thought back to the pictures. "Maybe we found another clue to Abigail's hidden life. Her literally hidden life." They had gone through most of the pictures on the wall and Riley noticed that the card had been found on the wall directly opposite where the photos were hidden. "There... and..." She walked to the corresponding picture on the north wall and took it down. Behind the back, she found a long strip of black cloth.

Priest had followed her lead and taken the picture off the south wall. She found a red strip that matched the black one in length.

"What do you think?"

Riley took out the photographs, removing them from the baggie and envelope so she could examine them closer. "Look at this picture. You can see her feet." She turned it around and Priest, after initially looking away from the nudity, focused on the feet tucked under Abigail's body. There was a strip of black cloth tied around her right ankle.

"But where's the red one?"

"I think that whoever took the picture is wearing it." She held out an evidence bag and Priest lowered the cloth inside. Riley put the black cloth into its own bag. If Abigail's club partner had tied the cloth around her ankle, then there might be evidence on the material that could lead them to whoever it was.

She looked at the evidence they had gathered and nodded. "Not bad for an afternoon of rooting around someone else's place. Let's get out of here and see if we can figure out what this card goes to."

The desk sergeant had a printed-out list of all car accidents during the time frame Riley requested, and she scanned the list as she went upstairs. "Rear-ended, no injuries. Car versus pole, pole won. Driver was treated at the scene but no passenger reported." She blew air through her lips as she looked at the rest of the entries. "There's a chance that the accident didn't get reported. If it happened in No Man's Land after dark..."

They stopped by Vice and showed the card around; none of the detective had ever seen one like it, but they promised to keep their eyes open.

Riley filed the card and everything else they'd found in the office with evidence.

Priest put her hands in her pockets as she followed Riley upstairs. "What now?"

"Now we go back to our desks and start calling the people who worked with her. Maybe one of them will know about the pictures or recognize the card."

"As well as it was hidden, I would be surprised if she shared that part of her life with them."

"Maybe she *shared it* with them." She shrugged. "S&M is a two-person game. Abigail definitely had a partner, and it had to be someone she trusted. It's either someone she knew from work or from home. Her sister said she didn't have any current boyfriends, so it stands to reason it was a coworker."

"Or barring that, a coworker may have known more about Abigail's personal life than her sister. I doubt her sister knew about those photographs."

"Right. It's going to suck bringing this up with the people she was closest with."

They sat at their desks and Riley took out a copy of the address book she'd gotten on the first trip to Abigail's studio. Priest had one of her own. "I'll start with the back, you start at the front and we'll meet in the middle again."

Priest gave her a thumbs up and picked up her phone. Riley went to the back of the list, found the number for Yeager-comma-Donna, and dialed. "Mrs. Yeager? This is Detective Riley Parra. I'm calling about Abigail Shelby..."

Riley glanced up, as if she'd sensed her partner's approach, and watched as Gillian walked across the bullpen. "Thank you, Mr. Janssen. We'll be in touch if we need anything else." She hung up and smiled. "Hey, darling."

"Sweetheart." She smoothed her hand over Riley's hair. "I've got an early night, so I thought I'd hop a train back home."

Riley looked at her watch and saw it was a reasonable enough quitting time. "No, don't do that. I'm just going through~"

Priest waved her off from her desk. "I'll take over. You've done more than half the book anyway. Go home. I'll call if I find anything."

"You sure? Thanks." Riley stood up and took her jacket off the back of her chair.

"Thanks, Caitlin. See you tomorrow." Gillian waited until Riley was ready and then extended her hand. Riley took it and led Gillian from the bullpen. She waited until they reached the stairs before Gillian spoke again. "Rough day?"

Riley shrugged. "It never really recovered after Ann Tucker came in. I hate dealing with the family. I'm always worried I'm going to call someone's sister or daughter 'the body' or 'it.' People don't understand that cops have to inure ourselves to it, and it comes off as callous. I hate it."

"I know you do." Gillian squeezed Riley's arm. "What about the investigation? Did you get any leads?"

"Ah, some. A couple of racy photos and a weird card."

Gillian squeezed Riley's hand and chuckled. "Ooh. Racy photos, huh? What kind of weird card?"

"It's blank except for the word 'right' on front and a number on the back. No one in Vice recognized it."

Gillian slowed down, forcing Riley to stop a step below her and look up.

"Right like the direction. Like..." She lifted her right hand.

"Yeah. Why?"

Gillian nudged Riley forward and they continued down the stairs. They walked together across the lobby and out into the chill of twilight. Gillian moved Riley toward the building, out of the wind, and looked down the street.

"You're not going to like this, but keep the commentary to a minimum. Please?"

Riley shrugged without agreeing.

Gillian exhaled and looked to make sure no one was in earshot. "About five years ago, I was dating a woman. She got off on power games. She... liked to tie me up. Sometimes she would take me to this club where we could..." She cleared her throat and shrugged her shoulders. "It was called Lotus. It was a club for people like her. They had cards like the one you're describing. You'd run your card through the scanner to get in. Everyone had a number. The card you found, it had five digits?"

"Yeah. 61242, I think. I'd have to check."

"My card was 45345."

"You remember the number?"

Gillian tilted her head at Riley. "She made me use the card a lot, Riley, okay? It's not something I tried to memorize. I hated that place, but I cared for her, so I tried to make it work. It was the reason we eventually broke up."

"What does Right or Left mean?"

"It shows whether you're... dominant or submissive. Right is for a top, Left is for a Bottom. A horizontal line means that you can be used for whatever by whomever."

Riley winced and looked toward the corner, wanting to ask but unable to bring herself to say it.

Gillian answered anyway, her voice soft. "My card said Right. It was the only way I'd agree to go there with any regularity. But it meant that my girlfriend was a Line, so I had to watch while she and... other women..." She shuddered. "It's a bad place, Riley. It's buried in No Man's Land, and just being inside the building gave me the creeps. I would shower for half the next morning after we came back from their just to get the stink off of me."

Riley stepped forward and embraced Gillian. After a moment, Gillian returned the hug.

"If you have to go there for anything, even just to question someone, take Priest. Take Sariel, too, if she'll show up. You want to know why I so easily believed demons existed when you told me three years ago? It's because I'd been in that club. S&M is one thing; I think it can be a healthy part of a mature relationship. It's why I went along for so long. But that club is something else. Something... wrong. I got hurt there, and I was forced to do things I didn't really want to do."

Riley stepped back and brushed her fingers over Gillian's face. "I should go tell Priest all of this."

"Go ahead. I'll take the el home."

Riley took the keys from her pocket. "I'll take the train. You get home, make yourself a nice warm bath, get something to drink. Wrap yourself up in a towel and curl up on the couch. I'll be there to wake you up and take you to bed."

Gillian smiled. "Promise?"

"I swear."

They kissed, and Riley felt Gillian relax in her arms. She broke the kiss. "Better?"

"Much. Thanks for not freaking out."

"It was five years ago. Five years can be a lifetime. Trust me, if anyone knows that..."

Gillian laughed. She kissed Riley's forehead and squeezed her hands. "You should go tonight. As much as I hate saying it, that club is... most active at night. It's already been a day and you can't afford to lose any more time on this case. The club isn't far from the waterfront, and you can probably find the address in the files upstairs. So take Priest, be on your guard, and go to the club tonight. Other people in the club will show you if they're a Right, Left or Line by showing their hands. All you have to do is show the same hand they do, and they'll leave you alone. Tops don't want a top."

"Okay. Thanks."

Gillian nodded. "Be safe. I won't hold you to the promise to tuck me in, but you better be there in the morning."

"That I can do."

Gillian took the keys and stepped out of the embrace. "I'll see you at home. Promise me."

Riley held up two fingers and then crossed her heart with them. She watched Gillian walk away, making sure she got to the garage safely before she went back into the building.

Narcotics had an actual wardrobe closet for undercover operations, and their lieutenant let Riley and Priest borrow two outfits for their trip to Lotus. Riley ended up in a white tank top under a hoodie and newsboy cap while Priest chose a T-shirt cinched at the waist by a wide belt and a pair of strategically ripped jeans. Riley slumped against the wall, waiting to be let into the club, with her hands hooked in the pockets of her baggy borrowed jeans.

Priest reached up and ran her fingers through her hair. Riley pushed her hands down and lowered her voice. "Stop fussing. You have to look like you belong. Just relax and act normal."

Priest hunched her shoulders and wrapped her arms around herself. "There's nothing normal about this place. We're not even inside and already I feel... anxious. It's going to be a very uncomfortable night."

"Just remember what I told you. If someone shows their right hand, you do the same. Just copy whatever they do and no one should bother you."

They got to the front of the line and Riley straightened. The bouncer, a monolith carrying a small tablet computer, looked them up and down before waving them forward. Riley scanned the card she'd checked out of evidence and the light showed green. The bouncer pushed the door open.

The bouncer looked down at the screen of his tablet. "Have a wonderful evening, Ms. Shelby."

Riley slipped her arm around Priest's and guided her into the club. Immediately Riley could smell evidence of several kinds of drug, as well as the stink of sweat and sex. A waitress passed them carrying a tray full of drinks, dressed only in a white dickey that covered her breasts. She smiled when she saw Riley watching and she lifted her right hand. Riley immediately did the same, as did Priest.

The waitress chuckled and kept walking. "Just saying hi,

ladies."

"Oh." Priest cleared her throat and watched the woman walking away, blushing when the woman turned and caught her staring. Priest looked at Riley. "This is a very uncomfortable place."

"Hopefully we won't have to be here long. Come on."

They moved deeper into the crowd. To her surprise, Riley saw that the nudity wasn't restricted to the women clientele. Riley saw one woman approach a man and begin touching him, the crowd gathering to watch the display. It was hard to tell if the open area on the far side of the bar was a dance floor or a designated orgy pit.

Riley nudged Priest forward. "Don't look too hard. You may turn into a pillar of salt."

"I'm sorry. I didn't expect to have this reaction. Sex is still... very new to me. I'm intrigued by all the aspects of it."

"Yeah, well, trust me. Some aspects of it aren't exactly for the faint of heart. Even if you're interested in S&M, this isn't it. Don't take notes." A woman looked pointedly at Riley's breasts and raised her left hand. Riley did the same and the woman shrugged and moved on. "Hand signals. I guess it's better than just coming out and asking if you want to bang."

They made their way toward the bar, lifting their right and left hands intermittently like drivers signaling turns on a serpentine roadway. They were almost to the bar when Riley lifted her left hand to a disappointed bottom, and her hand was immediately grabbed from behind. Her left arm was pinned behind her back, and she was pulled tightly against a stranger's body.

Riley turned her head just enough to see the woman, her black hair cut short and feathered around her face. The woman was wearing a black leather jacket, and her dark eyes were full of lust as she tightened her grip on Riley's arm. Riley knew she could get out of the hold, but not without causing a scene and possibly injuring this woman.

"You can to play with me, little bottom. Safe word?"

"Cop."

The woman's bright red lips spread to reveal dazzling white teeth. "That's one of the strangest I've heard in a while, but I'm game. Do you want your friend to watch?"

"I'm... a cop, lady. Let go of me right now."

The top sighed. "Cop or fireman, you're still a bottom in here, girl. I saw your hand. So you'll call me 'ma'am.'" She brought her free hand up and curled her fingers around the collar of Riley's tank top. Her arm tensed, preparing to rip when Priest grabbed the woman from behind. Her arm went across the woman's neck, and Priest threw her weight back until the woman lost her balance. Riley's shirt ripped, but not enough to cause an exposure problem. Priest wrestled the woman to her knees and lowered her lips next to the woman's ear.

Over the hum of the crowd and the throb of the music, Riley couldn't hear what she said. Finally, the woman nodded and Priest let her go. She looked at Riley with regret and then faded off into the crowd. Priest straightened her shirt and put her hand on Riley's arm.

"Are you okay?"

"Yeah, fine. What did you say to her?"

"I said a woman was dead because someone had taken the game too far, and we were here to make sure they paid for their crime."

"Good thinking. Maybe we should have just worn our badges and saved ourselves some trouble." She watched a woman in a short black dress as she was grabbed from behind on the dance floor, half-carried to a booth where she was thrown down onto the vinyl. The woman was shaking her head and struggling. Riley started over but, before she could move, the apparent victim wrapped her arms around one of the men and drew him down on top of her. It took all of Riley's strength not to run over and intervene anyway, and the rest to keep herself from imagining Gillian in this place.

A waitress had appeared with two glasses of beer, smiling as she held one out to Riley. "Abbess didn't tell me what you like to drink, so I took a guess. Are you right or left?"

Riley didn't take the glass. "I'm sorry, who are you?"

"I'm Charlie." She looked at Priest. "Is your friend joining us, or just watching?"

Riley realized this woman hadn't indicated a hand, so Riley couldn't send her away with a flick of the wrist. "Why do you think Abbess sent me?"

"You have her card. Stan at the door told me." Her expression loosened a bit, and Riley saw the real person behind the club persona. "The Abbess didn't send you? Why do you have her card?"

Riley looked at Priest and then stepped closer to Charlie. "Is there someplace quiet where we can talk?"

Charlie's facade had completely crumbled, and she nodded quickly as she turned and scanned the crowd. She handed her drinks to a passing bare-bottomed waitress and motioned for Riley and Priest to follow her. They went up a metal flight of stairs to an upper room furnished with beds and fainting couches instead of booths and tables. Most horizontal surfaces were occupied by people going farther than the people on the ground floor.

"Over here." Charlie gestured at a large bed that was blocked off by a half-wall. Charlie sat on the edge of it and Riley discovered the din of the club was slightly lessened. "It's the best we can do without actually going someplace else. Why do you have Abigail's card? What happened?"

Riley introduced herself and Priest before getting to the hard part. "I'm afraid Abigail was in an accident. She didn't make it."

Charlie's eyes widened and then became wet. She shook her head in vehement denial. "No. No, that's not possible. I-I saw her last night."

"What time was that?"

"Um, around eight? Or nine? It was early and the club had just opened. She was here for a little while but then she left."

Priest was standing with her back to the room, blocking Charlie and Riley from the crowd. "Did you see who she left with?"

"No, I mean, I didn't even see her leave. But she just kind of vanished. I assumed they finally let her go."

Riley frowned. "Who let her go?"

Charlie blushed and looked down at her hands. "Last week, Abigail's boyfriend came up with a game called Mascot. He gave Abby to the club, and she was going to be their... plaything, I guess. So once a night, every night last week, Abby would be brought out onto the bar and they would, uh... they would play with her."

Riley remembered Gillian's report indicating a lot of sexual activity in the past week. "And that was consensual? Abigail was up for it?"

"Well, yeah, absolutely. Nothing happens in this club without the consent of everyone involved."

"You don't exactly sound sure."

Charlie's shoulders slumped. "I don't know. When I asked, Abby said everything was fine. She told me to stop worrying about her. But she had to stay here the whole week. She couldn't go home or to work, and she had to stay in her room like a prisoner. At first I thought she was getting off on it. But the last few nights, her performance was a little... off. Like she wished it would all just end."

"I heard this place doesn't have safe words. Was there any way for her to end the game if it got to be too much?"

"The establishment doesn't require safe words, but only the most hardcore people go without one. Most people here respect it. Abby's was bluejay." She smiled a little at some memory invoked by the words. "I just told myself that if there was a problem she would have said it. The owners would have let her go in a heartbeat."

Riley heard moans and cries coming from elsewhere in the private area. It was hard to ignore them, but she forced herself to focus on Charlie. "You said this game, Mascot, was her boyfriend's idea. Who was he?"

Charlie closed her eyes. "You're going to get me in so much trouble."

"Whatever you tell us is confidential. We won't reveal where we got the information."

"At first he was just this guy that came around at the same time Abby did, but they knew each other. I mean, from the outside world. They had these ribbons that they wore on their ankles. Black and red. It meant they were a couple. I assumed he was someone who worked at her photography studio, but I'd never seen him there."

"You went to Abigail's studio?"

"Oh, sure. It's where I got my family portrait done for last year's Christmas card."

Riley looked at Charlie and tried to place her, trying to figure out which sweater-clad soccer mom in the display pictures was now sitting in front of her in a low-cut corset and fishnet stockings.

"Anyway, they started meeting here and after a while they started hooking up."

"Do you know his name?"

"I know the name he uses here, but that won't help you. Abby was Abigail Shelby in the outside world, but she was the Abbess in here. Her boyfriend was Brother Tuck. That's all anyone knew about him."

Riley straightened slightly and looked at Priest. "Are you sure about that name?"

"Yeah. I thought it was weird he didn't go by Friar Tuck, but..." She shrugged. "I thought it was some cutesy way of connecting himself to Abby's character. The nun and the monk. I wish I could be more help."

Riley's expression had darkened considerably. "I think you've helped more than you know, Charlie."

Riley didn't want to waste time going back to the station to change. She had a windbreaker in the backseat and zipped it all the way up to cover what she'd worn to the club. Priest followed her up the front walk, hands in the pockets of her jeans, and kept her chin down. "I hope you're right about this, Riley."

Riley was looking toward the driveway, at the single minivan parked in front of the closed garage. "Really? I hope I'm so far off base I'm not even in the ballpark anymore." She also hoped there was a second car just out of sight.

She rang the doorbell and stepped back so she could be seen through the narrow windows on either side of the door. The curtain was pulled back slightly, and then the door opened to reveal Ann Tucker in her pastel blouse and jeans. She was barefoot, and her hair was wet from a recent shower. She tucked a wet strand behind her ear and looked hopefully at them.

"Yes? H-have you found something?"

"Maybe. Mrs. Tucker, is your husband home?"

Ann furrowed her brow. "Robert? Uh, yeah, he's in the back with the kids. Why?"

"We'd like to speak with him if we could."

Ann seemed confused, but she nodded and motioned the detectives inside. Riley stepped into the brightly lit foyer while Ann walked to the hallway. "Rob? Can you come here for a second, please?" She tugged on the hem of her blouse as she walked back to where Riley and Priest were waiting. She looked between them, obviously at a loss for why they were standing in her house so late at night.

Robert Tucker came around the corner with a smile on his face, undressed down to a T-shirt and jeans. His feet were bare, obviously on his way to bed, and he looked at their two guests in confusion. "Hi. Who's this?"

Riley and Priest both raised their right hands, palm front, in greeting. Rob's smile wavered and his face went slack.

"Detective Riley Parra, Detective Caitlin Priest. Mr. Tucker, where's your car?"

"Uh, it's at the shop. I had a bit of a fender bender." He tilted his head slightly. "What's this all about?"

Riley hated being right in situations like this. "Mr. Tucker, my partner and I would like to ask you a few questions about your sister-in-law and a club called Lotus."

Rob wavered on his feet like a tree caught in a strong breeze. He turned and pressed his shoulder to the wall, his body slumping. Ann was staring at him, confusion dominating her features.

"Rob? What is Lotus? What does it have to do with Abigail?"

Riley stepped forward. "Everyone wanted to protect Abigail. But Abigail hated being treated like something fragile. She wanted to prove she was strong. So that's why she started going to the club as a top. But she wasn't going to go someplace like that by herself, so she asked someone she trusted to come with her just in case. How long was it before you started sleeping together?"

Robert closed his eyes. The blood had drained from his face, making the stubble on his cheeks stand out. "It wasn't like she was Abigail. She was a different person in the club. We both were. We realized pretty quick that there was... something between us." He ran his hand through his hair and looked down at his feet. "We were just going to do it that once, as part of a group thing. But the next time we went, we~"

Ann's voice was shrill. "Shut up, Rob, what are you talking about?"

"Things got out of control, didn't they, Rob? You started seeing her outside of the club. At her apartment. Is that why you ransacked it? You were looking for something you might have left behind that would reveal what you'd been doing. Maybe Abigail had been writing a diary and mentioned you. You couldn't take the chance."

Rob's voice was weak. "I was going to go back and clean it up."

"What happened after the Mascot game went bad?"

Ann was looking between Riley and her husband, both of them now strangers to her.

"I did it as a game. Abby was always saying how she wanted to completely give up control, just once. So I gave her to those men~"

Ann made a sound of utter grief and turned to walk away. She only made it as far as the living room before she dropped into a crouch and put her hands over her head. Priest walked to her and knelt beside her, a hand on Ann's shoulder for comfort.

"~for a week. And I told her that she couldn't use her safe word to end things. She was excited at first, but then she called me. She said she couldn't do it anymore. She wanted out. She tried saying her safe word but one of the men just covered her mouth and kept going.

"I drove to the club and I picked her up. She said she wanted to leave the club behind. I said I didn't want to lose her, and that... she gave me... She told me that she wanted me to leave Ann." Riley could hear Ann sobbing now. "She said she loved the kids, and she loved me, and she told me that we could be a real family. I told her absolutely not. We were arguing, and I was speeding and not paying attention. I hit a parked car."

Riley kicked herself for the oversight of not looking into hit and run accidents.

"I knew she was dead. I... checked everything and I... couldn't handle it. I panicked. I don't even remember driving into No Man's Land, and I don't remember dumping her like that."

Riley motioned for him to stand up. "Robert Tucker, you're under arrest for manslaughter and illegal disposal of a body. You have the right to remain silent." She looked at Priest and Ann, who were still crouched just inside the living room door. "Cait, are you staying?"

Priest nodded, still touching Ann's quaking back.

Riley hauled Robert around and guided him toward the front door as she continued reciting his Miranda rights.

No one in Lotus saw when the brunette arrived, but they were all drawn to her. She kept her arms at her sides as they approached, attempting to entice her by showing their right or left hands. They all wanted her, men and women both. She allowed their hands to touch her clothes and her body, and a few reached out for her hair. A thumb brushed her bottom lip, and lips alighted on her bare shoulders as she passed through the crowd.

The woman simply closed her eyes and continued toward the center of the room.

This was a place of evil and debauchery. What occurred here had nothing to do with love or desire. In her time, the brunette had seen all variations of sexual intercourse. Some methods were harder to understand than others. What was happening within these walls was little better than rape. She opened her eyes and a woman touched her cheek. The woman smiled, and the brunette smelled the stink of demons on her. Everyone in the crowd had been touched by demons. Something that could have been beautiful was forever tainted.

One of the revelers gathered the courage to speak. "Haven't seen you in here before."

"A friend suggested I come and see it for myself."

The stranger pressed against the brunette's side. "Mm. I'm glad you listened. What's your name, sweet thing?"

The crush of bodies had become almost unbearable. The brunette could barely breathe, but she smiled. "My name is Sariel. And this is for the greater good."

Her wings extended, and every eye in the club widened. The crowd fell back, and Sariel released a burst of radiant white light that filled every corner, every crevice, and every dark space in the club until only light remained.

It was midnight before they got done with booking. The manslaughter charge held, since Robert Tucker's reckless driving led to Abigail's death. He finally broke down when they were taking him to holding, but Riley was beyond caring at that point. She had liked Ann, and now she'd lost her sister and her husband in the same two days. Riley hoped some judge would be able to upgrade Robert's charge to second degree murder, but it was doubtful.

When Riley got home, she found Gillian still asleep on the couch, wearing a towel around her body. The lamp beside the couch was the only light in the room, casting glow and shadows across Gillian's features. Riley smiled at the sight and then knelt next to the couch. She brushed the hair away from Gillian's face and touched her cheek until Gillian's eyes opened and focused on her.

"Hey."

"Hi." Riley held up her hand, keeping it as a flat line. Gillian smiled and mimicked the move. Riley clucked her tongue. "Looks like we're at an impasse."

"We'll figure something out."

Riley turned her hand and laced her fingers together with Gillian's. They kissed hello and Gillian brought Riley's hand to her cheek. "How did the club go?"

"It was hellish. But we caught the bad guy."

"Good girl."

Riley shook her head. "Manslaughter and dumping the body. She died in an accident. How long do you think he's really going to serve?"

"That's not for you to worry about. You caught him, and you brought him to justice. That's all you can do. It's like when I looked at that poor girl's body and I knew what she'd gone through. There was nothing I could do about that. But I'm luckier than you are."

"Oh yeah? How so?"

"Because I know that when I'm done, it's going into your hands. And I know I can trust you to do what needs to be done."

Riley kissed Gillian again. "Let me carry you to bed."

"I'm heavy."

"You're a twig. Besides, I'm strong." She picked Gillian up off the couch and her towel fell away. "Whoops."

"I'll have to change into pajamas."

Riley raised an eyebrow. "Now, now. Don't be so hasty."

Gillian laughed as Riley carried her quickly into the bedroom and kicked the door shut behind them.

Priest tried to slip into bed without waking her partners, but Chelsea was far too alert for that. She greeted Priest with a kiss, which quickly turned into something more. Soon Kenzie was awake, watching while she worked her hand between her two partners to lend a helping hand. Afterward, Priest fell asleep with a woman on either side of her, Kenzie's unscarred cheek against her back and her own head on Chelsea's chest.

She dreamt.

The land was flat and, in the distance, she could see water on three sides. It wasn't an island; there were other landmasses very nearby but not yet connected to this spot by bridges. Two men approached where Priest was standing, both of them trailed by invisible armies. The sky was rolling, wild and frantic. She understood it was a time before weather, when anything could happen anywhere, without warning. She saw lightning flashing far away and the echo seemed to make the ground tremble in its wake.

The emissaries stood facing one another. Priest saw no difference between the two, no indication of who was the hero and who was the villain. One wore a simple white cloth tied around his waist. The other wore a tunic that covered his chest and most of his legs. The air was charged with electricity from the storm. The man in the tunic lifted his hand with two fingers pointed forward.

Both armies howled.

The man in the loincloth knelt and drew a circle in the dirt. His fingers seemed to dig and tear at the hard ground like a farmer's plow. He stood, and the man in the tunic lifted his foot and smashed his heel into the circle. The ground cracked and collapsed, and both men and their armies backed away as the ground opened. Instead of darkness, the hole opened up onto light. Blinding and pure light that carried toward Heaven before falling to the height of a campfire.

The men turned and left the area, but the fire still burned. Priest was pushed through time quickly. The sky rolled too fast to see. The land flooded and became parched from drought. Settlers arrived and were quickly banished. A fortification was constructed around the odd light, and then it was destroyed. Another wall went up, it was also destroyed. Finally, stone was used to contain the light, and it held. A building was constructed around the stone vault. Priest recognized the building, but she told herself that it wasn't possible. Other buildings rose around it.

Priest watched as a settlement turned into a town and became a city. She watched as streets were laid out and then paved. Cars appeared. She watched as the anonymous spit of land became civilization.

She watched as it became unmistakably familiar.

Priest woke with a gasp, disturbing Chelsea.

"What's wrong?"

"It's here." Priest was surprised to find she was drenched with sweat, something she had thought wasn't possible after regaining her divinity. She pushed her hair out of her face, staring wide-eyed into the darkness. "It was this city. Something happened here a long, long time ago and I think... it's calling out to me."

In the middle of the night, it was harder to tell the city center from the worst parts of No Man's Land. The main difference was the sound; no squealing tires or breaking glass or gunfire. Priest was dressed in a blouse and slacks, barefoot in the courtyard of the mysterious building she and Riley had explored earlier that day. Her wings were fully extended to either side of her, the feathers rippling gently in the breeze.

She looked up at the windows of the building, flat and dark like the eyes of a dead dragon. But there was nothing dead about this building no matter how abandoned it might appear.

Priest crossed the courtyard and dropped to one knee in front of the door. She bowed her head and closed her eyes. She heard a sound behind her and looked back to find two men watching her from the stone archway. One wore a tunic of the finest cloth with his long hair waving in the breeze, and the other wore a simple loincloth. She remembered them from her dream, but this time she recognized them for who they were.

The Michael she knew wore a different face; this was how he had looked when the most ancient books were still unwritten.

The other was the Favorite.

Priest didn't back down. "I'm going inside."

Neither angel tried to stop her. She turned and put her hand against the door. It swung open at the slightest touch, and Priest inhaled sharply as she looked into the darkness. Then, curling her wings inward just enough to make it through the entrance, she walked inside. As soon as she was gone, Michael and the Favorite vanished from the scene.

PECULIAR GRACES

AT FIRST, she thought it was dawn. She looked up at the sky, gauging the light before she realized that the sun was actually setting. She'd lost an entire day inside the building, and she had nothing to show for it. The light of the lost day faded quickly as Caitlin Priest left the courtyard of Bethel Luz and took wing. She didn't have time to be subtle or deal with mortal restrictions.

She needed Riley's help.

No one at the table smoked, but Kenzie had brought cigars she had been saving for a special occasion. Riley had taken one, alternating between sticking it in her mouth and using it to make a point during stories she was telling. The living room furniture had been moved out of the way to make room for the poker table, borrowed from the police station for the occasion.

Chelsea and Kenzie were sitting across from Riley close enough that their shoulders were touching. They were playing the same hand since Chelsea couldn't see the cards well enough to play on her own. Gillian was to Riley's right across from Lieutenant Briggs. The game was rounded out by Gillian's best friend Maureen Spenser, who had arrived earlier that afternoon to attend the wedding.

Riley rested the unlit cigar in the ashtray and made her bet. "Now this is a bachelorette party. I'll call."

"The only part I hate is taking all your money right before you get married." Kenzie added her chips to the pile. "Doesn't mean I'll back out, but I'll feel real bad about it."

Riley grinned. "I promise I'll think of you when I spend your cash, Kenz."

Kenzie pursed her lips and blew a kiss at Riley. Riley waved her hand in the air as if clearing smoke.

Gillian, who had already folded, patted Riley's hand as she got up. "Another beer?"

Riley checked her watch and the three empty bottles already standing in front of her. "Switch me to soda, please."

"Anyone else? Beer?" Briggs and Chelsea both asked for tea and Maureen asked for a soda. "Coming right up." She was only halfway to the kitchen when there was a knock on the door. She changed direction and looked through the peephole. "It's Caitlin."

"Oh, good." Kenzie grinned and clapped her hands. "This party needed a stripper."

Riley tossed a peanut at her former partner. "You need to switch Kenzie to soda, too, babe."

Gillian ignored them and opened the door. "Caitlin. We were getting a little worried about you. Riley said you weren't at work, Kenzie and Chelsea didn't know where you were."

Priest nodded. "I apologize. I was distracted by something for a lot longer than I expected to be." She cleared her throat and looked past Gillian into the main room. "Would it be possible to take Riley away from the party?"

Gillian stepped closer and lowered her voice so that Maureen couldn't overhear. "Are you okay? Is everything... *all right?*"

"Everything's fine. I just need to speak with her."

Riley was already up and crossing the room. "What's wrong?"

"Nothing, maybe. I just need your opinion. If we hurry we can be there and back in an hour."

Riley smiled. "Jill and I are in the middle of our bachelorette party, Priest. Can it wait?"

Priest looked into the room, weighing her options, and then eventually nodded. "I suppose it can wait until the party's over. But we can't leave it until morning."

"Okay. Come on in. We have beer, soda, tea~"

"I'll take a glass of ice water."

Riley motioned for Gillian to go back to the table. "I'll get it. Introduce Priest to your friend."

Gillian took Priest into the living room. "Mo, this is Caitlin Priest. She's Riley's partner on the force."

"Ah, the other woman." Maureen smiled and stood to extend her arm across the table. "Maureen Spenser. I knew Jill back when she was just a wild heiress."

Gillian laughed as she took her seat. "Back home you were considered wealthy if you had two televisions in your house."

"And the Hunts had *three*."

"But the working one in the parlor was sitting on top of the broken one. So it balanced out."

Priest held Maureen's hand for a moment and then let it go. "It's nice to meet you, Maureen."

Riley put a bottle of water in front of Priest and pulled up another chair. "Come on, I'll deal you in. I can teach you the rules if you need me to."

Priest cleared her throat. "I... I don't think I should gamble."

"Well, we are playing for high stakes here. Kenzie's down forty cents."

Kenzie jabbed her cigar at Riley. "For the moment."

"Come on, Cait. It's just good fun. No money actually exchanges hands at the end of the night." She watched Priest, noticing how tense she had been from the moment she arrived. Whatever she had come to tell her was obviously weighing on her, but some things were sacred. It would hold until they were done. "C'mon. I'll even spot you for the first hand."

Priest finally relented and sat down. "Just one hand won't hurt."

Forty minutes later, Priest was up two dollars and fourteen cents. Riley had leaned back in her chair, her shoes off, her feet sliding up and over Gillian's ankles under the cuffs of her jeans. Gillian bet, swirled her cigar with her tongue, and conversed without acknowledging Riley's game, but occasionally she would respond to Riley's touches with her own foot, lifting her leg and curling her foot until it was caught in the leg of Riley's pants.

They wrapped up the game when half the players were out of chips, and Kenzie declared it was time for her and Chelsea to hit the road. Briggs agreed that it was time to call it a night and the crowd moved toward the door. Priest looked at Riley with anticipation but tried not to look too eager. Gillian kissed Riley and smoothed down the front of her blouse.

"Go ahead. Mo and I will clean up. Don't stay out too long."

"I'll do my best. See you when I get back." She kissed the corners of Gillian's mouth before she turned to Priest. "Is this official business?"

"You should probably prepare for the worst, just in case."

Gillian sighed. "Love hearing *those* words before my fiancé heads off into the night." She let Riley get her badge and gun, and then grabbed her collar. "Don't be a cliché, all right? All those movie cops who are one day away from retirement or getting married next weekend and they get shot down in a hail of bullets. Don't be one of those movies."

"I'm too old for that shit." She kissed Gillian to seal her promise, smoothed her hair, and whispered a goodbye and a "love you" before she followed Priest out of the apartment.

"Thanks for waiting."

"It's different now that I'm not just posing as a mortal. I understand how important things like that party can be. I enjoyed meeting Maureen."

Riley smiled. "It's nice getting some insight into Gillian when she was a kid. She's going to be her maid of honor at the wedding."

Priest nodded. "Will you have a best man? How does that sort of thing work?"

"Actually, I was thinking of a best woman. And I thought you could do the honors." Priest turned at the bottom of the stairs and looked at her. "I've known you longer than anyone else I've ever met. Even when I didn't know you were there, you were there. You've saved me more times than I can count. If anyone deserves the position, it's you."

"I would be honored, Riley. Thank you."

Riley clapped Priest on the shoulder and guided her out of the building. "Let's go see what kept you occupied for so long."

Riley felt a twinge of apprehension as they approached the building. The Abigail Shelby case had distracted her from Priest's unusual draw to the building, but now the memory came flooding back. An empty building in the middle of the prosperous center of town, curiously ignored by real estate agents, tenants, and squatters alike. Riley glanced at Priest as she parked curbside, the sidewalk abandoned despite the fact it was barely past ten.

Priest seemed more agitated than she'd been at the party, looking up and down the street as she unfastened her safety belt. "Damn. I thought I had closed it up again, but perhaps they sensed it while I was inside. They're here."

"Who is here?"

Priest was silent so long that Riley thought she was just not going to answer. Finally, she sighed and shook her head. "Gail Finney and Gremory."

"Oh, wonderful." Riley tried to keep a lid on her anger. "Are you going to be okay?"

"I'll be fine. Gremory had me under her hold while I was a mortal, but it won't be an issue now. She has no power over angels."

Riley nodded. "Good to know." Thanks to their encounter in Jon Casady's office, Riley knew that she could also resist Gremory's succubus mojo now that she knew what she was dealing with. "Still, probably best to be on alert."

They got out of the car and Riley pulled her jacket back so her gun was clearly visible. They walked under the stone archway to the courtyard and found Gremory and Gail standing by the fountain. Gail wore a turtleneck and black jeans, her hair pulled back and her face scrubbed free of makeup. She looked irritated and tired. Gremory, on the other hand, looked like someone had cut her out of a magazine and pasted her into reality. She turned and cocked a hip, her lips curling into a sly grin.

"Well. The two sides meet again. Caitlin, I regret I didn't get to taste your sweet juices." She ran her finger along her bottom lip.

"Save your games, whore." There was a roughness in Priest's voice that surprised even Riley.

Gremory gasped and put her hand against her chest. "Well, Zuzu's bells are ringing loud and clear. You got your wings back. How lovely for you."

Priest stepped forward. "Leave this place. What's inside is not for you."

"It's not for you either, child." The flirtation was gone from the demon's voice. "Just because you were the one to break the seal gives you no sovereignty over this place."

Riley whistled and held her hands up. "Okay, time out. What the hell is going on here? What's so important about this building?"

Gail looked at Gremory. "That's what I would like to know. We've been here for an hour looking for a way in, and she won't tell me a damned thing."

"You'll be told when the time is right." Gremory spoke without breaking eye contact with Priest. "You've had a day to dig through this building, cherub. You had your chance and now it's our turn."

"Like hell."

Gremory laughed. "Exactly." She turned her head and met Riley's eyes. "Hello, Detective Parra." Riley suddenly received a mental image of Gremory, naked but for a strap-on, and her knees went weak. Gremory laughed with a sound that was more like an orgasmic moan. "Like what you see?"

Riley forced the image away and managed a dreadfully weak smile. "Like? Not really. But I am glad it'll be so easy for you to go fuck yourself."

Gremory's smile turned into a sneer. She looked at Priest again. "This building is neutral. Gail and I are not leaving, and I can assume you and Detective Parra won't leave while we're still here. So I suggest a compromise. We both go inside and whoever finds the cheese at the end of the maze first is the winner."

"How do I know you'll stand by the terms of your agreement?"

Gremory laughed loud and hard at that. "To ask me that in this of all places... you have my word, Zerachiel. Do I have yours that you will step aside if we are victorious?"

Priest looked at Riley and then extended her hand. Gremory took it and they shook. Gremory brought her other hand up and it glowed red for a moment before Priest closed her free hand around it. The red glow intensified, mixing with white and gold. The ground began to tremble and Riley realized the angel and demon were the epicenters of the quake.

"Riley..."

She didn't have to be told twice. She raced toward the door, the plywood cover loosely placed over the opening. She slid it out of the way and ran blindly into the dark building. She heard the slapping of Gail Finney's footsteps on the ground behind her as she ducked to one side of the door. She timed it as best she could and shot her right arm out just as Gail crossed the threshold. She ran into Riley's fist and went down hard, flat on her back.

Riley didn't take the time to see if she was all right before she ran deeper into the building. She didn't know what she was looking for, just that a demon and angel coveted it equally.

Anything that could cause a truce between those two was definitely something she wanted on her side.

Riley unlocked the door to her apartment. What a wasted night that had been. The building was nothing and she was tired and sore. She rolled her shoulders as she stepped into the apartment and turned on the light.

Gillian gasped, her voice surprisingly high-pitched. She was on the couch, which had been made up for Maureen, and she clutched at her sweater to hold the unbuttoned sides together. Maureen turned to one side and tugged her jeans back up over slender hips.

"You were supposed to be gone for... a-an hour." Gillian's face was beet red, her freckles showing as she looked at Riley with regret and horror. Her hair was mussed by someone repeatedly running it through their fingers.

Riley tilted her head to the side in confusion, and her voice had no anger in it. "What's going on, Gillian?"

She turned her head away in shame as she buttoned her jeans. "Maureen was my first, Riley. I guess I just had to get her out of my system." She looked at Maureen and tucked her hair behind her ear. She kept her head down to avoid Riley's gaze.

Riley rolled her shoulders, looked at her watch, and shook her head. "I don't even know what to say. This is... this is really pathetic."

Gillian looked up. "Riley, you don't have to be hurtful..."

Riley ignored her and directed her next statements to the ceiling. "If you want to break me, stop pulling this shit. Gillian cheating on me? That didn't work with the mara and it won't work now." She turned and scanned the apartment. "I thought we had a truce."

The apartment darkened and flickered like burning film on an old movie reel. The darkness of the building replaced it, and Gremory's face hovered in front of her. "It was worth a try. A truce doesn't mean we have to play by the rules."

Riley rushed toward the demon, but Gremory swung her arm and knocked Riley to the side. She hit the wall and landed in a pile of rubble as the air rushed from her lungs. Gremory advanced on her, but Riley rolled to one side and avoided her grasp. She grabbed Gremory's right leg and tugged, knocking the demon off balance long enough that Riley could get to her feet.

"So what exactly are we fighting over? Is there a chance we

could split it fifty-fifty and get me home in time for Letterman?"

Gremory had hit the wall and wiped drywall dust from her shoulders. She smiled and shook her head. "I would have thought the angel stopped keeping secrets after what happened last year with the Angel Maker."

"She's been a little busy." Riley put her fists up. "You want to brawl and leave Gail to find the precious by herself?"

Gremory glanced down the hall, obviously rethinking her plan. "You and I will dance soon enough, Detective Parra. Trust me on that."

"Save the bad guy cliches and get the hell out of here."

Gremory ran down the hall, and Riley didn't relax until she was out of sight. Riley scanned the area and stepped into a room that was missing its door. The windows were painted black and she had a flashback to the building where Samael had held her captive for her "trial." *Priest let you walk right into that trap, too.* She pushed aside her misgivings and backed out of the room. The building was strange. The floors didn't correspond precisely to the exterior, and it seemed like the corridors stretched on much farther than they should have. Every room she had looked into so far was empty, but with the vacant feel that told her nothing had ever been there.

This building wasn't just abandoned. It had been utterly ignored since being built.

When she reached the stairs, she saw Priest coming up to greet her. Priest raised her hand in greeting and Riley saw that the tips of her fingers were blackened. "Are you okay?"

"I'll be fine. Gremory is a bit more powerful than I thought. I won't be underestimating her again."

Riley nodded. "You want me to hum a few bars of 'Amazing Grace' to get you back up to fighting speed?"

Priest shook her head. "Thank you for the offer, though. Come on, I think it's this way."

"What is this way? What exactly are we fighting over?"

"It's a very long story. I'll tell you, but I want you to be prepared." She looked into an empty room and motioned for Riley to follow her to another flight of stairs. "Do you know the origins of this world?"

"You mean Adam and Eve, God created the Heavens and the Earth in seven days?"

"That's the myth, yes."

Riley raised her eyebrows. "Did you just call one of the biggest stories in the Bible a 'myth'?"

Priest shrugged. "God created the world in seven days, right? What's a day?"

"What's a *day*? Give me some credit, Priest."

"A day is measured by the length of time it takes the Earth to make a complete revolution on its axis. The planet hadn't started yet, let alone started to rotate. Why would God measure something by an event that had yet to happen even once? The universe was not created in one flash of light. It was a slow, methodical process. 'Day' is used so humans can wrap their minds around the event. In the beginning, God created the heavens and the Earth and the Earth was darkness. This is all from the point of view of Man. Before the darkness, there was more in the Heavenly realm. Much more. God and the angels coexisted there in harmony. God had created the angels but he wanted something more. Angels were perfection, so he decided to open the mortal realm and use it to create something more interesting and... less perfect."

"So humanity exists because God was bored one morning."

"Does that make you upset?"

Riley snorted. "Actually, no. It makes a lot of sense."

They had reached another level. Priest paused her story as she examined the layout of the floor before motioning Riley back down the stairs.

Riley prompted Priest to continue the story. "So I guess making our little imperfect world went over well with the older kids."

"Less well than you know. Several of the angelic elite were horrified he would attempt something so shocking. To improve on angels by creating something inferior to them was almost blasphemous."

"Can God blaspheme?"

"There was a lot of debate on that subject. One faction decided that things were fine as they were. They asked God to rethink his decision, but he declared they were blaspheming for questioning his decisions. The darkness spoken about in the Bible refers to this time, when angel stood against angel and God was being questioned by his perfect creations. The mere fact that they were questioning him proved they weren't perfect, so why did he need to create mortals?"

They reached a lower level and Priest led the way across the floor. She stepped into a large room and turned in a slow circle before kneeling.

"So what happened?"

"The angels were on the brink of a civil war that would have torn Heaven apart. The Father washed his hands of everything and turned his back on us until we came to a solution. The two leaders decided to meet in the wasteland that God had created for his new children. Michael met with God's Favorite on a desolate piece of land."

Riley frowned. "They met on Earth?"

"They met in the mortal realm before it became Earth. Before it was even truly a planet as you would recognize it. Imagine something sitting in a kiln awaiting the sculptor's touch. The two angels stood on the unformed ground and made a decision. Those questioning the creation of humans would leave. They were sent away to live outside of God's realm."

"Kicked out of the house for disagreeing with Dad? Sounds like the apple didn't fall far from the tree."

"You would be surprised how human angels can be." Priest stood up and brushed off the knees of her trousers. "The spot where they met, where they reached the detente that turned a faction of rebellious angels into demons, was here."

"Where?"

"Right here, this town, where this building is standing."

Riley's eyes widened. "You're fucking with me."

Priest shook her head. "A nexus was created in order to facilitate the meeting. It was called the Ladder. This allowed the angels into the newly created mortal realm and, when the agreement was reached, it was used to send the demons to their own realm. Heaven, Earth, and Hell, all connected at a single point in space. A containment dome was built around the nexus, and another shell was built around that. Then a town began to form, people drawn by the energy of the nexus without realizing it. This town was constructed around this spot, Riley. You said this was the center of town and you are right. This building is the exact center of town.

"The Ladder can never be destroyed, so it is still open. It's open right now, somewhere in this building. Because of the shielding, neither Gremory nor I can trust our senses to locate it so we're stumbling blind."

Riley followed Priest back out into the corridor. "What does that mean?"

"It means that demons could potentially enter into the realm of Heaven on their own terms. It means Gremory could walk in, grab Michael and Raphael, and drag them back to Hell for an eternity of torture. It means that the demons could tear the door to Hell wide open and let Hell spill onto the streets of this city. It would be like turning on a faucet. The city center would flood with hate and evil and No Man's Land would surge forward. This war would be finished in an afternoon."

"And you just agreed to let Gremory have it if she found it first? God, Priest, what were you thinking?"

"Desperate times. If we fought her outright, we couldn't win. This way we at least stand a chance."

"All right. What's the plan when we find it first? Tear it open and let the angels flood the city with peace on Earth, goodwill to men, God bless us everyone?"

"No. We do our best to shut it down once and for all. Or at least contain it so that no one else can use it in the future."

"It's been open since the dawn of time. What chance do we have?"

Priest turned to face Riley. "I've discovered why I'm having such unusual dreams and uncertain memories of things I shouldn't know. Selaphiel did more than protect my divinity. He opened Zerachiel's mind to what he knew. I've been gifted with knowledge of this city, this war, and this world that I was never a part of before. It's why I know that you have a chance, Riley. If any champion were to uncover the Ladder, it would be you."

"All right. The Ladder. That's the one mentioned in the Bible, right? Jacob's Ladder?"

Priest nodded. "That's how I realized what was being hidden here. The name of this building is Bethel Luz. Those were the names of the place where Jacob had his dream."

Riley stopped moving and listened to the building. "So this building was created to keep people from just randomly stumbling over the Ladder and causing problems. It's hidden behind walls, or locked away in some dark room, or basically out of sight. So why aren't we hearing Gail and Gremory knocking down everything in their way to find it first?"

Priest listened to the silence all around them. "Perhaps they are being cautious."

"Or perhaps they're following us, letting us do the heavy lifting so they can step in at the last second." She drew her gun and spun around, aiming into the darkness at the top of the stairs. "I'm going to start firing in five seconds unless you show yourselves."

She didn't really expect them to come slowly down the stairs with their hands up, but she was completely unprepared for Gail launching herself out of the darkness like some vampire wannabe. Gail shouted as she slammed into Riley, who could only drop her gun in an attempt to catch the flying woman with the minimum amount of damage to them both. They hit the wall and Riley twisted to toss Gail to the ground as Gremory raced down the stairs and slammed into Priest just as hard. The angel and demon were thrown into an empty room, Priest's quickly extended wings impacting the doorway as she went through.

Gail rolled onto her hands and knees and glared up at Riley. "Looks like this is it, Parra. The final showdown, with the fate of~"

Riley kicked Gail in the head, knocking her sideways.

"Just shut up already." She grabbed Gail by the collar of her shirt and hauled her to her feet. "Gremory said you guys were playing by the rules, right? Well, fine. You're under arrest for assaulting a police officer. You have the right to~"

Gail shoved away from the wall and rushed Riley, grabbing her around the waist and knocking her backward. Riley hit the opposite wall and got the air knocked out of her once again by Gail's weight. Gail twisted to face Riley, grabbed a handful of her hair, and forced her head down. She brought her knee up and hit Riley in the forehead, making her loopy when Gail let her go. Riley stumbled, one hand to her head as she tried to regain her bearings.

"This is it. Gremory and I are going to open this fucking portal, and the city as we know it is going to fall. It'll be magnificent."

"How'd she get to you?" Riley felt a trickle of blood coming from her eyebrow and cursed. It would be tough explaining that one to the wedding photographers. "What did she promise you for this? What could possibly justify joining forces with a demon?"

"You heard the little story that your angel told you. The good guys are just brownnosing kiss-asses who couldn't stand up to Daddy. The demons lost their little scuffle, so they'll always be the bad guys even though we are led by God's Favorite angel. It's time they were given a chance to stand up and claim their birthright as God's favorite children. It's time for the mortals to accept they are a failed experiment."

Riley tried to scan the ground for her gun without being obvious. "There's a little flaw in your 'death to the mortals' plan."

Gail smiled. "I won't be mortal when this is all over. Gremory and I have a little deal."

"Oh, I can already tell this is going to be good."

"She's possessed her current host for far too long and she's becoming bored. When we win this skirmish, she's going to possess me fully. I've been given tastes and..." Her eyes rolled back and she shivered. "It's exquisite."

"That nice, warm feeling you have? It's wool being pulled over your eyes." She found her gun and lunged for it. Gail intercepted her and wrapped an arm around Riley's throat. She threw her weight back, pulling Riley with her, and they both hit the floor.

Something impacted the wall hard enough to crack the plaster, sending waves of dust down on the two mortals in the building. Riley and Gail both looked toward the disturbance just as Priest was shoved through the wall. Riley bent forward and tossed Gail off of her before running to Priest's aid.

"Riley, don't~"

Gremory picked Riley up and tossed her out of the way. Riley hit the wall and slumped to the floor, the pain radiating from her shoulder telling her that something had been jarred loose. "Oh, not good..."

Gail crossed to where Riley had fallen while Gremory picked Priest up off the rubble. Gail bent forward and pressed Riley's head against the wall hard enough to make Riley's skull ache. "This is what happens to the good guys. They have their time in the sun. They become complacent. And then the bad guys rise up and take over. History cycles. The bad guys rewrite the rule book when they take charge, so the good guys become outlaws. And everything starts all over again."

Riley couldn't see what Gremory was doing, but she heard a sickening crack and Priest cried out in pain.

"This is the way it should have been in the beginning." Gremory adopted a deep, resonant voice. "I can already see the new version of the Creation story. In the beginning, God decided to toss aside his perfect creations for new toys. His original creations weren't very keen on this idea, and they decided the time had come to break away from the old man." Another crack, but this time Priest only whimpered.

"God was banished." Crack, groan. "The creatures who would be called demons stepped up to fill his seat. We ruled."

Priest was whimpering now.

"Mortals remained in the caves where they belonged,

amusements for the newly reigning seraphim. The end."

Gail laughed and bent her knee, placing it in the center of Riley's chest. She took Riley's hands in hers and leaned back, pulling her arms while pinning her torso against the wall. The ache in her shoulder grew into agony and she bit back a cry of anguish.

Riley heard the sound of a body dropping and Gremory appeared behind Gail.

Gail smiled. "Like picking the wings off a fly."

Gremory laughed. "Now there is an interesting idea." She turned. "You lost your wings once, little angel. How would you like to lose them again so soon after getting them back?"

Riley turned her hands around and gripped Gail's biceps. Her fingers were numb, but she managed to grip the arm tightly. She forced herself to ignore the pain and tightened her grip, digging her fingernails into the soft flesh Gail. Gail's smirk turned into a sneer and she shook her head, her hair falling limp into her eyes.

"What is this, a prank? We're not in the fourth grade, and I'm not your big sister."

Riley opened her eyes. "The classics stick around because they work." She spit in Gail's face.

Gail recoiled and pulled her knee slightly away from Riley's body. It was enough for her to turn the tide, taking advantage of Gail's awkward position to knock her flat on her ass. Her left shoulder felt like it had been dislocated, but her right arm was just sore. She stooped to pick up a piece of the broken wall, stumble-running across the corridor as Gremory pinned Priest to the floor. Riley pulled her arm back and brought the piece of drywall down on top of Gremory's head. It shattered on impact.

Gremory slowly turned to face her. "You'll regret that you~"

Riley threw the remaining handful of drywall dust into Gremory's eyes. She screeched and twisted away from her just as Gail slammed into Riley from behind.

"We have a rodeo now!" Gail shouted.

Riley twisted her lower body and spun around quickly. Gail tried to hold on but she was sent flying. Riley was dizzied by the move and dropped onto her hands and knees, crying out as she put weight on her shoulders. The pain was quickly forgotten when she spotted her gun lying within arm's reach. She grabbed it, twisting around just as Gremory recovered from her blindness. She looked at the gun as Riley pulled the trigger.

Gremory was hit in the head, knocked back and grabbing

blindly for the banister as she fell down the stairs. Riley shifted her aim to Gail, sighting the barrel in the center of her chest. "You want to try it? I'd love for you to try it."

"This isn't over." Gail backed away and then ran down the stairs to recover her wounded but still alive partner.

Riley lowered the gun, exhausted from the effort of holding it up so long. She got to her feet and grunted at the various aches and pains that announced themselves as the adrenaline faded. Priest's arms and legs were twisted in ways that shouldn't have been possible, and it made Riley nauseated to look at it. She knelt near Priest's head and touched her throat to feel for a pulse. Priest opened her eyes at the touch and then cried out. "Riley, ahh..."

"Don't try to talk."

Priest ignored her. "Did we win?"

Riley kept her own wounded arm pressed tight to her chest. She felt like everything from her elbow to her shoulder had been pounded into dust. "I think that's up for debate."

Riley managed to get Priest into a room without adding too much damage to either one of them. She propped Priest against the wall and sat down beside her, massaging one shoulder for a few minutes before switching to the other. Both shoulders felt dislocated at the very least. She had an image of herself trying to carry Gillian over the threshold and grunted in irritation at herself. She looked at Priest, who seemed to be in much worse shape.

"I don't suppose you brought any water with you."

Priest shook her head. "Sorry."

"And here I thought you said angels were perfect creations."

Priest offered a weak smile. "I was recently a mortal. I'm forever tainted by the imperfection."

Riley sighed and stared at a spot across the room. "I take it you're out of commission."

"Gremory broke both my legs." She reached down with one hand to massage her thigh. The other sickening cracks Riley heard had been the fingers of Priest's left hand. "I could hover, but I wouldn't be an effective fighter. I'm sorry, Riley, but I'm afraid I won't be moving from here until you bring in some reinforcements."

Riley took her cell phone from her pocket. It was miraculously undamaged from her multiple impacts with the wall and floor, but the screen showed no signal. "Looks like the Ladder makes a hell of a dead zone. What about Sariel?"

"I attempted summoning her while I fought Gremory. She didn't respond."

"Is that because of interference or because you two are having some kind of tiff?"

Priest sighed. "I don't know. I haven't seen much of her since I rejoined Zerachiel. I don't think she approves of the situation. Or it could be that my return means she's no longer necessary here. I'm your guardian angel again, so there's no reason for her to stay. I spoke with her after we visited Lotus, but I don't know if she responded."

Riley had used the time Priest was talking to take stock of her own wounds. "Speaking of you being my guardian, do you have a comment card I could fill out regarding your performance?"

Priest smiled. "I'll get one for you."

Riley tried to lift her left arm and cried out in pain. "Gillian is going to kill me. Literally end my life. I don't think the suit I chose for the wedding will fit over a full-body cast."

"Gillian would marry you if you were just a head in a jar."

"She may have to settle for that."

Priest grunted and looked down at herself. "You have to take it again."

"Take what?"

"My divinity. It was returned for a reason. If I give you my divinity, your wounds will be healed. You can find the Ladder and prevent Gremory from getting her hands on it."

Riley had already started shaking her head. "Nope. One time thing. You brought me back, now you're put back together... everything is how it should be. I'm not going to use your divinity like an extra life in a video game."

"We can barely move, Riley. Gremory is healing as we speak, and soon she will be strong enough to crush us so she can find the Ladder at her leisure."

"Is there any way you can give me a little, let it heal me, and then take it back?"

Priest shook her head. "Under normal circumstances I could heal you. But after Gremory worked me over, I feel I wouldn't have much left after that."

"If saving my life means sacrificing yours, then I won't do it. It's not even an option."

Priest reached over and touched Riley's hand. Riley squeezed it and rested her head against the wall.

"Maybe this whole thing is a trap. We all run in here willy-nilly and get our asses kicked. Then we can never get out and we die in here. It's a tar baby."

"I don't believe that. It let me out to get you, didn't it?"

"Yeah, and then it got three more people to ensnare."

Priest was shaking her head. "It's here. I know that it's here, and that it can be found."

Riley sighed. "Okay. Then why are we on the third floor? If the Ladder was created before this building was erected, why aren't we looking on the ground floor or the basement?"

"This isn't a typical building. It was created for the express purpose of concealing the Ladder. It's been here throughout recorded history, conforming to its surroundings so no one notices it doesn't fit in. The interior is just as tricky. Rooms change, the layout is inconsistent, and it is larger than it appears from the street. I've been through this entire building and I've found nothing."

"Okay. So the basement..."

"There is no basement."

Riley thought about that. "There has to be."

Priest looked at her. "I looked, Riley. I've spent this entire day exploring this building and I've found no sign that there's a basement."

"But that's not possible. Look, this place was built at the beginning of time, before there was even a city. Right?" Priest nodded. "Then the spot where it was originally built has to be in the Underground. When the city was founded, today's ground floor would have been thirty or forty feet in the air."

Priest's eyes had widened. "I can't believe I didn't realize... you're right. Of course you're right."

"So there has to be a way down there."

"You should go before Gail or Gremory has the same idea."

Riley shook her head. "No way. I'm not leaving you here."

"Gremory will manipulate any weakness in order to gain an upper hand. Right now, your weakness is the fact you won't leave me behind. She expects you to sit here beside me, watching an empty hall, while she and Gail find the Ladder. Go. As long as you're looking for the Ladder, they won't bother coming back to find me."

Riley grunted as she stood up, angling her body forward and getting her legs under her so she wouldn't have to push with her arms. She got to her feet and rubbed her shoulders once more. "Geez. Okay, I'll see you as soon as I can."

"Be careful, Riley."

She nodded as she walked to the door. She peered into the hallway to make sure Gail and Gremory weren't lying in wait. As she descended the stairs, she thought about the possible ways into the Underground. There were a lot of buildings in the city with Underground access that even the tenants didn't know about. She'd been in a lot of them during her patrol days, and she tried to remember the trickiest hiding spots. Her mind was occupied by Priest and her injuries, and the fact that Gremory and Gail were somewhere in the building.

When she reached the ground floor, she moved toward the back of the building. The floor was tiled, and she occasionally stopped to tap her heel to see if any spots were hollow. She went into what would have been a utility closet in a regular building and felt the tile sag under her feet. She stepped back and used the butt of her gun to chip away at the tile, pulling it away one square at a time. Using the light from her cell phone's display screen, she saw a wooden ladder leading straight down into the dark. It was flanked on both sides by earthen walls that formed a tight tunnel into the Underground. Riley's shoulders almost shouted loud enough for her to hear as she hung her legs over the edge.

"Maybe this is the ladder Priest meant. Maybe I don't have to go down there." She shook her head. "Just do it, Parra. Don't be a wuss." She took a deep breath, her ribs joining the protest, and stepped onto the ladder. Halfway down, the pain across her shoulders was almost unbearable. She was about to step off the ladder when she heard movement above her. She looked up as two dark shapes blocked the slightly less-dark light coming from above.

"Oh, you gotta be kidding me."

The bright side was that she would be able to lie in wait for them at the bottom. Of course in the condition she was in, they would probably be able to knock her down without breaking a sweat. She rested her head against the rung, trying to think of the option with the best chance of success. She stepped off the ladder, her hand instinctively going to her left shoulder to rub the knot that had formed there.

She thought of Gillian in that green slip, straddling her waist and working out all of these kinks. *"How do you do this to yourself, baby? You're always so tense..."*

"Not the time for distractions," she muttered as she moved away from the ladder access. She crouched next to a wooden support strut and kept her gun at the ready. She heard Gail and Gremory's descent and tensed as they came closer. She ran her thumb over the engraving on the grip of her weapon and considered a non-violent approach.

Gail reached the bottom rung first. She took a flashlight off her belt and shined it in all directions. Riley ducked back out of sight until the light passed her. She saw the light playing over the ground and knew they were looking for footprints in the dirt. "Which way did she go?" Gremory asked as she reached the bottom.

"I don't know. A surprising amount of people have come this way recently. Don't you feel something? Like a tug, or~"

"Quiet."

Gail obediently shut up as Gremory scented the air. Finally she pointed to the northern path. "This way."

Riley waited until they had entered the tunnel before she left her hiding place. She looked toward the ceiling to get her bearings. Priest said that the building had been constructed to protect the Ladder. Whoever or whatever had put the building together wouldn't tuck the Ladder away in some far corner. They would have surrounded it as much as possible on all sides. She walked toward the middle of the building, moving slowly and silently so she wouldn't alert Gremory to her true position.

The path hugged a curved brick wall, several corners of the brick sticking out to achieve the angle. The trail Riley was following ended abruptly in a solid stone wall that stretched to completely block the tunnel. She stepped forward and ran her hand over the smooth blockade and was surprised by how warm it was.

Someone stepped up behind her and shoved her head into the stone. Pain exploded from between her eyes and she dropped to her knees, shoved aside by Gremory as she stepped forward to examine the wall. "Thank you, Detective Parra. You saved us a lot of time of fumbling in the darkness. Here it is. Right behind this wall." She smoothed her palms over the stone and hung her head. "So close. Soon, Gail."

Riley saw the spot where her head had made contact, the starburst of blood dripping down the surface. Gremory spread it with her fingers and the stone seemed to groan.

"We need more... Gail, acquire more blood from the champion, if you would..."

Gail stooped to pick up a rock. "It would be my pleasure. I'm going to really enjoy this, Riley..."

Gail lifted the stone over her head. Riley waited until her arm was fully extended before she fired, keeping the gun by her hip where she'd drawn it. The bullet hit Gail in the right arm and the force of impact knocked her backward. Gremory spun at the sound of the shot, took in the situation, and shrugged. "It doesn't matter which champion supplies the blood..."

Gremory looked at Riley and licked her lips.

Gillian sank to her knees taking Riley's pants down as well, and Riley rested her shoulders against the wall~

~Gremory knelt down and cupped Gail's wounded arm with her hand. The blood poured over her palm, coating her hand and fingers. Riley tensed her finger to shoot, but instead~

~she tightened her hand in Gillian's hair, pulling her lips back against her teeth as Gillian's tongue touched her~

Gremory spread the blood over the stone. It cracked where she applied the blood, spreading to reveal a golden light pouring from within. Riley squinted and turned away, remembering what the Holy Grail did to the Nazis in that Indiana Jones movie as the fantasy faded from her mind. *Oral sex from Gillian. At least the demon is getting better at finding ways to distract me.* Gremory pushed with both hands and increased the gap between the two halves of the stone.

Riley saw Gail, slumped across the tunnel from her, trying in vain to stop the bleeding from her arm. She was distracted by the light show from within the stone. Riley lifted her gun and lined up a shot, aiming dead center between Gail's eyes. *Championship match. Only one can survive, right?*

She lowered the gun without firing just as something slammed into Gremory's side. The demon was pressed against the still-opening barrier, her face twisted into a grimace of anger and pain. Gremory tried to push away from the stone, but Priest was using all of her strength to keep her pinned. Priest squeezed, her teeth bared as she pulled Gremory away from the ever-widening opening in the stone.

"We... had a deal... Zerachiel!"

"A deal which you broke. Riley found the Ladder."

Gremory managed to fight Priest off and threw her to the ground. She brought her foot up and slammed it down on Priest's broken leg. Priest's shout of anguish tore at Riley, but she was finding it increasingly difficult to move. "Parra found the barrier. I'll find the Ladder, and the first thing I'm going to do is send you to Hell. A lot of your old friends would like to say hi." She ground her foot down on Priest's leg and Riley cringed at the sound as well as Priest's increased cries.

Riley closed her eyes. *Sariel, you bitch, if you can hear me, then hear this and tell me you're okay with what's happening. Tell me you're fine with Priest being tortured this way. And if you are, then maybe I'll let Gremory take you self-righteous bastards to Hell.*

When she opened her eyes, Sariel was standing in front of her. Gremory looked up just as Sariel extended her wings. The tunnel filled with light that was only matched by the glow coming from within the barrier. "You will not touch her again."

"Sar~"

The entire tunnel seemed to shake, and Gremory was hit by the shockwave. It threw her back against the barrier. Gremory's eyes grew dark and she brought her hand up to meet Sariel's attack. She lunged forward.

Sariel's fist sank into Gremory's chest. Gremory widened her eyes and opened her mouth in an almost human expression of shock and horror.

"No, no, no."

Sariel's eyes flashed. Her wings seemed to glow even brighter. Gremory's look of shock and horror faded as her flesh was charred and darkened by smoke. Sariel pulled her arm back and Gremory imploded. Her shriek echoed in the tunnel until Riley and Gail both had to cover their ears. When they could look again, Sariel's glow had diminished drastically. Her skin was ashen, her movements slow and unsure as she dropped to her knees beside Priest.

"What did you do?"

"I destroyed her." Sariel's voice was distracted as she stroked Priest's face. She had gone unconscious during the attack, but she stirred at Sariel's touch. "The nexus will be sealed. This building will be sealed. The nexus will not be accessed through violence." She looked up, her unblinking eyes locked on Riley. "Thank you. For calling me."

Riley dipped her chin in acknowledgement.

Sariel gathered Priest's broken body in her arms, still looking at her face.

"Sariel... we're going to die down here unless you help~"

Riley turned and saw Gail Finney standing a few feet away. Gail's arm was intact, and Riley realized that her own various aches and pains were also gone. She looked at her watch and saw that it was a half hour after she'd left her apartment. "I guess time works differently in there. Along with everything else." She rolled her shoulders just to make sure they were in factory condition and checked her gun. The bullets she'd used inside were missing, but it was otherwise fine.

"Do it."

Riley looked up at Gail's voice. "Do what?"

Gail was sobbing with her both hands limp at her side in surrender. "Finish the job you started down there. Finish it."

Riley holstered her weapon. "Go home, Gail."

Gail lunged forward took a swing at her. Riley easily dodged the punch, grabbed Gail's arm, and pinned her against the side of her car. "It's been a rough night for everyone, okay? So let's just call it a draw and go to our separate corners. There's no need for any more bloodshed, all right?" When Gail didn't answer, Riley tightened her grip. "All right?"

Gail grunted affirmatively and Riley let her go. Gail stumbled a few steps away before she turned around. "Think about what happened down there. Think about if things had gone a little bit differently, and you watched another demon slaughter Zerachiel that way. Then just try and imagine how I feel right now. This isn't over, Parra."

"No, I don't suppose it is." She sighed heavily. "But for tonight, let's put a pin in it, huh?"

Gail walked away, hands shoved into her pockets and her head hung. Riley looked to the sky as if she expected to see two angels in flight. She could only hope that Priest's injuries had been healed as fully as hers and Gail's had been.

Riley got behind the wheel of her car and took a moment to enjoy how soft the seat felt against her back. The pain had gone away, but the memory of it was still vivid. She probably needed a good night's sleep to let it fade fully. She took her cell phone from her pocket and dialed her home number.

"Hey. I thought I'd get a chance to nag you about staying out all night with other women."

If you only knew. "Sorry. I'm on the way back now."

There was silence and then a rustling, and Riley knew that she'd moved the phone away from where Maureen could overhear her. "Hey. You all right? You sound weird."

Riley leaned back against the headrest. "Long night."

"Wanna talk about it? Mo is about to camp out on the couch, so we could sit up and talk in the bedroom."

"No. You know what I want?" She rubbed her eye with her free hand. "I want to sleep with you tonight and then, when we wake up, I want to go marry you."

More silence. "Is th~"

"Don't say we're not ready. We have the suits, we have your friend here, we have..." She looked at the empty seat where Priest would have sat. "We have everything we need and, if we don't, we can improvise."

"I wasn't going to say that. I was going to ask if there's anyplace open tonight who could do it. But I like the sleeping together thing, too."

Riley smiled. "Love you. I'll see you soon."

"Don't speed. Get here soon, but get here in one piece."

"Will do. I love you, Jill."

Gillian laughed softly. "I love you, too. See you soon."

Riley hung up and tapped the phone against her thigh. "All right, Cait. Now you have to come back. I need my best woman."

When there was no reply, Riley started the car and pulled away from the curb.

Priest woke slowly, aware first of hands on her legs and then the lack of pain. There were still aches, but they were minimal compared to what she had been expecting. A hymn was playing quietly on a stereo, and it sounded like there were a multitude of speakers all over the room. She opened her eyes and scanned an unfamiliar room, the slanted window above the bed looking out on a deep night sky. She could see more stars than she would have thought possible in the middle of a city, blurred by the dirt and grime on the glass but still awe-inspiring. She grunted as a pair of hands adjusted their grip on her calves and lifted her head.

Her trousers and shoes had been removed, leaving her in her underwear and socks. The tails of her shirt covered her modesty well. Sariel was sitting on the edge of the bed, her fingers wrapped tightly around Priest's legs as if she was trying to choke them. The harder she squeezed, the less the broken bones hurt.

"You came."

Sariel opened her eyes and met Priest's gaze. She looked quickly away. "Riley called me. I couldn't ignore her calling."

"Is she all right?"

Sariel nodded. "I removed Riley and Gail Finney from the chamber. The nexus has been resealed. The mortals have been healed of their wounds. You're fortunate that the area around the nexus is so malleable or I wouldn't have been able to pull off some of what I did."

"Thank you."

"You and Detective Parra didn't give me much of a choice."

Priest pushed herself up and winced; Sariel hadn't healed her ribs or hand yet. "I thought perhaps you had left."

Sariel met Priest's gaze. "Why do you do these things? Rush into such dangerous situations? It's a miracle that you survived even your short time as a mortal."

"I'm Riley's guardian angel. It's my purpose to be with her in times of great danger."

"You do more than that. You have become ingrained in her life. You've taken a mortal name and a profession. You have assumed all the entrapments of a human being. Why?"

"Because I love her. I've had many charges over the years but Riley is different. Her protection is more than an innate urge. She is a powerful force. The reason I go into these dangerous situations with her is because I know that she would go alone if she had to. I respect that side of her. That fearless part of her."

Sariel let go of Priest's leg and the tingling in the flesh faded.

"Thank you for healing me."

"It's taking longer than I thought. You were very badly injured, and I was weak from... everything else I did this evening."

Priest tilted her head to the side. "Healing Riley and Gail?"

"And destroying Gremory. She's gone."

"That must have taken a great deal of power. You shouldn't be conscious right now."

"I took your advice. I've been hiding out in the bell tower of a church." She licked her lips and took Priest's broken hand. She laced their fingers together and squeezed. Priest gasped at the pain, and sighed as it began to lessen. "You were right. The power you feel even when the building is empty. It's as if the worship seeps into the stonework."

Priest smiled. "I was worried at first that it would be like a drug. And the~"

Sariel leaned forward and kissed Priest. The power flowing between their hands intensified briefly, a flaring light in Priest's body. When it faded, her hand felt strong and whole again. She didn't loosen her grip, and Sariel's fingers squeezed her tighter. They parted and Sariel closed her eyes, her lips parted as she tried to catch her breath.

"Thank you."

"Embracing the mortal part of myself has been difficult. It feels like a betrayal to my angelic side."

Priest shook her head. "When we assumed this form, it became part of us. Caitlin Priest is just a facet of Zerachiel, and vice versa." She tucked a strand of hair behind Sariel's ear. "We have to eat. Not as much as actual mortals, but we do. So why should we ignore our other instinctual needs?"

"I love my brethren, but it's different with you. My feelings for you are confusing. The reason I came when Riley called is because I heard you. I heard your anguish and I couldn't stop myself from acting. I couldn't stand the thought of you in pain." Priest leaned toward her, but Sariel retreated. "You are in a relationship."

"What I have with Kenzie and Chelsea is unique. They are a couple, and I'm... an occasional participant. Their commitment is to each other. They would understand how much I would really like to kiss you now, Sariel."

"I don't know."

"My hand has healed, and yet your grip hasn't lessened." Sariel looked down. When she looked up again, Priest kissed her. Sariel let go of Priest's hand at last, cupping her face with both hands as she lowered her down onto the mattress. Sariel twisted her hips to climb onto the bed and stretched out beside Priest. Their kiss became more passionate as Sariel lifted Priest's shirt and ran her hand along her flank. She cupped Priest's ribs and Priest arched her back as her broken bones knit together.

Sariel moved to straddle Priest, breaking the kiss to sit up and gaze down at her.

"What are we doing?"

"We can figure that out as we go." Priest sat up and began unbuttoning Sariel's blouse. Sariel took the hint and began to undo the buttons of Priest's shirt as well. They kissed as they shrugged out of the sleeves, tugging their hands out of stubborn cuffs before touching each other again. Priest moved her lips to Sariel's neck, down to the curve of her shoulder as Sariel undid her bra. Sariel's ears were bright red, and Priest sucked the lobe into her mouth as she cupped Sariel's small breasts in her hands. The nipples hardened under her fingers and Sariel gasped.

"It feels like worship, doesn't it?"

"So it must be sacrilege."

Priest smiled. "No. It's just the closest a mortal can get to feeling what we feel." She pecked Sariel's bottom lip and smoothed her hand down Sariel's back. She kept her eyes open as she leaned back, working a hand between them to undo the catch of Sariel's pants. The material sagged open, and Priest slid her hand inside. Sariel looked down, chin against her chest, and gasped as Priest touched her.

"Oh..."

Priest took Sariel's hand and moved it to her own lap. Her fingers were trembling as Priest flattened them against the material of her underwear. "Here... stroke me here, like this. Like I am."

"How many? How many fingers?"

"Two." Priest was gasping now, also stroking with two fingers as Sariel began to mimic her movements. "Inside... you can put them~" Sariel used her thumb to pull aside the cotton, and then her fingers were on flesh. Priest rolled her head back and groaned, pushing one fingertip inside of Sariel. Sariel rested her head on Priest's shoulder and stroked the smooth flesh with her tongue. Priest turned her head and kissed Sariel's temple as the two women moved together.

Sariel lifted her hips and sank down on Priest's hand, forcing her fingers as deep as they would go. She curled her free arm around Priest's neck and looked into her eyes. "I... I feel... Caitlin..." Sariel's wings exploded from her back, spreading as far as they could. The feathers were splayed, her body glowing in the ambient light cast from them. Priest opened her own wings, which emitted a slightly brighter glow than Sariel's, the two of them crying out their orgasms in harmony. Priest lowered her head to Sariel's chest, and Sariel pressed her lips to the top of Priest's hair.

They separated from each other, their wings folding and disappearing as Sariel crawled out of Priest's lap and lay beside her on the mattress. She ran her hand down Priest's arm without looking, Priest lifting her hand until their palms pressed together. Priest stared up at the slanted window overhead and her lips curled into a smile as she let the sensations of what they had just done fade. It was remarkably like worship; the good feelings sometimes lasted for hours afterward.

"How long?"

Priest glanced at her. "Until what?"

"Until we can do that again. How long d-do we have to wait?"

Priest smiled and propped herself on one elbow. She kissed Sariel, dragging her free hand between Sariel's breasts before she followed it with her lips and tongue. Licking Sariel's erect nipples, spreading her legs as she settled between them. "I think we've both waited long enough, don't you?"

Sariel tried to answer, but the words were cut off by a gasp. She dropped Priest's hand so she could grip the sheet with both hands, lifting her body to meet Priest's lips and tongue.

Riley slipped into the apartment with her shoes hanging from two fingers. Maureen was sitting up on the couch, her lower body wrapped up in a blanket. She smiled when she looked up and closed her book on her thumb. "Hey. Jill told me that there'd been a change in schedule. Guess you can't wait to make it official, huh?"

"Yeah. No time like the present."

"I'm surprised it's taken you this long. Thanks for waiting long enough for me to get here. And... for a long time, I wondered if there was a person worthy enough for my best friend in the whole world. Thanks for being that person."

Riley smiled. "I'm trying to be."

"Have a good night."

Riley shrugged. "It can only go up from where I just came from." She waved goodnight as she crossed the living room, still rubbing her shoulder even though the pain was a distant memory. She still couldn't get her mind around the events of the night. Even if Sariel had somehow erased the events, the Ladder still existed. It was a hell of a dangerous thing to just leave lying around.

She went into the bedroom and closed the door, glancing toward the bed. "Jill? You awake?"

"Hi."

Riley turned and saw Gillian standing in the bathroom door. None of the lights were on, but in the streetlight glow through the window she could see the lacy cut of Gillian's nightgown and her long, bare legs. Riley licked her lips. "Hey."

"It's our wedding night."

"It's the night before our wedding." Riley smiled. "There's a difference."

Gillian shrugged and stepped into the room. "Well, correct me if I'm wrong, but shouldn't one of us have gotten a sexy, naked lap dance from a beautiful woman in honor of this occasion? Not that I didn't enjoy the bachelorette party but... wasn't it missing something?"

"Now that you mention it."

"Sit on the bed."

Riley took off her coat and tossed it, sitting on the edge of the bed. Gillian bent down, her hands on Riley's shoulders, her lips peeling back in a smile as she raised an eyebrow.

"I don't have any singles."

"It's okay. I don't have a G-string..."

Riley cleared her throat as Gillian straddled her and began to roll her hips. Gillian's breasts were in front of Riley's face, and her hands naturally came to rest on her thighs. She licked her lips and began to stroke as Gillian moved on top of her.

There was something to be said for a traditional bachelorette party, after all.

She turned her head and spit, shoving the gun away from her. She'd never been told about the gun metal taste, the oil on her tongue. She supposed that most people who tasted it weren't around to describe the experience. Gail Finney wiped her thumb over her bottom lip and turned toward the chair that Gremory usually took when she came over. "Come back. Come back." She'd been trying to summon Gremory all night, to no avail. The silence was crushing her.

She pressed two fingers against her shut eyes, trying to stave off the tears threatening to flow.

"Come back. Alyssa, I love you, come back to me."

Gail slipped off her chair and hit her knees, moving her hands to clutch the back of her neck. She shuddered and sobbed openly.

In time, the tears stopped. Gail lowered herself to the floor and clutched herself as she pulled her legs up against her chest. This would not stand. Riley would pay for this, would suffer for taking Gremory from her.

"For you," Gail whispered. "For you, Gremory..."

Her lips curled into a smile as she began planning. Riley Parra would pay, and then... she almost felt pity for the poor people of this damned town.

Reign in Hell

The Demon holds a string. He licks the pad of his thumb, wets the string, and begins to coil it. "What is the worst thing I could do?" The loops of the string are tight. "The worst possible scenario you could conceive. What do you suppose that would be?" The string forms legs. He twists, going back over the body he's already created to form arms. "I could kill everyone you know. I could kill them in ways more painful and traumatic than you would believe." He uses wide loops to create a bulbous head. "I could do all of these unspeakable things to them, but leave them alive."

He takes a small white cloth from his coat pocket and wraps it around the doll. He holds it up to admire his handiwork, and the doll appears to be wearing a wedding dress. He smiles at his creation, licks his thumb again, and uses the saliva to keep the string from unraveling. He picks up the hair he'd earlier taken from the shoulder of a coat, a long and curled strand of chestnut-colored hair, and wraps it around the doll's head.

The doll isn't large, spanning just a little more than the length of his index finger, and he completely encloses the doll in one hand and begins to squeeze. Blood seeps between his fingers and drips to the ground between his feet.

He makes eye contact. Sustained eye contact with a demon has instant consequences for a human. The churning stomach of nausea, strength *seeping from your body as if from a tap.*

"What do you think? Are those the worst things I could do? You're wrong."

He opens his palm and tosses the doll to her. The doll is pristine.

"The worst thing I can do is make you do it instead."

Riley looks down at the doll in her hand as it begins to bleed.

Earlier

"Riley?" The justice of the peace raised an eyebrow, and her lips had a slight curve to them. She leaned forward to make sure Riley was paying attention to something besides Gillian. Riley nodded for her to continue. "I promise to listen to your voice and your heart."

Riley repeated the words as best she could without her voice trembling. Her biggest fear had been looking ridiculous, and now she was afraid people would think she wasn't treating the moment respectfully enough. She continued to repeat the words recited by the justice of the peace, but she spoke them directly to Gillian.

"To respect you, to stand beside you in sorrow and in happiness. To offer strength and understanding, and to provide comfort in times of need. I swear to make your needs my own, and to love and honor you for as long as we both shall live."

"Gillian?" the justice said. She began the vows again, and Gillian smiled as she went through her own recitation. Riley bit the inside of her cheek to keep from tearing up as she squeezed Gillian's hands. Gloves. Whose idea was it for the bride to wear gloves? She wanted to feel Gillian's palms against hers. When the vows were finished, Riley turned and took her ring from Priest. Priest smiled proudly, and Riley winked at her before turning back to face her partner.

"Riley Jacqueline Parra, do you take Gillian Eleanor Hunt to be your partner?"

"If she'll have me." She swallowed. "Sorry. I mean, I do."

The justice laughed. "It's all right. There's no need to stand on ceremony. Gillian..."

"Yes, I do, I do."

"Then exchange the rings that will symbolize your unity, your love, and your commitment to one another."

Gillian removed the glove of her left hand and extended it to Riley. Riley slipped the ring onto the third finger. Gillian took the ring from Maureen and placed it on Riley's finger.

"By the power vested in me vested in me, I now pronounce you married. You may kiss–" Riley cupped Gillian's face and kissed her lips. "Well, it's a good thing we're not standing on ceremony."

Riley smiled but didn't break the kiss. The witnesses cheered, and Riley felt white rose petals raining down on them from both sides. Riley kissed both of Gillian's cheeks and then rested their foreheads together. Gillian squeezed Riley's hand, and they stepped off the altar and walked toward the door hand-in-hand. Priest and Maureen followed a few steps behind. The group moved through the lobby of city hall, Riley reluctant to let go of Gillian's hand even to open doors.

The sky was clear when they finally stepped outside, only a few clouds marring the perfectly blue sky. Riley squinted up and then turned to her partner. Her spouse, her wife. A few rose petals had caught in her hair and Riley started to pluck them out before she realized they looked perfect. She brushed Gillian's cheek, started to kiss her, and then pulled back.

"What's wrong?"

"Nothing. I've just always had this thing about being with married women. I may need some time to get over the mental block."

"Let me help." She put her arm around Riley's neck to keep her from backing away and kissed her hard. Riley sagged against Gillian, her arms tight around her waist, and kept up the kiss until Priest politely coughed a 'you remember you are in public, right' reminder.

They parted and Riley brushed her nose against Gillian's. "Hello, Dr. Gillian Parra."

"Hi, Detective Riley Hunt."

Priest frowned. "Wait, you're taking... wait..."

Riley laughed. "No. We'll keep our own names. I just wanted to hear how it sounded." She kissed Gillian again. "I think it sounds pretty close to perfect."

Maureen whistled and clapped, drawing the attention of someone entering the City Hall behind their group. Riley moved down the steps so they would be out of everyone's way. She'd worn a black suit and white shirt, while Gillian was in a beautiful teal gown. It wasn't exactly traditional, but when something looked that good, tradition could take a flying leap.

"So what's the plan now?" Maureen asked. "Honeymoon, month-long vacation?"

"If only." Riley had her right hand in Gillian's left, the thumb of her left hand idly and unconsciously stroking the new ring on the its third finger. "We get the rest of the day off and then it's back to the grind tomorrow. But we can do plenty with an afternoon and an evening."

Gillian laughed and pressed herself against Riley's side.

Maureen smiled at her friend. "In that case, I will definitely stay out of your hair for the rest of today." She turned to Priest. "Want to get some lunch?"

"Uh, sure." She smiled at Riley and Gillian, stepping forward to embrace them both. "Congratulations, you two."

"I'm glad you were here, Cait. I wasn't sure if your, uh... religious beliefs would let you be involved."

Priest nodded. "Anywhere love is declared, God is there. A wedding of any kind is a celebration of love. It's more problematic when it comes to divorce."

"No worries there."

Priest turned to Maureen. "Let's get out of their hair. I can show you around a little, show you the good hotels and which streets to avoid."

"I appreciate it." She waved goodbye as she led Priest down the sidewalk to her car.

Gillian returned the wave and then grabbed the lapels of Riley's jacket. She pulled her in for a kiss, sighing when they parted.

"I figure it'll take us about fifteen minutes to get back home. Figure we have to eat at some point today, so maybe an hour for lunch~"

"A half hour if we order takeout."

"Brilliant. Half hour, then. Maybe a shower or two, shared of course. Maybe a little sleep?"

"Cat naps."

Gillian nodded. "And we don't have to be anywhere until eight o'clock tomorrow morning. Assuming forty-five minutes to shower, dress, and drive to work. So I figure that gives us... about nineteen hours for a honeymoon."

"Then what are we waiting for? Time's wasting."

They ran to the car.

Jimmy was scratching the back of his head with both hands when the door to the studio finally opened. He stood up so quickly that his chair rolled across the production booth, thudding quietly against the wall as he stormed out into the corridor. "It's about goddamn time. Where the..." He looked Gail over and made a face. "God, what the hell happened to you?"

"None of your damn business." Gail's hair was unwashed, her blouse buttoned wrong. She was wearing torn blue jeans and sneakers and she hadn't even attempted makeup. Her eyes were still red from crying all night. "It's radio. People will picture whatever the hell they want. Are we good to go?"

Jimmy rolled his eyes and ducked back into the booth. "We're live in thirty. As in thirty seconds. As in you got here thirty seconds before~"

"It's my fucking show, Jim, so shut your goddamn trap." She dropped into her seat and put her headphones on. She rested her elbows on the table and pressed her hands together in front of her face as if she was praying. She hadn't rested a minute since watching Gremory's destruction. The empty ache in her chest kept growing and growing until she wasn't sure her body was big enough to contain it.

She had tried contacting Gremory countless times through the night. Her forearms were wrapped with bandages from all the cuts she had made, scribbling useless designs on her apartment's floor. Several of her incantations had resulted in a pounding headache, like receiving an injection from a syringe with an air bubble. It was then she realized that she was succeeding with her calls, but there was no one to respond.

Jimmy's voice came through her headphones, soft and velvet compared to his barely-above homeless appearance. "Coming to you live across the airwaves, exposing the truth behind the conspiracies, it's the Gail Finney Show. And now, journalist, author, and truth-seeker... your host, Gail Finney."

Gail brushed her hands over her cheeks and faced the microphone. When she spoke, there was no trace of a tremor in her voice. "Good afternoon, my fine people. Today we're going to take a bit of a different tactic. We're not going to focus on the corrupt and inept police, not directly. This afternoon, we're going to focus the gross incompetence of the Medical Examiner's office. Flawed analysis, mishandling of evidence, falsifying evidence, cronyism... this is all just the tip of the iceberg of what you can find if you dig deep enough into the Office of the Chief Medical Examiner.

"The Chief Medical Examiner works directly with the police department to investigate homicides. They do the autopsies and gather the evidence and basically decide whether or not foul play was involved. Their evidence is crucial in sending criminals to death row, or forcing them to spend their entire life behind bars. And you probably don't even know her name. Well, I'm going to enlighten you. The Chief ME is named Gillian Hunt. Her evidence has led to seven people - seven - being given lethal injection.

"When I say she works directly with the police, I should have been a bit clearer. Dr. Hunt works *closely* with one detective in particular. A detective I'm sure many of my readers and listeners will recognize. Detective Riley Parra. And what, pray tell, are Dr. Hunt and Detective Parra doing on this fine day? They're engaging in a lovely bit of playacting down at City Hall where they'll exchange rings and say meaningless words and then prance off into the sunset."

Gail leaned back in her chair and looked at Jimmy through the glass. He was shaking his head, looking down at his console, his lips moving as he muttered to himself.

"So we have one of the most secretive, rogue cops in the department on one hand, and the woman who decides which criminals live or die on the other. And now they're bound in... well, not *holy* matrimony, but something similar. I'm terrified, ladies and gentlemen. I'm horrified at the possibilities of this union. Now all Detective Parra has to do is go to her honeylamb and say, 'This guy I'm chasing, oh, this guy is a real tool and I think he should go down whether he did it or not, and if you could manufacture a little evidence that would point to him, well... well, that would be really swell of you, babyface.'"

Jimmy pulled his microphone to his face. "Sorry to interrupt you, Ms. Finney, but we have to pause for station identification."

Gail pinched the bridge of her nose. "God, Jimmy. My listeners may be imbeciles, but they know what fucking station they're listening to."

Jimmy mouthed a curse of his own. "We'll be right back with more of the Gail Finney Show after these messages." He jabbed a button. "What the hell are you doing, Gail?"

"What I always do."

He lifted his phone, showing that he had been searching the web. "There are zero complaints against either the Office of the Medical Examiner or Gillian Hunt in the past five years. None. There is nothing to substantiate your claim that the office is in any way corrupt."

Gail gestured at her booth. "Since when have we cared about *proof*, Jimmy? Everything we do here is smoke and mirrors. Taking a little slice of fact and twisting it to our own means. Don't tell me you've been falling for the same bullshit I've been spouting to these jagoffs. The phone lines are lighting up, aren't they?"

Jimmy sighed and looked down at his console.

Gail motioned for him to turn on her microphone and he rolled his eyes. He timed the end of the commercial and leaned forward. "Welcome back to the Gail Finney Show. Now it's time to take a few callers."

Gail slapped the table hard enough to make Jimmy jump. "Bring 'em on, Jimbo. I'm feeling confrontational today."

Twelve and a half hours into their honeymoon, Riley decided they should have something to eat. She called for pizza while Gillian took a quick shower. They both reeked of sweat, but neither seemed to mind the smell too much. Riley was sitting on the floor with her back against the bed, her legs stretched out in front of her. From her position, she could see into the bathroom where Gillian was standing under the spray.

"Sorry about your shoulder."

"What?"

"I said I was sorry about your shoulder."

"Don't be. Hurt so good."

Riley smiled. She was about to suggest helping Gillian with her hard-to-reach places when the doorbell rang. "Ah, pizza..." She got up and made sure she was sufficiently covered. She had just thrown on a button-down dress shirt and a pair of boxers, not willing to delay further games with Gillian just to avoid traumatizing the pizza boy.

She took her wallet off the counter and opened the door, surprised to see Priest waiting with their order.

"Did you take a second job and not tell me?"

Priest handed the pizza over. "I was waiting downstairs when I saw the delivery man. I knew it was for you and I assumed if you were eating it would be all right to... disturb you briefly."

"Did you pay for it? How much do I owe you?"

"I don't mind. I consider it a fee for intruding. I have to tell you something, but you have to promise you won't fly off the handle. And you have to swear you won't leave this apartment until tomorrow."

Riley leaned against the door. "Oh, boy. You better tell me."

Priest took a folded newspaper from her back pocket and held it out. "I will stop you physically if I have to. This is Gillian's day, and yours, and you deserve it. I just thought you should know what was going on as soon as possible."

"Riley?"

"Be right back." Riley stepped into the hall and closed the door behind her. She was reading Gail Finney's article. "What is this?"

"A transcript of her radio show from this afternoon. Watered down, of course, without the cursing."

"Gillian Hunt... *corrupt* medical examiner's office...? This is all bullshit."

Priest nodded. "I know. The good news is that she actually touched a nerve this time. The State Board of Health issued a statement saying that Gillian's department has received no substantiated complaints and that Gail's statements are entirely without merit. Gail's own bosses asked for verification of the content, and she refused to hand it over."

"She attacked *Gillian*."

"Right. But you cannot~"

Riley handed the paper back to Priest. "Go home."

"What are you going to do?"

Riley ran her fingers through her hair. "I don't know. I think maybe we'll try a few toys that we haven't used very much. Variety and all that. We still have about seven hours left in our honeymoon, and I'll be damned if I'll waste one more minute on Gail Fucking Finney. Screw 'er. I won't let her ruin this day."

Priest was smiling. "Being married has changed you, Riley Parra."

"Yeah. I'm a real pushover now. You want a slice of pizza?"

"No. Like you said, seven hours... you'll need your energy."

Riley smiled. "Night, Priest."

"Goodnight, Riley."

Riley went back into the apartment and picked up the pizza as she closed the door. She crossed through the living room and into the bedroom where Gillian was lying on the bed, wrapped up in blankets that hinted at her nudity but didn't reveal anything. Riley, who had spent the better half of the last day exploring every inch of that body, found herself desperate to see more. "Hey."

"What took you so long? I got lonely."

"I was trying to figure out a way to make eating pizza erotic."

Gillian sat up and the blanket fell to expose one breast. "What did you come up with?"

Riley tossed the box onto the foot of the bed as she climbed on top of Gillian. "Leave it until morning and eat it cold."

Gillian laughed as she wrestled with Riley, wrapping the blanket around them both. Riley settled on top of Gillian, feeling her body through the thin layer of clothes she was wearing. Gillian was still wet from the shower and her skin was supple and smooth to the touch. Riley bowed her head to kiss the curve of Gillian's breast before pressing her forehead to her cleavage. Gillian put her legs around Riley, cupped the back of her head, and stroked her hair as Riley began to kiss her chest.

"Stay with me."

Gillian chuckled. "That's kind of what that whole deal this morning at City Hall was about. But here's a promise. I'll stay as long as you do. And in that case I'll only leave to hunt you down."

"You'd do that?"

"It's right there in my name, baby. Gillian Hunt... hunter"

Riley moved up Gillian's body and kissed her. "I thought it would feel different. Making love to you now that we're married."

"It doesn't?"

"No. Maybe I've been married to you a lot longer than I thought."

Gillian smiled. "Could be." She took Gillian's hand and kissed the fingers. "Want to eat some pizza?"

"We do need to build up our energy."

Riley kissed Gillian's shoulders and gestured at the blanket entangling them. "See you back here in about fifteen minutes?"

"It's a date."

"We need... mm. We need to sleep." Gillian glanced at the clock. They had three hours before they had to report to work. She brushed Riley's hair away from her face and ran her thumb over Riley's bottom lip. "One of us has to be the realist in the relationship."

"I guess. But just because you're sleeping doesn't mean I'll be able to keep my hands off you."

Gillian pressed her lips together, deep in thought. She slid across Riley's body to her nightstand and pulled open the drawer. While she searched, Riley kissed her shoulder and back. Finally, Gillian found what she was after and twisted to hold up the handcuffs.

"Will I have to resort to desperate measures?"

Riley grinned.

Priest looked up from her desk when Riley finally arrived in the bullpen. She smiled and made a show of looking at her watch. "I thought maybe we shouldn't expect you in today."

"It's only noon." She pulled her chair out and sat down, now wishing she had taken Gillian's advice and gotten more sleep. Still, when faced with a pair of handcuffs and a beautiful naked woman... "Is Briggs pissed?"

"She said it was extenuating circumstances. It's fine. Do you want a report about the... Gail Finney situation?"

Riley groaned. "That depends. *Do* I?"

"Oh, I think you'll want to hear this." Priest tossed the newspaper to Riley's desk. "All the complaints got to the radio station's boss. Gail's foul language on the air, combined with her baseless accusations led to the Board of Health and the O.M.E. to call for her immediate termination. The station has suspended her without pay pending a review of the situation."

"What about the paper?"

"That's the morning edition you're holding. I'll let you read it yourself."

Riley unfolded the paper and looked at the space usually occupied by Gail's column. "'Until the unpleasantness has been resolved, Ms. Finney's column will no longer appear...' Wow."

Priest raised an eyebrow. "If you'd gone out looking for revenge last night, the headline would be much different. Police detective assaults reporter. She would be a hero to her followers. Now, it looks like her fans are turning on her."

"I didn't register for it, but I'd call that a damn good wedding present. How did you and Maureen get on yesterday?"

"Just fine. It's clear to see how she and Gillian became friends. They are extremely similar." She tapped her pen on the edge of the desk. "Could we maybe speak about something private soon?"

"Sure. What's up?"

Briggs came out of her office before Priest could respond. "Happy wedding, Riley."

"Thanks, boss."

"You sure you don't want to take an extra day or two off?"

Riley smiled. "I think it would do more harm than good. We

needed to come up for air."

"Are you and Priest up for a case?"

"Hit us."

Briggs held up the file she had brought out. "A landlord found a renter dead in his apartment when he went to collect the rent. Look it over, see if there's any evidence of foul play. Could just be a routine overdose."

"You're going easy on me."

"I could hand it off to Booker."

Riley took the file. "I'm not above being coddled. Let's go, Priest." She waited until they were at the stairs before she spoke again. "So what did you want to talk about?"

"The night before last, when we were at Bethel Luz... Sariel came in and saved us. She healed your wounds and then took me away."

"Yeah. What happened there?"

Priest cleared her throat. "We became intimate."

Riley stopped walking, forcing Priest to stop as well. "That means something different to you guys, right? You, uh, worshipped together or something?"

"We made love."

"Two angels. Wow." She started walking again. "That must have been something."

Priest blushed. "I'm unsure what it means."

"What about Kenzie and Chelsea?"

"I spoke to them about it. They understand. I was never a part of their commitment; it was always them and me. Now if this... situation persists, I will simply become a part of a couple."

"You and Sariel, moving into a little starter apartment, picking out curtains and china?" They reached the lobby. There weren't a lot of people milling around, so Riley noticed the civilian in a hoodie stepping away from the desk sergeant's station. "It could happen. She's a little young for you, though."

"We're approximately the same~"

Priest stopped herself mid-sentence and suddenly grabbed the collar of Riley's shirt. She shoved, and Riley tripped over her own feet on the way to the ground. Before she could even formulate a protest, gunfire filled the lobby. It sounded like a cannon firing as the retort echoed off the walls and tile. Priest stepped between Riley and the shooter, and the bullets exited her body in a spray of red blood. Priest went down to one knee, and Riley saw the shooter's face.

Gail Finney.

Ken Booker had just entered the building when the gunfire started. He drew his weapon and dropped into a firing stance. "Freeze! Right now, drop the weapon!" He was standing between Gail and the exit, so she aimed her gun at him as she ran.

"Booker, get out of here!" Riley shouted. She was on her knees, gun drawn, but she wouldn't risk shooting with so many innocent people in the way.

Gail and Booker fired at the same time. His bullet grazed Gail's arm, but she got luckier with her shot. Ken twisted at the waist and dropped to the ground with a flower of blood blooming on his chest.

Riley grabbed Priest and put a hand to the sticky blood on her blouse. "Cait..."

"I'm faking." Priest spoke through clenched teeth, her face pale. Riley lifted her hand to reveal that the wound under the torn cloth of her blouse was already beginning to knit. Priest jerked her head toward the door. "Get her."

Riley got to her feet. The uniformed officers who had been in the lobby were tending to Booker. As she passed him, she saw that his eyes were open, but the sheer amount of blood on his shirt didn't make her hopeful. He locked eyes with her and nodded, once. Riley didn't understand what he was trying to convey, but she returned the nod and mouthed that she was sorry before she ran out into the sunshine.

A crowd of people were frozen at the bottom of the stone steps, obviously still reacting to the sound of gunshots. Riley motioned them toward the door. "Get inside right now. Go, now!" She reached the sidewalk and saw the hoodie just a few dozen yards ahead. She broke into a sprint, the adrenaline making her forget the fact she'd been up most of the night exhausting herself, arms pumping as she thought of Priest and Booker lying bloody in the lobby of the police station.

Gail went around a corner and Riley put on an extra burst of speed to lessen how long Gail was out of her sight. She reached the corner and slammed hard into what felt like a solid brick wall. She went down hard, flat on her back for the second time in five minutes, and Gail dropped onto her. She straddled Riley's neck and pressed the barrel of her gun to Riley's forehead. The weapon was still hot from shooting in the station.

"Partners should have been off limits. Remember that when your put your new bride in the ground." She looked up and saw policemen in uniform running toward her. She raised the gun and fired indiscriminately, forcing them to take cover. She stood up and swung her foot to the side, kicking Riley in the temple. Her vision blanked, and her head filled with ringing from the impact of Gail's hard sole against the shell of her ear.

When she recovered enough to sit up and look around, Gail was gone. The street was a madhouse, and she realized that her weapon was missing.

"Great. Really great first day back."

The officers who saw blood when Priest was shot were assured they were suffering from a form of mass hysteria. Obviously she had to have been wearing a bulletproof vest in order avoid injury. She had changed clothes simply because she didn't want to walk around wearing a shirt with holes in it. Ken Booker hadn't been so lucky. One of the uniformed officers had arrived seconds after the shooting, but even their best efforts hadn't been enough. He died before an ambulance could arrive.

Gillian examined Riley and gave her a clean bill of health. Briggs agreed to hold the briefing in the morgue so they wouldn't be overheard by other officers. Riley was sitting on an exam table with Gillian by her side, Priest and Sariel standing silently to one side while Briggs held court in the middle of the group.

Booker's body had been covered with a sheet and placed in one of the drawers so he would be out of sight, but everyone's eyes continuously drifted over to the closed door. Riley tried to condense the information she had into an easily-digestible format

"Gail is my counterpart for my bad guys. I have Priest watching my back, and she had a demon named Gremory. A couple of nights ago, Priest and I got into a little skirmish with Gremory and Gail. Things got pretty heated and it had gotten to the point where we were basically toast. I could barely move and Priest was... basically she was already dead."

Gillian turned and walked away, keeping her back to the room as Riley spoke. Riley watched her and regretted keeping this part of the story from her.

"Sariel," Riley gestured to her, "came in to save the day. She healed me and Priest, and she... basically she destroyed Gremory. Gail was torn up pretty bad. That led to the article, which led to her getting fired, which I guess led to..." She gestured toward the drawer holding Booker's body. "I attempted to pursue, but she kicked me in the head and the rest..."

Briggs looked at the angels. "Patrol cars are searching for her. What about you two? Can't you fly around and find her?"

Priest shook her head. "No, for the same reason the demons can't just scan the city and pinpoint Riley's location. Gail is protected from us the same way. If she wasn't, she would never have gotten so close this morning."

Sariel cleared her throat. "We can't track her directly, but there's a chance we could find a trail. If she's leaving a wake of destruction, we could possibly track that and find her."

"Good. Thank you... uh, Ms. Sariel. The officers said that Gail spoke to you, Detective." Briggs faced her again. "What did she say?"

Riley looked at Gillian and couldn't bring herself to voice the threat. "Nothing. Just nonsense about how I was going to pay."

"I've got a firestorm on my hands here. The press is howling. For once, though, I think they're on our side. A disgraced journalist opening fire on a room full of cops is kind of hard to spin, even for them." She ran a hand down her face and sighed, her gaze drifting back to where Booker was laid to rest. "I always thought she was just a goddamn nuisance. Find her, Riley."

"Will do, boss."

Briggs left to do the official press conference. Priest and Sariel moved closer, and Gillian returned to Riley's side. She took Riley's hand and squeezed hard. Riley used her free hand to cover their joined fingers, rubbing Gillian's knuckles with her thumb. "So what now? What happens when one champion goes gunning for the other?"

"Bad things." Sariel looked furious and confused, pained and pissed. "It would be like the leaders of warring countries leaving their offices to duke it out on a street. The fighting is usually left to the various armies."

"So we're just figureheads?"

"No. That was a poor analogy." Sariel rubbed her temple and Riley realized that she was flustered. She wasn't thinking straight because of what had happened to Priest. "Perhaps generals. You're the generals of the battle."

"All right. Priest, last year you mentioned that this has happened before, and it's always connected with something huge.

World Wars, pandemics, that sort of thing."

"Right. But those were extended conflicts between two champions. The fighting would start in No Man's Land and the surrounding environs, but it would quickly spread to encompass the state, the country... But if we end this expediently, we could be able to avoid worldwide consequences."

"Then let's end this expediently. I can go after her directly now, right? She threw down the gauntlet and I'm just picking it up."

Gillian's voice was soft. "You could just leave it where it is."

Riley leaned again her and looked at Priest for an answer.

Priest nodded. "Yes."

"And what happens? I mean, if one of us wins, the city would be down to one champion. What happens then?"

"The side that wins would assume victory for the current war."

Riley blinked. "So the war could have ended if Gail shot me?"

"For the rest of her lifetime, yes. The demons would have free rein of the city until she passed away. In that time they would gain such a stronghold that the angels would have little chance of pushing it back once hostilities were resumed with new champions."

"But if Gail dies~"

"Riley." Gillian squeezed her hand.

Riley squeezed back. "I don't have much of a choice here, Jill. She's going to keep coming after us. If I can bring her in safely, then I will. I don't think she's going to come easily. If I have to..."

Gillian put her head down on Riley's shoulder. She looked at Priest. "If Gail dies..."

"Marchosias will have to lay down arms. The demons would stop fighting and the angels would have dominance. We could push back No Man's Land for good."

"Just that easy?" Riley asked.

Priest looked evasive. "No. But those are the broad strokes."

She kissed Gillian's forehead. *Partners should have been off limits. Remember that when your put your new bride in the ground.* "Then we'll do what we have to do. Gail's gone off the deep end. We need to stop her before anyone else gets caught in the crossfire."

Sariel left, but Riley told Priest to give her a few minutes with Gillian. Gillian sighed and shook her head, and Riley kissed her hair.

"I'm sorry, Riley. I'm acting stupid. We're the same couple we were last week. Just because we went to City Hall yesterday... I mean, it's like we paid a parking ticket. It shouldn't change who we are."

"But it did. It is different now. I'd be hurt if you weren't concerned for me."

Gillian sat up. "I can't ask you to not to anything stupid. That's just part of the Riley Parra I fell in love with."

"Thanks."

Gillian smiled. "But I'm going to worry. And I'm going to complain. And if I can, I'm going to ignore whenever you guys are planning something reckless. But the Riley I fell in love with also wouldn't kill a woman in cold blood."

"Cold blood? She killed Booker. If Zerachiel hadn't come back, then she would have killed Priest, too." The thought was almost as unbearable as imagining Gillian getting hurt. "I want to bring Gail to justice but she might not give me that option."

"Then promise me something."

"Anything."

Gillian took a deep breath and let it out slowly. "Kill her first. Don't let her get the drop on you just because you're worried about how I'll react. Whatever decision you make, I'll know it's the right one."

"I'm yours now. I'm not about to let Gail Finney destroy your property."

"And maybe if that happens, you and I can have a real marriage. No wars, no angels and demons, none of this nonsense. We'll head out to the suburbs and get a nice house with a white picket fence."

"I'd love that, Jill."

Gillian smiled and kissed Riley. "Thanks for humoring me. Now go on... find her and make her pay."

"Yes, ma'am."

She slid off the table, leaving Gillian to the unpleasant task of Kenneth Booker's autopsy.

The newspaper and radio station both issued statements before the noon hour. Gail Finney's employment at both was effectively terminated following the "tragic events." Her coworkers at the station were dissecting the situation and trying to figure out what had happened to cause Gail to go so completely off the deep end.

Riley led Priest to the car and waited until they were safely on the road before she asked her question. "What Sariel did... destroying Gremory that way. That's not unusual, right? It's happened before."

Priest kept her eyes on the road through the windshield. "It's basically the same thing I did with the Duchess."

"Basically, but not exactly."

"Sariel acted out of an emotional charge. Destroying a demon like that takes an immense amount of power. She shouldn't have been able to do it, plus heal you, me and Gail. Fortunately she had spent several days inside of a church so she was like a super-charged battery."

Riley nodded out of politeness. "That's not what I'm asking, Cait. I know you and Sariel and Gremory are soldiers in a larger army. Sariel basically assassinated a pretty high-ranking officer in Hell's army. Are they going to just let that drop?"

"Probably not."

"She always struck me as by the book. Don't get me wrong, I'm grateful. We both probably would have died in those tunnels if she hadn't stepped in. I just can't understand why she would do something so drastic."

"Because she's in love with me."

Riley had to force herself to keep her eyes on the road.

"She was willing to risk the consequences in order to keep me alive. I'm not sure how I feel about that."

"It's how I feel about Gillian. I'd break rules to protect her. Hell, I'd do a lot of things to save her." She looked at Priest. "Do you love Sariel?"

"I don't know if I'm in love with her, or if I'm just... lusting for her physical form. I'm not sure I know her well enough to say that I'm absolutely in love with her."

"Don't underestimate lust. It gets you over that first hurdle. Getting to know someone can wait a little while." They stopped at a red light. "What's the plan to find Gail?"

"I have one. But I don't think you're going to like it very much."

"One of those plans, huh? Can't wait to hear it."

"You're right. I hate this plan."

Riley was standing on the rocks of the waterfront, just high enough that the tide wouldn't wash over her feet. Her hands were in her pockets against the chilly breeze coming off the water as she turned and scanned the road. Priest was closer to the road, scanning for signs of their enemy.

"I thought you meant I'd hate it because it was dangerous~"

"It is dangerous."

"~but this is literally standing still. Gail Finney is out there somewhere, and she has a cop's blood on her hands."

Priest turned to look at her. "The waterfront is neutral ground. If she'll meet us here, she won't be able to inflict harm on you. Maybe we can talk some sense into her."

"How long are we supposed to wait?"

"Without Gremory to guide her, Gail won't have a way to find us through her ordinary channels. It may be a while. You'll just have to be patient."

Riley started up the shoreline. "You know me way too well to think I'll just stand here and wait. If she can't find us, then we'll have to find her."

"She'll be planning for that. If we engage her on a field of her choosing~"

"I know all about home field advantage, Cait. But we're not going to get anywhere by standing in our separate corners daring the other person to make their move first."

Priest followed Riley to the car. "She's irrational and angry. She wants you to pay for what happened to her partner."

"Yeah, well..." Riley's voice trailed off. "My partner."

"What?"

Riley pulled out her cell phone and dialed the station. "Yeah, this is Detective Riley Parra. I'm at the waterfront. I need you to look up the nearest plant shops, seed shops, gardening supply stores, anything like that."

Priest shook her head. "Gardening?"

"Flax seed. Gail told me she was going after my partner. I just assumed Gillian was the only target she had because she mentioned 'my new bride.'"

"You think she's set up a trap for me and..."

"Call Sariel."

"I'm trying." Priest looked down the street and closed her eyes. "Damn it, come on."

Riley got into the car and Priest followed. She folded her hands in her lap and closed her eyes, lowering her chin to her chest. "Please, Sariel... please..."

"Yeah, I'm still here," Riley said into the phone. "Polk Street... yeah. Can you text me the entire list? Good." She flipped the phone closed and pulled away from the curb.

"She's not answering, Riley. I'm sorry."

Riley didn't say anything. She didn't want to make Priest feel worse about her plan, didn't want to point out how much time they had lost just standing around. She could only hope they were in time to save Sariel from paying the price for killing Gremory. Instead, she handed her phone to Priest when it announced a new text had arrived.

"Start calling these places. See if any of them sold a lot of flax recently."

Priest took the phone and used the text to dial the numbers on her own cell phone. She had just started talking when Riley's phone rang.

She took it back and only glanced at the screen before answering. "Yeah, boss."

Briggs sounded ready to explode. "Turn on your radio. Finney's station. Now."

"Shit." Riley turned on the radio and scanned until she found the right frequency. Gail Finney's voice came through her speakers, and Riley fought the instinct to turn the radio off.

"~insanity. I wanted to tell my side of the story. There are things people don't know, okay? Things I can't go into. I wasn't trying to kill that cop today. I was trying to kill Riley ... Parra." The pause indicated an expletive had been censored, which meant the rant was either taped or on a delay. "This is all going to end when Riley is dead. Riley comes to me and faces up to what she did, and I'll turn myself in for the other shooting. Riley, if you're listening to this, you can end it all right now by coming to meet me."

Briggs spoke through the phone Riley had forgotten by her ear. "She's given the address several times. She wants you to meet her at the Cleveland Street el station." Riley cursed quietly; it was the only station in town that was completely enclosed so it couldn't be seen from the street. "We have officers surrounding it, but someone claims they saw a hostage. They're not going to make a move until you get there."

"Thanks, boss. I'm on my way now." She had to pull a U-turn in the middle of the street, prompting a symphony of car horns blaring at her in protest.

"She has Sariel."

"Don't worry, Cait. We'll get her back."

Priest nodded, but she didn't seem convinced.

Cleveland Street wasn't far, and traffic was blocked well in advance of the seized station. Riley and Priest showed their badges and were waved through by the officer who was directing traffic. As they approached, Riley eyed the stop from a tactical viewpoint. It was accessed by stairs, like every other el station, but the tracks passed through a small building designed to look like a covered bridge trestle. It had been the first in a projected series of quaint additions to the city's elevated train system in the eighties. Only one was constructed before the project ran out of money.

Riley parked and leaned back in an attempt to look through the windows. One of the officers on duty shook his head. "It's no good, Detective. They all have shutters. Supposed to be there for, what do you call it, uh, athletics."

"Aesthetics," Riley muttered.

"Yeah, them. But she got 'em closed. We sent someone up to take her out, but she opened fire on 'im. He only got a quick look, but it was enough to see that she had a hostage with her."

Priest said, "A pretty woman, brown hair?"

"Yeah, sounds right."

Riley opened her trunk and took out her vest. Priest took hers out as well. "Have you stopped the trains?"

"First thing we did. We got 'em backed up a few miles back. If this isn't done by rush hour, we're going to have a lot of pissed off people to deal with."

"I'd rather have that than let a cop killer slip away." She secured her vest and then spotted a SWAT team member a few yards away. She whistled for him to come over. "Can I get a couple of helmets?"

"Helmets?"

Riley nodded at the station. "We're going to be coming up from floor-level. I don't want her to shoot us in the head."

The SWAT member came back with two helmets. Riley took one and handed the other to Priest. "Anything else?" the man said. "We have a couple of stun grenades if you want to just take her out."

"We'll keep that option in mind. We want to make sure the hostage is safe above all else." She knew Sariel wouldn't be affected by the stun grenades, but she didn't have a clue what kind of trap Gail had set up. She didn't want to make any drastic decisions before they knew exactly what they were dealing with. She secured her helmet and headed for the stairs. She stopped at the bottom and leaned forward, looking up into the darkness above.

"Gail Finney! This is Riley Parra. Is the hostage safe?"

There was a long enough moment of silence that Riley thought she wasn't going to get an answer. Finally, Gail chose to respond. "Come up!"

"I'm not going to do that until you assure me you're unarmed."

"Come up now or I'll kill your little angel."

Riley debated her options and started reluctantly up the stairs. "I'm coming up. I am armed. Don't make me use it, Gail. Understood?" No answer. Riley looked back and saw Priest was following her. She wished they weren't surrounded; it would be a lot easier to let Priest spread her wings and come into the station over the tracks. She crouched when she reached the station's entrance. A railing stood on three sides of the access hatch and Riley made sure Gail wasn't in sight before she took another step.

Gail was standing in the corner of the station, well away from the shuttered windows. Sariel was flat on her back in the middle of the waiting area. She was surrounded by a smoldering ring of flax seed. She was pale, her lips parted to allow her rapid, shallow breaths. Riley kept her gun on Gail's center mass as she moved up the remaining steps and reached the flat platform. The peaked roof overhead and the shuttered windows filtered the day's sunshine down into a dreary gloom.

"Hi, Gail. Nice of you to turn yourself in."

Gail laughed. "I want you to watch your little friend here pay for what she did."

"We were all in pretty bad shape. She didn't have to heal you, you know. She could have left you like that."

"I wish she had. Don't come any closer. Stay over there. By the tracks."

Riley did as Gail expected. "The trains have been stopped. You're not going to escape. So just let Sariel go."

Gail pushed away from the wall. She took a gun from her belt, but left it hanging by her side. "I'll make you a deal, Riley. If your other angel sacrifices herself, I'll let this one go."

"What?"

"I've decided to call it seracide. The act of seraphim ending its existence. I want Caitlin Priest, Zerachiel, to end herself. That's the price of my surrender."

Priest's voice was quiet. "You'll let them both go?"

"Cait, shut up."

Gail laughed. "I guess I was negotiating with the wrong person.

That's the deal. Your life for hers."

"I'm willing, Riley."

Riley moved between Priest and Gail. "I'm not. We aren't trading lives here, Gail. You're cornered. This isn't a negotiation. It's surrender. Put your weapon down and place your hands on your head."

Gail looked down at Sariel. "Do you even understand what she did to me? Or does it not matter, because Alyssa was a demon? My entire life I waited for someone who understood me and made me feel less alone. I loved Alyssa with all my heart."

"She was a succubus. She made you feel~"

"She didn't do that with me. She couldn't. I needed to decide to be their champion of my own free will."

Riley glanced over her shoulder and Priest confirmed the information with a nod.

"Not all of us associate with the side of the angels. Alyssa was intrigued by the idea of someone loving her of their own free will. We were made for each other. I'll never find another partner who understands me the way she did. So I want you to know that pain. Both of you. Zerachiel already died once, so it's time for her to finally pass on for good."

"I'll do it, Riley."

"The hell you will. Priest, Sariel and I are all walking out of this station in one piece. Your life is the only one that's debatable."

Gail looked down at Sariel. "It comes down to this, huh?" She smiled and looked at Priest. "Did she tell you what happens at the end of all this? If you win?"

Riley shrugged. "Yeah. If I win, the angels take over."

"I meant what happens to you. What happens to the champion in a war that's no longer being fought?" Her smile widened. "She didn't, did she? Well, I suppose it's for the best. All's hell that ends hell." She swung up her gun and fired, hitting Riley in the vest. Riley returned fire but Gail was already on the run. Instead of making a break for the stairs, she moved to the left and went out onto the tracks.

"Stop!" Riley pursued her, leaving the station.

Gail only ran about thirty yards beyond the station's entrance before she turned around. The wind caught her hair and clothes, and Riley heard a commotion on the street below.

"I never knew how easy it could be to end a war."

"Gail, don't... don't!"

Gail took two steps to her right, spread her arms to either side, and tilted. Gravity did the rest. Riley lunged toward her as Gail's feet left the track and she tumbled into empty air. The people gathering on the outside of the barriers screamed, and Riley heard a member of the SWAT team barking orders as Gail fell. Riley heard Priest approaching from behind her, the sound of running steps vibrating through the tracks.

She expected the moment to drag on as if in slow motion, but it was over in a flash. One moment Gail was falling and, the next, she hit the top of a police car. Her arms were spread out, her hands overhanging the roof on either side with the fingers curled.

Riley couldn't look away. "Cait..."

"Sariel is safe." Priest's voice was quiet, respectful. "Riley... you've won."

"Good for me." Riley finally tore her gaze away from the horror below them and looked at Priest. She was holding up a barely-conscious Sariel. "Come on. We're going to have to give a lot of statements for this one."

Gail was miraculously still alive after her fall, so the commander in charge of the scene called an ambulance instead of the ME. Riley and Priest gave their statements, and then gave them again when Briggs showed up on the scene. Internal affairs showed up as a precaution, but several camera phones had captured the entire exchange and revealed that Gail made the plunge of her own free will with Riley standing at least ten feet away from her. Riley explained that Sariel was Priest's new girlfriend, Sara Elmore. The EMTs insisted on checking her out, but Riley and Priest both assured them she was fine. Since her color had returned and she didn't have any physical injuries, they decided to drop the issue.

The press was clamoring for an interview with Riley, but Briggs successfully held them off. Riley and Priest helped get Sariel to the car, laying her in the backseat and making sure she was comfortable.

"Do you know where the closest church is?"

"St. Benedict."

"Okay, we'll drop her–" Riley was suddenly hit by a surge of pain, clutching her shoulder as she dropped to one knee. Priest came around the car, seemingly unconcerned as she helped Riley back to her feet. She leaned against the car and put a hand on her forehead. "What the hell was that?"

"A shooting pain? Did it originate from your tattoo?"

Riley looked at her. "How'd you know that?"

Briggs jogged over to where they were. "Riley, Priest. We just got word. Gail Finney just died on the way to the hospital."

Priest looked at Riley. "That's what you felt. You've won."

Briggs raised her eyebrows. "So that's it? It's over?"

Sariel shook her head. "Not exactly."

"You'll fill me in later, I assume." Briggs didn't look happy about being left out of the loop.

Riley said, "As soon as I know what the hell is going on, I'll tell you."

"Okay." She held out her hand. "Whatever happens, you're the last one standing, I guess. Congratulations."

Riley shook her hand. Briggs went back to where the reporters had converged while Riley and Priest got into the car.

"We'll drop Sariel off at St. Benedict and then we have to make another stop."

Riley pulled away from the curb. "Gail was telling the truth, wasn't she? There's something you haven't told me about this whole business."

Priest nodded.

"Did you lie to me?"

Sariel answered. "No, she didn't. She merely left out a piece of information for your peace of mind."

Riley sighed. "Do I have time to call Gillian before we make our other stop?"

"Yes. Of course."

Gillian was starting her report on Ken Booker's autopsy when her cell phone rang. She smiled at the display, took off her gloves, and closed her eyes when she saw the name on the display. Her eyes were wet with tears when she opened the phone. "Hello, wife."

"Hello, wife. It's over."

Gillian's smile wavered and she leaned against the table. "What?"

"Gail committed suicide. She died on the way to the hospital. I'm the last woman standing."

Gillian covered her mouth with her hand, eyes closed. Tears rolled down her cheeks. "Are you okay?"

"Yeah. Priest says we have to do something else before I come back, though. I don't know how long it will take. I just wanted to let you know I love you."

"Oh, Riley. I love you, too. Good job, baby."

"I don't think it's over yet. Not quite. I'll let you know what's going on as soon as I know. I don't think Priest has been entirely truthful."

Gillian scoffed. "There's a shocker."

"Do me a favor. The EMTs are taking Gail to the hospital for her autopsy. They said they would let you do it if you requested it, but... I don't want you to. She said she was going to take out my partner. Somehow I don't feel safe even though she's dead. Who knows what deals she made before she jumped."

Gillian trembled at the thought of another body in her morgue coming to life. "Hey, I'm always willing to turn down work."

Riley laughed. "I love you, wife."

"I love you, too, wife. I'll make dinner for the conquering heroine."

"Thank you, baby. Priest is getting impatient, so I should~"

"Yeah. See you tonight."

Riley said, "Yeah. Bye, baby."

"Goodbye, sweetheart."

They left Sariel at St. Benedict's in time for the evening service. Riley made her call from the narthex and then led Priest back out to the car. Priest directed her without telling her where they were going, but Riley started to get a bad feeling as they entered No Man's Land. She parked in front of a very familiar building, the entrance still under construction after she'd driven a car through it almost two years earlier. The entire block felt bad and made her want to call for backup. "Marchosias?"

"The end of the war has to be made official. If Gail had emerged victorious, this meeting would have been between her and Michael."

"Well, let's get this over with. The less time spent in No Man's Land, the better."

They got out of the car. "The demons won't be here. Marchosias would have sent them away. We're coming here in neutrality, like negotiating a treaty. But I can't advise you once we're inside. You should know that before we go in."

Riley nodded and let Priest lead the way inside. Memories of her first visit to the building flooded back to her.

The atmosphere of the building seemed heavier than outside. Her head felt wrapped in cotton, her vision swimming slightly as she climbed the stairs. At the first landing, she turned to the right and began checking the rooms. Every room was an apartment, fully-furnished, but none of the doors were closed. It was as if the residents had just packed up and left. Trash and dirty dishes lined every horizontal surface, and trash cans overflowed onto the floor.

"Are you okay?"

"This is the place where I got hurt so badly I went to Gillian. So it has a happy ending. I'm fine."

Priest nodded and scanned the lobby. "Marchosias!"

"No need to shout, angel." The demon had appeared on the second floor landing. He wore a dark suit, his blonde hair smoothed back. He smiled as he started down the stairs. "Well done, Detective Parra. I knew you had it in you. Gail Finney and Gremory have both been defeated while you and Caitlin Priest, against *all* odds, are standing here. You both died last year, and now here you stand. I suppose it goes to show that you can never underestimate the underdog."

"Save it, Marky. I have a dinner date."

He put his hands into his pockets when he reached the lobby. "Right. Far be it for me to keep you from your second night of wedded bliss. How is Gillian, by the way? Does she know you have me, and the demons who nearly slaughtered you here, to thank for your relationship?"

Priest's voice was firm. "Get on with it, Marchosias."

He waved her off and focused on Riley. "The time has come to make a decision. End the war for the remainder of your lifetime and let the angels have dominance... or allow me to choose a new champion for evil and continue hostilities. The choice is entirely up to you."

"And the catch?"

Marchosias laughed and stepped forward. "The catch." He took a piece of string from his pocket and licked the pad of the thumb on his other hand to coil the string. "What is the worst thing I could do? The worst possible scenario you could conceive. What do you suppose that would be?"

Riley had her arm flung across her face, her feet flat so that her knees were bent. She was comfortable, lying in a spot of sun, and she was loath to move. But she knew she had to, so she sat up and stretched her back. Caitlin Priest was sitting at the nearest desk, turned around in her chair to face the bench where Riley had been laying. "God, don't watch me sleep. It's creepy."

"Sorry. I was debating whether I should wake you."

Riley yawned. "What time is it?"

"Almost four."

Riley was wearing her uniform, the badge on her chest still feeling odd. She wanted it on her hip, wanted to wear street clothes, but certain requirements came with being sheriff. Priest seemed to enjoy her uniform as deputy, but the entire thing made her feel like the lead in an all-woman Andy Griffith stage show.

"Any calls?"

"None. I would have woken you."

"I know." Something was gnawing at her. Something was amiss. She walked to the front door of their small office and opened it to look outside. No cars, a few pedestrians. There were three bicycles chained in front of the diner across the street, and Riley had a sudden urge for one of Mae's delicious burgers. She rubbed her stomach. "Did I have lunch?"

"You don't remember?"

"I just woke up. Humor me."

"You had a yogurt and said you were trying to eat light."

Riley grunted. She could have a burger and call it an early dinner. Maybe she would skip the fries. Over the buildings of Main Street, she could see the skyline of the city in the distance. It looked fake, sheathed with clouds and immaterial. It was hard to believe that she had been a detective there so recently, that she had ended the war between demons and angels. The city was at peace.

She wondered if Gillian would let her have the burger for dinner. That thought stuck in her mind for some reason and she turned to Priest.

"Where's Gillian?"

Priest delayed answering for so long that Riley turned to make sure she'd heard the question. "Probably at work."

"Here?"

Priest looked up. "No. In the city. It's safe enough now that the war is over. And it's not like there's a big call for a medical examiner here in White Stream."

"Right." She looked outside again. "Who knew that peace would be so boring?"

"Do you want to walk down to the high school and see if any of the kids are smoking marijuana?"

The thought depressed Riley more than doing nothing. "Nah,

let them get high." She looked up and down the street and stepped back into the office. She couldn't help but think she was forgetting something important.

As she walked back to her desk, her thumb toyed with the naked skin at the base of the third finger on her left hand. She didn't notice it, unconsciously folding her fingers into a fist as she sat down. "I think I'll have a burger in about half an hour. Call it an early dinner."

"Sounds good."

Riley nodded and tried to think of what was bothering her. But try as she might, she couldn't think of anything that was wrong.

She cupped her left fist with her right hand and idly stroked the naked third finger. If she had forgotten it, it must not have been all that important.

FALSE IDYLL

Must I thus leave thee, Paradise?—thus leave
Thee, native soil, these happy walks and shades?
~ Paradise Lost

The afternoon dragged on. Riley stared blankly at the far wall of the office with one foot up on her desk, occasionally looking at either the phone or the front door. Priest seemed happy enough at her desk, jabbing at the keys of an antique typewriter that filled the office with clacking noises. At one point Priest got up for a cup of coffee, offering the pot to Riley. She took a cup mainly out of fear she would fall dead asleep without the caffeine. "So this is our life now, after the end of the war?"

"You said you wanted peace and quiet. The people of this town required a sheriff."

Riley stood up, carrying her cup to the window. The city was still there, wrapped in a mist of haze. "Where is Sariel?"

"Still in the city keeping an eye on things. It's much calmer since you ended the war."

Riley nodded. "And where's Gillian?"

There seemed to be a long pause before Priest's answer. "She's at work, Riley. I told you that already."

"Right. Sorry." She turned her back to the window. "This isn't right."

Priest looked up from her typewriter. "What isn't right about it? You ended the war, Riley. Afterward you decided you deserved peace and quiet and we all agreed. Lieutenant Briggs accepted your resignation. You moved here to White Stream to fill their vacant sheriff's position. I came along to keep an eye on you just in case things weren't as quiet as you thought."

"And that was how long ago?"

"Five weeks, Riley."

That sounded right, but she couldn't make her head accept it. Riley held up her hand, looking at the palm. "The doll."

"What?"

"Marchosias gave me a doll." She closed her eyes and tried to remember. It had barely been a month; surely something as monumental as making a deal with a demon wouldn't fade from her memory that quickly. "He gave me a string doll."

Priest stood up. "No, he didn't."

Riley looked at Priest with suspicion. "Who are you?"

"I'm Caitlin Priest. I'm Zerachiel." She spoke slowly, as if this was something she'd gone through several times. "I know what you're thinking. The mara, and Gremory playing tricks with your mind. But this isn't a hallucination, Riley. It's not a fantasy concocted to make you give up. You won the war. You're the sheriff of White Stream~"

"Then why doesn't anything feel right? Tell me something only the real Caitlin Priest would know."

Priest sighed and rested her hands on the desk. "This is ridiculous, Riley."

Riley put down her coffee cup and went to the door. "Then I'll go into the city and get some answers there."

"Kenzie cries sometimes when she has an orgasm." Riley stopped with her hand on the door. "It embarrasses her, so she puts her arm over her face so her partner won't see. And please, Riley, don't say that's just something I could have pulled out of your subconscious. This is real. Think about it. Does this feel like a fantasy? Look at the little things."

Riley took a slow scan of the office. There were drops of coffee near the pot where Priest had spilled. She could hear the hum of the air conditioner. There were scuff marks on the tile floor, and cobwebs in the corners. She looked at the door jamb and saw the nails pounded into the surface of the wood surrounded by years of scuff marks. She shut the door and stepped into the room.

"What the hell is going on? Because it feels like I'm losing my mind."

Priest lowered her head. "I'm sorry, Riley. I thought it would last longer than this."

Riley felt something inside her head and she closed her eyes, picturing a wall beginning to crack. She had a memory, sudden and sharp, of Priest standing in front of her. They were in the sheriff's office, standing a few feet apart, and Riley was furious. No. She was shattered. Weeping.

"*Make me forget. Just wipe it out.*"

"*I... I can't do that, Riley. It wouldn't work.*"

Riley was sobbing in the darkness. "It would be better than it is now."

Riley opened her eyes and saw Priest standing in front of her. "What did you make me forget? Where's Gilli~"

Priest touched the side of Riley's head and she immediately lost consciousness.

Riley reached for the alarm when it went off, but her knuckles bounced off a solid wall. She woke up, stared at the unexpected wall, and rolled onto her back. The alarm clock was on a side table she had apparently forgotten about. She turned it off, threw back the blankets, and sat up with the blankets wrapped around herself.

Her cheek was wet, and she glanced down to confirm the pillow was as well. "Drooling. Very attractive, Riley. You'll definitely get a girl that way." She pushed her hair out of her face as she untangled from the blankets and walked to the bathroom. The bedroom was more familiar to her now that she was actually awake.

She started the shower and undressed. She reached for the third finger of her left hand, and then frowned at it. It was almost like she was trying to take off a wedding ring. What the hell had she been dreaming about?

She put the thought aside and showered quickly. She found her uniform and put it on, braiding her hair in front of the bathroom mirror. She glanced down at the supplies spread around the sink, the toothpaste and brush, the comb. Something was missing. She reached down and rearranged things, trying to find the empty spot. Had someone been in her house? She tried to remember if she'd had a one night stand since moving to White

Stream.

Absolutely not.

Riley was surprised by her mind's vehemence at the idea. Something was definitely wrong.

"Yeah," she said to her reflection. "You're losing your mind."

As she passed her bed, she looked at the pillow and realized that her chin had been dry. Only her cheeks had been wet. If she had been drooling... She brushed her cheek with the back of her hand, like wiping away a tear, but that was ridiculous.

Why would she have been crying in her sleep?

Outside, the day was overcast and chilly. The sun was trying valiantly to break through the clouds, but it only succeeded in making everything look gray. Riley locked the door behind her and went to the cruiser which, like the house, had been given to her by the city. It was beat up and needed a paint job, but it was hers. She liked the gold star on the driver's door. Priest was sitting on the trunk of the car. She smiled, but the expression seemed foreign on her face. "Good morning, Riley. Did you sleep well?"

"Yeah. How'd you get here?"

Priest pointed across the field that made up Riley's back yard. There was a small yellow house on the other side of a one-lane dirt road. "We're neighbors, remember?"

Riley smiled. In the city, a distance like that wouldn't even be on the same block. "Gotta love the suburbs." She hooked a thumb over her shoulder. "I'm just going to say goodbye to..."

Priest tensed as Riley's voice trailed off. "To who?"

Riley thought and then shook her head. "I don't know. I was thinking of... I don't know. I think I just need a good breakfast."

"Right."

"Are *you* okay? You seem bummed about something."

Priest looked at Riley, her eyes full of sadness. "No. Just a little tired, that's all. I'm fine." They got into the car and Riley backed out of her driveway. It was still odd, after five weeks, to have an actual house. When summer came, she would have to buy a lawnmower or pay a neighbor kid to do it for her. Or on second thought...

"When the grass starts growing, how about you come over and mow it for me?"

Priest laughed.

"I'm not joking. It's all part of being human. You can wear a tank top and cut-off shorts, get all sweaty. Gillian will make you some lemonade."

Priest's smile faded. "Will she?"

"Hm?"

"Riley... what... what if I don't like lemonade?"

"Then I'll make you ice tea instead. Come on, save me the twenty bucks or whatever the teenage swindlers are charging for yard work."

Priest looked out the window. "I'll consider it."

"What's gotten into you?"

"Nothing. It's just been a very long day already."

Riley reached the stop sign and looked to the left and right. There wasn't another car in sight. "Yeah, these small towns can really get to you. Don't worry. Once we get to the office I'll let you take a catnap in one of the cells."

Priest smiled. "I think I'll take you up on that offer."

Riley pulled up in front of the police station and saw Sariel standing by the front door. "I thought she was in the city."

"I asked her to come by. There's something I want to discuss with her."

Riley parked and led Priest up the sidewalk. "Hey, Sariel. How's the city?"

"Much quieter these days. It's nice." She put her hands in her pockets and stepped to one side so Riley could unlock the door. "People feel safer, even if they don't quite understand why. People are venturing out onto the streets of No Man's Land after dark. Goodwill toward their fellow man has been restored. What is it mortals say? I never thought I would live to see the day."

"Well, you're welcome." Riley went inside and turned on the lights. She had a feeling the day would never quite get bright enough to leave the lights off, even with all the windows the office had.

Sariel closed the door. "That's why I can't allow you to endanger that peace."

Riley looked at the two stone-faced angels. She tried a smile. "What? What are you guys talking about?"

Priest looked distraught. "I'm sorry, Riley. It's what you told me to do."

"How drastic are we talking?"

Priest shook her head. "Let's not get into that. Let's just hope the easy way works and then we won't have to worry about the last ditch option."

Riley closed her eyes against the sudden, unexpected memory. "What the hell is going on?"

"You're remembering." Sariel moved closer. "I was against this from the beginning. If you insist on knocking down the walls that Zerachiel formed, it's the only way."

Riley looked at Priest. "What the hell did you do to me?"

"Only what you asked, Riley."

She was on the floor, her hands balled into fists between her knees. She was sobbing. Priest was kneeling beside her, one hand on her back. "Make it go away. Just take it away from me. All of it."

"What happened?"

Sariel grabbed Riley, but she pulled away. The angel moved behind her and pinned Riley's arm behind her back. Riley fought, but Sariel was too strong. She kicked the back of Riley's knee and she went down. Priest walked forward and looked sadly down at Riley. "I am sorry, Riley. We warned you about all of this. I told you that~"

"You told me and then you made me forget. You say I agreed to this before? When?"

"Two weeks after you made the deal with Marchosias. The pain was too great for you. You asked if there was anything we could do." Sariel spoke without strain, as if it was nothing to hold Riley down. "The only option was permanently damaging. Zerachiel attempted a less drastic version in the hopes it would be enough. It wasn't. But the cards have been dealt. She has no other choice now."

Priest was standing in front of Riley now. "You will still be the same person. Trust me. I wouldn't have even suggested this if it would change who you are."

"Wait." Riley pulled on her arm, but Sariel didn't budge. "Can you make me remember? Whatever it is you did first, can you undo that before you do the Big Bad Thing?" Priest looked at Sariel. "Look, I obviously agreed to this before. Just let me know *why* I agreed to it."

Sariel shook her head. "It's up to you, Zerachiel."

Priest put three fingers on Riley's forehead. Riley felt like she'd been hit in the face, the starburst of light and dying neurons filled her vision. Her body went limp in Sariel's arms, and the angels guided her to the floor as her memory flooded back.

Five weeks earlier

Marchosias was making a doll. He was using a single piece of string to form a human figure. When he spoke, his voice was casual.

"What is the worst thing I could do? The worst possible scenario you could conceive. What do you suppose that would be?"

Riley remained silent. She glanced at Priest, who gave a subtle shake of her head. She couldn't help in this situation. She could just be a witness to events.

Marchosias continued. "I could kill everyone you know. I could kill them in ways more painful and traumatic than you would believe. I could do all of these unspeakable things to them, but leave them alive. There are things demons can do to a human's psyche that makes even me sick. They can... oh. I call it a ticking time bomb. Imagine the worst thing that's ever happened to you replaying over and over in your mind like a movie stuck on repeat."

Marchosias took a white cloth from his pocket, wrapped the doll in it. He admired his handiwork; it looked like a voodoo doll bride. He reached into another pocket and produced a hair. He wrapped it around the doll's head. The demon closed his fist around the doll and squeezed, and blood began to seep through his fingers.

He made eye contact with Riley, and she felt the tug at the back of her skull. She fought the urge to look away even as she wanted to curl into a ball and sob.

"What do you think? Are those the worst things I could do? You're wrong." He tossed her the doll. "The worst thing I can do is make you do it instead."

Riley looked down at the doll just as it started to bleed. She dropped it and took a step back, eyes wide in horror. For a moment, just a moment, the doll had borne Gillian's face.

Priest's voice was tempered. "Just stick to the agreement, Marchosias. There's no need for games."

Marchosias laughed. "The good guys. No flair for the dramatic in any of them." He held his hands out palm-up. "You won. You defeated my champion. Or, more accurately, you stood by while another human being committed suicide. Good... job? But the method doesn't matter. You won, you're the last champion standing, and now you have a choice to make. Option one, you can end the war right now. Option two, you can allow the war to continue by granting me license to choose a new champion. Once the new player is on the board, our little dance can continue."

Riley looked at Priest. "You can't advise me, but can I ask you questions?"

"Yes and no only," Marchosias warned.

"Okay. Has this ever happened before? One champion beating the other?"

Priest looked at Marchosias. "Yes."

"And they always got the same offer?"

"Yes."

"And they all chose to continue the war?"

This time Priest just nodded, averting her gaze.

Riley looked at Marchosias. "What's the catch?"

He grinned. "I won't lie; it's a big one. I want the war to continue, so choosing that would put me in your debt. Ending the war is in your best interest, so to choose that, you will have to make a sacrifice."

"Here we go. What's the cost? My life?"

"Nothing so gauche. No, you won fair and square. It would be a bit ironic to ask for your life, wouldn't it? No, to end the war, you must sacrifice the most precious thing in your life."

Riley looked at the bloody voodoo doll on the floor. Her heart clenched.

"I won't kill her."

He waved his hands. "No one said anything about *killing* her. All you humans think about is death, death, death. Why do you assume death is always the worst thing? I merely said you had to sacrifice the most precious thing in your life. And you're close, but I'm not talking about Gillian Hunt. She is one half of the most precious thing in your life. What I want, the price for ending the war, is your relationship."

Priest gasped and muttered, "Oh, you son of a bitch." She folded her arms and turned away from the scene playing out in the lobby of Marchosias' building.

"If you agree, you and Gillian Hunt will never meet. You'll never fall in love or get married. Your entire relationship will be erased from the history books. Cut from the golden loom of the Fates. Dr. Hunt won't remember anything, but you would know."

Riley stared at the doll. Possessed by the Duchess, permanently scarred by the experience... allowing herself to be possessed again a year later in order to stop a bombing attempt. All the Hell Riley had brought to their door... "Would she be safe?"

Priest turned around, shocked. "Riley..."

Riley didn't look at her. "I'm talking to the demon. Would Gillian be safe from the demons if I agreed to this?"

Marchosias nodded. "The demons would stand down due to

your victory but, beyond that, she would never have met you. My minions would have no reason to pay extra attention to her."

Priest moved closer. "Riley, think~"

Marchosias swept his hand to the side, and Priest was thrown back as if the center of gravity had shifted. She hit the wall and fell to the floor in a pile.

"No advising." Marchosias buffed his fingernails on the lapel of his jacket, his voice calm. "So, Detective. Can I go out and pick my shiny new champion now?"

"I choose to end the war."

Marchosias' eyebrows rose. He smiled.

Priest hung her head. "Oh, Riley, what have you done?"

Riley was trembling, her hands balled into fists. "Gillian would be safe. The city would be safe. The only one suffering would be me." She straightened her shoulders and looked the demon in the eye. "End the war. Take your price."

Marchosias pointed at her left hand. "The ring."

Riley looked down. It was the plain gold ring that she wore to work, not Gillian's priceless family heirloom. Still, she was reluctant to part with it. She looked at Priest, who was silently crying. "I had to, Priest. The greater good."

Priest only nodded, refusing to meet Riley's gaze.

Riley stepped forward and placed the ring in Marchosias' palm. She felt a tremor, barely felt before it was past, and Marchosias closed his fingers around the ring.

"Pleasure doing business with you. I'd apologize for taking so long, but it's not like you have that dinner date any more." He looked at Priest. "You are free to go, angel."

"You seem pretty happy for someone who just lost a war," Riley said.

Marchosias shrugged. "Who doesn't like time off? Besides, the human lifespan is pitifully short. So we'll lose a few decades. It's fun to be the underdog sometimes." He waved goodbye, and Riley realized that he was using the hand she'd placed the ring in. It had disappeared. "It was a pleasure negotiating the treaty with you, Detective Parra. Now please leave. I have an army of unemployed demons who will be crawling to me for something to do."

Riley went to Priest and helped her up, taking her weight as they walked out of the building. Priest shoved away from Riley as soon as they were outside. "How could you do that?"

"Gillian will be safe. That's all that matters. When I married her, I promised I would keep her safe, and if I can do it this way..."

Priest closed her eyes. "Oh, Riley, that's not..." She looked away, tears in her eyes. "You'll remember her. You'll remember loving her, and losing her. And you can never see her again, not even to say goodbye."

"I'm the champion. I might not have signed up for it, but it's my burden to bear. Not hers." She looked up toward the sky. "The city doesn't feel different."

"Yes, it does. To me, to every other angel in the city limits. You changed everything, Riley. Congratulations."

Riley had never heard that word sound like such a defeat, such an insult. She took Priest's extended hand and squeezed.

"So now what?"

"Now the city begins to heal. Angels can focus on helping rather than fighting. The demons will lay down their arms. It's like Marchosias said; a human lifetime is a small thing when it comes to a war like this. They'll use their time strategizing and preparing. Then the moment you're dead, we'll have a new champion and they will take one of their own. And the dance begins again."

Riley nodded. "And what happens to me? I can't..." Her voice broke, and she waited until she trusted herself to speak. "I can't see Gillian, so I assume we can't work together anymore."

"We'll figure something out. For right now, Sariel has a place. You can get some well-deserved rest and we'll come up with answers in the morning."

Riley kept her face turned to the shower spray even after the hot water ran out. It helped her ignore the fact that her eyes were burning, that her face was hot from holding back tears. *The winner, and still champion...* No matter which way she turned it, she knew she had made the right decision. Gillian was safe. The city was safe. How could she have chosen one person over an entire city? It's what Gillian would have wanted. And this way there was no heartbreak. How can you pine for a lover you never even met?

She finally got out of the shower and shivered in the cold of Sariel's bathroom. The walls were bare brick, the pipes running exposed along the wall. Her feet left amorphous wet prints on the concrete floor. She toweled off, thinking of all the times Gillian had wrapped her hair in a towel and 'scruffy-rubbed' her. That brought back the tears, so she pushed the thought aside for better options.

The city was safe. How many people would sleep soundly

tonight after a lifetime of fear? How many people would walk confidently out their front doors without clutching their purses and wondering if this was the night the bad guys got them? She had done the right thing.

She did the right thing.

Riley changed into the T-shirt and sweatpants Priest had left for her and went into the main room of the loft. Priest and Sariel were sitting in the small kitchenette under the sloped window, holding hands in the middle of the table. Priest saw Riley's entrance and let go of Sariel's hand, making her turn around.

"I think I'll just go to bed."

Priest looked at the clock on the wall. "It's still early."

"Yeah, and it was a hell of a day. Am I on the couch, or...?"

"The guest room is next to the bathroom," Sariel said. She glanced at Priest. "You did a great thing today, Riley. You did something very few champions have ever accomplished."

"Go Team Parra. Good night."

Priest said, "Good night, Riley."

She found the guest room, a glorified closet with a bed and a nightstand. A narrow window looked out onto the alley. A quick glance told her that there was no fire escape on this side of the building, and she wondered if that was why Sariel had put her here. The blanket and pillows were folded neatly at the foot of the mattress and Riley began putting together her bed.

As she tucked the sheet around the mattress, she realized she could hear Priest and Sariel in the other room. She remained still, focused, and tried to make out the words.

Priest was speaking. "I couldn't tell her. After everything she did for us, everything she sacrificed, it just didn't seem right. I told her she can never see Gillian again."

"If she ever does, she'll understand the truth."

"Riley made right choice. We should just focus on that and everything will be fine."

Riley went to the window and tested to see if she could open it. It was old enough that she was afraid it might have warped to the frame. She pressed her palms flat against the glass and winced as she pushed upward. There was a quiet squeak as the window opened a crack.

"Riley?" Priest, from the living room.

"Just wanted some fresh air. It's a little musty back here."

She waited to see if Priest was coming to investigate. She

pushed the window the rest of the way up, used the nightstand as a step, and squirmed through the narrow opening. She may have grown a few inches and gained some pounds since first liberating herself from the Parra family apartment, but she still had some tricks up her sleeve.

She stood on the apron of the window and twisted to look up to the roof. There was a pipe running vertically along the side of the building and she eyed the rivets holding it in place. It wouldn't hold her weight. But if she countered some of her weight with the broken brick... it left a gap just wide enough to make a handhold. She reached out and pressed on it with four fingers, braced against the window in case the brick shattered. It didn't, so she took the step.

Part of her weight on the brick, her free hand gripping the pipe, Riley felt like she was hovering in midair. Her heart pounded and she warned herself not to look down as she pushed herself up. She used the bricks with her right hand, her fingernails quickly becoming broken and bloody during her ascent.

Riley reached the top of the building by sheer grace, scrambling over the edge and rolling onto the rooftop. She lay flat on her back, panting and staring up at the stairs while she caught her breath. Finally, she knew she had to move. Her escape wouldn't go unnoticed long, and Priest could find her in a split second. She got to her feet and ran for the fire escape.

Riley knew that Priest and Sariel would look for her in one of two places; the morgue or Gillian's apartment. She didn't plan on going to either. She went to the marketplace, a strip of stores that had expanded onto the narrow sidewalk running in front of them, and bought a cheap baseball hat and sunglasses. Then she went to the Eighth Street station and bought a ticket for the el. She sat on one of the benches running along the back wall with her hands in her pockets.

She had always denied it at the time, but she'd had a crush on Gillian for years before they finally got together. There were things she knew, tiny tidbits of information that were rolling around her mind for no reason. She had known that Gillian liked to eat in her office, that she occasionally took a long weekend for a trip back home, and that she walked four blocks from the station to take the Eighth Street el home.

Gillian didn't have to take the train as often anymore; she usually managed to get a ride from Riley at the end of the day. But if they never met, then she was gambling on one routine remaining the same.

Other commuters started to fill the station. She turned sideways on the bench to watch people as they approached the station. She was about to give up hope when she saw a familiar green overcoat. Her eyes burned from sudden tears and she looked away, tugging the baseball cap down to cover her face. Gillian climbed the stairs and it seemed like everyone else faded away. They were just background noise with Gillian taking center stage. She cleared her throat, excused herself as she slipped past someone and took a seat to wait for the train.

Riley risked a look. Gillian was facing away from her, head lowered so she could work on something in her lap. A notebook or a file or something. Riley looked at the curve of her neck, the strands of hair that had come loose from her ponytail, the way she brought her hand up and scratched behind her ear with her pinkie finger.

The train arrived. Riley waited until Gillian was on board before she followed. She was just another commuter, a nameless face in the crowd. She found a seat and put her arm across the back of it, slouching and using her arm to cover the lower half of her face as she looked to where Gillian had sat. She was holding a newspaper, folded to the article she was interested in. She was wearing her glasses. She rearranged the paper to look for something else to read, and Riley saw her left hand was bare. The ring had been brand-new, but Riley still felt a twinge in her chest at its absence.

The train lurched out of the station and Riley closed her eyes. She tried to imagine what the past three years would have been like without Gillian. The time Gillian spent in Georgia had nearly killed her. But it would be easier now. She made the necessary sacrifice. Gillian was living in a peaceful world with no demons trying to kill her just to make a statement.

They reached the next station and the doors slid open. Gillian looked up as a blonde Riley had never seen before boarded, and she smiled and waved. She stood, and the two of them moved to a bench where they could sit next to each other. Gillian held the blonde's hand and, when they sat down, leaned in and kissed her lips in greeting.

Riley barely contained the angry shout that threatened to boil out of her, sliding down so that she couldn't see over the back of the seat. She cupped her hands over the brim of her new hat and tried to sort through her feelings. She thought that if she could categorize them, she could lessen their grip on her. She steadied her breathing and told herself it wasn't a betrayal. How could you cheat on someone you'd never met?

"Dear?" The voice was that of an old man. "Are you all right?"

She waved him off and she heard his feet shuffling away.

Someone sat next to her feet, and Riley kicked at them. "Seat's taken."

"No, it's not."

Riley groaned. "How'd you find me?"

Priest shook her head. "It wasn't that hard. You're still the champion." She looked over her shoulder and then down at Riley. "She never met you."

"I know."

"This is why I didn't want you to see her. In addition to the fact that it could cause certain... issues. Are you okay?"

Riley sat up, but kept her back turned to Gillian and her "friend." She sighed and shook her head. "No. I can't stay in this town. It's going to be like a sore tooth, knowing she's here. I'm going to keep touching it, even though it hurts. And it's going to kill me." She rubbed her face and looked out the window at the town speeding by. "I did it. I saved it. But it's gonna kill me."

Priest took Riley's hand. "We'll work something out. There's no reason for you to stay here in the city now that the war is over. We can go somewhere else. Not too far, but... far enough."

Riley closed her eyes and nodded. Somewhere else sounded extremely appealing to her right then.

Apparently in a world where she never met Gillian, Riley lived in a fortress of an apartment. The walls were covered with protective sigils, the windows were blacked out, and it seemed like she only lived in one small interior room that didn't share any walls with neighboring apartments. The rest of the space was filled with various weapons and books about fighting demons and possessions. She stood in the middle of it all and looked at the axes hanging on the walls.

"Looks like I was hardcore."

"You didn't have anything to distract you. So you took the war to the demons." Priest picked up a book and dropped it onto the couch. "The end result was the same, however. Gail Finney's meltdown and suicide. So it looks like the way you were doing it was just fine. I mean, the way you~"

"I know what you meant." She went into the bedroom and packed her meager things into a bag. She searched her dresser drawers and the closet, frowning as she dug through the sometimes torn and smoke-damaged clothes. Priest came into the bedroom and watched.

"What are you looking for?"

"My red blouse. It's my favorite; I can't find it anywhere."

Priest was silent for a moment. "Didn't…"

Riley stopped searching. "Right. Jill bought that for me." She picked up her bag and slung the strap over her shoulder. "Okay. Let's get the hell out of here."

White Spring was the first town outside of the city limits, separated from the outer edge of No Man's Land by scattered few houses and trailer parks. Priest was the one who heard about the job opening; she didn't say how and Riley didn't care. She took the position and, a day later, she was being escorted around the little town by their mayor. He was a chubby man with round eyeglasses and a speech impediment that made him chuckle after everything he said.

"You probably had quite a lot of excitement in the city, huh? Big detective and all?" He laughed. "We got a couple of stories in the paper about you earlier this year. That whole Angel Maker thing?" Another laugh.

"Uh-huh."

"Well, you won't get much excitement like that around here. Couple of break-ins and drunk 'n' disorderly." He laughed. "But we're happy to have ya. Yes, ma'am. Lucky to get someone like you. Heh-heh." Riley scanned the dashboard for something to stuff into the man's fat mouth and came up empty.

He pulled over to the curb in front of the house where they had started the tour. Riley's new home, if she agreed to take the job.

"Well, that's the tour. It's not much, but it's what we got." Another laugh. "And if you take the job, well, I can't promise you we could afford a deputy…"

"That's okay. I know someone I can get, and she works cheap."

He looked at her. "That mean you'll take the job?"

Riley exhaled and nodded. "Yeah. I'll take the job."

Riley knocked on the door and then took a step back, a practiced move that she doubted she would break any time soon. Now it was easier for whoever was inside to tell she was a cop; instead of a badge on her hip, she wore it on the chest of her desert-sand tan uniform blouse. Her hair was braided, which she hated, but it was part of the White Stream's dress code for their uniformed police force. She resisted the urge to touch it as the door opened and a kind-faced woman peered out. Her skin was unblemished, her dark hair falling around her face like curtains. Bright blue eyes blinked at her.

"You must be Robbie's replacement. I'm Sheila, his wife."

"Hello. De~ Sheriff Riley Parra. I was just getting settled, and there were some things in your husband's office that I thought you should have." She bent down and picked up the box by her feet.

"Oh. Thank you so much. You didn't have to come all this way." She opened the screen door. "Please, come in. Let me get you something to drink."

Riley thought about arguing, but she didn't want to make Sheila carry the box herself. "Thank you, ma'am." She stepped into the house and felt the temperature plummet. It was cold outside, and downright freezing inside. The front door led into a hallway between the living room and kitchen.

"You can set that stuff down anywhere. Uh, I have water, juice, some coffee..."

"Water would be fine. Thank you."

Riley carried the box into the living room and sat it next to the coffee table. It was full of the previous sheriff's personal items; awards, photographs, some books she had found tucked far back in the desk drawers for lazy afternoons. She picked up one of the framed photos and looked at it. Robert and Sheila Lynch in happier times, standing in front of a stone formation wearing sunhats. Robert was a beefy man, all smiles in the photograph.

Five months earlier he had fallen asleep at the wheel while he was on patrol. Since then the city had gone without a police force, an experiment that had gone well but the mayor was eager to end. Sheila returned with two glasses of water. "It's from the fridge, so it should be nice and cold."

"Thank you. This is just pictures, some plaques... things your husband had in the office when he..." She pressed her lips together. "I thought you'd want it back."

"Thank you. The mayor has wanted me to come down there

and pick it up, but I just couldn't bring myself to do it. Packing up Robbie's things would have meant he was really gone."

Riley could have kicked herself. "God. I'm sorry, I didn't think."

"No. It's good. It's been long enough. Are you married?" Riley thought she remained stoic, but Sheila immediately backpedaled. "Oh, my God, I'm sorry."

"It's fine. I... was married. Briefly. I guess no matter how long you get, it seems too short."

"I never thought I'd call seventeen years short, but you're right. You're very right, Sheriff."

"Call me Riley."

Sheila smiled. "What was your husband's name?"

Riley debated for a moment and decided on the easiest course of action. "Gil. He was a doctor."

"I'm sorry." She laughed. "God. I'm so sick of hearing that from people, like it was their fault Robbie stayed up half the night and then worked double shifts. 'I'm sorry for your loss.' What does that even mean? Anything? Everyone dies eventually." She used both hands to push the hair out of her face and hunched her shoulders. "I shouldn't dump all of this on you."

"Well, if anyone will understand, it's me. I won't take any more of your time."

Sheila walked her to the door. "If you ever want to share stories... talk about the men we lost... you could call me. It would be nice to talk with someone who knows what I'm going through."

"Yeah. I'll keep that in mind." She held out her hand. "Thank you, Mrs. Lynch."

"Sheila."

Riley nodded and stepped off the porch, welcoming the cold breeze that felt warm after being in the Lynch house.

They were sitting together on the back of the cruiser, looking toward the city. Riley was almost finished with her bottle of beer, but Sariel was too distracted by the label to drink. "What do the names mean? Rolling Rock and Heineken and~"

"The names don't matter. They're just labels. Drink, Sara."

Since the end of the war, Sariel had embraced the human name Priest had bestowed upon her. When in White Stream, Sariel became Sara Elmore. She was Priest's out-of-town girlfriend, a cop in the big bad city. The mayor had suggested turning the police force into a three-man ("Excuse me," he had laughed, "a three-woman operation."), but Sariel refused. She was wearing a blue sweater and jeans, her ankles bare underneath the rolled-up cuffs of her jeans. The more time she spent with Riley and Priest, the more she seemed to also accept her human side.

"How have things been lately?"

"Good. I've been kind of hanging out with the last sheriff's wife. Sheila." Riley looked down at her beer bottle. "We talk about loss and the things... that we'll have to learn to live without. I still haven't told her that my partner was a woman."

She looked toward the horizon again, remembering long nights sitting in the Lynch house trying to keep control as she talked about Gillian. It was sometimes harder knowing Gillian was still alive, still out in the world, but just unavailable to her.

"Do you have feelings for her?"

"God, no." Riley sighed. "She's straight. And I was just married to the love of my life. I don't think I'm ever going to just get over that." She looked at Sariel. "Would you? I mean, if you could go back to being the angel you were before you met Priest, would you?"

Sariel was utterly still, her eyes locked on the sun as it lowered in the sky. Finally, she shook her head. "I wouldn't want to go back to before her."

"Right." She held up her beer bottle. "To the women who changed us for the better. Now you're supposed to..." She sighed and tapped the neck of her bottle against Sariel's. "We have a lot to teach you, Sara."

"Well, we have time."

The thought was like a punch in Riley's gut. "Yeah. I guess we do."

Priest finally forced the back door when Riley didn't answer after the fifth knock. The lights were out, the curtains drawn, and Priest smelled rotten food in the kitchen. She took the time to seek out the old takeout containers and wrap them in plastic bags before she went into the living room. Riley was sitting on the floor with her back to the couch, staring off into space. Her service revolver was in her right hand, resting casually on her thigh like it was a can of beer. Priest stared at it as she crouched beside her friend.

"You've been missing for three days. The mayor is pissed."

Riley lifted the gun and aimed it at the window. She squinted one eye shut and curled her lip as she sighted the sash.

"You know what sucks? I have to feel this bad. Every day. Every day." She lowered the gun. "If I kill myself, the war gets two brand new champions and the war starts over again. So it would make my sacrifice pointless. So I have to live to be at least a hundred and ten." She looked at Priest. "I did the math. That's the earliest I can die and feel like it was worth it. Some people live to a hundred and fifteen or something, but I haven't been taking care of myself like I should have been. So, one-ten. That's, what, twenty-seven thousand more nights staring at the ceiling and crying myself to sleep and twenty-seven thousand more mornings waking up with that split second thinking she'll be next to me."

Priest held her hand out and Riley grunted as she placed the gun in it.

"Sariel is worried for you, too."

"Yeah, I'll bet she is." Riley's voice was barely louder than a whisper. "Make me forget. Just wipe it out."

"I... I can't do that, Riley. It wouldn't work."

"It would be better than now." She closed her eyes. "Gillian forgot everything. Over five years of memory completely rewritten. So just do the same to me."

Priest closed her eyes. "I can't do that, Riley. I could~"

Riley looked at her. "What?"

"There's a way, but it's permanently damaging. You would never be the same person afterward. It's like placing an ice cube in a glass of water, allowing it to melt, and then trying to take the water from the ice out. You may succeed, but you would remove a lot of the original water as well. It would be brain surgery with a, a melon baller. But there is something we could do. I could put up a wall around all your memories of Gillian. They would still be there, below the surface, but you wouldn't be able to dwell on them. And if the walls ever cracked, you would be devastated."

"The other option... the permanent damage one. How drastic are we talking?"

Priest shook her head. "Let's not get into that. Let's just hope the easy way works and then we won't have to worry about the last ditch option."

"If you can do that, then... do it."

Priest reached out and touched Riley's temple.

Riley was locking the front door to the police station when Sheila Lynch pulled up in the visitor's parking space. Riley smiled politely and waved on her way to her cruiser. Sheila got out and waved, taking some sort of covered dish from the passenger side of her car. Riley waited for her to cross the distance between them and she smiled. "Evening, Mrs. Lynch."

"I told you, call me Sheila."

"Right. I forgot. What can I do for you?"

"Well. I got used to cooking for two. I thought maybe we could split it and talk about our mutual losses."

Riley furrowed her brow. "Ma'am?"

Sheila got the look of someone who had stumbled onto a sensitive subject but didn't quite know where she'd gone wrong. "Ah... m-my husband, Ro~"

"The former sheriff. Right. I'm just not sure what you meant about mutual."

"Well, your-your husband. Gil."

Riley blinked at her. "I'm gay, Mrs. Lynch. Who told you I had a husband?"

Sheila looked completely humiliated, stunned, stupefied. She looked away from Riley and cleared her throat. "I'm sorry. I thought you~ I don't know. I'm very sorry, Sheriff Parra. I've spoken to a lot of people recently and I guess I just... thought you were someone else."

"Happens a lot."

Sheila went back to her car, refusing to look at Riley as she backed out of the space and drove away. Riley watched her go, a confused smile on her face as she got into the cruiser. Priest was coming over for dinner, so Riley stopped at the grocery store on the way home and picked up a few things she was lacking. She set out the plates and silverware, rinsing everything in the sink and drying it if just in case they were still dirty. She wasn't used to doing the dishes.

"I guess doing the dishes was Gil's job back when I was married," she muttered, chuckling at her joke. She looked down at a water-beaded fork and her smile faded. "Gil."

Detective Parra? I'm Dr. Gillian Hunt.

When Priest arrived a half hour later, she found Riley on the floor of the kitchen. She was holding a fork hard enough that the tines had cut her skin. There was only a small trail of blood trickling down the inside of her wrist. Priest took the fork away from her and cupped Riley's face. "Riley? Riley, look at me."

Riley had been sobbing. An entire relationship had flooded her mind, all the feelings and love from her entire life with Gillian rushing in... and then the pain of losing her crushed it all back down. "Jill used to do the dishes."

"Oh, Riley."

"Make it go away. Just take it away from me. All of it."

Priest closed her eyes. "Riley, if it doesn't work this time~"

"Do it." It wasn't a demand or even an order. It was a plea.

Priest closed her eyes and prayed. Seconds later, Sariel knelt beside Riley and looked into her eyes. "It didn't work."

"I know it didn't work. She wants to try again."

Sariel shook her head. "Impossible. If it didn't work this time, then what makes you think it'll work? Besides, the trauma would be irreparable."

"Riley... this would be the last time, do you understand? If this fails, we'll be forced to take drastic measures. Forcibly removing every memory of Gillian from your mind. It could cripple you mentally. Everything associated with Gillian Hunt would be affected. Your mind would be like Swiss cheese when we're done. We could leave things as they are now. You could learn to live with the loss. But if we take the next step, it would mean there's no going back."

Riley kept eye contact with Priest throughout the speech. She finally nodded. "Do it."

Sariel shook her head. She grabbed Priest's hand when she tried to touch Riley's forehead.

Priest looked at her with sad eyes and shook her head. "Don't stop me, Sara. This is what she wants. I'm going to do it for her whether you approve or not."

"I wasn't going to stop you." Sariel looked down at Riley. "I just... wanted to tell you to make it as strong as possible this time."

Priest nodded. "Riley, you'll be unconscious for a few days. When you wake up, there's a chance you'll remember Gillian in bits and pieces, but do not pursue those memories. You'll know they're painful. You'll know to avoid them, and Sara... Sariel... and I will make sure you don't pursue it. But if you fight the erasure~"

"Yeah. Melon ball lobotomy. Do it. If you can make the hurting stop, just fucking do it."

Priest put her hand on Riley's forehead, and Sariel covered it with her own.

Now

They had moved Riley to one of the bunks in the cell while the memories flooded back. She spent most of the day reliving the past month, curled under blankets while her angelic wardens occasionally visited and checked on her. When it was done, Riley fell into a deeply troubled sleep. Riley woke to find Priest sitting in a chair next to the bunk, watching her with an apologetic look on her face.

Riley sat up and hung her head, her fists pressed against her temples. Priest waited to speak. "Do you feel like you need to throw up?"

Riley shook her head.

Sariel came into the cell. "You know what we have to do now."

Riley looked at her, and then looked at Priest.

"The damage is too great. We shouldn't have tried messing with your memories. The only option now is a complete eradication."

"Can I... have a minute? Just in case I don't come back in one piece from this... eradication?"

"Sure, Riley."

Riley stood up and went to her desk. She took a pack of cigarettes and a lighter she had confiscated from some high school kids out of the locked drawer. Priest and Sariel were standing in the open cell door. Priest frowned.

"You don't smoke."

"Last cigarette before an execution. I'll be right outside." She left the door open and stood on the porch of the building. She looked at the city in the distance as she put the cigarette between her lips and flicked the lighter. She had smoked before, but she was out of practice. The way her hand was trembling didn't help matters any. Finally, she got it lit and she put the lighter back into her pocket.

Everything about Gillian, gone. She would never remember the woman who liked ducks, who on rare occasions liked to be spanked in bed, who wore glasses that made her look like a refugee from a fifties B-movie. She would forget the time she had taken the glasses off and gasped, "Why, Miss Haversham, you're *gorgeous*." The way Gillian sometimes rubbed her left calf with the bottom of her right foot when it itched.

Gone.

It would be like she was killing Gillian Hunt.

Riley took the pack of cigarettes from her pocket and tore away the plastic. She turned it upside down and a powder fell out. Riley spread it across the opening of the door before she faced the angels who were still standing in the office. "Sorry, guys."

Sariel started forward, but Priest wasn't sure what was happening. "Riley~"

Riley dropped her cigarette. It landed in the flax she had poured from the cigarette pack. Five weeks ago, when she first arrived in White Stream, she had put together this backup plan with no real expectation of ever using it. The entire building was circled by a thick layer of flax, and Riley had made absolutely sure the ground was coated with it. Now she had finished the circle, and her lit cigarette ignited the powder.

Sariel slammed into the invisible barrier, her face twisted in anger. "Riley, this is wrong. You know this is wrong. Do not do this."

"It's the only thing I can do. Sorry." She looked at Priest. "I am sorry, Caitlin."

She jogged down the front steps and climbed into the cruiser, ignoring the sound of Sariel shouting after her. Riley pulled away from the curb, the tires screaming as she drove toward the edge of town as fast as she could.

Riley drove slowly through the streets that had so recently been No Man's Land. Stores that she remembered being boarded up now stood open, with signs announcing their grand re-opening. She still saw a few drug dealers on the streets, but nowhere near as many as she was used to seeing. *This is the price. This is what I gave up Gillian for. All these people who have new leases on life.* It hardly seemed fair for her to risk their new lives just because she was sad. But she needed closure. Just one last glimpse of Gillian before she stepped off the cliff.

It was Thursday, so she knew exactly where she could find the love of her former life. She parked in front of the apartment building, resisting the urge to pull into the tenant-only garage, and walked purposefully through the lobby to the stairs. She went to the laundry room, so intent on her mission that she almost didn't notice the yellow tape stretched across the door. She panicked slightly until she saw it was just "CAUTION" instead of marking off a crime scene.

A note was taped to the door at eye level. "We are sorry for the inconvenience, but the laundry room is closed for repairs at the moment. - Thanks, the mgmt."

But it was laundry day. Would Gillian skip laundry under circumstances like this? She thought for a moment before she walked back to the stairs. The irony of going all this way, making all this progress, only to come up on a dead end was too much for her. She couldn't drag herself back to White Stream and call it fate. She had to see this through to the end. She got back in the car and stared down the street.

The closest laundromat was two blocks away in a strip mall. Riley tried to imagine Gillian going there, but the idea of her using those machines on her clothes... Gillian wasn't a fashionista, but she liked to take care of her things. A subpar washing machine would not touch anything she owned. There was another laundromat that shared space with a veterinarian and a law office. It took up much of the first floor, a corner storefront with windows that looked out onto two streets. It was well-lit, it was clean... it was where Gillian would go.

Riley made the drive in a daze. Her plan was just to watch Gillian again, like she had on the train, but she wasn't sure she'd be able to follow through. The need to hear her voice might be too great. Could she risk the new and improved city for a chance to say goodbye to the woman she loved?

The sky was dark, so the fluorescent light of the laundromat made it look like an aquarium. Riley pulled into the parking lot, found an empty space facing the building, and got out of the car. She rested her hands on the roof with her eyes closed, and then finally looked when she had summoned the appropriate amount of strength.

Gillian was wearing scrubs, her hair was down, and she was loading her clothes into a washing machine. She poured in the detergent, set the machine, and carried the mesh hamper back to one of the seats that ran along the window. She sat down, crossed her legs, and rested her chin on the fist of her right hand.

Riley's heart broke. In their past life, she would have sat down, put an arm around her, and asked what was wrong. There was just something in her demeanor, in the way she was carrying herself, that made Riley want to punch whoever had hurt her. Gillian's posture was absolutely defeated.

She heard a rush of air and then two soft footfalls on the pavement behind her. She didn't have to turn around to see who it was; there were only two options.

"How'd you get out?"

"The mayor stopped by. We asked him to break the circle." Priest was standing on the passenger side of the car.

Riley nodded. "Are you here to drag me back?"

"That's what I told Sara. But you would just end up back here again. And again. You need to do this. You need to see her."

"Why..." Her voice broke and she lowered her head. "Why is she so sad?"

"She's heartsick."

Riley frowned at her. "What? She's with someone, I saw them..."

"That was her girlfriend for that week. She hasn't had a meaningful relationship in years. She sabotages them, pushes them away, because they're not right. Their voice or the way they laugh is just wrong. She doesn't know why, and she doesn't know what she's looking for. So she's unfulfilled."

Riley glared at her. "You swore she wouldn't remember."

"Marchosias said that. But Riley, you and Gillian shared an oath. You married one another. Sometimes that can just seem like a word, but it's important. Your souls were bonded. You took yourself out of Gillian's life, but your souls are still attached. You were lucky because you knew the reason your heart was hurting. Gillian doesn't have that luxury. She's pining for someone she's never met, and she doesn't know why."

"You should have told me~"

"I couldn't. Once you made your agreement, I thought it would be kinder to not tell you."

Riley looked at the laundromat again. Gillian had stood up and was checking a load she had already put in the dryer. She held her hand out. "Give me twenty bucks and I'll call it even."

"What?"

"A twenty. Or whatever you have."

Priest took out her wallet and handed Riley a twenty dollar bill. "What are you planning to do?"

"Don't worry. I'm not going to give anything away. This is just something I have to do." She folded the money and jogged across the parking lot. She was still in her uniform, so she zipped up her jacket so it wouldn't be quite so conspicuous. A bell rang as she opened the door, stepping out of the dim gray light of twilight to the artificial glare of the building. It seemed to shine off every surface, reflecting from the machines and the tile floor.

Riley went directly to where Gillian was, her heart pounding as she closed the distance between them. It had been five weeks since she touched, smelled, spoke to Gillian, and she felt like a junkie trying to tie off a vein. She needed this so badly she wasn't sure she'd be able to do it.

Riley cleared her throat. "Excuse me."

Gillian hesitated as if she thought someone else was being spoken to, and then she turned. She straightened and met Riley's eyes. It was like being faced by a stranger, and Riley resisted the urge to cry. She swallowed and held up the money.

"You dropped this."

"I don't think so." Gillian looked at the money and then at Riley. "Do I know you?"

"No. I just... I think this fell out of your pocket when you were sitting over there."

Gillian smiled. "I don't carry bills that large when I do laundry. Was it under the seat, or..." She looked around the room. "Someone might have been sitting there before I was. It's probably theirs."

"You sure? I... could have sworn..."

"No." Another smile. "You could just keep it."

Riley shook her head. "No. I'll turn it into the owner..."

"Well, you *know* they'll keep it." She winked. "I say keep it. Maybe it's fate, and you were supposed to have it. Thanks for trying, though. Nice to know there are still honest people in the world."

Riley nodded. "Yeah. Sorry to bother you."

Gillian shrugged. "There's nothing to apologize for."

"I was just trying to do the right thing. And I am very sorry."

Gillian frowned at her, but Riley turned away before she could ask anything. She was almost to the door when Gillian spoke again.

"Wait a second, please. What's your name? Hey..."

Riley moved faster, pushing through the door and crossing the sidewalk with two strides. She had her keys out, tears burning her eyes as she half-ran across the parking lot.

The bell over the door rang behind her.

"Hey! Stop!"

Riley stopped, halfway between the building and her cruiser. Priest closed her eyes and shook her head, turning away from the scene and crossing her arms on the top of the car. Riley slowly turned to face Gillian.

"I thought you were going to turn the money in to the

laundromat owner."

"I... I didn't..."

"That was your money, wasn't it? You didn't see it under the seat. You walked in there and asked me if I'd dropped it. Why?" She moved closer. "Why do I feel like I know you?"

"I have one of those faces." Her voice was so subdued she wondered if Gillian even heard it. "I have to go."

Gillian shook her head. "You were just trying to do the right thing. What does that mean? The right thing."

"Jill, I can't~"

"No one calls me that." Gillian was crying now. "So why... isn't that odd to me that you just did? Why does it sound right?" She pressed a hand to her forehead. "Why is the only strange thing here the fact that I don't know your name?"

Riley started backing away. "I have to go."

"Riley, wait." Gillian's eyes widened. Riley felt like she had been punched. She turned to Priest and...

Priest felt the stillness even before she realized Riley and Gillian were frozen. She felt his presence behind her and reluctantly faced him. Marchosias was sitting on the trunk of Riley's cruiser, toying with a small red piece of plastic. "Five weeks. Your girl lasted five weeks." He clucked his tongue. "I had my money on two. I mean, sure, she cheated with the mind wiping thing. But still, kudos to her for sticking with it for so long."

"You son of a bitch."

Marchosias whistled. "You kiss your Father with that mouth?" He slid off the trunk and looked at Riley. "She's destroying herself. You know that. And you also know that tearing Gillian Eleanor Hunt from her mind will leave her a frothy-mouthed vegetable in a padded room. Nice way to spend the next seventy years. You and Sariel changing the former champion's diaper. Feeding her applesauce and wiping it off her chin. Fun times for everyone involved." He tilted his head to the side. "Speaking of Sariel, how is the sex? I imagine it's quite explosive..."

"What's your game?"

"I'm trying to be a nice guy here, Zerachiel. I'm here to make a one-time only, limited time offer. We can go back. Five weeks. We can erase Riley Parra's original answer and continue the war as it was meant to be. I get to choose a new champion and everyone goes home happy. Well, other than the poor folks in No Man's Land, of course. If you agree to the plan, I'll owe you a boon." He gestured at Riley. "I can heal the damage you and Sariel caused by messing around in your pal's mind. She'll be right as rain, the lovers will be together again, and it'll be like these past five weeks never happened. Well. They'll have happened. But not the way our little group remembers."

He snapped his fingers and Riley came unfrozen.

She looked at Gillian and turned around, eyes flashing when she saw Marchosias. "You."

"Hello, Riley. How has your month gone? We really should try to keep up better. Do you have email? A blog, perhaps?"

Riley lunged at him, and Priest caught her. "Riley. Wait."

"What do you mean, wait?"

"Marchosias has an offer." Riley scoffed. "I think you'll want to listen to this one."

The demon smiled and stepped forward. "I'm here to make a one-time only, limited time offer..."

Gillian was lonely. She tried humming to herself, but it wasn't the silence that bothered her. She finished with her laundry, loaded it into the mesh hamper, and carried it outside. She glanced at the beat-up old police cruiser parked in the lot, reading the name on the door and wondering what a White Stream cop was doing here. She unlocked the door of her car, put the clothes in the backseat, and started humming again as she pulled out of the lot.

She drove home and parked in the garage, lugging the clothes to the elevator rather than haul it up the stairs.

When she got to the apartment, she hesitated with the key in the lock. She took a breath, held it, and pushed the door open. She braced herself for heartbreak when she opened her eyes.

Riley was sitting at the dining room table. "You should have called. I would have come down and helped you with the laundry."

Gillian left the door open, knocking over the hamper as she ran across the room. Riley stood up and caught her. They kissed, the tears flowing down Gillian's face to their lips. When they parted, Gillian pressed her forehead to Riley's. "I wasn't sure. I don't know why, I heard the offer and I saw Marchosias and~ I wasn't sure you'd really be here."

"You should have looked at your ring. That's what I've been doing."

Gillian sniffled and looked down at their rings. "So what really happened? All I remember is just a flash, and then it was like a door was opened in my mind."

"I made a deal with the devil." She kissed Gillian's cheeks. "It just means I have to stay here and keep fighting this war."

"But you were at peace."

"Peace is dull. And pointless without you." She wiped away Gillian's tears. "It's not paradise unless you're there with me."

Gillian shook her head. "Does it seem like a dream to you, too?"

"Yeah. I know that I made the right choice five weeks ago. I know that Priest and I went back to work, we got cases... but I have these memories of White Stream. I know a woman named Sheila Lynch. But at the same time, I know it didn't happen. You?"

"I have a lot of memories that I don't really trust. They're already fading." She ran her hands over Riley's face. "I cannot believe I forgot you. I can't believe he could do something so awful to me." She kissed Riley's lips. "But the war~"

"The war has to end one day. I'll find a way to end it right, without games or tricks. I'll end it and then I'll buy you a house in White Stream."

Gillian smiled. "I would love that."

"It's not a bad little town."

"I love you."

Riley kissed Gillian. "I love you, too." She slid her hands down Gillian's arms and took her hands. "Why don't you close the door and take me to bed?"

Gillian smiled. "I think that could be arranged." She pecked Riley's lips again and reluctantly pulled away from her. She closed and locked the door, stooped to pick up the hamper, and turned as if she expected to see that Riley had vanished.

Riley seemed to anticipate her fear and had crossed the room. She cupped Gillian's face in her hands. "I'm still here."

Gillian smiled and kissed Riley's left palm. Then she slipped her hand into it and guided her to the bedroom.

Outside, the war raged on. Demons and angels waged a war that was echoed on the streets. In muggings and robberies, in assaults. No Man's Land rolled on, forgetting the peace it had so recently enjoyed. In the morning, Riley would go back to war. For tonight, she enjoyed the only kind of paradise she would ever want or need.

The war would take care of itself for one night.

ABOUT THE AUTHOR

Geonn Cannon lives in Oklahoma. He is the author of several novels, including the Riley Parra series which is currently being produced as a webseries for Tello Films, and two official Stargate SG-1 tie-in novels. Information about his other novels and an archive of free stories can be found online at geonncannon.com.

MORE FROM GEONN CANNON

"*Cannon's prose is beautiful. This isn't the most plot-filled of his novels but highlights the splendour of everyday life that it's so easy to take for granted. It's there to remind us that love can sometimes happen, not at first sight, but through the captivation and enmeshment that comes from truly listening and being heard by someone out of reach.*" - Jo at **Goodreads**

For the next two years, Colonel Noa Laurie - the sole survivor of a disaster which destroyed the International Space Station - will be orbiting Earth in an experimental craft called ODIE. Her mission: to clear away the treacherous minefield of space junk that has accumulated around the planet and endangers future missions. Her only lifeline during this mission will be the radio connecting her to the command center and whoever happens to be assigned to the communications desk.

Or so she thinks.

Because tucked away and almost forgotten in an Indiana woodshop is an antique radio. Its owner, Jamie Faris, occasionally uses it for eavesdropping on the truckers passing by on the highway. One day in the third month of Noa's mission, Jamie uses the radio to vent her frustrations by screaming into the ether. She screams and rages and curses into the thick static knowing it won't matter because no one will hear, but she's wrong... someone is definitely listening.

And she's about to say hello.

~ **Can You Hear Me**

CPSIA information can be obtained
at www.ICGtesting.com
Printed in the USA
LVHW040813250319
611719LV00032B/885